# Queen of Thieves
## PART 1

By Kimathi Khama

This is a work of fiction. The authors have invented the characters. Any resemblance to actual persons, living or dead, is purely coincidental.

If you have purchased this book with a 'dull' or missing cover—you have possibly purchased an unauthorized or stolen book. Please immediately contact the publisher advising where, when and how you purchased this book.

Compilation and Introduction copyright — 2011 by
Triple Crown Publications
PO Box 247378
Columbus, OH 43224
www.TripleCrownPublications.com

Library of Congress Control Number: 2011920127
ISBN: 978-0-9832095-1-5

Author: Kimathi Khama
Graphics Design: Hot Book Covers
Typesetting: Eric Pasini
Editor-in-Chief: Vickie Stringer
Editor:21st Street Urban Editing: Brandie Randolph
Editorial Assistant: Christopher Means
Special Thanks: Jane Eichwald

First Trade Paperback Edition Printing 2011

10 9 8 7 6 5 4 3 2 1

Printed in the United States of America

This book is dedicated to the three blessings in my life

Monica Christine

Sean Michael (Jair)

Audley Kimathi Khama, Jr.


Daddy loves you

# *A*cknowledgments

*All praises must be given to the creator -* THE ALMIGHTY GOD. *My finite mind may not be able to grasp your infinite wisdom in this creation called life, but my conscious allows me to see that it's there. I am eternally grateful for the blessings.*

To my parents:
*Granville & Monica Watson:*
**Father** *(RJP) – I can't thank you enough for the knowledge you've imparted in me. You taught me knowledge as a child, yet it took for me to be a man to appreciate it. Thank you.*
**Mother** *– You always had my back, even when I was dead wrong; always washed me with the undying love of a mother, regardless of the dirt I got in. You are truly the mother of creation. I love you.*

To my family:
*My big brother,* **Granville** Seretse *– You have been the most powerful influence in my life; always the light when I ran head first into the darkness; cleaned me up when I ran with that crew, savage in the streets; been there every step of the way as I spent over a decade in a cage. Big bro, I love you.*

To my lil' sis, Samora *– You grew up on me fast. Sorry I wasn't there for you and my nieces. But, the love is always there.*

To the entire Watson family:
**Nikki Watson** (Atl), Long Island, New Jersey, Miami, Jamaica.

Carol Diana Mulvey:
*Almost 20 years of blood, sweat and tears. You gave me the most precious gift I could ask for: my beautiful daughter. Thank you. Held me down when I needed it the most, from freedom to a cell, almost a decade. I owe you for that. Thank you. It took me time to see that even the hate I have for you is love. Love is love.*

Saira Dominguez:
*You blessed me with the first heir, (Jair) Sean Michael, the young God. The irony in life reveals itself by showing that our separation actually brought us closer. You will always reign as Queen. Love is love.*

Mayda Rodriguez:
*You believed in me when I barely believed in myself. Rode with me through pushing a bicycle petty hustling to pushing chromed out cars and flipping weight. You taught me the true definition of a ride or die chick. I got your back for life. Love is love.*

Crystal Simmons:
*You gave me a beautiful son, Audley Kimathi Khama, Jr. I'm sorry I allowed the streets to take me from you both. You tried to make a man of me, but I resisted every step of the way. I wasn't ready for you. You were ahead of your time. I respect your decisions. Love is love.*

*To all those who walked with me (mentally) in my darkest hour:* **Troy Johnson** *(Lil bro, get your weight up),* **Heather Bolling** *(Defacto wifey, trust – I got you),* **Kiesha Hernandez** *(I ma see you),* **Audrey Martin** *(Keep that beautiful head up),* **Kim 'Earth Tranquility Purnell** *(we will break bread),* **Tina Wilson** *(Green eyes),* **Madeline Dejesus** *(I didn't know what I had in you),* **Jona Huard** *(Bre'anna—that's my life).*

*I must pay homage to* **Althea Seaborn.** *You helped make this possible, gave me those positive words of encouragement. You are a Queen in your own right. Thank you.*

*To all the heads that I've crossed paths with in this journey called Corrections: It's too many to name, but I must pay homage:* **Donald Seaborn AKA lil' Dee** *(Althea and that support was a real good look),* **Gary (Malik) Sadler & George Figueroa** *(Legal minds at work),* **Michael (Fortune) Walker, Timothy Iassogna,**

**Danny Beverly** (You can be touched. *Keep writing, my brother. Let's get it from in here.* Respect*). Ne'Knowledge is key!*

To all the rest:

**Hold your head up.** *When them visits and letters stop, and them blocks get put on them calls –* **Hold your head up.** *When that lil' shorty get fed up cause that time slowly (or quickly) beat her down, so she left you for self –* **Hold your head up.** *When that State appointed 'counsel' keep playing games with your case –* **Hold your head up.** *When them C.O.'s try to beat you down (mentally), think smarter, think harder –* **Hold your head up.** *Do something with that time, value yourself. There's wisdom in that old adage:* **If you fail to plan, you plan to fail.** *Do something constructive. Know that you're worth it. ONE.*

Heavy respect to:

**Michael McClean** *aka* **Milly YOT** *(Let 'em know records—***Definition of a crook***), and* **Vaughn Walker** *aka* **Biggz Diablo** *aka* **Da Legend** *(Lion's Den records—***Da makings of a legend***). That joint merger:* **Tale of two hoodz***, is a problem! Y'all were right—this is a movement! Heads can either fall in line, or fall victim! I respect the grind. On the* **surface***, it's just money (let's get it), but underneath, it's much, much deeper. Few will understand. A-alike, B-alike, so we C-alike. One.*

*A special shout out to the whole* **CT-Hartford: the Heartbeat** *(North) The Vil, Nelton Court, Chapel, Westland, Barbour, Garden, Jungle, Enfield, Vine, Bowls Park, The rotten Ave, Bedrock (Bedford), The Square (rip), Dutch point, The Sands, Blue Hills, (South) Park Street, Frog Hollow, Rice Heights (rip), Ward, Charter Oak (rip), Flatbush, Hillside, Zion.*

*To all my* **New Haven** *affiliates: Vil, Trey, Elm, Jungle.*

*The Port* **(Bridgeport)***: P.T. Barnum (rip) Marine Village, The Terrace, The Hollow All the rest: Waterbury (Dirty Water), New Britain (Juan Vazquez—Cool J; Aurora Vazquez aka Audi), Norwalk, Stamford, New London...All of Connecticut STAND UP!!*
*A special big up to HOT 93.7 Y'all stay shouting out brothers on lock. The love is reciprocated. To ALL the DJs, rep CT to the fullest. ONE.*

*I can't forget **Jane Eichwald** (Ambler Document Processing) for being so patient with me while editing this project. It's been a journey, but you stuck it out with me. Thank you.*

*Lastly, to that C.O. that popped me out my cell late night, traveled with me, seen my vision, seen the depth in me, critiqued my work, gave me that positive feminine advice in that negative environment of darkness, I got 'nuff love for you. We will always share that **Secret**. I'll see you on the other side. ONE.*

*Enjoy*

*Kimathi Khama*

# Chapter 1 | Conundrum

There was complete silence in the GMC Suburban as four sets of eyes watched an animated couple walking hand in hand through the shopping plaza's parking lot, heading towards their vehicle. Oblivious to the eyes watching them, a middle-aged man playfully slapped his companion on the rear, producing a faint chuckle from her, before opening her passenger door.

11:39 P.M.

Olu's BVLGARI ASSIOMA spun with precision as he turned to focus on a pair of headlights approaching: a blue and white patrol car. Olu watched the cop car from the back seat behind the driver; the marked patrol car quickly inspected the parking lot before cruising up the street.

*Right on time. Like clockwork.*

Olu prepared months for that night. Everything had to be done with accuracy in order for his plan to work. Their last gig had flaws, glitches in scheduling and planning.

11:42 P.M.

Olu looked down at his watch again before turning to Shakim. Shakim was Olu's right hand man, his dedicated soldier. At twenty-six, one year younger than Olu, Shakim sat, eerily attentive, waiting on a signal from Olu.

"Time. What do your watches read?" Olu called out in his deep voice, to no one in particular.

"Eleven forty-five." Shakim answered first, sitting to the right of Olu.

"I'm on. Eleven forty-five." Keithy followed in turn from the passenger seat.

"Same thing; I'm good," the driver announced.

"Keithy, repeat to me the first thing you gonna do," Olu demanded, his voice stern.

"We all hit the front door. We have to be in by eleven fifty, sharp. Shakim will immediately secure the guard: disarm and cuff him," Keithy narrated, "while he's doing that, I will disable both cameras and pop the security door behind the counter. This all has to be done within a minute and a half. By this time, you and Shakim will take the counter, hit the drawers, the safe, and the red box. Bag the money, gag both clerks, and by eleven fifty-five, we out!" Keithy ended, self-assured.

Olu remained silent, stone-faced.

He had long lost full confidence in Keithy, the confidence needed to assure constant, positive results in their line of work. Keithy had a tendency to slip, to get sloppy, and his flaws now jeopardized the security of the whole team. But, that night, his involvement was vital. His connection to a skilled get-away driver who knew the drill and his intricate knowledge of the check cashing place that they were about to rob, was unique.

11:47 P.M.

Olu lowered the black ski mask over his face; the rest of them followed behind him. The black truck crept through the darkness; its headlights off, snaking its way to the side entrance of the building. A sawed-off shotgun; Olu pumped the handle, checked the ammunition, and lodged a shell into the barrel. The chrome, snub-nosed .357 sparkled in Shakim's right hand as his left reached over to the handle of the door. Keithy, almost in sync, followed suit.

Approaching the entrance, Olu studied the well-lit insides. Three clerks total: two female, one male, behind the counter at his seven, eight, and nine o'clock, and one security guard to his three o'clock by the door. One more clerk than anticipated. No problem. The place was empty of customers.

11:48 P.M.

"Keithy, stay focused. Don't forget to…wait a minute…look!" Olu announced, for all eyes to zero in on the security guard who removed a pack of smokes from his pocket. He exchanged a few laughs with one of the female clerks and then approached the door, cigarettes and lighter in hand. Shakim immediately turned to Olu. Olu didn't blink.

"This is better. Sha, creep him. Snatch him up and rest him to the side, quiet."

Shakim slid from the vehicle and, with cat-like reflexes, snuck up behind the guard who was in the process of putting a flame to his cigarette, only for Shakim to swing down the handle of his gun with skull-crushing force to the back of the guard's head, knocking him out instantly. Shakim caught the guard in mid-air before he could hit the pavement and easily dragged his body to the side of the building behind a large, green, metal trash bin. Emerging from the darkness, Shakim gave the truck a confirming nod. Keithy yanked the charging handle on his TEC-9 and, with Olu's shotgun in hand; they exited the vehicle with lightning speed to storm the front doors.

"What the...aagggg!" Screamed one of the female clerks the moment she witnessed three masked men burst through the entrance.

In his true fashion, Keithy deviated from the plan almost immediately, sprinting directly to the door leading behind the counter. Keithy tried his memorized code, frantically pushing buttons on the door handle to disengage the lock. The male clerk behind the counter, despite the sudden robbery attempt, remained calm enough to begin locking the tills of money, looking back and forth from the tills to the man fumbling with the lock on the door.

"Gissele! Push the fuckin' alarm and hide in the back–now!" The male clerk screamed, fumbling with the last till. Keithy locked into the man's eyes before he stepped back from the door. In a hail of gunshots, Keithy unloaded half the clip around the door handle, shredding the wood grain on the door, ripping the hinges from its foundation. Shakim, who was armed, manning the door, jumped at the sound of gunshots. He looked over his shoulder to see Keithy viciously kick at the tattered door. After three violent kicks, the door flew open for Olu to shove Keithy out of the way and rush behind the counter.

"Here! Take it!" The male clerk cried, offering Olu the last till of money that he failed to lock.

"The key to the safe. Give it to me," Olu demanded, eerily calm.

"The locks, they're set on a timer. They can't be..."

Olu violently slammed the handle of his shotgun in his mouth, knocking him back on his ass.

"Just give him the fuckin' key!" The female clerk screamed, "the key, it's around his neck!" She continued, "just take the money and leave!"

Olu ripped his blood stained shirt open to reveal a single key attached to a beaded chain around his neck. The chain was easily popped and beads showered the floor. Olu tossed what was left of the chain attached to the key in the female's direction for it to fall to the floor by her feet.

"I'll give you five seconds to open it, or he dies!" Olu growled at her, holding the barrel of his gun inches from the man's face. With trembling hands, she managed to open the safe, and then fell by the side of her male co-worker on the floor.

"Thirty seconds! Time!" Shakim barked over his shoulder.

Olu dropped a black duffel bag on the floor by the safe, filling the bag with money. Keithy began to raid the last open till that the man couldn't close, stuffing the few stacks of bills into his pockets. Shaking the other locked tills, Keithy turned down to the female in frustration and screamed, "open them! Open the fuckin' drawers, now," then snapped the ratchet on his gun again.

"Time! Time!" Shakim announced thickly, giving his last and final warning. Olu's head popped up from the safe. Although there were only four more stacks of bills left in the safe, Olu grabbed the duffel bag filled with cash and, without hesitation, headed back out the door leading behind the counter. Shakim held the front door open for them in anticipation of a quick getaway as Olu rushed towards the door. But, Olu paused in mid-step. He stood frozen as he watched Keithy lower his gun down to the clerks on the floor.

"Time! Let's go *now!*"

The black, wool, knit mask concealed Olu's face, but, not the one-inch slit that revealed his eyes and the menacing stare that he pierced Keithy with. Their eyes remained locked before Keithy's eyes sliced back down to the couple on the floor.

Olu didn't get a chance to say another word before the flame from Keithy's TEC-9 lit up, slicing into the couple hidden behind the counter. Shell casings jumped in all directions from the side of Keithy's weapon to fall and bounce around his feet, with the last bullet tearing into the male teller's face, blowing a piece of his skull out the back of his head. Silence fell over the room. Keithy lowered his gun, a faint trail of smoke leaked from the tip.

"Now we can go," Keithy slurred with contempt, followed by an insolent strut past Olu and Shakim.

"What the fuck happened in there?" The driver questioned the trio nervously. The GMC cruised in darkness down a long, deserted road. All four passengers had remained silent since the lethal outcome at the check-cashing place. Immediately following the robbery, Olu struggled with the urge to unload his weapon on Keithy after his reckless display. Olu knew Keithy was a risk, but, he never expected Keithy to resort to something so drastic. Keithy was well aware that Olu had one cardinal rule when it came down to pulling jobs: *No killing unless absolutely necessary.* Olu made that point loud and clear when they were first introduced.

"They fuckin' seen me, bro'! What else was I supposed to do?" Keithy explained, from the passenger seat.

"How tha fuck they see you? You had your mask on!" Shakim barked angrily, from behind the driver's seat, his eyes burning a hole in the back of Keithy's head.

"They…Man! They shouldn'ta did that stupid shit! That nigga shoulda just fell the fuck back and gave us the money according to protocol. But,, naw, he wanna be a hero an' start locking drawers an' shit! That nigga brought that upon himself!" Keithy growled, never taking his eyes off the road.

Olu had remained silent and perfectly still behind the passenger seat from the time they drove off. His staid eyes sliced back and forth from the driver to Keithy sitting in front of him; his mind projected him back to the last image Keithy gave him at the scene. Keithy crossed him and jeopardized their whole team, their plans, reacting childishly, fueled solely on emotion. That was something Olu found impossible to tolerate. Ironically enough, Keithy's own words began to ring eerily in Olu's mind: *He brought this shit upon himself.*

"Olu, you know that nigga fucked up. That wasn't on me," Keithy expressed, his voice detached from emotion.

"You did what you felt you had to do," Olu said, finally breaking his silence. The truck slowly rolled to a stop at an intersection. "Forget the cameras. What was up with the door, Keithy? The coded locks? You assured me, us, that the code was the same. That we would have easy access behind the counter."

"Yeah, that. I…I don't know what happened. My source, my inside contact gave me that code, four, three, one, seven, five. I drilled it into my memory. Four, three, one, seven, five. Four, three, one, seven, five."

"Then what happened?" Shakim said.

"I don't know. I don't have any excuses for that, Olu. I can only go by what my source gives me," Keithy explained, unsympathetically.

"Well, obviously, somebody screwed up. Either you or your alleged source. And as a result, two people are dead," Olu stressed. Keithy remained silent.

"Yo! You been fuckin' up lately, Keithy!" Shakim spewed.

"Relax, soldier," Olu uttered, casting a glance at Shakim. "Keithy reacted to a situation that he thought could potentially become hostile."

"And it could have become hostile. That other female escaped out the back. He was pushing alarms on shit, fuckin' shit up! Who knows what the fuck else woulda happened if we left them breathing?" Keithy cast a quick glance over his shoulder at Shakim.

"I just hope you deal with your source as well. You know, so there won't be any further discrepancies in the future. I'm going to trust you and believe that this wasn't your fault. So, I can only attribute any faulty information on to your source."

"Olu, I promise you, that wasn't on me. And you better believe I'm gonna deal with that."

"Then it's settled. By the way, when you hit that last drawer, what did you get? Let's divide these funds up and pay people what they have coming to them." Olu rummaged through the duffel bag on the ground between his feet.

"Oh, yeah, that. I almost forgot about that. Let me see...," Keithy snickered, digging his hand in his pocket, "... looks like, about fifteen hundred," he quickly counted the bills in his hand.

"The other pocket, Keithy. What about the other pocket?" Olu questioned, noticing how Keithy only withdrew the contents of his left pocket. Another annoying chuckle escaped Keithy's lips.

"Nothing seems to get by you, huh? I was just getting to that," Keithy stated, reluctantly reaching into his right hand pocket. "Thirty-seven hundred." Keithy emerged the stack with the other bills in his hand.

Shakim's lip curled. He clutched at his weapon, his eyes intent on Keithy. Shakim felt partially responsible for the upset at the check cashing spot, mainly because he was the one to introduce Keithy to Olu. Shakim vouched for Keithy, recruited him, and assured Olu that he could be counted on.

Yet, their last two heists, this one included, convinced Shakim that Keithy was quickly becoming expendable. But, acting on this was a different story. Shakim respected Olu's position, the position of leader to their small clique, having full confidence in his ability to determine their next course of action. As a result, Shakim refused to act without Olu's approval first.

"Keithy, I'm waiting. Pass that back here so we can divide this up," Olu repeated.

"Well…um…sure. No problem, Olu," Keithy stuttered. The truck slowly rolled to a stop in a scarcely lit parking lot in the back of the projects. Olu counted the stack of bills that Keithy handed to him, throwing inconspicuous glances at Shakim every now and then. The looks were ambiguous and confusing, as Shakim waited on Olu's next move. Casting a glance out the side window, Olu spotted his Cadillac Escalade parked in the second parking lot over.

"What does it look like back there, Olu?" Keithy casually picked his weapon up from the floor. He made brief eye contact with Shakim in the rear-view mirror. Shakim noticed Keithy's actions, but, it was the glint of Olu's chrome Desert Eagle that caught Shakim's attention.

"Everything is just fine. Here you go, payment in full," Olu called out. Keithy turned around completely to face the back seat.

*Blap! Blap!*

Two shots spit out like fire into Keithy's face. His head exploded. Chunks of bone burst out the back of his skull, painting the windshield with blood and fragments of his brains.

"Yo, hold up! Wait, wait!" The driver screamed in vain, as an eruption of explosive blasts in the tight quarters flashed like lights as Olu and Shakim unloaded their weapons on him. Bullets tore through the leather upholstery of the driver's seat and headrest, riddling the driver's body with lead. Seconds later, two sets of black leather gloves opened the back doors as Olu and Shakim emerged from the truck. He scanned the area to see if their disturbance attracted any unwanted attention. There wasn't a soul in sight. Olu reached back in the truck for the duffel bag and after slamming the door behind him, rounded the back of the truck to meet up with Shakim.

"I understand. That had to be done," came out of Shakim's mouth, before Olu had a chance to speak.

"He was a threat to the operation, to us. He had to be eliminated," Olu returned, receiving a slight nod from Shakim. "The only weapon involved in the incident is still with him, in the truck. Leave it there. Let the police find it on him. Give them a little pleasure to know that the gunman and the weapon used are no longer a problem. I have the money. You do trust me to fairly divide this up, don't you?"

Triple Crown Publications presents... Queen of Thieves *PART 1*

"Olu, we have been brothers for years. There is never any issues of trust between us. I trust you with my life," Shakim said with sincerity.

"And you with mine, brother. Tomorrow, come by the house and we will divide this. I trust you can handle this situation." Olu reached forward to give Shakim dap and a tight hug before he headed towards his vehicle. Disengaging his car alarm, Olu sat in the driver's seat of the large truck, tossing the duffel bag carefully over to the passenger seat. He removed the wool, knit ski mask that was lifted up around his forehead and used both hands to pat down a sea of waves spinning on his head before attempting to make out his image in the rear-view mirror.

Within one block of driving away, he could hear the distinct sound of a massive explosion, followed by a succession of car alarms screaming into the night from the blast. A faint grin formed on Olu's face now that he was assured that Shakim properly disposed of the truck.

Olu pulled into his designated parking space at his girlfriend's condominium complex.

12:41 A.M.

Shaking his head, Olu grabbed the duffel bag from the passenger seat and headed out of the truck. The truck's door swung open to illuminate the back, a dark blue, pinstriped suit covered in transparent plastic hung from a hinge in the back window.

Finding a spot underneath a stairwell, Olu began to quickly pull the blood spattered black hoody from over his head, followed by the matching sweatpants down around his ankles. The cool, fall night caused a chill to run down Olu's spine. Olu got dressed within a matter of seconds. Jingling his keys in his hand, he opened her apartment door and stepped in to see his woman sleeping on the couch in front of the television.

The flickering images on the screen popped flashes of light in her dark living room; an infomercial could be heard whispering from the set. Olu moved in silence as he pushed his keys in his jacket pocket, placing his briefcase next to a closet door in the foyer. He leaned in and reached for the television remote on the coffee table in front of her.

From the first time Olu spotted Maliaka, "Liaka," Sikes, moving in a hypnotically rhythmic dance at a nightclub in New York two years prior, he knew he had to make her a permanent part of his life. He stood over her

Triple Crown Publications presents... Queen of Thieves
*PART 1*

admirably and, with vivid recollection, remembered their first encounter. Her skin tone was the first thing that captured his attention, her complexion that of dark milk chocolate. Being extremely dark himself, Olu found the glow of her dark skin wildly exotic, original. Strangely enough, her initial resistance to his advances was the second thing that he found so attractive about her; she played hard to get.

In the beginning, their long distance commute from Olu's residence in Queens, New York, to Liaka's residence in West Hartford, Connecticut, put a strain on their relationship, resulting in Olu ultimately relocating to Connecticut to be closer to her. The move was also financially beneficial to Olu. He recently opened his second Mercedes Benz/BMW car dealership in Farmington, Connecticut, less than a year ago. The first dealership he opened four years ago was in Queens.

Olu stored away that last image of Liaka sprawled out on the couch; a large, white T-shirt alluringly hiked up to her flat stomach, some fire-red cheeky panties atop her voluptuously thick thighs, and a multi-colored silk head wrap holding her hair in place. Olu sneered in lust before pressing the power button on the television remote. Darkness and complete silence fell over the room.

"O…Olu? Is that you, baby?" Liaka mumbled, before Olu could make it out of the room.

"I didn't want to disturb you. You looked so peaceful lying there," Olu said thinly, making his way back to her side. He nonchalantly rested the duffel bag at the end of the couch. Liaka reached up to click on a light on an end table above her head.

"You're getting in pretty late," Liaka sighed. She wiggled her body around, flipping herself over to rest her head on his lap. She made herself comfortable on his thigh. Olu removed the scarf from her head to run his fingers through her hair. Liaka's first instincts were to stop him. Now she would have to take the time to brush her hair back down and wrap it back up before she went to sleep. But, his firm strokes were relaxing, and she soon found herself purring at his touch.

"Yeah, it was a long day at the lot. It got pretty hectic today. This one couple came in, requesting our latest model CLS, but, we didn't have any in stock. So, I had to go out there myself to try to convince them that the Mercedes S-Class is our most requested model. But, they were persistent. They had to have the CLS. You know the saying: The customer is always right. But, this

time of year, when its inventory, it always seems to get crazy. Trying to push this year's models off the lot to make room for next year's arrivals is always stressful. The sales, the paperwork, the competition."

"I'm sure you'll make out fine. You always do. I have something in the fridge from earlier. Are you hungry? I can warm it up for you," Liaka suggested, raising her head from his lap.

"I'm all right, love. I didn't mean to wake you now."

"Olu, come on. You have to eat," Liaka said, swinging her legs out to stand up.

"No, really, I'm okay. You don't have to…"

"Baby, it's not a problem. It'll only take a minute," Liaka insisted, walking off to the kitchen. He found it humorous as he struggled to find some type of defect or flaw on his woman. In his mind, there were none. In his eyes, she was perfection in every sense of the word. Twenty-two, five-six, one-hundred and thirty-five pounds; thirty-six, twenty-two, thirty-six. Olu envisioned her to be the epitome of a woman.

Liaka wasn't awake, or attentive enough, to look back to notice Olu luxuriating in the way her ass swayed in cadence under her flimsy shirt. As she disappeared around the corner to the kitchen, Olu smiled. Reaching for the straps on the duffel bag, Olu weakly stood to his feet and headed off towards her bedroom. He began to peel his blazer from over his shoulders for it to fall heavily to the floor. His shirt was next. Unbuttoning and peeling the shirt from the tuck in his slacks, Olu opened it, and then plopped down to lie across the bed.

"Oh, bay, I forgot to tell you what happened to Asia today," Olu heard Liaka call out from the kitchen. He wasn't sure if it was actually her voice or a product of his imagination as his eyes quickly became too heavy for him to hold open. A weak struggle with the inevitable and Olu's body succumbed to the sleep he so desperately needed. His last visions were that of clouds transforming into solid images of Keithy and the driver, the looks on their faces as the flashes of gunfire faded him into unconsciousness.

Liaka scooped the last wooden spoonful of red beans and rice from a crock-pot to place it next to two pieces of baked chicken breasts with collard greens on the side. A tall glass of iced tea—Olu's favorite—was added to a bed tray as Liaka clicked off the kitchen light and headed for the bedroom with his food.

A silhouette of Olu passed out on her bed. She silently placed the tray on a nightstand next to his head. His body was statuesque: six-, four inches tall and two-hundred and thirty-seven pounds of chiseled muscle. Liaka reached out to make contact with his flat stomach; her manicured fingernails crawled up underneath the bottom of his tight wife-beater. Her hand caressed lovingly over his stomach, her fingernails sliding over the indented grooves of his six-pack. Tickling a trail of hair that led from Olu's belly button to his pubic area, he grunted, and then let out a sigh turning over to his side.

Liaka let out a faint giggle.

She began to undress Olu. After placing his second size-14 *Phat Farm* sneaker on the floor, Liaka was suddenly overcome with a curious feeling. She quietly clicked the power button on her television and pressed mute. His sneakers coupled with his suit? Liaka vividly recalled Olu leaving that morning with a pair of Gucci loafers.

Liaka looked up, her eyes returning to the face of a peacefully sleeping Olu. Her eyes then found themselves traveling down to his waist. His zipper was down and the whiteness of his boxers could be seen through the slit of his slacks. The corner of Liaka's lip curled, her eyebrows raised. She leaned up to the side of Olu's neck and took a sniff. Nothing. Liaka boldly lowered her head to his waist, her nose hovering less than an inch from the open zipper of his crotch. She inhaled deeply. Nothing there either.

*Could he be cheating on me?* Outside of that night, Olu's fidelity never caused Liaka to even raise a proverbial eyebrow. Liaka found herself growing uncomfortable thinking of those images, the image of another woman in Olu's arms. She shrugged it off.

*What was I thinking? The way I put it on him, he couldn't possibly be thinking of another*, Liaka joked to herself. Reaching over to the tray of food on the nightstand, Liaka was about to return the tray to the kitchen before she mistakenly kicked something on the floor. A large duffel bag at the foot of her bed.

Liaka watched Olu for a few seconds before returning her gaze to the bag. Olu's breathing grew shallow. Liaka quietly placed the tray back down on the nightstand. She moved in silence as she lowered herself to her knees at the bottom of the bed, gently pulling the bag between her thighs. Liaka thought about it. An annoying voice in the back of her head was telling her that she was doing the wrong thing: invading his privacy. But, the voice quickly faded out of existence as she reached for the zipper. She exaggerated two coughs;

trying to mask the sound of the zipper being pulled open.

*It's just clothes*, Liaka said to herself with a sigh of relief, from seeing what appeared to be a crumpled sweat suit. A hint of guilt came over her. Yet, no sooner did Liaka start to feel better about the situation did she see what appeared to be blood, droplets of blood splattered across the chest of the sweat suit. She carefully lifted it up out of the bag to examine it, only to be startled by what she saw next, money! Bundles and bundles of money covered by the soiled clothing. Liaka peeked over the bottom of the mattress up at Olu. He was still sleeping, his deep breathing now a humming buzz of a snore. She removed the entire sweat suit and placed it on the floor next to her.

If she had to guess, she would have estimated, from the size of the bag, that it held at least seventy to eighty thousand dollars in large bills. Each bundle was strapped together in green and white bank tape. Her breathing began to increase, her heart raced, and butterflies churned in her stomach.

She found herself reaching to pick out a stack of hundreds. Her thumb fanned through the stack. The bills were crisp, new. She did it again. It sounded like a single shuffle on a new deck of playing cards. But, there was something else in the bag. Taking the single stack out revealed a brief twinkle, a metallic object beneath the other stacks of bills. She dug her hand within the bills to wrap her fingers around the weighty object.

*A gun! A gun stained with blood!*

Liaka immediately dropped the weapon. It fell heavily back into the bag, the piles of money cushioning its fall. Liaka slowly rose to her feet. She stood motionless, staring down at Olu, one thought now in the forefront of her mind, *Who is this man that I fell in love with?*

# $C$hapter $\mathcal{M}$aliaka
2

The bright morning sunlight broke through the blinds to shine its radiant light into Liaka's bedroom. She squeezed her eyes tighter. The sounds of some light jazz played from a clock radio on her nightstand. Liaka didn't know why she left the radio tuned into the jazz station for her morning alarm; the soothing sounds actually produced the opposite effect. Instead of giving her that sharp jolt she needed to wake her from her sleep, the light horns and smooth, harmonious saxophones put her more in a state of peace.

It wasn't until Liaka attempted to roll over and reach up to hit the snooze on the alarm did she realize that Olu's arm was secured tightly around her waist. Peeking over her shoulder, Liaka could see that he was completely undressed aside from his boxers. Liaka looked down to see, and feel, his raging morning erection pushing a tent in the front of his boxers, until a slight shift of his body caused his manhood to pop through the front slit.

Eleven inches.

Eleven inches of the thickest, blackest, vein-covered, muscular piece of flesh Liaka ever feasted her eyes upon throbbed inches from her backside. Liaka was more than familiar with every inch of Olu, but, she still found herself mesmerized by his manhood. She could feel her insides moistening, the muscles of her vagina inadvertently squeezing, clutching, almost calling out to it.

Liaka's eyes rolled up to look at Olu's face to see that he was still fast asleep. It was like her ass had a mind of its own as she found herself inching her waist back towards it, until his massive member found a home between her fleshy thighs. Olu let out a faint moan and unconsciously pushed forward. Liaka cursed herself for going to sleep the night before with her panties on, only imagining how nice of a treat it would be to just back up on him to feel the length of him inside of her as a way to start the day.

She flashed back to the first night when she felt the full length of Olu penetrating into her. If she didn't know any better, she could have sworn that he penetrated *past* the depth of her vagina, breaking through her back-walls to the bottom of her stomach. But, within a few short weeks of Olu *custom-fitting* himself between her thighs, the initial throe of accepting him was substituted by an ecstatic feeling unparalleled to any other pleasure she ever experienced. But, great pleasure always seemed to have its price and Liaka was stuck, no pun intended, with the dilemma of potentially ruining herself to other men. How could she ever be driven by a *compact* again when Olu drove her so lovingly in his stretch?

Liaka's left hand slowly reached back to circle and curl around him. She had to have him, now! Liaka knew that Olu wouldn't have any complaints of her waking him up like that. What man would complain of being awakened by the pleasures of her tight, wet silk? Her manicured fingernails could barely close due to this thickness.

She was reluctant to let him go, but, she needed both hands to wiggle her panties down her sides. The temptation to slide her panties to the side, revealing her now soaking wet opening, was fetching. But, there would be no impediments that morning, nothing to frustrate what she had in mind. Wiggling out of her panties, Liaka's breathing grew shallow as she positioned him, slowly easing herself back, preparing to inch his thickness into her, until…

"Shit!"

The snooze let up on her alarm clock for the sounds of a *Nina Simone* song to overshadow Olu's light snore and her growing breath. Liaka looked up at the alarm clock.

6:35 A.M.

"Damn!"

She quickly weighed her options. One: she could simply ignore the time and slide back on him, knowing after she filled herself with him and gave a few rhythmic grinds, that he would wake up and give her the morning quickie she so desperately craved. But, knowing Olu, it wouldn't be a quickie, as a quickie by Olu's definition could take up to a half-hour! Entertaining that option would definitely make her late for work. Or, two: hop up out of bed to take a quick shower and rush to make it out to work by seven A.M. The decision shouldn't have been a difficult one to make, especially after arriving late to work six times in the last two months; four of them the sole result of indulging in the very same thoughts she was having at the time. But, it was. She couldn't think of a better morning workout or a better excuse to be late for work than to be filled with Olu's love.

Liaka sighed heavily.

As much as she hated to accept it, she had to choose door number two and get up out of bed to get to work. She looked up at Olu's sleeping face with a grin, thinking he may have never known how close he came to enjoying the pleasures of her flesh that morning. A cold shower was definitely in order that morning or the thoughts of what she planned on doing to Olu when she got home from work that night would distract her all day at work.

The flimsy T-shirt Liaka wore to bed fell into a crumpled ball around her feet on the bathroom floor. Liaka shivered as a million droplets of cold water burst from the shower nozzle to rain over her body. The shower was quick, but refreshing and, most importantly, it served its purpose.

Leaning forward into her bathroom mirror, Liaka examined her face, taking inventory of any possible blemishes that may have sprung up overnight. There were none, still the flawless complexion of a chocolate *Hershey's Kiss*, a little treat Olu insisted that she tasted like. Liaka smiled. Just thinking about the way Olu seductively bathed his tongue over every inch of her body provoked the same illicit thoughts that she had before taking her cold shower. She shook them off; knowing the slightest entertainment of those thoughts would have rendered her cold shower useless.

A clear, sunny day, expected to reach the low seventies on that second week in September. A charcoal gray *Calvin Klein* skirt with matching blazer, Liaka laid them out across the bottom of her bed. A white dress shirt was next as Liaka slipped it on, followed by squeezing into her waist-hugging skirt. It was tight. A little too tight according to Liaka's recollection. Those last two weeks of *Wendy's* and those double Swiss cheeseburgers with extra-large fries were

beginning to catch up to her.

Liaka brushed it off.

6:49 A.M.

She knew she would never make it to *Dunkin Donuts* for her morning mocha latte and Boston Crème doughnut, so she had to be content with the large glass of orange juice that she drank as she grabbed her brown leather attaché case and headed out the door.

Liaka's pearl-white, two-door *Acura TL* rolled to a stop in her usual parking spot. Hertzberg, Hertzberg, Fox, and Green. Liaka had worked as a paralegal for over a year and a half for one of the senior partners, James Hertzberg. Liaka loved her job, but, remaining a paralegal wasn't in Liaka's future. Under the guidance of her mentor, her boss, she planned to study for the Bar exam with the hopes of becoming an attorney one day. Liaka always felt she was blessed with the gift of gab, so litigating a case in a courtroom was right up her alley.

Resting her attaché case on the floor next to her computer, Liaka took a load off in her office swivel chair, sliding up to her computer. Before Liaka could power up and log-on, she was stuck momentarily on a 4 x 6 picture of herself and Olu sitting in a picture frame on her desk.

The picture had sat on her desk for close to a year and it became somewhat of a ritual for Liaka to view it every day before she focused on her work for the day. But, today, something was off, it was different. Decked out in a cream Armani suit, with Liaka by his side in a cream Chanel dress, the picture was taken to capture a night out on the town, attending the opening of a new stage play at the local coliseum.

There was a wily smirk on Olu's face. *Who is the man in this picture? The man that I'm hugged up with? The man I fell in love with? Who is he?*

The duffel bag that she went through the night before came to her mind. The blood stained clothes, the bloody gun and the tens of thousands of dollars now flooded Liaka's thoughts. What began to puzzle Liaka even more was her current reaction to it. She found herself extremely turned on by the whole concept of it. She couldn't quite put her finger on it, but, instead of fear or a logical desire to end the relationship and part ways with this now mysterious man, she found herself intrigued by the sheer mystery of it all.

*Whose blood was it? Is the person dead? Could Olu be the killer? Could he*

Triple Crown Publications presents... Queen of Thieves *PART 1*

*actually take the life of another human being? Most importantly, could he possibly be living a second life, a second life outside of the monotonous relationship she thought they had?*

Liaka was approached, almost exclusively, on a daily basis by the thugs, the ballers, the hustlers, and the big money drug dealers to the point that she began to think that she was somehow equipped with some type of homing device that exclusively attracted those types of men to her. But, of all the attention she received, Liaka never found herself too fond of those particular types of men, and would only associate with them for *entertainment purposes.* That's why she found herself so attracted to Olu. In comparison to these men, he possessed some of the same traits – the 'take no shit' attitude, the confidence, the fearless soldier, the street-smart smooth gentleman – but, he was also different.

Olu wasn't limited to those of personality traits. He had the edge of a hustler, but, he could also blend in without the faintest of detection into the elite of the upper class. Liaka knew she needed that in a mate: a street-smart hustler who could apply his intelligence on a *legal* level. Was Olu everything she ultimately wished for in a man? Or, was her knowledge of this man only limited to the outward image that he provided her? Liaka knew she had to put those thoughts out of her mind. It was way too early for that. She had a mountain of paperwork to get through and she hadn't even had her cup of morning joe.

11:25 A.M.

With half the morning gone, Liaka knocked out the most important cases she had to prepare. Motions were typed up and ready to be mailed and the preparation for four cases were out of the way. Liaka was able to distract her attention from Olu long enough to get her work done, but, now that she had a few moments of free time, she knew she needed a second opinion.

"You have reached the West Hartford Police Department's main office. Our business hours are from eight A.M. to five P.M. For directions to…Beep!" silenced the recorded message as Liaka pressed a button on the receiver, "you have reached the property department. If you know your party's extension, please enter it now. If you…beep, beep, beep…one moment, please."

"Kadiajah Wilkins, may I help you?"

"Asia, hey girl. It's me, Liaka."

"Liaka, whassup?"

Kadiajah 'Asia' Wilkins, was one of Liaka's closest friends. At twenty-six, Liaka made acquaintances with Asia some two years back when they happened to run into each other at their favorite hair salon, Innovations. Their initial encounter was something they could make fun of in the present, but, in the past, it was a totally different story.

Frequenting the same salon on a regular basis, they happened to run into each other on a few occasions. But, it took their main stylist, Sasha, to make a mistake and schedule them to get their hair done at the same time for them to make first contact. With both of them being strong-willed and a little stubborn, neither one of them was willing to concede and give up their place in the seat. Fed up with their back-and-forth bickering, Sasha decided to cancel both of their appointments, leaving them standing in the middle of the salon, stumped.

Both at a loss for words, they could only watch in awe as another sister capitalized off their dispute, jumping in the stylist's chair to take their place. Those sudden turn of events , the woman now sitting in the chair, throwing a shit-eating grin at them both, caused Liaka and Asia to bond and spark up a conversation at their common aversion for the woman. They became friends in the process after they found out how much they had in common. Over the years, their friendship evolved to the point where Asia felt so close to Liaka that she named her godmother to one of her two children; her six-year old baby girl, Sky. Her youngest son, Donovan Junior, was four.

"We still on for this evening?"

"This evening? What's this evening?"

"The gym. We have abs, thighs, and calves to do. You know you better keep it tight to make sure you keep Donovan Senior happy."

"Girl, I'm about sick and tired of his ass," Asia sighed.

"Sure, sure, you are," Liaka said with a smile.

Liaka knew Asia was talking out the side of her neck because she would have done anything to get back with her baby's father. Donovan senior was Asia's first love, her first real boyfriend, and the father of her two children. He'd been good to Asia; owning up to his responsibilities as a father and treating Asia with the utmost respect. But, with that being Asia's first real relationship, she took advantage of him, played him soft because of his kindness and eventually lost him as a result.

"No, I'm serious, Liaka. I'm tired of running after him. He constantly holds my past over my head to make me feel bad. He knows the feelings that I have for him. And he knows that I want us to get back together. Maybe that's why he's such an asshole!"

"You know you don't mean that," Liaka said. "Does he have the kids this weekend?"

"Yeah. I think he's taking them to *Six Flags*," Asia answered, secretly wishing he invited her too.

"So, we can go out then. We haven't been out in a while."

"Uh huh, and just my luck, he will hear about it, and I'll *never* hear the end of it."

"Asia! You two are not together anymore! Why are you still living for him? He's moved on. You need to go out and have some fun yourself. Do you think *he's* at home every night worried about if you see or hear about him being at a club?"

"I know, I know," Asia whined.

What Asia kept secret from Liaka, because she knew Liaka would scream on her and never let her hear the end of it, was she still slept with Donovan whenever *he* felt like it. It was embarrassing to Asia that he would drop off the kids, proposition her for a quickie when he felt like it, only to leave her high and dry, whether she got satisfied or not.

It started with Asia being so used to Donovan's love that she didn't even feel comfortable with the thought of another man touching her, to her thinking that her loving would eventually bring him back home, to concluding that it was just easier to give him what he wanted, figuring her rejection would only cause tension. Asia knew there was something wrong with their relationship, but, was stuck so long in their routine that she felt it easier to go along than to fight it.

"Asia, we are going out," Liaka insisted.

"But…"

"But, nothing! This weekend, it's on! You ain't gonna have the kids, so, let's go out and have some fun. Girl's night out. Lianna was telling me about that new club they got in, New Haven. I think it's called *The Museum*. We should go and check it out."

"Lianna…uh," Asia sighed.

Guilianna 'Lianna' Gomez, was the third and only other female Liaka considered a friend. Prior to Asia, Liaka and Lianna were acquaintances. But,

Liaka wouldn't label Lianna a close friend for several reasons. The main reason was Lianna's lackadaisical attitude about life. Lianna, at twenty-three, was one year older than Liaka. Yet, unlike Liaka, who had goals to go somewhere in life, Lianna's main goal was to meet and land the ideal drug king-pen or gangster that would take care of her and support her: her smoking weed, drinking, and partying lifestyle. So, in those respects, they were just the opposite: Liaka strived for financial independence, while Lianna strived to marry a sugar daddy.

Another reason why Liaka wasn't dead set on becoming best friends with Lianna was because she was promiscuous – *very* promiscuous. Her reputation around the town was legendary. Liaka attended the same high school as Lianna, Hartford High, and had seen Lianna around the school, but, with their different circle of associates, they never managed to cross paths. Not until one day, four years ago, when they happened to attend the same house party.

The party was wack, the guys were corny, and the music was outdated according to them both. It was then that Lianna spotted Liaka out of the crowd, a familiar face from school, and sparked up a conversation with her, asking Liaka for a light for her blunt. It was that night of sharing the blunt together, along with the same sentiments of the party that their friendship blossomed.

Despite their obvious differences, which Liaka quickly came to be aware of, she still took a liking to Lianna. She fancied Lianna to a free spirit. Aside from being one of the funniest people Liaka had ever met, Lianna brought a side out of Liaka that she knew she would never have the courage to bring out herself. Liaka enjoyed the type of excitement and fun Lianna brought into her life. But, Asia didn't particularly care for her and made no qualms about her disapproval. As far as Asia was concerned, she tolerated Lianna and remained civil to her out of respect for Liaka. But, that was as far as it was going to go.

"Why you say 'uh'? Why you say it like that?"

"'Cause you know how I feel about her."

"But, you never even gave her a chance."

"Give her a chance for what? I don't give her a chance 'cause I know what she's about, nothing! And to be honest, I don't know what you see in her."

"'Cause she's funny and fun to be around. You gotta admit, that last time we went out, we had mad fun!" Asia remained silent with a huge smile on her face. "I didn't hear you."

"I can't front, I did have fun. But, not because of her," Asia replied, refusing to give Lianna any credit.

"But, you sure ate the hell outta that plate of shrimp and steak she got them brothers to treat us with after the club."

"Oh, your girl ain't stupid now. 'Cause them shrimps went down!" They both broke out in laughter.

"I think if you gave her a chance that you would like her," Liaka said sincerely.

"You might be right. And I would be more willing to give her a chance, maybe if she closed her mouth and legs a little more. Stop giving her goods away like it's going out of style or something."

"Hmph! She might say just the opposite about you! And say that you need to open your mouth and legs a little more!" Liaka returned.

"Listen, my supervisor walked by me like three times already, so I know he knows I ain't takin' to somebody about work," Asia explained, glancing up at her supervisor out the corner of her eye. "Plus, it's about lunchtime, so..."

"Wait! I almost forgot to tell you why I called in the first place. It's about Olu."

"I could have guessed that," Asia sighed. "You *always* talking about Olu. Olu this and Olu that. So, I already know any conversation with Olu's name involved is gonna take up my whole damned lunch! We got the gym today after work, so you can tell me then."

"Yeah, 'cause girl, you not gonna believe this."

# $C$hapter 3 | $B$e $B$orn $B$lack

$L$iaka entered *Bally's* at about six thirty in the evening. She got off work a little later than Asia, so she arrived at the gym to see Asia already dressed in a purple leotard bodysuit with a black sweatshirt wrapped around her waist. Asia was sitting on the floor with her legs spread apart, stretching. Leaned over completely with both hands grabbing her ankles, Asia didn't see Liaka walk right past her with a gym bag over her shoulder.

Locker 15 swung open. Stripped down to her panties and bra, Liaka peeked over her shoulder when she felt a pair of eyes locked onto her. If Liaka wasn't mistaken, a middle-aged white woman was brazenly staring at her body. Liaka looked over her shoulder again to lock into the woman's eyes. The woman was so lost in her gaze that it took a few seconds for the woman to turn away in embarrassment. Liaka rolled her eyes at her.

She took silent offense at the woman who she felt was observing her in lust. The last thing Liaka was about was taking auditions to play for the same team. She loved Olu and dick too much to even entertain the thought of being with another woman. Tying her shoulder length hair in a bun, Liaka removed a pair of *New Balance* sneakers from her gym bag, along with a stopwatch and locked her gym bag in the locker.

"Excuse me," Liaka heard over her shoulder. She finished tying her sneakers and rose upright to see the same woman who was fixated on her, standing

Triple Crown Publications presents...          $Q$ueen of $T$hieves
*PART 1*

only a few feet behind her. "Have you been working out in the gym for a long time?"

"Excuse me?"

"The gym. Have you been working out for a while?"

"Um...a few months. Maybe four or five, why?"

"I...I just noticed...and I don't mean to be so blunt, but, you have an amazing body," the woman replied, in a shy, but, fascinated, tone.

"I'm not gay," Liaka said bluntly, about to walk off.

"No! No, not anything like that! I'm not gay myself. I'm not coming on to you. I didn't mean it...I was just wondering, do you have any particular workout that you could recommend that may help to tone up my thighs. Maybe...um...help to accentuate my rear?" The woman explained, nervously probing.

Liaka fought the urge to burst out laughing in the woman's face. But, the woman was sincere, and Liaka knew her inquiry was genuine. Not to mention, a look down at the woman's flat rear end told Liaka that the woman needed all the help she could get.

"Well, I'm not a personal trainer or some expert in that department. But, I can tell you what I do. First off, I try to make it to the gym at least four days out of the week and, when I do come, I work out for at least an hour and a half. You have to burn the calories. So, I also have to watch my diet. As far as a workout, I stretch, then warm-up on the treadmill. Then, I hit the Nautilus Machine to tone up the inner and outer thighs. Finish that up by doing five sets of twenty lunges, followed by leg extensions. When you feel them burning, that's when you know you're doing something," Liaka said, with a smile. The woman listened to Liaka attentively, recording everything Liaka said into her memory.

"Believe me, that's more than enough. Thank you. I really appreciate that. And, again, you really do have a great body," the woman commented gratefully, smiled, and walked away. Liaka concluded from the woman's petite frame that she was going to have to do a whole lot more than squats to help. She exited the locker room to see Asia throwing a towel over the handlebars of a stationary bike.

"It's about time," Asia said.

"I was here. I was just in the locker room having the strangest conversation," Liaka said, taking a seat on the bike next to Asia.

"What are you talking about?"

"Making your ass bigger," Liaka said, playing with the computer display on the handlebars to set how many miles she was going to ride.

"Make your ass bigger? Girl, you are the last person who should want to get a bigger ass!"

"Shaddup!" Liaka laughed, playfully slapping Asia's arm. "I wasn't talking about me, smartass. It was for a lady in the locker room. A white lady. She was looking at me getting dressed and asked me for tips on, basically, how to get a bigger ass."

"Hmph! Let some woman be looking at me damned near naked! I woulda helped her ass all right–by beating her ass! I don't play that woman-on-woman shit. I only want the opposite sex looking at me. Anyways, why was she asking you?"

"First of all, in all likelihood, she asked me because, well, just look at this body!" Liaka joshed, lifting one hand from the handlebars to gesture to her body, "and second, who are you kidding, talking 'bout you only want the opposite sex looking at you? I guess your definition of the opposite sex is limited to Donovan."

"So, what, that's right! That's my baby. I bet when I lose these twelve more pounds that I'm shooting for and slim my waist up even more, he'll come crawling back," Asia said with confidence. "Alright, Miss Good-body, what type of advice did you give her?"

"Just what came to the top of my head: squats, lunges, jogging. That's about it."

"Do you know what you should have told her?"

"What?"

"You should have given her one piece of advice that would have guaranteed her a big ass–*BE BORN BLACK*!" Asia exclaimed, as they both broke out in laughter. Continuing her pace on the bike, Asia reached for her towel to pat a few small beads on her forehead. "So...are you gonna tell me what happened with Olu? I know you're just dying to tell me," Asia said, with a few pants from her workout.

"Yeah, girl, I almost forgot about that," Liaka sighed. "You not gonna believe this. He came in kinda late last night. But, that's not too unusual for him this time of year. But, when he came in he was so tired that, before I could even heat up something for him to eat, he passed out on my bed."

Triple Crown Publications presents...

Queen of Thieves
*PART 1*

"That's what I wouldn't believe?"

"No! Let me finish. Now, of all the people in the world, you know I trust my man. He never did anything for me to question his faithfulness. But, last night, I seen something that caught my attention. A duffel bag. A black duffel bag. I never seen it before and it was just so unusual."

"So, what? It's probably nothing. What do you think, he's cheating on you? Taking an extra pair of *jump-off* clothes to change up before he gets home?"

"I gotta admit, when I first seen it, that thought crossed my mind. So I checked him, smelled him *and* his clothes. I wanted to see if I could smell another woman on him. 'Cause if he's working all day, it should be no way that his dick should smell like soap!"

"Girl, you crazy!" Asia giggled.

"No, I'm serious. Olu has certain ways about him. And I know my man's patterns. He is super clean. You would think he has some type of compulsive cleaning, germ disorder. So, every time after we have sex, unless I put it on him 'til he passes out, he gets up and cleans himself, thoroughly. So, if anywhere below his belt smells like soap, I know he must have been having sex."

"Well, if it wasn't that, then what was it?"

"It was what was *in* the bag."

"Oh, no, you didn't. You didn't go snooping around in his stuff."

"Oh, yes, the hell I did! Shit, if he ain't doing anything wrong, he should have nothing to hide or worry about, right?" Liaka expressed righteously.

"I guess so. But, ooohhh, if he would have caught you going through his stuff, um!" Asia said, shaking her head.

"Come on now. Your girl ain't stupid. I made sure his ass was out cold." Liaka assured. "But, when I went through the bag, I found clothes. Clothes with blood on them."

"Blood? What do you mean, blood? Blood like he was fighting? Or, blood like he cut himself?"

"No, it was too much blood for him to have cut himself. Plus, I didn't see any cuts or bandages on him. But, even that wasn't it. When I took the clothes out, there was money, *lots* of money. Bundles and bundles of money," Liaka explained. Asia remained silent as her steady pace in pedaling slowed down. "Not only that, there was also a gun."

"A what?" Asia blurted, for her pedaling to stop altogether.

"Don't stop working out," Liaka said, nervously looking around, "just keep going while I tell you," she whispered, then continued her pace on her bike. "I was stuck. I mean, I didn't even know what to do."

"So, what did you do?"

"What else could I do? I just put it back the same way I found it."

"You didn't tell him?"

"Tell him? Yeah, I can see it now. Uh, hey, baby, by the way, when you were asleep, I was snooping through your stuff and stumbled upon a bag full of money, bloody clothes, and oh, yeah, a gun. But, enough of that, how was your day at work?"

"Well, you can't just do nothing! You have to find some way to talk to him about it."

"How? How do you break the ice to something like that?" Liaka chuckled, in a nervous tone. "If I tell him, he's gonna know that I was going through his stuff behind his back. Then he might think that I've been going through his stuff the whole time that we've been together and I haven't! Or, say nothing, and have the man that I love walk around me every day, knowing that he had that stuff on him," Liaka narrated, confused at how to solve the dilemma she found herself in.

"Maybe...maybe he'll just tell you. It was late when he came in, right? And you said he just fell asleep. So, maybe when you get home, he'll explain everything to you."

Liaka turned to Asia with one eyebrow raised. "Apparently, you don't know Olu," Liaka sighed, "but, I have to admit," Liaka continued in a low tone, "it... it did kinda turn me on."

"Excuse me? I don't think I heard you correctly. Because I thought I heard you say that that turned you on."

"Well, it was sorta...mysterious, you know? I thought I knew everything about this man. From the way he eats, to the way he grumbles in his sleep. I even know how he shakes his damned dick after he pisses! But, this. I woulda never expected something like this from him. So, I guess that little something gave him that mysterious edge again. I don't know, Asia. I just got turned on by that shit." Liaka beamed, as she reflected back on the events of the last twenty-four hours.

"Okay, now, it's official, you're crazy! You've completely lost your mind!" Asia pronounced with a smile, shaking her head.

"Now, come on, Asia. Don't you think that's *kinda* sexy? Even a little?"

"Oh, yeah, sure. Sexy in a gangsta, serial-killer sorta way," Asia snickered.

"He's not a serial killer!"

"How do you know? Because whatever you *thought* you knew about this man, you were obviously all wrong! Liaka, he's been lying to you the whole time. Doesn't that bother you?"

"Well...it's not like he actually lied to me," Liaka said unconvincingly.

"Dress it up anyway you like. But, that's not gonna erase the fact that he may kill people. Do you hear me, Liaka? He may kill people! And even if you think you are safe in his presence, which now, I don't know how you can think that. But, even if you think you're safe from him, what makes you think you're safe being *around* him? He may have enemies for all you know," Asia stated, receiving no response from Liaka.

Yet, Liaka heard her every word. She was listening, intently. But, a response was as elusive as the approach in which she planned on confronting Olu. Liaka continued pedaling on the bike, a thousand thoughts racing through her mind, the most prominent being: *Who is this man that I fell in love with?*

# $C$hapter 4 | $B$rothers

T his is the spot right here," Olu stated firmly. He pointed to an object on a makeshift diagram of a bank with a metal rod. All eyes were on the rod as Olu, Shakim, and their newest member, Diesel, circled around the table, hanging onto Olu's every word.

The diagram they stood around took over three weeks to make. But, the end result was an exact replica of the bank and a few surrounding streets. A large spotlight hung over their heads to shine light on the layout. Their details of the insides, which could be seen due to the open roof, were meticulous. Plastic human figurines represented the bank tellers, the security guards, and even potential customers. Matchbox cars were used to represent the possible flow of traffic leading away from the bank, down to a miniature toy truck replicating the armored truck. There were even miniature trees cut out to depict the amount of foliage surrounding the scene. The diagram was over four-feet by four-feet squared, and it took up a good portion of Shakim's basement, seated atop a wooden board on an eight-foot pool table.

"This is our blind spot," Olu continued.

"Not really," Diesel announced. "If you look here…," he pointed to a spot on the diagram, "…there is a large, global mirror on the corner wall. It would appear that it's only function is to reflect the view from around the corner. But, it's not. There's a small camera behind it. So, aside from the three cameras

Triple Crown Publications presents…    $Q$ueen of $T$hieves
*PART 1*

strategically placed in plain view on the east, west, and south corners, we also have to consider this camera as well," Diesel narrated. Olu nodded.

"Real good," Olu said flatly. "This is a big job, so every precaution has to be made, every detail worked through. D, can you positively verify the schedule of the armored truck?"

"Two fifteen, every Thursday, side entrance. You can set your clock to it," Diesel returned, with a hint of arrogance in his voice. He pointed down to a spot on the diagram. "Three guards: two in the cab, one in the back—all with state issued 9mm glocks. Their protocol dictates two procedures: one, fire on command, if they can retreat and recover safely; or two, if no other recourse, surrender with no hostility. This is all contingent on them following protocol. But, under such circumstances, you know us humans can be very unpredictable," Diesel stated, then reached into his jacket pocket for a pack of smokes. He tapped the back of his cigarette on the table to finally look up and see Olu and Shakim staring at him.

"What? What's going on?"

"Don't light that," Olu said thinly.

"Why?"

"The smoke. I can't stand the smell of smoke, weed or cigarettes. It makes me sick," Olu expressed, his lip curled at the thought. Diesel turned to Shakim who returned a blank stare back at him. He returned the cigarette to the pack along with the lighter. "To continue, is there anything else we should know about the armored truck?"

"No, that's about it. They still seem to mimic their same movements from six months ago when I worked for them as a security guard. Their truck, their drop-off times are all the same. I even know the two guards."

"What about the security guard uniforms?"

"I got that covered." Diesel walked over to a bag by the basement stairs. Removing some clothes from a *Starter* backpack, Diesel neatly displayed an exact replica of the security guards uniform, the hat, the jacket, the pants, and matching shirt, all brown with gold trim. He laid them in their proper sequence on the floor, and then followed by removing a security belt that went with the outfit. "As you ordered. I got one more of these where this came from."

"Shakim, this is yours. Make sure it fits because this is what you'll be wearing. Once you're inside, you're our guard." Olu commanded, for Shakim to nod in agreement. "We move in as scheduled. Two o' eight, we take the bank. Shakim, you're up first. Take down the guard. He will be stationed approximately twenty-two feet from the front door. You know the routine—shock and awe! Hit him before he even knows what hit him. Lethal moves, only if necessary. Your next move is to secure the surveillance, the cameras, all of them. Understand?"

"Understood," Shakim returned bluntly.

"D, me and you will then move through this course right here…," Olu described, trailing the rod through a course in the diagram, "…we should end up here at the safe by two oh nine," Olu stated, tapping a dollar symbol on a tiny square. "I will secure the manager who has the main key to the safe. He should have already prepared the delivery for the truck and the truck's total inventory. Because of this, he should be in his office: southeast corner, third room towards the back. The safe is holding twenty-five point four million, mainly in denominations of twenties, fifties and one-hundreds. It's too heavy and it will take too long to get it all. So, if we calculate this correctly, we should get about eighteen million within one and a half to two minutes. Diesel," Olu stopped, his voice became harsh, "don't get greedy! The money is useless behind bars, or dead! Do you understand me?"

"Olu, I…"

"Do you understand me?" Olu repeated, raising his voice.

Diesel stared at Olu before answering. "I understand."

"We can't have any issues with anyone taking it upon themselves to deviate from the plan. Issues cause confusion. Confusion leads to misunderstandings, and misunderstandings leads to prison or people getting shot or killed. We must be one mind, moving as one unit, one body. Because once we get the money from the safe, if we time this correctly, at that time the truck should be arriving.

"The truck should be holding close to fifteen million on arrival. The truck's inventory will also compensate for the money we leave in the bank. Shakim will be at the door mimicking the security guard's actions to lure them in. And once they get within twenty feet of the door, you, Diesel, and me will strike at that point—ambush them! But, we must act fast because there will only be two of them, the third one will remain in the vehicle. So, again, it is vital that we calculate this accurately. Is there any questions?" Olu stated, scanning from Shakim to Diesel. They both remained silent. "So, I should take it that your silence is indicative that you know the plan inside and out?" Olu turned to Diesel.

"I have no questions. We went over this before, a couple of times."

"Good, good. So, I'm sure you'll be able to answer this: say the security guard activates the alarm, which will automatically set off the security system to lock the main doors. What will you do?" Olu questioned. Diesel revealed his reluctance to answer. Then, the answer dawned on him, a light went off in his head.

"We don't have to worry about the security guard activating the alarm, silent or otherwise, because the security guard, unless he's doing a tour *behind* the counter, does not have access to the alarm. He can't tour behind the counter because protocol dictates where he can and can't tour. Security clearance only," Diesel returned.

A trick question.

The corner of Diesel's mouth revealed a hint of a smirk. He began to search for any sign or expression from Olu, anything that would expose an indication of emotion from him. But, there was none. Nothing. Olu remained silent, stone-faced. His only response was to signal Diesel's correct answer with a slight nod. Diesel passed a glance at Shakim.

"I've worked with Shakim on almost every job that I've done. His loyalty is unparalleled, coupled with his ability to take and follow orders without question. He has the dedication and ambition of a warrior! I trust him with every ounce of blood that pumps through my heart. So there's no need for me to question him," Olu declared, reading Diesel's thoughts. "Then it's settled. Thursday, twelve noon, we convene here at Shakim's to prepare. That should be about it," Olu ended. With a nod only directed at Shakim, Olu moved up the stairs and out of the room in silence. Diesel trailed Olu's movement with his eyes until he disappeared out the room.

"I know what you're thinking," Shakim said, "but, trust me, he's at his best when he's like that. I've dealt with many types of people and personalities, but, I've never met someone so focused in my life. Once he gets into that mode of thinking, that frame of mind, it's like that brother is some type of fuckin' robot or something."

"What up wit' all that intellectual, trying to be all proper shit? Fuck, man, we niggas! Niggas don't talk like that! Who the fuck that nigga think he is, Bryant Gumbel or some shit?" Diesel spit, finally putting a flame to the tip of his cigarette. "The nigga fucked around and got *me* talkin' like a white boy!"

"Naw, he's just on some self-educated shit. That brother stay reading books. Every time I swing by his place, if he's not working out, he's reading. Either some type of strategy, or war, or some type of book on politics. Man, the brother hold conversations with me and, sometimes, I gotta fuck around and get a dictionary to understand him!"

"That shit don't impress me, dun," Diesel slurred, exhaling a cloud of smoke, "if that nigga wanna impress me, let's get this fuckin' money! Get these mil's and split the pie three motherfuckin' ways! If we pull this shit off, that's when that nigga would impress me. Then, I would be willing to break bread with that nigga. Shit, if we do this right, niggas can get a couple of blazin' bitches and blow they backs out—in Brazil!" Diesel said sharply, then leaned into Shakim with his hand extended. They laughed, giving each other dap and a tight hug.

"Trust is a hard thing to come by in this line of work," Shakim sighed, as he held Diesel close to his chest. Diesel broke their embrace and leaned back to look Shakim in the eye. He noticed how Shakim still held his hand tightly in his. "Some might even say the word *trust*, associated with what we do, is a contradiction in terms. But, I told Olu that I had faith in you. Don't let me down," Shakim ended, releasing Diesel's hand. Diesel's only response was a smirk as he put the cigarette in the corner of his mouth, nodded, and walked out. Shakim clicked off the overhead light that shined on the diagram and walked upstairs from his basement.

"What I said was true." The sound of Olu's deep voice startled him as he turned to see Olu standing in the doorway dividing the living room and kitchen. "When I said that there was never any need for me to question you that was the truth." Olu pushed himself from the wall and walked slowly towards Shakim.

"How long have you been there?"

"Long enough."

"So you heard…"

"Everything I needed to hear and everything I needed to see. So, now I ask you one question: my brother, do you believe he can pull this job off? Your word is all I need," Olu said with a firm stare at Shakim.

"I wouldn't have allowed him into our cipher if I didn't have confidence in him. He will do what has to be done."

"I believe you. And your assurance is all I need. But, if some twist of fate does arise, causing him to deviate from the plan, don't hesitate, not even for a second. Take him down!" Olu expressed sharply, with Shakim agreeing with a nod.

# Chapter 5 | Just Be

The chrome spinners on Olu's jet-black Benz continued to spin as he pulled his car to a stop in Liaka's parking lot. The meeting that he had with Shakim and Diesel went off without a hitch. Olu wasn't too comfortable working with Diesel on such a big job. But, with Shakim giving Olu his seal of approval on Diesel, Olu felt a little better about the mission.

Shakim's word was good enough for Olu; Shakim's word was blood. Plus, Olu needed Diesel for several reasons. Firstly, because this was one of the biggest heists Olu planned on pulling off. Such a large bank *and* the armored truck in one hit was new territory for Olu. He needed a well-skilled driver, now that Keithy was no longer available. Also, someone who had intricate knowledge of the inside workings of a bank. For that, Diesel was perfect.

Olu was familiar with and had hit a few banks in his time, even pulled off a job more than three years ago on an armored truck, all with remarkable accuracy. Olu knew to hit them both at the same time would require every measure of his skill and expertise. But, it had to be done. Olu knew when he got into the mission that it would be his last. He was a soldier, and as the business goes, Olu put in his work.

He was tired.

But, not only that, he began to notice things about himself. The brief two years that Olu found himself with Liaka, he began to notice the changes

Triple Crown Publications presents... Queen of Thieves
*PART 1*

within himself, his way of thinking. Yet, the changes were subtle and swift. He found himself thinking about her throughout the day. Hours lost as she consumed his thoughts. Her skin, her style, her smell, her body, her smile.

There were occasions where Olu thought if he concentrated hard enough, he could actually *taste* Liaka on his tongue, her essence, the sweet nectar between her thighs, despite not being in her presence for hours. One thing was for sure, Olu knew he never experienced the feelings he was having for Liaka with any other woman in his life.

Liaka was different. She revealed things to Olu that he didn't even know existed within himself. Beauty, ugliness, darkness, light, pain, and pleasure, were all amplified in her presence. He knew, without question, that he wanted to spend the rest of his life with this woman. Olu stepped from his vehicle with a different sense of self. Once inside, his first sight was the back of Liaka walking out of the living room to disappear into the kitchen. She didn't hear him come in.

Olu tossed his leather *Wissam* coat on the recliner and followed her into the kitchen. She was bent over, reaching for a bowl of strawberries on the second shelf in the fridge. Olu licked his lips as he watched Liaka in silence. She was wearing one of his shirts. It was over-sized on her body, but, short enough to ride up to reveal the crotch of her white G-string, the tail of the string disappearing invitingly between the flesh of her cheeks.

Liaka could feel the energy of his presence behind her, his eyes clinging to her every move. A slight smile spread across her lips. She could see the tips of his shoes between her ankles as she slowly raised upright, closing the fridge in front of her. With her back still to him, Liaka said, "do you normally make it a practice of watching me in silence?" gazing over her shoulder, plucking a strawberry from the bowl to place it between her lips. She kept her back to him, giving Olu the view she could see he was enjoying.

"If you only knew," Olu slurred.

"Really? Should I be worried?" Liaka said sexily, kissing the strawberry from her lips.

"Maybe," Olu declared, approaching her from behind. Within seconds, Olu was at Liaka's back. He reached around her to pick a strawberry from the bowl. For the first time in their relationship, Liaka felt a distinct feeling that she never felt in Olu's presence—fear.

In the past, being with Olu provided just the opposite—the semblance

of security and comfort. But, ever since Liaka found Olu's duffel bag, she questioned the very essence of the man she shared her bed with. Liaka began to sprinkle sugar over the bowl of strawberries, fighting the nervous feeling brewing in the pit of her stomach. She resisted the urge to turn around and face him, afraid that she would reveal the fear now evident in her eyes.

Olu's breath made contact with the back of Liaka's neck as he lifted her hair from her shoulders. The peach fuzz on the back of her neck stood on end, goose bumps raised on her arms. The coolness of the tip of the strawberry made contact with the side of Liaka's neck as Olu drew a small circle on her flesh. Liaka closed her eyes and remained perfectly still as Olu replaced the coolness of the strawberry with the heated tip of his tongue.

She could feel her legs turning into putty as she felt his wet tongue trail a deliberate line up her neck to the base of her ear. Olu's lips gently trapped the tip of her ear lobe only for him to remove his lips and whisper, "Maliaka, I love you." Liaka's eyes popped open. In the two years that she'd been with Olu, she never heard Olu speak those three, monumental words.

"What did you just say?" Liaka spun around to face him. "Olu…"

"Shhh…," Olu whispered. "Don't speak. Just let me talk." Olu embraced her hand and dropped down to one knee. "Maliaka, you are my oxygen because I need your breath to breathe. My food, for your nutrients feed me. You give me reason to exist, to live, to breathe, and to hope for. You give me life because, without you, I see nothing but misery and death. Maliaka, I love you and I never want to part with you. I want to share the rest of my life with you. Do me the honor and accept this." Olu removed a small, black, velour box from his pocket. "Be my wife, Maliaka and I promise you, I'll make you the happiest woman on this planet." Olu opened the box to expose a three-karat diamond surrounded by four one-karat canary diamonds, encased in platinum.

A tear rolled down Liaka's cheek. She was speechless as she stared down at Olu on one knee, slowly sliding the ring onto her ring finger. It was surprising that he even managed to get it on her shaking hand. Liaka couldn't even take a look at the massive rock glistening on her hand, her eyes remained fixated deep within Olu's eyes. Olu cracked a faint grin to reveal a row of pearly white teeth.

"If you need some time to think, I can…"

"No!" Liaka blurted, "I mean, YES! Of course, I will marry you, Olu. Yes!" Liaka cried. Olu rose to his feet for Liaka to throw her arms around him.

"Wait! No, wait!" Liaka said sharply, breaking their embrace. "I need to know something first. I have to ask you something and I need you to be honest with me. PLEASE, be honest with me," Liaka pleaded, staring up at Olu through tear-filled eyes. "Is there anything that I don't know about you? Anything that I *should* know about you?"

"Anything you don't know about me? I...I don't understand," Olu said. "You do know that I love you, don't you?"

"Yes, Olu. I do believe that you love me. With all of my heart and soul, I believe that you love me. But, I want to know who you are. Who you really are," Liaka said, her hands circling around his. Olu remained silent. The tension grew as Olu felt Liaka's eyes pierce into the depths of his, into his soul. Olu began to turn his head away. "Olu! Look at me!" Liaka cried out, reaching for his chin. "Look me in the eyes and tell me. Is there anything about you, and I mean *anything*, that I should know about you?"

Olu could feel something shattering within himself. Gazing into her eyes, Olu could not bring himself to lie to her. To conceal his double life from Liaka had become more and more of a difficult task as the days passed. The worry of his fears had come full circle: reveal the truth of his life, everything, the good, the bad, and the ugly. Or, possibly begin the rest of his life with the woman that he loved based on a half-truth—genuine love concealed behind a life of lies. Olu felt he had the strength to do almost anything. But, he couldn't do it; he could not continue to look into the eyes of the love of his life. Olu slowly began to walk off.

"Where are you going?" Liaka said painfully. Olu released his hand from hers.

"Come with me," Olu said in a flat tone, walking to the living room. Liaka followed his every move until he made his way to the edge of the sofa. His large frame rested heavily into the cushions, his sigh revealing the weight of his confession. Liaka seated herself close to Olu, her body pressed tightly against his, both of her hands reached out to rest on his thigh.

"Maliaka, whatever I tell you, I want you to understand that my love remains the same. Promise me that you will never lose sight of that," Olu implored, his voice trailing off, his eyes down to the floor. Liaka's movements were deliberate as she immediately slid off the couch to slide in between Olu's knees, squeezing herself between his legs. She twisted her head to get under his, lifting Olu's head with a kiss.

Triple Crown Publications presents... Queen of Thieves
*PART I*

37

"Baby, my love, my feelings for you are eternal. So, yes, I promise you. I will never forget that you love me, as I love you," Liaka assured, through innocent eyes. Olu inhaled, his exhale a sign of total release.

"I'm not a car salesman. But, I do own the couple of car dealerships that you know about. But...but, that's not the main thing," Olu stated, his eyes now lifted up to hers. "I do jobs. I'ma stick-up artist," Olu stated, his words coming out flat and direct. Olu began to search Liaka's eyes for any change, any hint of her immediate thoughts. But, there was none, just a blank stare in his direction. Until a moment passed and a twinkle appeared, her eyes refocusing as if she suddenly returned from some mental trip.

"What does that mean?"

"It doesn't mean anything because it doesn't change anything! I still love you. But, I do certain jobs. They started out as contracts, but, then I went independent."

"How long have you been doing...jobs?"

"Before I continue, Maliaka…," Olu started, "…I'm not gonna lie or hide anything from you anymore. So, anything you ask me, I'm gonna be brutally honest in my response. Because of that, please, do not ask me something that you really don't want the answer to. There are some things that I personally think would be better left unsaid."

"How long have you been doing that?" Liaka repeated.

"About four years."

"So, when we first met, you...you…"

"Yes," Olu said, his voice now devoid of emotion.

"Have you ever hurt anyone?"

"Yes."

"Have you ever...ki...killed anyone?" Liaka stuttered, lowering her eyes in anticipation of the answer he was going to give her. Olu paused to take a deep breath, but kept his gaze remained on her.

"Yes."

He searched her face again for any change. A few seconds passed before Liaka raised her eyes back to his, and he could have sworn that a slight grin formed. Unbeknownst to him, the moment Olu confessed that he was a stick-up artist; an explosion went off in Liaka. Not an explosion of anger or fear, or even resentment. It was an explosion of excitement, of raw, unbridled passion for him. Everything suddenly fit. The duffel bag and its contents, his mysterious demeanor and behavior, all made sense now. Liaka slowly rose to her feet to stand in front of him. Olu followed directly behind her, standing to face her.

"Maliaka, please, say something. Anything. Just tell me…"

"Don't talk. Just be," Liaka whispered.

Beginning with the third button on her dress shirt, she started to slowly unbutton each button until she slid the shirt from over her shoulders. The shirt fell lightly to the floor to expose Liaka's naked chest, her breasts standing firm, her nipples erect. A mischievous smirk spread across Olu's face. He proceeded to unbutton his shirt, then leaned forward, guided by his tongue to make contact with her shoulder. Liaka quivered, her eyes closed, and she allowed Olu to completely have his way with her. She sighed when she felt the tip of his tongue trail a wet path between her shoulders. A soft moan escaped Liaka when Olu wrapped his lips around her right nipple.

Liaka's eyes parted slightly. Her drunken gaze peered down on the top of Olu's head, then to his shirtless back as he stripped his shirt from his body. The metal of Olu's belt buckle clinked on the floor as his pants, along with his boxers, fell around his ankles. Liaka finally felt the elastic strap of her G-string being peeled down around her waist as Olu gently guided her body down to the plush carpet between the couch and the coffee table.

# $C$hapter 6 | $R$ules to the $G$ame

$A$ proposition / thoroughly analyze the contents of my conversation / Yin and Yang—Bonnie and Clyde / the birth of an organization / the most important skill / MASTER YOUR EMOTIONS / your physical attraction is necessary / but your mental, intelligence is mandatory / first rule–**loyalty** / we will become one / second rule–**honestly** / it's irrelevant to lie / deception among us will only divide / our past stays that in order to enforce the laws we live by / comprehend? / let's begin / our goal within three years is to make three million / blend / chameleon status / switch our identity / mix in with the lifestyles of high society / **Power rule number–one** is self-explanatory / *Never put too much trust in friends, learn to use your enemies* / be wary of friends / they will betray more quickly / for they are easily aroused to envy / adopt a former enemy / a strategic move / for your loyalty they will have more to prove / **Power rule number–two** / *Always say less than necessary* / with words, if you are trying to impress / bite your tongue, say less / you'll achieve the opposite of your goal / exposed, you seem less in control / study and analyze body movements and facial expressions / realize **Power rule number–three** / *Conceal your intentions* / thrown off balance / never reveal the purpose behind your actions / with no offense, there's no defense / remain a mystery / **Power rule number–four** / *Play to people's fantasies* / a siren at first glance / understand the ingredients to manufacture romance / become the focal point, overwhelming / emphasize sexuality over rationality and clear thinking / driven by lust, you accomplish your purpose / **Power rule number–five** / *Make all your accomplishments seem effortless* / as you please, your actions must seem natural, executed with ease / artistic, the awesome and extreme, realistic / you're too good to be true / **Power rule number–six** / *Discover each person's thumbscrew* / usually an insecurity / an uncontrollable emotion / the shy are sometimes dying for attention / train your eye for detail / the hidden message and take advantage / use that secret pleasure to keep them in the dark / **Power rule number–seven** / *Play a sucker to catch a sucker, seem dumber than your mark* / the trick, make your victim's feel smart / intelligence is vanity / the wisest man knows how to make use of stupidity / **Power rule number–eight** / *Cultivate an air of unpredictability* / turn the tables deliberately / this strategy can intimidate / behavior that has no consistency / a smoke screen / **Power rule number–nine** / *Keep your hands clean* / a paragon of civility / never soiled by mistakes, a spotless identity / of course you'll make them, a human endeavor / the key is to shift the blame, remain clever / an alluring specimen / **Power rule number–ten** / *Know who you're dealing with, never offend the wrong person* / beware of the serpent with the long memory / if hurt or deceived, you'll receive vengeance with no sanity / study your opponents carefully / a delicate position in this game of constant duplicity / never trust anyone / never discriminate who you study / mimic actions / a mirror reflection / the next class is victim selection / master the act of deception / dissect these laws and you'll be ready for seduction.

"First things first. Always go in order."

"Okay, I think I got it. Release the clip to make sure it's loaded…" Liaka started, ejecting the clip on a black 9mm glock, "it's fully loaded, so I insert it back in 'til it clicks, to secure the …magazine, right? Then chamber the round. CLICK-CLACK. Release the safety, and I'm ready," Liaka rehearsed, holding the fully loaded weapon in her hand.

After spending half the night engaged in the most intense sex they ever experienced, Liaka and Olu sat up most of the other half with Liaka questioning Olu on every aspect of his double life. To Olu's surprise, the more he indulged into his past, giving detailed descriptions of the events that shaped his days as a stick-up artist, Liaka appeared to grow more intrigued with each story, clinging to his every word.

From Olu's recollection, he would only be able to make it to every second or third story before Liaka would mount him in mid-narration and literally ride the remaining story out of him to a glorious climatic finish. He also noticed that Liaka wanted details: gory, explicit details. The more descriptive, the more graphic, the more animated, the more Liaka seemed to be stimulated.

By the end of the night, things were unmistakably clear to Olu—Liaka was incredibly turned on by the fact that he was a ruthless killer. Being aware of Olu's alternative lifestyle, Liaka now found herself sensitive to his touch. In the aggressive manner in which Olu took her, Liaka envisioned Olu robbing a bank or violently overpowering a strong man when he ravished her sexually. The irony of his revelation left Liaka feeling more protected in Olu's presence, than the opposite of feeling the need to be protected from him.

"So, is that right? Did I get it right?" Liaka questioned optimistically, from across the kitchen table.

"Yes, Maliaka. That time you got it right," Olu assured her, carefully removing the loaded weapon from her hand. "But, that's not very becoming of you: guns. It's not becoming of any woman, But, especially you. Guns are coarse, rough. Guns are so cold and unforgiving. You, on the other hand, are warm and merciful. Guns take lives. And you, you bring life forth," Olu stressed, replacing the cold steel of the gun with the warmth of his hand.

"I wanted to teach you a little about guns so you could protect yourself. Not to destroy, but, for self-preservation. Of course, if I am there, I would unleash the wrath of hell upon anyone who even thought about bringing harm to you. But, I'm not always going to be there. So, if I can't be there to protect my *investment*, my investment must be equipped with the knowledge to protect herself," Olu delivered, with sincerity in his eyes. Liaka began blushing.

"Oh, so I'm your investment now?" Liaka said with a smile, squeezing his hand over hers.

"Yes, you are. My most treasured, my most cherished, my most valued investment. My lifelong investment. An investment that I hope will bring me several *smaller investments* in the very near future."

"Oh, really?" Liaka said, with one eyebrow raised.

"Absolutely. Three boys and a little girl."

"Wow!" Liaka gasped, her mouth dropped open. "I don't know if my body could handle all of that."

"Sure you can. Those hips were made to bear my seeds."

"Hey!" Liaka giggled, playfully slapping his arm. "Don't make fun of my hips. You know you love them."

"Loving them is an understatement. But, now that I think about it, you still never answered my question. My proposal?"

"I thought I did. But, if I didn't, of course, Olu. Of course, I will marry you," Liaka leaned across the table to kiss him. "But...what if something…"

"Nothing. Nothing will happen to me if that's what you're wondering. Once I decided to propose to you, I decided that I'm officially out of that lifestyle. Well, not exactly."

"What do you mean, 'not exactly'?"

"I have one more job to complete. It's a big job. But, once it's complete, I'm done. I informed all of my contacts that, for lack of a better phrase, I'm resigning. Before, there were no strings, no obligations. With you, I now have one."

"So, you're getting out...for me?"

"Yes and no," Olu said bluntly, "I played with the idea of leaving the business for some time now. But, with you accepting my proposal, agreeing to be my wife, you just solidified it. So, now that I think about it, yes, ultimately, I am doing it for you."

"Can I ask you a question?" Liaka posed, "what is your last job?"

"Don't ask me something like that," Olu spit curtly. "I shared with you a few instances from my past. But, for your own protection, I will not share that with you." Liaka was taken aback. Her facial expression changed. "Please don't look at me like that. You make me feel guilty," Olu stated, noticing the strange look she gave him. "Maybe in a few months, or on our honeymoon in Barbados, I'll give you every single detail. Because, from your behavior last night, I can tell that you like details," Olu said, cracking a smile. "But, aside from that, you can ask me anything."

"Anything?" Liaka said, her voice warming back up to him again.

"Yes, Maliaka, anything."

"Okay, let me see. Oh, okay. How did you feel, you know, the first time you did it?" Olu sighed from Liaka's question and reclined back in the kitchen chair to make himself comfortable.

"Nervous. I was nervous. I don't think it was so much the job that made me nervous, but, the unknown of what was going to happen. But, once you're successful, once you complete your mission, you feel better. But, then, the more you do it, and the better you get at it, you begin to grow more confident, until you reach a point where it becomes second nature."

"You make it sound like it's a real job," Liaka said, with a slight chuckle.

"To some, it is. In this line of work, you must look at it like a job. It's not something that you can jump in and out of. It becomes a lifestyle. Might I add, an addictive lifestyle. The adrenaline you get on every mission is unparalleled. It also takes a certain frame of mind and training to assure success."

"What do you mean, training?"

"The way you think. You have to train your mind to think on different terms, to be sensitive to different things that you pass over every day. You have to learn to study people, pay attention to their details, their mannerisms. Their exterior is relevant, but, only to a small degree. Why? Because people put on masks. Different masks to suit their purpose."

"So, to be effective in this game is to be able to see through the masks people put on. Once you learn to study the subtle clues, you will begin to pierce that veil, that cloak that they use to try to shield themselves to the world. Pay attention to such things as their clothes, their gestures, a certain look in their eyes, their off-handed comments."

"Imagine a person being a broken jigsaw puzzle. Their outward appearance is one piece, their style another, their attitude, yet another, their comments, one more. The key to mastering them is to put all the pieces together in one composite whole. The way you do that is to get them to talk. People love to talk about themselves: their mate, their children, their friends, their jobs, their entire lives."

"Interesting. What else? Tell me more," Liaka asked, glued to his every word.

"Well, your frame of mind. You have to learn to put yourself, your mind, in a certain mode. Think of any aggressive sport. The players don't go in thinking, 'I'm gonna lose'. At least, not any *good* player. They would think, not only have I won, but, how I'm gonna celebrate my victory! Because, if your inner self can't possibly see yourself achieving something, then it would be almost impossible for your outer self to manifest that into existence. For every job I've done, even in the beginning, there was never one time where I thought I wouldn't be able to succeed. I…," Olu paused, throwing a strange look at Liaka. A mischievous grin spread across his face. He remained silent for a moment as he studied her.

"What? What happened?"

"And the hunter becomes the hunted," Olu said with a smile. "Get them to talk. Yeah, you got me. You sure are a sharp one, Miss Maliaka. Trying to outfox the fox," Olu slurred, a chuckle escaped his lips.

"No! What are you talking about? We were just talking," Liaka said innocently, unable to mask the smile on her face.

The doorbell rang.

"Saved by the bell," Olu stated, rising from the table.

"Hold on! We ain't done talking yet! It just started getting good," Liaka called out to him as he headed out the kitchen. "Don't think I'm letting you off the hook! We are gonna finish this later!" Liaka called out even louder as he disappeared around the kitchen corner. Liaka stood from the table herself, quickly snatching up the 9 mm as they pounded on the door.

"Yeah! I hear you! I'm coming!" Liaka yelled out, searching frantically to hide the weapon. Scurrying off to the bedroom, Liaka hid the gun in the middle of some clothes in her dresser drawers then rushed back to the front door.

"Damn, girl! What took you so long?" Asia snapped. Both of Asia's kids bolted past Liaka, with her son sprinting straight to the bathroom. "Little Donny had to go to the bathroom for like a half hour now. I kept telling him to hold it 'til we got here. And you got the nerve to be taking all day to answer the door," Asia said, pushing her way past Liaka with shopping bags in both hands.

"Auntie Likey, can I watch TV?" Asia's daughter asked, looking up at Liaka through innocent eyes.

"Of course you can, Sky," Liaka said warmly, then relieved a handful of bags from Asia's hand.

"Thank you," she chirped happily, running from them to jump on the recliner chair, grabbing for the remote.

"So, what do you have here?" They took their seats on opposite ends of the couch with shopping bags between them.

"Stuff for Sky! That lil' girl is gonna drive me crazy! She woke up this morning insisting that she has nothing to wear."

"I don't like those clothes anymore," her daughter spoke up sadly, from the recliner.

"Um, well, life doesn't work that way, Sky! I would love to rearrange my whole wardrobe every time I didn't like my clothes anymore, too! But, I can't. Money don't grow on trees," Asia returned sharply to her daughter, ending by rolling her eyes at her. Asia's daughter mumbled something under her breath as she clicked through the TV stations. "Excuse me? Did you say something?"

"I didn't say anything," her daughter sighed.

"Oh, okay, because I still got ALL the receipts to those clothes! And I ain't got no problem bringing them back! Anyways," Asia snapped, returning to Liaka, "I went out to buy Miss Fashion Diva a few outfits. I got her this cute lil'...oh, hi, Oluwan," Asia cooed, as she looked up to see Olu enter the room. Asia's entire demeanor changed. Her body language shifted, her voice became softer, her eyes locked into his.

"How are you, Kadiajah?" Olu stepped into the room, sipping on a glass of iced tea. "Maliaka, I see you got company, so I'll give you women some time to be alone. I have a couple of errands to run anyways. I'll be home by dinner, all right, love," Olu said, gulping down the rest of his drink, standing over her back.

"Dinner? Okay. But, please be home by six. Because, after dinner, I was hoping we could catch that new *Tyler Perry* movie. Remember?" Liaka looked up at him, over her shoulder.

"Not a problem, love," Olu stated, then leaned over to plant a firm peck on her lips. "Nice to see you again, Kadiajah. Bye-bye, little girl," Olu ended, as he nodded to Asia, then waved at little Sky, before he disappeared into the back bedroom.

"I didn't know Olu was here. I knew I shoulda called first. But, I was right around the corner from here, so I just stopped by."

"You know I don't care about that. I was hoping to see you today anyways, so I could show you this," Liaka said happily, pushing her engagement ring close to Asia's face.

"He didn't...I know this isn't..."

"Yes, he did! And, yes, it is!" Liaka cheered, as Asia's eyes widened. She embraced Liaka's hand to get a closer look at her ring.

"Oh, my God! Oh, my God! Liaka, I'm so happy for you!" Asia threw her arms around Liaka. Asia's son returned from the bathroom to see Liaka and his mother bouncing in their seats, locked in an embrace. He giggled at their gestures as he jumped up next to his sister on the recliner to join her watching

TV. "Let me take a look at that ring again," Asia said happily, reaching for Liaka's hand again. "Wait a minute, girl. 'Cause I gots to get my sunglasses to stare at this!" Asia joked, squinting her eyes, twisting Liaka's hand to examine each angle of the ring.

"It's nice, isn't it?" Liaka said, with an indelible grin on her face.

"It's beautiful, absolutely beautiful. Liaka, I'm so happy for you," Asia sighed sincerely.

"When did this happen?"

"Last night. He just walked up behind me and...Asia, it was so romantic. He got down on one knee, told me I was his breath, his nourishment, his food. And girl, the way he made love to me after...oohhh," Liaka said with a shiver.

"Auntie Likey, I'm thirsty. Can I have something to drink?"

"Girl, don't you see grownups talking?" Asia snapped at her daughter.

"Of course, Sky," Liaka said.

"Sky, go get yourself something to drink. And get something for your brother, too. 'Cause right when he see you drinking something he's gonna miraculously get thirsty, too," Asia said curtly, then focused back on Liaka. "This is all so sudden, Liaka," Asia continued, her smile returned, "but, what about the bag? The duffel bag that you found? Did you ask him about that?"

"Th...the bag?"

"Um, yeah, the bag. A gun, bloody clothes, filled with money. Is that ringing a bell?" Asia said sarcastically. "Let me guess, he popped the big question on you, pushed a huge rock on your finger, and you forgot all about that? Does that sound about right?"

"No! No, that's not what happened. Girl, you know me better than that."

In the excitement of their celebration, Liaka forgot all about the fact that she told Asia about the duffel bag. Liaka knew she couldn't tell Asia the truth; that Olu robbed banks as somewhat of a hobby. Asia began to notice the change in Liaka's demeanor, her body language, her facial expression, the sudden change in the tone of her voice. Asia felt she had known Liaka long enough to determine when she was lying or telling the truth. From what she knew of Liaka, she was lying through her teeth.

"Okay, so what did he say?"

"Nothing really. He…"

"'Nothing'? What do you mean, 'nothing'?" Asia snapped, then leaned back to get a better look at Liaka.

"Um, why you say it like that?"

"Because! What do you mean, 'nothing'! How's he not gonna say something about the bag? You know what I think—I think you didn't ask him. I think he proposed to you and your head was so high up in the clouds that you didn't even care about the bag anymore. Bag? What bag?" Asia teased, her hands waving in the air as she looked up at the ceiling.

"Shaddup!" Liaka laughed, playfully pushing Asia on her shoulder. "Well, you know what, you're wrong! I did ask him about it and he told me everything," Liaka assured.

"Okay, then what did he say?"

"It wasn't his. There! You see, it wasn't even his. So, we were making a big deal about it and it wasn't even his. Are you satisfied?"

Asia just looked at her. "Are you gonna feed me then change my diaper, too? Maybe burp me? Because you must think I was born yesterday if you think I'm falling for that!"

"Well, get over my shoulder and get prepared to be burped, 'cause that's the truth. He told me the bag wasn't his and I believe him."

"Liaka, don't you think you should…"

"Look! Asia, please," Liaka spit, "just…let me have this moment. Just trust in me to know that I know what I'm doing. Please," Liaka pleaded, reaching out to squeeze Asia's thigh. Asia got the message.

"So, you're happy?"

"I don't think I've ever been happier," Liaka said fervently, embracing Asia's hand. Asia threw her arms around Liaka again. Liaka whispered, "thank you," in Asia's ear.

"Okay, okay, don't get all emotional on me. No need to get all teary eyed," Asia said with a smile, using her thumb to wipe the tears that swelled up in Liaka's eyes.

"Auntie Likey, why are you crying?" Asia's daughter asked. She walked in from the kitchen, carefully carrying two glasses of soda.

"I'm okay, Sky. I'm just happy."

"If you're happy, then why are you crying?"

"Sky, she's fine," Asia assured her, "sometimes when grownups are really, really happy, they cry. You can say they are tears of joy," Asia explained to her daughter who handed her brother a drink, a confused look still on her face. "So, did you guys set a date?"

 Triple Crown Publications presents...    Queen of Thieves
*PART 1*

"No. We're not even close to that. I think we just might take some time to enjoy the moment, enjoy the engagement period."

"Enjoy, huh? I think I know just what you mean when you say *enjoy* the engagement. Just make sure he don't enjoy you too much. You know what they say: why buy the cow when the milk is for free," Asia smirked.

"The milk might be for free, But, the milkshake isn't," Liaka said, with a mischievous smile.

"Girl, you a mess," Asia laughed.

"Enough about that. What's been going on with you?" Liaka asked, standing to walk towards the kitchen.

"Nothing much compared to your news. Just the same ol' thang. Me and Donovan had a long talk last night. We were on the phone for like three hours."

"Really? That's good. What did he have to say?" Liaka said, with a raised voice from the kitchen.

"Sky! Stop pulling at your braids! Come here." Sky popped up off the recliner at the sharp tone of her mother's voice and quickly sat on the floor between her legs.

"It itches," Sky whispered, looking up at her mother. Asia sucked her teeth and twisted Sky's head forward to watch TV as she began to take her braids out.

"We were just talking about everything. The past, the kids, the future, what happened between us," Asia said, as she took out two braids and ran her fingers through her wavy hair. "Donny, go in the bathroom and get mommy a brush for me, okay?" Jumping off the recliner in a second's time, her little energetic son ran out of the room to the bathroom.

"And? What was the final outcome?" Liaka pressed, walking back in the living room with a bowl full of chocolate chip cookies.

"Uh, uh! Now, you know you wrong!" Asia hissed, watching Liaka place the bowl on the coffee table.

"Auntie, can I have some cookies?"

"See? Now, you knew that was gonna happen when you brought them in here! You ain't slick!"

"Of course my little niece can have some," Liaka said, pushing the bowl in front of her. Sky dove into the bowl without asking her mother, stuffing a whole cookie into her mouth. Liaka looked over at Asia, pushing her tongue

49

out at her, teasing her.

"Oh, don't worry. I will get you back! When you have your lil' Olu's and lil' Liaka's running around her, I'm gonna spoil them to death!" Asia threatened, nodding her head.

"Yeah, yeah, I know. But, until then, finish telling me what he said," Liaka said, walking off to the kitchen again to return with two glasses of milk.

"You know how he is. We talked about everything and nothing. But, we did talk about why we couldn't seem to get along," Asia said, leaning forward to pop one of the cookies in her mouth. "So much for us watching our figures," Asia chuckled, then popped another cookie in her mouth, taking a sip of milk to wash it down.

"Forget about that! Did he talk about getting back together?" Liaka asked, snatching a handful of cookies herself.

"Not really. I think he was just calling for a booty-call," Asia snickered. Donovan Junior walked back into the living room and handed his mother the brush, then filled both hands with cookies and jumped back up on the recliner. "All he had to do was ask, 'cause I sure woulda gave him some," Asia confessed, running the brush through her daughter's hair.

"I know you woulda," Liaka smiled, "you know how it starts. First, it's just a couple of late-night booty-calls. Then, he's spending the night, waking up to the kids. Then, before you know it, he's moving back in."

Asia played on Liaka's words. A smile spread across her face. "Maybe you're right."

"I know I'm right! You know how men are. Their pride won't let them say they're sorry or that they were wrong. So, they always beat around the bush waiting for us to fix things. So, fix it! The next time he calls late-night, tell him that you'd rather talk in person than over the phone. Then, when he comes over, girl, put it on him 'til he's begging you to take him back! Go get your man back, girl."

"Girl, you ain't never lie!" Asia laughed, as they gave each other a high-five in the air.

# $C$hapter 7 | $S$phinx

$W$e have the place surrounded! There is no chance of escape!" blared over a police bullhorn, barely audible over the confusion of police sirens, and TV camera crews, along with their news reporters. The *First National Bank of Connecticut* was surrounded with commotion. Olu peeked out of a side window.

A large, black, trailer-type truck—S.W.A.T. It was parked about a block down the street. Yellow police tape was wrapped around the perimeter of three buildings within the area of the bank, with lines of people curiously watching on the other side. At least three television camera crews were visibly on the scene, their white vans lined front to back just inside the police tape.

Over fifty uniformed police officers scrambled in various areas on the scene, all taking orders from two plain-clothed detectives posted by a gold Crown Victoria. On the roofs of the adjacent buildings across the street, Olu spotted three snipers, setting up their high-powered rifles: one atop the roof of a dry cleaner, one to the left, about a block away in the top corner window of a real estate office, the last, camouflaged in the bushes about a half a block down.

Olu had stepped back from the blinders lowered in the windows once he had seen the snipers fully set up, his last vision that of a cop on one knee behind the open door of a marked police car, shouting orders through a bullhorn in front of the bank. Olu looked around the bank.

The security guard was shot, and possibly dead, from the looks of it. He laid lifeless as a male and female customer of the bank, now covered in his blood, propped his head on her knee, while the male applied pressure to the gunshot wound in his upper chest. Shakim, in a security guard uniform, and Diesel, dressed down in a black three-piece suit with a black ski mask, were both holding the seventeen customers at gunpoint.

The bank customers, now hostages, were all lying face down in the center of the bank with Diesel pacing back and forth on top of the teller counter with an AK-47 pointed down at them. Shakim was by the door with a sawed-off, double barrel shotgun in hand.

Olu and his team were in trouble.

Olu, dressed in a black three-piece tuxedo as well, paced the room in silence, his mind racing, trying to come up with some miraculous idea as to how they could make it out of there—alive. Their problems started from the time they entered the bank. Moves were miscalculated, positions were altered.

Shakim entered the bank and took down the security guard perfectly, just as planned. Or, at least, he thought it was perfect. Diesel and Olu entered the bank shortly behind to storm the counter. The only signal that they were given to alert any sign of danger was a blaring shriek from a female customer causing all three of them to turn around in shock to see the security guard's hands unfastened with his gun drawn on them.

This set off a chain reaction of events: Olu, Shakim, and Diesel reacted with all three of their guns being drawn on the security guard in a type of modern day Mexican stand-off, and the bank manager running for cover yelling out to a teller behind the counter to press the alarm. The security guard revealed how nervous he was, his hands visibly shook as the gun bounced back and forth between the three of them. Out of the three, the guard had no idea who he should keep the gun fixed on. Shakim and Diesel kept their positions, stiff as statues, their guns aimed at the security guard's head.

Olu slowly lowered his weapon.

"I give you my word, lower your weapon and place it on the floor and you won't get hurt. We both don't want any accidental shootings. I don't want anyone to die here, and I'm sure you don't want that either," Olu related to the security guard, with slow, calculated steps in his direction. There was a slight nod from the security guard as he began to lower his gun, only for a 'pop' to tear through the silence.

The guard spun to his side and was thrown back about ten feet as a bullet from Diesel's AK-47 tore through the right corner of his shoulder blade. The gunshot was enough for the security guard to squeeze off one shot of his own. The shot ricocheted off the white marble floor just inches passed Olu's head to embed in the wooden teller counter before he dropped his gun. Strangely enough, the loud ring of gunshots didn't startle Olu or cause him to jump from the explosion. His only response was a deliberate turn in Diesel's direction with a look of repulsion in his eyes. The minor standoff in the bank immediately erupted into a frenzy of screams and hysteria, with several customers bolting headfirst out of the front doors.

Olu's first response was to abandon the mission and cut their losses. But, within ten feet of the front doors, Olu paused in mid-sprint when three marked cars screeched wildly in front of the bank. A marked cop car even parked directly in front of their getaway car, blocking them in.

As the police quickly exited their cars to take cover behind their hoods and trunks, their guns aimed at the front doors, Olu shook his head as he backtracked inside of the bank. Before Olu had enough time to think, the bank was completely surrounded by a swarm of police and television crews.

"Number one, talk to me!" Shakim implored to Olu.

"Just relax. Everybody keep a calm head. As of now, we have the situation contained," Olu delivered calmly.

"And how tha fuck do you know?" Diesel challenged.

"Because we aren't dead yet!"

"What are your plans?" Shakim added, and for the first time, revealed signs of tension.

"We wait. I'm sure from the few that escaped, it's been related that the security guard is shot, possibly dead, and that there are several more hostages in here. Hostages changes the rules. And, with the TV crews out there, they can't afford any unnecessary civilian casualties. Somewhere along the line, the Feds were contacted. Give it another half an hour. Hostage negotiators will be contacting us," Olu related confidently.

"Then what? Then, what tha fuck we gonna do? How tha fuck we gonna get outta this?" Diesel barked, gesturing to the security guard and the terrified hostages shaking nervously on the floor. Olu watched Diesel's movements; his fidgety actions, his insistent pacing, his angry rants wielding a large assault rifle, and, most importantly, the reactions the hostages were having as they watched him.

"Believe this," Olu started, "losing control will only complicate things. And losing control, acting on emotions, is the last thing we need now. Is that clear?" Olu delivered sternly. Diesel was hesitant, but his silence indicated his understanding.

"Can I have everyone's attention?" Olu announced loudly. Complete silence swept over the room. "As you can see, we have a situation. I don't want to be in this position just as much as you. Because of that, I'm going to ask that everyone remain calm and, most importantly, to remain silent. I repeat, to remain silent. Question: does anyone here have any immediate medical issues?" Olu called out to the crowd. Of the seventeen hostages, three hands slowly rose over their heads. "You, what's the problem?" Olu asked an older black woman.

"I...I'm on dialysis," she stuttered nervously, then lowered her hand.

"You?" Olu gestured, to the next middle-aged white woman.

"I'm a diabetic and I don't have any insulin. I..."

"Okay, and you?" Olu spit, pointing at the last man.

"I'm...I'm sick..."

"Speak up!"

"I'm sick! I have HIV," the man stated shamefully. The comment the man made produced the exact effect he was trying to avoid; most of the eyes were now glancing back and forth at him.

"You three...," Olu stated, as a single phone at a corner desk rang, "... stand up. Get the guard and move over there," Olu demanded. They quickly complied.

"But, wait! What about us?" A white man in his mid-twenties cried out, then jumped to his feet. Shakim was the first to swarm down on him.

"Number two!" Olu blurted, causing Shakim to stop dead in his tracks. "He's right. Bring him over here." Shakim walked the man over at gunpoint. An immediate buzz of grumbling came from the others in the crowd.

"I have three kids!" one woman cried.

"I'm also a mother!" from another. Other cries began to erupt from the crowd as Olu raised his hand to bring silence over the room.

"In time. But, I want him, specifically. He was the first to speak up, so he gets preferential treatment," Olu delivered to the crowd as the man cheerfully walked with the other three to the security guard. The phone continued to ring before Olu went over to the desk to answer it.

"This is special agent Tom Berkewitz. May I ask who am I speaking to?"

"Sphinx. You can call me, The Sphinx."

"Okay, Sphinx. Is there anyone hurt, injured?"

"We have a total of seventeen hostages among us. There is one, the security guard. He is critically wounded. We have another three requiring medical attention."

"Okay, Sphinx, that is very good. I see that you have an assessment of the situation," the detective said assuringly. "What would you like? How can we resolve this as safely and quickly as possible without causing any further incidents?"

"I have a hostage that will be coming to the door. Stand down!" Olu demanded.

"Everyone! We have a hostage coming out! Lower your weapons! No one is instructed to fire! I repeat, they are releasing a hostage!" Olu heard the detective scream out before he dropped the receiver on the desk.

"Come on, you, let's go," Olu commanded at the man. Several of the hostages began to grow restless as they watched the man quickly abandon the group with the medical issues, even the wounded guard, and approach the front door. Olu followed the man closely behind until they reached the back of the glass entrance doors. "Don't run. Just walk casually and, when you get out there, you tell them that they are to follow my every command. Got it?" Olu instructed, as the young man looked back with nervous eyes, then slowly pushed the front doors open.

"He's coming out!" the detective screamed at the sight of the front doors slowly opening, "I repeat, he's coming out! It's a hostage! Nobody..."

BOOM!

...tore through the tense silence as an M16 round from Olu's weapon threw the young man face forward about twenty feet towards the steps. Every cop, spectator, and camera crew in the vicinity dropped to the ground or jumped for cover behind any solid object upon hearing the gunshot. The young man's body sluggishly rolled down the fifteen steps, leaving a bloodstained trail behind him.

As people began to slowly rise from their cover, gasps and shrieks pierced through the crowd upon the first sight of the man's grotesquely contorted figure at the bottom of the steps. The front of his chest was completely blown off, revealing a hole the size of a volleyball where his chest used to be. His eyes were still open, staring off blankly into eternity. A glance up at the bank's front doors revealed the shadow of a masked Olu who quickly vanished back inside.

"Are you still there?" Olu spoke calmly into the phone once he returned to the desk. There was a brief pause before the detective responded.

"Wha...what the fuck's going on? I thought we were coming to an understanding?"

"From this point on, *you* will now determine the amount of casualties we have."

"But, why? Why did you…"

"That was a message. It was unfortunate, but, it had to be done. You must understand the extreme importance of complying to the letter of my demands. Do you understand?"

"Bu...but,...how, how do we know that you will not harm any other hostages?"

"You don't!" The detective remained silent. "Your silence can only indicate that you are contemplating your two options. Let me see if I have this correctly: being that a hostage has been killed, you can proceed to use lethal means to secure the bank. But, the flip-side to that is the potential, and I assure you, numerous casualties that will occur. I'm sure you don't want to be responsible for a blood bath. Your second option: continue with your hostage negotiations with the hopes of sparing as many innocent lives as possible. Is this correct?"

"What do you want?" The detective sighed sadly.

"I want the same thing you want. For this to be over. Do we have an understanding?"

"Sphinx, the last thing I want is for anyone else to get hurt. I…"

"Listen, we're wasting time. On good faith, I'm going to release the hostages with the medical issues and, also, the wounded guard. In fifteen minutes, you can call back and report your status."

"But, wait, what about the…"

*CLICK!*

Olu placed the phone back on the receiver. Walking back over to the hostages, they all seemed to cringe once Olu got back within their personal space.

"I will not harm you. It is unfortunate that you had to witness that. But, I

 Triple Crown Publications presents... Queen of Thieves *PART 1*

gave each of you direct instructions to remain silent. Unfortunately, he failed to comply with that very simple demand," Olu announced. "You three," he gestured to the group with the medical issues, "you can go. Take the guard and carry him out with you." The older black woman slowly rose to her feet, her lips quivered in anticipation to speak. All of them stared at Olu with a look of utter fear on their faces, unsure if that was their time to be released, or if they were to share the same fate as the first hostage.

"I give you my word; I will not harm any of you. Now, go!" Olu delivered sharply. The older black woman nodded behind tearful eyes. She helped the other woman and the man as they lifted the security guard to place his arms over their shoulders and walk off towards the front doors. The boisterous crowd outside quickly quieted to a low rumble as the front doors slowly opened to reveal the three hostages carrying the security guard.

From the middle of the bank, Olu, Shakim, and Diesel watched as the S.W.A.T. team, in full combat attire, carefully advanced to the hostages with bulletproof body shields covering themselves, to surround the hostages and quickly usher them away. The older black woman broke down in tears and collapsed upon first sight of two other S.W.A.T. team members dragging the dead man from the bottom of the steps by both arms.

Some members of the crowd let out cheers of relief, some even collapsed, as heavy, dark-brown wool blankets were thrown over the hostages once they were whisked away to safety. Once the hostages disappeared from sight, safe in police custody, Shakim turned to Olu.

"Now, what?"

"We wait," Olu answered, staring off at a clock hanging high up on a wall. "Now, we wait."

# Chapter 8 | Guilianna

D amn, Liaka! What the fuck, did you fall up in there?" Lianna shouted to Liaka in her bathroom. Seconds passed before the toilet could be heard flushing as Liaka emerged to meet Lianna in the living room. Liaka rubbed circles over her stomach with a slight moan from the diarrhea she'd been experiencing all day. She sunk heavily into the plush, leather interior of the sofa next to Lianna who was splitting a blunt down the middle with the thumbs of her French-tipped nails.

Lianna was a good-looking woman as far as Liaka's view of beauty was concerned. According to Liaka's unique standards, that was pretty good. Lianna was half-Peruvian and half-Haitian. A product of being bi-racial, Lianna was a perfect mixture of her very dark-skinned father and her olive-skinned mother, resulting in Lianna having a rich, caramel skin tone, resembling someone of Indian descent. Most of her other physical features were a direct reflection of her mother: five feet, five inches, extremely long, jet-black hair, and unmistakable green eyes.

Growing up all of her life on the North end of Hartford, Lianna was reminded, on nearly a daily basis, that she was easily a dark-skinned replica of her mother. Lianna vehemently denied that fact, but, aside from the skin tone, she was, in fact, a spitting image of her mother in every way. Lianna had her reasons for her extreme dislike in being compared to her mother, mainly because of her mother's promiscuous reputation around the neighborhood. Ironically, the image of a promiscuous woman that Lianna came to hate about her mother was the very same image that she mimicked, albeit an image that she could not see herself in. She ultimately became the person that she hated the most.

Lianna had a little brother who was two years younger than her, Angel, who was rumored around the neighborhood to be the product of an extramarital affair. Lianna knew in her heart, coupled with Angel's uncanny resemblance to a local light-skinned drug dealer from a different housing project, that Angel wasn't a spawn from the loins of her father.

Her father, who worked as an out of state truck driver, spent most of the year on the road, which left Lianna growing up for years, watching countless different men frequenting her mother's bedroom when her father was away. So it wasn't too farfetched for the rumors to be true. That was one of the major factors in Lianna's dislike for her mother, but, there was another.

Aside from her scandalous reputation and the infidelity on the part of her father, Lianna despised the treatment her mother gave her. Lianna felt that her mother neglected her, ignored her, and emotionally abused her, more concerned with the current man that she was sneaking around with than the well-being of her own kids. This left Lianna with feelings of resentment towards her mother. With her father being absent throughout most of her life, Lianna numbed the pain of her reality by any means.

"Coming out feeling about ten pounds lighter, huh?" Lianna teased, singing the lyrics of an *Ice Cube* track as she licked the blunt closed.

"It must have been something I ate last night," Liaka complained, with her face scrunched up.

"I got a cork in the kitchen if you wanna sit on it."

"Ha, ha, very funny."

"No, seriously, I have some Pepco Bismol in the medicine cabinet in the bathroom. But, whenever I don't feel good, this always does the trick," Lianna winked, then flicked a lighter to the tip of the blunt. Lianna, being an experienced weed smoker, inhaled deeply, filling her lungs completely with the intoxicating smoke. She passed the blunt to Liaka who hesitantly accepted it.

The trail of narcotic weed smoke danced from the tip of the blunt to evaporate in the air, hypnotizing Liaka into a trance. Liaka was the opposite of Lianna in almost every way, with smoking weed being no exception. The

moist tip of the blunt made contact with Liaka's lips. She inhaled lightly. Lianna blew out the cloud of smoke that she held in her lungs, looking at Liaka with a smile.

"It always kills me to watch you smoke. You hold the blunt like it's gonna hurt you. Don't worry, it won't bite you."

Liaka exhaled, but, there wasn't a sign of smoke coming from her lips. "I'm sorry I ain't you, Miss Bob Marley," Liaka jived, then handed the blunt back to Lianna.

"Shiiit! I woulda smoked his ass under the table!" Lianna spit with a chuckle, quickly raising the blunt back to her lips. Lianna devoured the next inhale, the fiery tip of the blunt glowing bright red from the strong intake.

"I bet you woulda," Liaka smiled, watching Lianna handle the blunt.

"If you would stop acting like you scared of the damned thing, then maybe you would learn to get your smoke on, too!" Lianna took another drag before she passed it back to Liaka. "Even when I first started smoking, I wasn't acting all like that! After the third or fourth time, most people just get used to it. It ain't nothing but smoke," Lianna stated nonchalantly, with a shrug. Liaka inhaled again, this time with more confidence, her second intake consuming more smoke. The intake was more than she could handle, Liaka choked and fought the urge to cough.

"Just relax. That's why you ain't doing that shit right! 'Cause you acting like it's a big deal," Lianna explained, as she shook her head at Liaka, then attempted to remove the blunt from her hand.

"I got...(cough)...got this," Liaka choked, pulling her hand back. Liaka wiped her watery eyes then took a deep breath. She gently placed the blunt back to her lips and carefully inhaled. For once, she had to admit, Lianna was right. With Liaka forcing herself to relax a little more, the next intake went down much smoother, despite ingesting more than double the smoke the last time around.

Another thing Liaka had to agree with Lianna on was the blunt making her feel better. Considering the result after all the coughing, choking, and teary eyes, Liaka found the weed affecting her to the point where she forgot all about the pain in her stomach. Liaka took another drag with confidence then handed it back to Lianna.

"I told you," Lianna said.

"That's enough for me," Liaka sighed, the few drags left her head spinning.

"That's another reason why I like smoking with you. It's almost like I'm smoking by myself," Lianna said happily, looking forward to enjoying the other two-thirds of the blunt by herself. Faint sounds of 50 Cent's "*When It Rains It Pours*" could be heard playing from a distance, but, gradually increased in sound and intensity as it neared close enough to rattle Lianna's second floor living room windows.

Lianna stood from the couch to approach her front windows, sliding the blinds up to peer out to the street below. It was her little brother, Angel. He rolled to a stop in front of Lianna's apartment building in his *Honda Prelude* with the hatchback open, blasting the music from his trunk. Lianna watched her brother as Angel and two of his boys exited the car upon the sight of a group of females approaching. They quickly surrounded the group of teenage females, randomly selecting their desired choices from the crowd. Lianna opened her window and leaned out to the street below.

"How you gonna talk to another bitch like that right in front of my house? I hope you at least brought some Pampers home for your kids you got up here!" Lianna snapped at Angel. The whole crowd looked up to see the lone female ranting out the window. Angel rolled his eyes up at Lianna and ignored her, then continued to spit game at the female in front of him. "Oh, you just gonna still keep talking to my man, bitch? Yeah, bitch, I'm talking to you! The one with the multi-colored shirt on that should read 'I'm a hoe' right on the front. Yeah, you, bitch!" Lianna cursed, pointing to the female in front of Angel.

"Lia! Why don't you stop fuckin' playin'!" Angel barked.

"You can deny me, papi. But, please don't deny lil' Angel, little Lianna, and the twins. Don't do that to your kids, papi," Lianna whined from the window in a sad tone. The female talking to Angel heard enough. She strongly pulled her hand from Angel's hold, rolled her eyes at him, and boldly walked away. Angel's pleas fell on deaf ears as the female and her girls separated themselves from the drama, walking off across the street. Angel shook his head watching the female's ass switch away, then turned up to a smiling Lianna in the window.

"What the fuck is wrong with you, you dingy-ass broad?" Angel cursed, as his boys pushed and laughed at him.

"Aw, shut up, nigga. Your game is wack anyways," Lianna laughed, withdrawing from the window.

"Now you know you ain't right," Liaka said, laughing herself as Lianna

made her way back to the couch.

"So, what? He know he got a girl. Serves him right!" Lianna said with no shame.

"Guess what?" Liaka blurted, standing up to walk towards the kitchen, "we going out this weekend."

"We are?"

"Yes. So, I'm trusting you to find the hot spot. You know how Asia is, and I'm tired of trying to convince her to let it go of her still sweating Donovan. So, I want us to go out and have some fun. You know, try to help her take her mind off of him," Liaka screamed from the kitchen, she returned to the living room with a glass of soda.

"Damn, bitch! You couldn't bring me something to drink?"

"And it's so refreshing, too," Liaka teased, then smacked her lips after she took another sip. Liaka and Lianna turned upon hearing a rattle at the front door for Angel and his boys to walk in.

"Angel, go get me something to eat. Please, I'm hungry," Lianna said, as soon as they entered her place.

"I ain't getting your stupid ass shit, puñeta! Starve!" Angel spewed. He dropped his keys on the coffee table, then headed straight towards her bedroom.

"Come on, Angel. I'm serious. Grab your sister a two-piece chicken or something. Please," Lianna continued whining. Angel ignored her, then disappeared into her bedroom. Both of his boys, who were Spanish, were draped in all red and blue apparel. If Liaka had to guess, they were most likely gang members: Los Solidos. Both of them made themselves at home without particularly being invited. One of them plopped down in Lianna's recliner, with the other being so bold as to squeeze in between Liaka and Lianna on the couch.

"Damn, chocolate! I bet you taste sweet as a motherfucka! Just like chocolate," the one between them said, licking his lips at Liaka. Liaka backed up and lifted one eyebrow at him.

"Carlos, believe me, you'll *never* find out!" Lianna snapped at him, then tapped him lightly on the back of his head.

"Ma, let a nigga hit that shit," Carlos said, once he noticed the half-smoked blunt in the ashtray. He instinctively reached for it, only for Lianna to quickly intercept it from him.

"Um, that's not gonna happen!" she blurted, lifting the blunt to her lips. "Y'all niggas ain't smoking my shit up," she took a deep inhale, then passed the blunt over to Liaka. Carlos turned back to Liaka with lust, followed by securing his hand around her neck. He licked his lips, staring at Liaka's mouth.

"Chica, let a nigga taste that smoke off them thick ass lips. Mira…"

"Ay, dios mio! Angel, would you come in here and get your stupid ass lil' friend? He act like he ain't never see a female before!" Liaka cursed, then reached over the back of the couch to strongly pull his arm from around Liaka.

"Yo, Lia! Where tha fuck my shit at?" Angel screamed from the bedroom. Sucking her teeth, Lianna stood from the couch, but not before throwing Carlos one last dirty look. Carlos simply smiled and winked at Lianna as she walked out of the living room.

"Now that Miss Hater is gone, what's really good, mamacita?" Carlos slurred, his body shifting closer to Liaka and his arm returning back over her shoulder.

"I got a man. In fact, I'm engaged," Liaka said flatly, removing his arm again.

"What that gotta do with me? I can keep a secret. Shit! I can definitely keep a secret when it comes down to you," Carlos stated in a seductive tone, placing his hand on Liaka's thigh.

"Well, unfortunately, I can't!" Liaka snapped, removing his hand. Angel came back out of the back bedroom with Lianna following closely behind him. He whispered something to Lianna before turning to his boys.

"Yo, come on. I got what I need. Let's bounce."

His boy on the recliner jumped up without a word as Carlos turned back to Liaka. He leaned in close to her ear and whispered, "chica, when you stop playing games and you ready for a nigga to lick you into luxury, holla at your boy," then flicked his tongue out at Liaka, followed by blowing her a kiss. Liaka fought the urge to burst out laughing in his face, and, instead, just smiled as he jumped up to meet Angel at the front door.

"Angel, please, pa. Grab me something on your way back," Lianna pleaded desperately.

"Lia, for real, I ain't going nowhere near the east side. You must ain't hear. It's like a thousand fuckin' cops and TV reporters around there! Some motherfuckas robbing a bank or something. Got hostages an' all that shit.

The ma'fuckin' police got that shit locked down! The S.W.A.T., the Feds. I'm surprised you ain't see it, that shit is all over the news."

Liaka's mind lit up.

It was something in the way Angel said it that caused a chill to come over her. She dropped the blunt in the ashtray and searched frantically around Lianna's place for the TV remote. The mere sight of the half-smoked blunt laying unprotected in the ashtray caused Angel to sneak his way back over to it. Liaka found the TV remote and clicked it over to the local news.

"LATE BREAKING NEWS! This is Keisha Grant, and if you're just joining us, we are live at the scene with explosive coverage of an unbelievably hostile hostage situation at the First National Bank of Connecticut. Minutes ago, our camera crew caught one of the most gruesome acts of violence this reporter has seen in her many years as a reporter, from an apparent police negotiation that went terribly wrong. I must advise you, the footage we are about to show you is very, very disturbing," the female reporter announced, as the TV screen flashed to the execution of the young man on the front steps of the bank. The image was blurred due to the cameraman catching every graphic detail as the gun-blast tore the man's chest open, but, it was enough to catch the man's violent execution.

"Oh, shit!" Angel barked, at the sound of the gunshot and the blurred image of the victim rolling like a rag-doll down the steps. "That shit was gangsta as fuck, nigga! Yo, them niggas is real as fuck! 'Cause they murdered that nigga, pretty-pretty, fa sho!" Angel screamed, followed by a sick laugh as all eyes in the room locked on the TV screen.

The cameraman, after gaining his composure to steady the shaking picture, zoomed in on the body at the bottom of the steps, then quickly to the blurry image of the gunman disappearing back inside the bank. Liaka felt her stomach drop. The little buzz from smoking the blunt immediately faded as she focused on the gun-wielding shadow backing into the darkness of the bank.

The shot of the apparatus was brief, a couple of seconds at the most, but, it was enough. Liaka looked on with sad eyes as she watched the man's movements; his particular style of dress, the suit he wore, and the most striking detail, his shoes. It was Olu. Aside from the ski mask, the clothes were all too familiar to Liaka. Visions of him raced through her mind; the warmth of his body next to hers that morning before she got up for work, his smell, the kiss he gave her before he left. The words that he said to her only days earlier hit her like a bolt of lightning: *This is my last job, I'm ending it for you.*

"Lianna! I have to go there! To the bank!" Liaka cried, jumping to her feet.

"What? Girl, are you crazy?"

"Damn, shorty! You wanna be on TV that bad?" The third kid finally spoke up, causing Angel and Carlos to break out in laughter.

"Lianna, please! I have to go there. I'm going!" Liaka was barely able to contain herself as she grabbed her coat and raced to the front door. Lianna shook her head.

"Liaka, wait up!" Lianna called out, stopping Liaka in her tracks, "Let me get my jacket. I'm coming with you," Lianna sighed, slowly standing to her feet. She went for her jacket not really knowing why Liaka found it so urgent to go there. Lianna returned to the living room to see Liaka bouncing, unable to stand still at the door.

"Damn, girl, what's the rush?" Lianna stated, as Liaka was practically out the door. "Let me just get the blunt," Lianna glanced back to the ashtray on the coffee table. It was empty, aside from a small mountain of ashes and cigarette butts. The blunt was gone, but not far. A trail of smoke rose from behind Angel's back. "Give me my damned blunt, boy!" Lianna snapped, then stormed over to Angel to snatch the blunt out of his hand.

"Oh, I thought y'all was straight," Angel chuckled, as Lianna rolled her eyes at him and headed out the door with Liaka.

# Chapter 9 | José Dominguez

A rust-colored Crown Victoria pulled up on the scene of the bank. The yellow police tape lining the area was lifted as the car rolled within the police barricade. Stepping from the vehicle, the lone driver removed his sunglasses. Overhead, two helicopters—one from a local news station, the other from the police department—circled like vultures around the area of the bank, recording every second of the activities below.

Blue and white wooden barricades that read POLICE! DO NOT CROSS! We're keeping the various news crews and spectators at bay. Several of the news crews on the scene were growing restless as they patiently waited on a report from the police on the current status of the hostage crisis. Upon sight of the lone detective, several of the TV reporters rushed in his direction with their camera crews close behind.

"Are the hostages still alive?"

"What do the robbers want?"

"When is this finally going to be over?" Came ranting's from various reporters as they surrounded him, shoving their microphones and cameras in his face. Several uniformed officers came to his aid as they parted the way for him. He was knocked side to side as he pushed his way through the crowd. Despite the cries from the reporters shouting out to him for answers, he remained silent as he departed from them. Traveling a few feet from their heckles, he spotted a group of plain-clothes detectives congregating around an unmarked car. But, before he could get to them, he stopped and took a look at the front of the bank.

The large white, Roman-style podiums lining the entrance stood like a setting from a distance past. The detective looked down from the beautiful architectural display to see a trail of blood lining the steps to form a pool at the bottom. His lip curled in anger from the sanguinary stained steps as the sight held him for a moment. He was momentarily lost in thought, only being distracted by the sight of a hand waving him over.

"Detective Dominguez, it's good to have you with us," the lead detective on the scene announced, with his hand extended. Detective Dominguez embraced the lead detective's hand in a firm shake as he entered their small semi-circle.

Detective Dominguez knew nothing of the current status of hostage negotiations, aside from the obvious pool of blood staining the bottom of the front steps. With so many different agencies on the scene, no one in particular wanted to sign off on or be responsible for the final and lethal means of storming the bank. No one wanted the potential civilian casualties on their hands, or their record. No one except for Detective José Dominguez.

Known throughout the squad as "The Cleaner," the Boston-raised Dominican was the lead detective of the Homicide/Special Crime Squad of the Hartford Police Department. Enlisted to the department three years prior, José took that particular unit by storm; his presence and tactics alone dropped the violent crime in Hartford by fifteen percent for every year he was employed there. He was crass, vile, and borderline illegal in the procedures that he used to clean up the crime on the streets but, to his superiors, the bottom line was he was effective. Public polls indicated that the city never felt safer.

Relocating from the Boston Police Department four years prior, José left the Boston P.D. under questionable terms. An investigation against him for allegations of indecent violent tactics to get suspects to talk, to unlawful conduct as an officer, and even allegations of inappropriate sexual misconduct with prostitutes were never confirmed-all on the condition that he turn in his badge and retire from the Boston Police Department.

This didn't stop him from joining the Hartford Police Department who ignored the previous allegations made against him. Their only focus was the

statistics of crime that his employment helped greatly reduce. The Mayor, along with the City's Chief of Police backed his every move, allowing him exclusive reign in his department, as long as he could continue to produce the same results.

It was results José gave them.

José took six months to handpick the most lethal, unorthodox detectives he could find to make his special unit. His motto being: "The crooks don't play by the rules, so we have to meet them on their playing field." As such, most of his tactics went unquestioned from his superiors due to his outstanding results. So, along with the enlistment of a few confidential informants on the police payroll, C.I's and 'snitches', Detective José Dominguez dominated the streets with his crew, leaving in their wake a trail of corruption, but, also, cleaner streets.

"What's the status here?" José inquired, to no one in particular. All heads on the scene remained silent, two detectives even bowed their heads.

"Please, excuse us, gentlemen," the lead detective said, leading José away from them, off to the side. Once they were a considerable distance away, enough where the other detectives couldn't get an earful, the lead detective said, "it's not looking good, José. We have two dead, the security guard and one of the hostages. The bastards actually executed the hostage right on the front steps, right in front of the vultures," he gestured to the TV reporters and their cameras.

"As we're told by the one who's calling the shots, they have another seventeen hostages inside. Their leader, he goes by the name of Sphinx. As of yet, he's unknown. We don't have his name listed in any of our databases. Even the FBI is at a loss. His M.O. is even new to us. So, as it stands, the guy's just that, a Sphinx, a fuckin' riddle! But, one thing's for sure, by the way he talks and the method that he's using, he's definitely not an amateur."

"Who has the lead?"

"We have the lead as it stands but, we're at the point where we're going to turn this over to the Feds. Let them deal with this shit!"

"Don't!" José expressed, "We can handle this. This is our fuckin' collar. Who's on negotiations?"

"Berkewitz."

"Berkewitz? That fuckin' mook! He couldn't talk a two-dollar trick out of her panties for twenty bucks! He's the fuckin' idiot you got talking to these

Triple Crown Publications presents... Queen of Thieves
*PART 1*

guys?" José barked, for the lead detective to nod. "And let me guess, the civilian got killed on his fuckin' clock, huh? Does that sound about right?" The detective regretfully nodded again. José shook his head in disbelief.

"First things first. Get those fuckin' news reporters back as far as you can! We don't need them up our asses, clogging up our crime scene. Any one of them give you a problem, arrest them! Two, tell the fuckin' gook suit squad, we got this! We don't need those stick-in-the-ass, by the book Feds telling us how to do our jobs! And three, patch me through to these fuckin' assholes so I can bring this travesty to an end!" The lead detective, secretly glad to be relieved of that position, ran off to comply with José's demands. Within moments, he sprinted back with a large portable phone housed in a black leather case.

"I'm sure you guys at least killed the main lines leading out of the building, right?" José took possession of the phone and rested it on the trunk of a vehicle.

"Absolutely. The main water was shut off as well. We were going to give them another couple of hours and kill the air. And if this proceeds into the night, we all had plans to kill the lights," the lead detective reported.

"Alright, patch me through," José declared, raising the phone to his ear as the lead detective dialed.

The hostages, Olu, Shakim, and Diesel looked up as the same single phone in the corner rang, shattering the silence in the room. Three hours had passed since the beginning raid on the bank, and Olu and his team were no closer to figuring out a way to escape than when they first began.

Diesel's initial fear transformed into a paralyzing panic as he reduced himself from pacing the bank, to fidgeting in the corner, to now being huddled on the floor in the corner with his weapon clutched tightly to his chest. Shakim was just the opposite. He remained calm, cool, and collected. His stance was militant as he patiently waited on orders from Olu. Olu slowly approached the ringing phone, with all eyes in the room following his every move to the desk in the corner.

"May I ask who I'm speaking to?" José said.

"Sphinx. Are you ready to negotiate?"

"This is Detective José Dominquez of the Special Crime Unit. Are the hostages still safe? What…"

"José? They called in 'The Cleaner', huh?" Olu spit over José with a chuckle.

José was speechless. He didn't think anyone outside of the department, and only within his unit, knew the nickname they gave him.

"Sphinx, did you say your name was? How did you...who told you...?"

"Do you really think this is the appropriate time to discuss where you have an obvious leak in your department? José, we have a situation on our hands, remember?"

"You're right. You're absolutely right. So, now I figure you obviously know who I am, that maybe we can stop playing games and I can get to know who you really are," José probed, totally uncomfortable that, as it stood, the man on the other end had one up on him.

"You don't need to know more than you already know. Just be confident that I, and most importantly, the associates that I work for, know who you are, Detective José Dominguez. Six years on the Boston P.D., three with the Hartford P.D. I see that you're doing pretty good for yourself. Especially considering the little mishap that lead to your, shall I say, dismissal from Precinct 432 in Boston. You moved up quickly, even taking over for Berkewitz, I see," Olu narrated to José. José remained silent, stewing in his own anger from hearing this unknown man recite his not so private past.

"Very good. It seems as if you did your homework. I'm impressed. Now what do you want?"

"I want what I came here for, the armored truck! Due to a discrepancy from the security guard, I was obviously unsuccessful in my interception of it. Give me the truck and this will all be over."

"The armored truck? We..."

"Listen, José. This isn't the time for stalling or pulling any of the evasive stunts that you attempt on the five-dollar dope fiends that you have a high success of busting. If this call made you believe in anything, believe that I'm intricately familiar with your little procedures. Am I making myself clear, José?"

José took a couple of seconds to digest what he was hearing, but finally said, in a low tone, "I understand you."

"Good. Now that we're on the same page, let's try to reach the same goal. Two things need to be established: One, we need the truck with its entire inventory—fifteen million dollars. Two, we need a jet, a Steinbrenner model, at the New Haven Tweed airport terminal with enough fuel to make it to South America."

"Then, what? What about the hostages?"

"As an act of good faith, I will release ten of the hostages. But, the other seven will come with us to the airport where the jet will be waiting for us. This is the deal, two hostages will check the money in the truck to make sure everything is clear. If they come back successful, we will take the truck and leave ten hostages. If those orders are complied with, to the letter, everything should go smoothly to the airport. At that time, once we arrive at the airport, I will have my pilot check the cabin and a quick survey of the plane to make sure we are safe to lift off. At that time, I will release five more hostages."

"But,...but,, what about the last two hostages?"

"One hundred miles out to sea, we will fly just below the radar and allow the last two hostages to parachute into the ocean. I'm sure you'll have the appropriate reinforcements to retrieve them."

"But, how do we know that they will be safe?"

"You don't!" Olu said sharply. "I'll give you thirty minutes to have the truck here, along with the rest of my demands," Olu ended, then hung up the phone. José looked at the disconnected receiver for a second then threw it along with its case as far as he could.

"*AAAAAGGGGHHHHH!*" José screamed at the top of his lungs as he totally lost it, kicking and punching the closest vehicle next to him, even punching out the side of a back window. All eyes within screaming distance instantly turned to catch the tail end of José's violent outburst.

"José! José!" The lead detective chanted, trying to grab hold of him to calm him down. "The cameras! The spectators! Look around, damn it! Get a hold of yourself!" Catching his breath, José looked around to see a few flashes from newspaper photographers and camera crews catching his every move.

"I'm gonna kill that motherfucker! I swear to you, I'm gonna fuckin' kill him myself!" José vowed, through clenched teeth. "If that little piece of shit thinks I'm gonna listen to even one of his fuckin' demands, he's crazy! I'll kill every hostage in there just to get to him!"

"What were his demands? What does he want?"

"I can tell you what he wants. But, I think it would be more appropriate to tell you what he's gonna get!"

# Chapter 10 | *I Can't Leave*

Liaka and Lianna found it almost impossible to find a parking space close to the bank due to the yellow tape and police barricades blocking the scene. She circled two blocks, then double parked in the closest thing to a parking spot she could find. She slammed the transmission into park, killed the engine and sprinted from the car at full speed towards the bank.

"Slow down! What's the rush?" Lianna cried, as Liaka separated the distance between them to fifty feet within the span of three seconds. Despite her heels, Liaka moved like she was wearing jogging sneakers as she made it to the scene within record time. Lianna, busy taking the last few tokes on the blunt, flicked the blunt roach from her fingers, then looked up to see Liaka quickly disappear into the crowd.

"Ma'am, I'm going to have to ask you to please remain behind the yellow tape," a uniformed officer said to Liaka as she squeezed her way to the front of the spectators, ignoring the makeshift barricade.

"But,...but, I know someone in there! My husband, he's in there!" Liaka cried to the officer who held her back.

"I'm sorry, ma'am. But, I can't allow anyone beyond this point," the officer explained sympathetically.

Liaka looked up at the sound of a helicopter over her head. Her hair blew wildly out of place from its massive spinning blades, throwing an uproar of wind upon anything within distance. Liaka felt the image on the TV screen that she had seen at Lianna's did the scene no justice. Being there, watching the scene first hand, Liaka now realized the seriousness of the situation. Liaka favored the scene to a war zone from all the police vehicles and police personnel on the scene. The cop that was holding Liaka back looked down to see the lost look in her eyes.

"Ma'am, this hasn't been confirmed, so please don't hold me to this. But, it has been rumored that negotiations from our best lead detective has led to the imminent release of at least ten hostages," he related in a secretive tone.

"Hostages? Please, just tell me what's going on!" Liaka pleaded.

"It was a bank heist. Apparently, things went wrong because the individuals who are holding the bank up immediately killed the security guard and later, in front of the cameras, killed an innocent hostage on the steps. But, recent reports lead us to believe that all the rest of the hostages are, at present, safe. So, it's very likely that your husband is okay now."

"What are they gonna do? What's gonna happen?"

"I don't know. The way the lead officers are handling this has not been conveyed to anyone. But, believe me, ma'am, these *guys are not going to get away with this!*"

Searching through the crowds, Lianna finally found Liaka with the cop and approached her from behind. "There you are! Thanks for leaving me!" Lianna said, embracing Liaka's elbow.

The cop glanced down at the female who broke into their conversation, oblivious to the fact that she was clearly trying to avoid eye contact with him. Unbeknownst to the officer, Lianna hated cops with a passion. An incident that Lianna encountered a few years prior in an abandoned alley left her jaded to all cops, all authority figures for that matter.

Noticing a young teen sprinting from a back project hallway, Lianna was curiously led by the sounds of groans and shouts to stumble upon the sight of a scuffle: three cops savagely beating a shadowy figure on the ground behind a dumpster. With each step, Lianna closed the distance between them to see each vicious blow being delivered by their nightsticks. Lianna was unsure as to why she was mysteriously drawn to the figure curled up on the ground and, in hindsight, couldn't understand how the cops didn't take the time to look up and notice an onlooker approaching them. Then it hit her like a bolt of lightning.

Flinching from another blow, the body on the ground lifted his head just enough for a street light across the street to shine its dim light on his face. It was Angel! The teen being savagely beaten on the ground, hidden to the world, was her own little brother. What happened next was still a little fuzzy to Lianna. All she could remember was charging one of them full throttle, jumping on his back with a fury of blows, and even biting at the cop's neck like a vicious animal.

After about a minute of scuffling with Lianna on his back, the cop wildly flipped her over his shoulder and slammed her violently on the cement below. The unexpected appearance of Lianna didn't thwart the cops on their mission. In fact, they only turned their anger and aggression on her, beating her and Angel within an inch of their lives.

With no resistance left from either of them, the cops left them both in the alley, bloody, lifeless piles of flesh, discarded like trash. Lianna's hatred for the police only heightened, coupled with other graphic stories from friends and family members who also suffered abuse from the hands of corrupt cops. In the end, Lianna was left with the position that all authority figures, especially cops, were the enemy. Liaka barely felt the gentle touch of Lianna who tugged on her elbow as the words of the cop repeated in her head. Those guys are not going to get away with this!

"Liaka! Liaka!" Lianna repeated, snapping Liaka back to reality. "Come on, let's get out of here," Lianna continued, trying to lead Liaka away.

"I can't," Liaka mumbled through sad eyes, "I can't leave him here."

Triple Crown Publications presents... Queen of Thieves PART 1

# $C$hapter 11 | $A$venge $M$e

$E$veryone up, now! Move!" Olu commanded, to a weary group of hostages. Groggy bodies snapped at attention as the seventeen hostages stood to their feet. All of them huddled in a cluster of bodies in the middle of the bank. The velvet ropes that were normally used to direct the banks' customers to different teller windows, were now transformed into a make-shift enclosure, detaining the hostages throughout the duration of the negotiations.

Now was the time. They knew it. Shakim and Diesel also reacted. They slowly stood to their feet. The few hours began to take its toll on them, with Shakim, for the first time, questioning Olu's methods on how they planned on getting out of that situation. Lifting the strap over his shoulder that held his assault rifle, Diesel approached Olu with Shakim close to his side.

"Olu, you know that I have never questioned your authority. Never have I doubted your procedures on how to handle our problems when they arise. So, I will not begin to doubt you now. Tell me that you will get us out of this situation and I will trust you. But, if you can't, give it to me straight, so we can end this thing with a bang," Shakim delivered, his face blank. Olu reached forth to rest his hand on Shakim's shoulder.

"My brother, I know you would. But, today is not your day to die, brother. You will make it out of this, alive," Olu returned. He spoke with conviction. The certitude put Shakim and Diesel more at ease. Shakim nodded. The hostages looked on in silence as the men spoke from a distance.

Olu went over his plan with Shakim and Diesel on his method for them to escape. It was a fairly simple plan, two-fold in the process. The first step was to gather and collect any form of identification from the hostages and threaten retaliation against their loved ones if they failed to cooperate; their family's safety was contingent on them following Olu's every demand without question.

Once that was established, Olu, Shakim, and Diesel would change into the clothes of some of the hostages, and be released posing as hostages, while some of the real hostages remained tied up inside the bank. Olu believed that once outside, with all the commotion of some of the hostages being freed, that the police would quickly usher them off the scene and away from the area. At that time, they could each separate from the scene to escape.

Diesel opposed the plan before Olu could even finish relating it. Diesel expressed how he refused to get that far to leave empty handed. He explained that, to walk out of the bank, according to Olu, as hostages, would leave them empty handed, exposing them to the mercy of the hostages, trusting that they would follow Olu's plan. Diesel refused, showing that he would not go along with Olu's plan by refusing to part with his weapon.

Shakim was seconds away from lashing out on Diesel before Olu stopped him. Open minded to other alternatives, Olu pressed Diesel for a better plan to make it out of there. To his surprise, Diesel began to narrate a detailed account of what they could do to make it out of there safe, and with the money intact.

Diesel began by relating that he would still release some of the hostages as an act of good faith, but, make sure to keep a few hostages behind . With the armored truck still being a part of the equation from the hostages being released, Diesel explained how the remaining hostages could be used as human shields, securing them safe passage out of the bank to the armored truck. He explained how each hostage would revolve in a circular motion around each of them, hindering the possibility of a cop, or a sniper, taking a clean shot on any of them.

Once in the armored truck with the money, they could drive to their escape, being dropped off at different locations to confuse the police. For a moment, there was silence. Shakim's first response was to turn to Olu; read his face, study his reaction. Then it came. Olu blurted flatly, "let's do it." Although

Diesel felt his idea was the best possible alternative to escape with at least a portion of what they came for, he was thrown off that Olu put up no form of resistance. With Olu's response being a flat, 'let's do it' and a solemn nod, his gesture settled it. Diesel's plan was the plan that they were going to follow. Like a distorted form of a football huddle, they broke off for the three of them to approach the hostages.

"After considerable negotiations," Olu started, addressing the group, "we decided to release some of you." The moment Olu finished his sentence, a vibration of voices grumbled from the group. Olu raised his hand and the grumbling quickly ceased. "You, over there. You and you. You...," Olu stated, pointing to different people in the group, directing them to separate themselves from the crowd. Olu's process consisted mostly of women and the hostages who were older in age, leaving the last of the slowly dwindling group to consist of all men. Despite two married couples being amongst the group, the only dilemma arose when Olu separated a middle-aged wife from her husband.

"No! Please! I...I won't leave him!" she cried out frantically, clinging desperately to her husband's side. Her husband reacted in anger, grabbing her hands to forcefully remove her from his side. His efforts were futile as his teary-eyed wife struggled with every ounce of her being, grabbing any article of clothing she could cling to, to remain attached to him. The group watched this ardent display in silence, fearful of the repercussions of intervening and for the fate of the defiant woman. Shakim was the one who finally reached forth to separate them.

"Please, don't hurt her! I'm begging you! Please, don't hurt her!" The man begged, raising his hands at Shakim. The woman crouched behind her husband at the approach of Olu.

"Wait," Olu announced to Shakim, who immediately stopped pulling at the woman. "Come here," Olu continued, beckoning the man over.

"Please! She didn't mean any disrespect! I...," The man stopped when Olu raised his hand. Unbeknownst to the husband, the woman's actions triggered something deep within Olu's psyche, something heartfelt pertaining to the sanctity of marriage; her refusal to abandon her husband's side, her willingness to share in any unknown fate that might befall him, her undying loyalty to her life mate. Olu could relate. He knew if he and Liaka were in the same situation, death would be the only thing separating him from Liaka's side.

"Your wife really loves you. Cherish that love," Olu stated, the crouching woman slowly stood up behind him. "Step over there with her," Olu continued, gesturing for the man to accompany his wife with the group of hostages being released. The six remaining hostages waited patiently; they anticipated being picked in Olu's process of selection. But, it was over. In order for Diesel's plan to work, they needed at least six hostages, so six remained.

"You six, over here," Olu commanded, gesturing them over to the desk where the phone for police negotiations took place. They each managed to make a circle around the table. "Remove all the contents from your pockets and place them here on the table."

A couple of the men looked over their shoulders at Shakim and Diesel, their guns clenched in hand, their eyes fixed in a menacing gaze. Slowly, an empty part of the table began to fill with a few wallets, keys, small bills and a variety of other items. Olu brushed objects aside as he sifted through the pile. Loose change fell to the floor as the wallets were picked up from the pile.

"William Hemmingway, 231 Longhorne Lane. Jeffery Lawrence, 35-A Blue Hills Avenue. Todd Richardson, 1254 State Street…" Olu recited, reading from each of their identifications. Each name being called was accompanied by a brief glance from Olu until each name was announced—the stack of IDs clutched within Olu's hand, ending by him stuffing them in his pocket. "Gentlemen, you have been selected to participate in our efforts to get out of this unfortunate situation. As such, the fate of your well-being, along with the fate of any loved ones located at these addresses will be determined by your full cooperation. Is this understood?"

"But,…but, what do we have to do?" a man spoke up from the group. The other men looked on in suspense.

"Detailed instructions will be given to you. What's important is that you follow these instructions to the letter. If this is done, you will all be home by the end of the night and this will all be over."

"Take cover! There's movement coming from the front doors!"

Close to a hundred guns and assault rifles were pointed at the front doors of the bank, resembling a firing squad. Silence instantly fell over the clamoring. A pin drop could be heard for fifty yards despite the crowds of spectators, along with numerous state and federal officers looking on. All eyes and every camera lens were glued to the bank's front doors as they gradually opened. Bringing the camera's focus into view, a blurry object took form to reveal an older woman being helped by a man at the top of the steps.

"Hold your fire! I repeat, hold your fire!" The voice of a cop shouted to the other officers at the first sight of the few hostages being released. Gradually, each hostage emerged from the darkness of the bank to slowly make their way down the front steps. S.W.A.T. instantly moved into action.

Most of the hostages had never experienced the excitement of helicopters, armored S.W.A.T. crews, and all the commotion, leaving them staring wide-eyed at the crowd and the amount of guns pointed everywhere. Guns still aimed at the bank's front doors, eight cops formed a circle around the hostages, fashioning a makeshift barricade ushering the eleven hostages out of the line of fire and into safety.

The few moments of silence was shattered by a huge uproar of cheers, claps, and whistles, the moment the hostages were guided behind six ambulances waiting on their arrival. Making his way to the back of the open ambulance doors, José approached the married couple still shaken from their experience sitting on a gurney.

"Hello, my name is Detective José Dominguez of the Special Crime Squad. I was hoping I could ask you a few questions," José said, addressing the woman, as two plain-clothes detectives walked up behind to join him.

"No! We don't want to talk about anything right now! We just want to get the hell out of here and put this damned nightmare behind us!" The husband delivered sharply, then jumped to his feet in front of his wife to shield her from their questions.

"Sir, I know that the both of you just experienced a very traumatic ordeal. And I wouldn't even begin to suggest that I understand what you are going through right now. But, in my experience as a detective, speaking to the hostages as soon as remotely possible will greatly improve our..."

"Didn't you hear what the fuck I just said? We don't want to talk to you! We don't have anything to say to you!" The man repeated angrily, staring down José and the other detectives behind him. José's lips twitched, one of his indicators that he was growing impatient, close to losing control.

The man's heated outburst was so close to José's head that a spray of saliva showered José's face. Instincts told José to grab hold of the man and slam him up against the back of the ambulance doors and beat any information out of him for his blatant display of disrespect. Luckily for the distraught gentleman, the ambulance personnel, coupled with the crowd of spectators, and the empathy he felt for the man, José maintained his professional demeanor and took a breath to curb his growing anger.

"They're dangerous," the woman spoke out, José and his colleagues were seconds away from departing to another hostage. Her words stopped them dead in their tracks. José turned back to see the woman standing up from behind her husband.

"Honey, you don't have to do this right now. Relax. Maybe later when you're…"

"It's okay. I have to say this. I want to talk to them." She rested her hand on her husband's shoulder.

"Ma'am, what were you saying?" José said enthusiastically.

"They're dangerous. Ruthless. I'm not sure how you're going to deal with this crisis, but, I hope you got a pretty good plan. Because I've never seen anything like that in my life! They are very dark, cold."

"What did they say? Did you happen to hear anything, and I mean anything, that they were talking about? Please, try to remember. Any little detail will help us."

"I'm sorry. All of their conversations were kept secret, very discreet. We were separated from them pretty much the whole time. From the looks of it, the tall one, I would say he's the one calling the shots. What I do remember is, when the phone call came through, not the first one, but, the second one, whoever he was talking to, that was the only thing to move him."

"Really?" José said, knowing he was the one to make the second call.

"Aside from that, he…"

"The front doors! They're opening!" A voice screamed from the crowd. The husband immediately threw his hands around his wife, pulling her into the safety of the back of the ambulance. José and the other two detectives drew their guns from their holsters and pressed up against anything solid to take cover. Camera crews instantly cut their interviews short from the few selected hostages stationed behind the ambulances, to spin their lens and focus back on the bank's front doors.

A middle-aged white man was the first person to emerge from the bank. His hands were raised. Even from a distance you could see that his hands were visibly shaking. He stopped at the top of the steps. A few hushed gasps could be heard coming from the crowd. Confusion began to set in as all the spectators remained intrigued as to why the hostage stood frozen, inches from the door, until a few more careful steps from the man revealed the reasoning behind the few gasps.

A shirt was tied snugly behind the man's neck with a knot in the back, holding the barrel of Shakim's shotgun fixed to the back of the man's head; Shakim's finger circled firmly around the trigger. The man's nervous demeanor became evidently clear to the crowd, as an accidental squeeze of the trigger would easily blow the man's head off.

A few more steps out of the bank's front doors, Shakim stood proud on the front steps, his head held high, his other arm leading to a .44 Magnum pressed to the chest of his second hostage. A duffel bag was strapped over his shoulder hanging tight on his back. It held a little over seven million dollars.

Shakim stood fearless; the hostages sandwiched him in the middle, their distance feet away from the huge pillars holding up the bank's entrance. The man took small careful steps as Shakim nudged him forward with the barrel of his gun. Once Shakim neared the edge of the front steps, leaving himself completely exposed in front of the bank, a brief scan of the entire scene revealed what appeared to be a hundred guns pointed at him. A perverted smile twisted up the corner of his lip. Separated from every vehicle within distance, Shakim's eyes stopped on his destination, the armored truck parked by itself in the middle of the street. The back doors of the armored truck were slightly ajar and appeared to be empty. Shakim looked over his shoulder then waved his head forward in a signaling motion to the others in the bank. Olu was the second to emerge, his guns attached to the hostages in the same manner as Shakim. Diesel was last.

"The one in the middle," the woman whispered, causing José to peek back at her. She stood frozen, paralyzed in fear, staring at the man that she knew she would never forget; the man now tattooed into her memory. "He's the leader. The one in the middle, the tall one," she continued, before her husband finally managed to pull her down back to safety. José nodded then turned back to face the bank, his focus now directed at Olu.

Side by side, the six hostages faced the crowd lining the top of the steps with Shakim, Olu, and Diesel shielded safely behind them. José held his gaze fixed, not on the hostages, not on either man standing on the outsides of their spectacle, but, on the center man, the one the woman so confidently pointed out. Another set of eyes were fixed on Olu, that of Liaka, blended into the sea of spectators.

Shakim was the first one to move again, his slight nudge provoking the hostage to take his initial steps down the stairs. The crowd, especially the police, looked on in confusion as Diesel quickly circled the six of them to take the lead, landing him in front of the group. Their movements were methodically coordinated, an alternating circular movement, with Shakim and Diesel circling Olu in the center as they headed down the stairs towards the truck.

Their ingenuity achieved both of their desired effects. The first was to greatly hinder any chance the police had for an open shot. The second was to protect the safety of their leader. It was working. There was complete silence as they moved in a circular course towards the truck. Diesel was the first to make it level on the pavement leading to the truck. It was only feet away, directly in front of him.

Diesel was tempted to disregard his hostages and flee blindly to the safety of the truck. But, he knew that the coast was far from being clear. He was clearly the most nervous of the three; his eyes bounced back and forth to all the guns aimed at him. The only semblance of safety came in the form of the bulletproof armored truck. A few feet from the side of the truck, Diesel's attempt to get a better look inside was thwarted by the length of his AK-47 strapped to the back of the hostage's neck.

"Check it! Tell me, is it clear?" Diesel yelled at the hostage in front of him, prodding the man forward with the barrel of his gun. Olu and Shakim stood in a triangular formation with their backs to the truck; their main focus still being the many guns being pointed at them. The man moved nervously, his hands still held in a surrender position, as he leaned forward to peek his head inside the side door of the truck.

The inside appeared to be as heavily armored as the outside, literally a rolling safe. Everything was metal, a dull, grey metal. The man panned to his right. A small, sliding metal door leading to the driver's seat was open. A deliberate scan to his left revealed a box, a four-by-four foot squared metal box. Then he saw it—movement.

The man's eyes widened as a S.W.A.T. team member rose slightly from the other side of the box. With the tip of his assault rifle exposed, pointed at him, he placed his finger over the mouth of his ski-masked face. Fear was evident from the look in the man's eyes, yet his actions, a nod so subtle that it was almost oblivious to the naked eye, feigned calmness.

Taking a deep breath, the man leaned back from the interior of the truck, looked over his shoulder at Diesel, and said, "yeah...yeah, it's clear." Diesel then looked back at Shakim and Olu. Their stares were blank, their demeanor anxious, as they waited for any signal from Diesel. Diesel nodded, followed by yanking the gun fixtures from both hostages to step up in the truck; they threw caution to the wind and ran off frantically the moment Diesel's guns were off of them.

"I got the driver's seat. You..."

*BOOM!*

...rocked the moment of tense silence as an explosion lit up the small back quarters of the armored truck. An M16 round from the hidden S.W.A.T. officer in the truck burst point blank into Diesel's chest, lifting him from the steps of the truck, throwing him back fifteen feet. Gasps could be heard coming from the crowd as everyone on the scene dropped for cover. It only took a second for Olu and Shakim to look down at Diesel and see the hole in his chest to know that he was dead before he even hit the ground.

Olu and Shakim looked up to see a swarm of black clad S.W.A.T. officers hovering down on them, one screaming, "take them! Take them now!"

Shakim was the first to react.

Click—*BOOM!*

Shakim pulled the trigger on his shotgun attached to the back of the man's head. His head exploded like a watermelon. Fragments of his skull mixed with brain splattered on everything within distance. The man's headless body crumpled hard to the cement. The second shot from Shakim's gun blared into the armored truck at the now exposed S.W.A.T. officer—he hit the floor behind the box to take cover. Like fireworks on the fourth of July, an explosion of gunfire erupted from every direction as every cop on the scene began firing on them feet away from the truck.

Shakim sprayed gunfire recklessly, dumping in every direction. A blast from his shotgun and two shots from his .44 Magnum leveled three cops before one of their bullets blew off a chunk of his shoulder. The shot tore into his flesh, which held the shotgun, spinning him wildly sideways and causing the shotgun to fall from his hand.

From the first chant of the swarming cops, Olu struggled to take cover in the truck with the hostages, hoping to avoid the hail of bullets flying in his direction. But, at the sight of a wounded Shakim, who painfully reached down to retrieve his weapon, Olu disregarded the hostages and went to his aid. Shakim never saw the cop taking aim for his head, feet from his body, but, he heard the shot.

*BLAP!*

A bullet from Olu's gun caused the officer to cry out in agony and collapse behind Shakim, thwarting his shot. The officer fell to one knee before another officer came to his aid, dragging his comrade to safety. With the skill of an expert marksman, Olu fired off single shots, each pegging off officers as he guarded Shakim's crouched body. One of Olu's guns emptied from his ceaseless fire. He dropped it to the ground to retrieve another weapon from the back waist of his pants and continued firing.

A symbol in the shape of an X was a blur, until the focus adjusted on the sniper's riflescope to reveal Olu in the direct line of fire. With one eye closed and the other squinted, the sniper steadied his hand as he prepared to fire. Without taking his eye off the target, the sniper carefully reached up to wipe a bead of sweat from his forehead. His hand returned to his weapon, his finger curled lightly around the trigger. The slight gesture of the sniper was visible to Liaka, prompting her to bounce on her feet from behind the safety of a cop car.

"Liaka! No! You'll get killed!" Lianna screamed, holding on to Liaka's clothes for dear life. Trying in vain to free herself from Lianna's hold, Liaka stopped and froze when a red laser sliced through the air from another sniper's weapon to bounce off Olu's chest. Liaka followed the red dot that danced on Olu's chest as it slowly rose to move in circles on the side of Olu's head. Everything became silent to Liaka. The crowds, the gunshots, the screams, everything. Liaka's eyes seemed like they blinked in slow motion. When her eyes slowly opened, she witnessed a sight which took a few seconds for her mind to comprehend; the sniper's bullet sinking into Olu's neck. The projectile pierced Olu's jugular vein. Blood squirted from his neck in spurts but, miraculously, Olu managed to remain on his feet, squeezing off the last few rounds from both of his guns.

From the corner of her eye, Liaka turned to see a lone detective running full throttle at Olu with his gun pointed at him. The detective was feet from Olu when Liaka witnessed a flash leap from his gun. The flash threw Olu's head back; a bullet entered the side of his face.

He stumbled drunkenly; both of his empty weapons fell from his hands to bounce heavily on the cement. A second passed before another shot from the sniper's gun dug into the back of Olu's bulletproof vest, throwing him forward, jostling him to his knees. Olu felt his breathing growing shallow. He knew with each breath, a little bit of life escaped him. He slowly looked around.

Shakim was only feet from him; puddles of blood on various areas of his body from the numerous shots he received. Two feet were the next thing Olu saw as his head bowed heavily to the ground. From out of nowhere, they appeared to be there. Olu traveled up from the shoes to look up to see Detective José Dominguez standing over him, his gun aimed inches from Olu's face. Olu felt a sense of peace come over him. Despite the several gunshots, he felt no pain; his body was completely numb. Olu cracked a slight smile.

Liaka's brief pause of resistance caused Lianna's hold to loosen. She broke free. Liaka never felt her body running or her legs moving, but she knew she was quickly closing the distance between herself and the detective standing over Olu who remained on his knees. Liaka managed to weave through and dodge every hand that tried to reach out and detain her, hands with no faces, her mind intent on getting to Olu. A single chant escaped her lips, "*NOOO!*"

Her screams were silenced by a blast from José's gun. A final shot ripped into Olu's cheek, knocking him heavily on his back. A team of at least four plain-clothed detectives surrounded José, then quickly ushered him off to the back seat of a waiting Crown Victoria. Another team, mainly of uniformed clad policemen, inched their way towards Shakim. At least ten guns were pointed at his lifeless frame on the ground. Two finely polished police shoes kicked away Shakim's guns that were by his side.

Despite the amount of officers littered on the scene, Liaka managed to sneak her way through the crowd of police to fall by Olu's side. Blood stained every inch of his clothing. Liaka crawled closer to him. Her hands were shaking, but she managed to lift Olu's head from the cement to rest it on her lap. Olu's eyes rolled in his head. The moment Liaka began to lovingly caress his forehead, the movement in Olu's eyes stopped.

They parted slightly.

He looked up into the blue sky to see clouds, a fragmented silhouette of the sun, and the face of what he thought was an angel: Liaka's face. His lips struggled to form a smile due to the hole in his cheek the size of a dime. The moment his lips parted to speak, a mouthful of blood spilled from his lips.

He began gurgling on his own blood when he tried to speak. A mouthful of pearly white teeth were coated in blood as Olu's lips began to move. Nothing came out, but he was trying to say something. Liaka lowered her face to Olu's lips hoping to make out the buzz that came from him.

"…I…I'm…sorry…," Olu whispered, then coughed a mouthful of blood in Liaka's face. A trail of his blood rolled down her cheek to mix with her tears.

"You don't have to be sorry," Liaka uttered between sniffles, caressing his forehead.

"Will…wi…will you still be my wife?" Olu mumbled. The words sang like a broken melody to Liaka.

"Yes! I'll still marry you!"

"Do you still love me?"

"Yes, Olu! I love you with all my heart!"

"Then don…don't let me die in vain. Get José! Avenge me, my wife!" Olu whimpered with the last ounce of his breath. The last words uttered from his lips drained the very life out of him. His partially opened eyes remained stuck on Liaka, but they no longer looked at her, they looked through her, through her to an existence unknown to consciousness.

Liaka raised her hand to bring it over his face to close his eyes. A light breeze could be felt over her body, like Olu's spirit was being carried away with the wind. She could feel the presence of someone approaching her from the side. It was Lianna. Yet Lianna, nor anyone directly around her, was Liaka's focus of attention.

Liaka stared off into the crowds, through the sea of blue and black uniforms, through the commotion, to the middle passenger in the back seat of the Crown Victoria. Detective José Dominguez was sandwiched between two other detectives as the vehicle broke through the yellow tape to speed away. Liaka followed the car with her eyes until it disappeared from view, then whispered to herself, "my husband, I promise you. I will avenge you!"

# $C$hapter 12 | $D$eath to $L$ife

$A$sia's car keys jingled and rolled to a stop at the bottom of a glass bowl on a side table in Liaka's apartment. The three of them, Liaka, Lianna, and Asia entered Liaka's apartment after they returned from Olu's funeral. Liaka headed straight to the sofa. She plopped down heavily in the middle cushion, then folded over to rest her face in her hands. Sniffles came from under her crouched frame, her back jumped from heavy breathing, but no tears came out; there were none left.

For the entire week and a half leading up to Olu's funeral, not an hour passed where a tear didn't roll from Liaka's cheek. Olu's death affected her in ways that she never imagined. Liaka missed every day of work since his death and even neglected her weekly visits to the hair and nail salon, something she hadn't done since the age of eighteen. She was drained, mentally drained. Liaka was doing badly and everyone around her knew it, especially Asia and Lianna.

Lianna headed straight to the kitchen. Snatching three cups from the kitchen cabinet, she grabbed the entire bottle of *Remy Red* from the fridge and headed back to the living room. Asia was busy fiddling with the stereo. Asia knew that whenever Liaka was feeling depressed that she turned to jazz to relax, the horns soothed her.

A song from *Billie Holiday* was playing and Asia turned up the volume.

Lianna handed Asia a half-full glass of *Remy Red* as they rounded both ends of the sofa to sit next to Liaka. Lianna poured another glass and sat it on the coffee table in front of Liaka. Asia began to caress Liaka's back lovingly, gentle circular massages as she took a sip of her glass. Liaka barely felt Asia's touch, her mind an image of complete darkness; her thoughts still clung to the scene of his funeral.

"Liaka. Liaka, it's gonna be all right."

The image of Olu's funeral evaporated from Liaka's thoughts. She raised her head from her lap with bloodshot eyes and adjusted to focus on a single glass resting on the coffee table in front of her. She quickly brought it to her lips and gulped. Liaka chugged the entire glass. A bead of the red liquid spilled from the corner of her mouth to roll down and drip from her chin. She regained her breath, then slammed the glass back on the table.

"Fill it back up!" Liaka spit sharply. Lianna and Asia passed glances at each other, but didn't say a word. Lianna just removed the cap from the large bottle and topped off Liaka's glass. Liaka raised the glass back to her lips. She filled her mouth, swallowed in gulps, until she downed half of her second glass before she placed it back on the table.

"It's gonna be all right," Asia assured her, her hand still on Liaka's back. The words hit Liaka hard. She leaned over to rest her head on Asia's lap.

"I've never loved anyone in my life the way I loved him," Liaka sighed, "there was something so special about him. Something…," Liaka took a deep breath, "…something that very few men possess. I don't know what it is. I don't even think it could be put into words. But, he had it. And I know I will never find anyone to replace him."

"Don't say that, Liaka! I know that Olu was very special to you. I saw the love you guys shared. But, don't say things like that. You deserve to be happy. Olu would want you to be happy," Asia replied. She continued to comfort Liaka, running her fingers through her hair. Lianna remained silent, steady nursing her drink. The music stopped.

Lianna approached the entertainment system, scanning through the selection of Liaka's music before she clicked on the radio. Hot 93.7. A reggae song from *Elephant Man* vibrated through the speakers, shattering the serene mood of the room.

"Lianna!" Asia snapped.

"Naw, it's okay," Liaka said, sitting up from Asia's lap. Lianna's head, then hips, began to gyrate to the music. The rhythm began to move her as she closed her eyes to feel the bass course through her body. Turning her attention from the array of blinking lights on the face of the stereo, she rhythmically moved back over to the couch, dancing herself to the other side of the coffee table.

Liaka and Asia looked at her with curious eyes as they watched the alluring dance she performed for them. Then Lianna opened her mouth. A terrible Karaoke attempt at a Jamaican accent spilled from Lianna's lips as she sang along with the song, her drink over her head chanting the words. Liaka and Asia looked at each other before bursting out in laughter.

"What? It ain't all that bad!" Lianna smiled. She didn't care that they laughed at her. She was only concerned that she accomplished what she set out to do, cheer Liaka up. Liaka couldn't help but to laugh at Lianna's antics because Lianna sure was making a fool of herself. Liaka thought for Lianna to be black *and* Spanish, that she sure didn't have any rhythm! Asia felt her phone vibrating in her pocket.

"It's Donovan," Asia said, looking down at the LED display. She flipped her phone open and left the room.

"Forget about her. Come dance with me," Lianna said, rolling her hips to the music. Liaka smiled, but shook her head with a resounding no. Lianna took one last sip of her drink, placed it on the coffee table, and danced her way over to Liaka, reaching for her hands.

Liaka's attempt to stuff her hands under her thighs was useless. Lianna danced a wildly provocative dance around Liaka who stood in the middle watching her. As the music changed, Lianna went from exotic, to straight silly, as she began to *wop* to the music. Liaka burst out in laughter.

"Don't front! You know you can't see me, girl!" Lianna expressed, her wop transformed into the *Running Man*. Liaka's perfectly still body began to give way, her stiff shoulders began to sway, her body slightly moved. "Oh, you want some of this?" Lianna continued, her *Running Man* transforming into some type of break dancing. Lianna 'up-rocked' in the middle of Liaka's living room, 'serving' Liaka. Asia emerged from the back bedroom.

"What the hell are you doing? Having a seizure?" Asia joked with a smile, witnessing Lianna jumping around the room like she was reliving a scene from *Beat Street*.

"What? You want some of this, too?" Lianna threatened, bouncing herself

over to Asia. Asia looked at Lianna jiggling her body in front of her as if Lianna had completely lost her mind. She passed a glance over her shoulder to Liaka who twirled her index finger over the side of her head suggesting that Lianna was crazy.

The music gradually faded out to reveal a commercial for some type of income tax firm. Lianna was winded. All the weed and cigarettes that she smoked quickly took her breath away. She walked over and plopped down on the recliner next to the couch, reaching for her drink.

"How's Donovan?" Liaka asked.

"He said he wants me to come and get the kids. He also said he has to talk to me. I asked what about, but, you know him, he always wants to act all vague and mysterious about everything."

"What do you think it is? Is it..."

"I don't know. But, I think so. All I know is, the last time he dropped the kids off, the kids weren't the only ones getting tucked into bed," Asia said slyly.

"I always knew you was a little closet freak!" Lianna spit from the recliner. Asia smiled. "And you one of the worst kinds! Because you *look* like you a nice, decent female, But, I know, you nasty!"

"Nasty? As opposed to an out-of-the-closet, open freak like you?" Asia returned.

"Shit! Ain't no shame in my game! I ain't doing nothing different than ninety percent of all them niggas out there! If a man got five girls and he's slaying all of them at the same time, then he's a playa—he's 'the man'. But, let a female do the *same exact thing*, and she's branded a skeezer, a freak, a hoe, a chicken head! I'm tired of that shit! Hell! I'll say it, just like them niggas like pussy, shit, I love dick!" Lianna announced with pride.

Asia and Liaka locked their eyes on each other and chanted in unison, "yeah! She's a hoe!" Then broke out in laughter.

"The sad difference is, Lianna, you are not a man. And you can't do everything a man can do. No one said it was fair that we have to live with that double standard, but that's reality," Asia said. "And just to clarify, don't mistake my comment to be an excuse for what some men do! Any man who sleeps with five different women at the same time is a hoe his damned self! It's just that society embraces their dog-like qualities, while a woman is shunned for that type of behavior."

"So, what? You want me to be more like *you*?" Lianna said with a chuckle.

"No. You don't have to be more like me. Continue being yourself. But, I'll tell you one thing—just because I have a church-girl image on the outside, doesn't mean that I can't drop it like it's hot and be a freak for my man behind closed doors," Asia said with a wink. "And speaking of my man, Liaka, are you gonna be all right here?"

"Yeah, I'll be fine. Listening to the two of you actually made me feel a whole lot better," Liaka answered. "Just do me a favor."

"Anything, what is it?"

"Go get your man back! Donovan's a good one. Fight for him. Don't let him get away," Liaka related, her melancholic tone returning. Asia walked over to Liaka and threw her arms around her.

"Thank you. And I will," Asia whispered in her ear. Liaka hugged her back, a long firm hug. Asia turned to Lianna. "Take care of my girl, okay?"

"You heard Liaka. Don't worry about us. Go get your man back!" Lianna added with a smile. Asia reached forward to give Lianna a hug before she turned to head out the front door.

# $C$hapter 12 | $L$ove $C$hanges

$D$espite Olu's funeral, Asia left Liaka's apartment in good spirits. The thought of whatever Donovan had to share with her put her in a cheery mood. Asia felt good that she left Liaka in better spirits; she knew Lianna would keep her head up until she handled her business. Asia merged into traffic on Interstate 91 thinking about her current relationship with Lianna. Over the past couple of weeks, Asia began to really warm up to Lianna, especially after she observed Lianna's recent loyalty to Liaka. Asia couldn't help but to smile as she traveled back to when they first crossed paths.

It was a Friday night, years ago, and mid-summer. Asia and Liaka stood glued at the bar of a nightclub; the dance floor was jam packed with heads ripping it up on the floor. It was the second night of the club's grand opening, which left the entire club wall-to-wall with people, forcing Asia and Liaka to fight for some room on the dance floor or secure a place at the bar, they chose the bar.

For the life of Asia, she couldn't understand the thrill that Liaka took in being squeezed in such tight quarters. On at least five different occasions, drinks were spilled on Asia, and it killed her to even think about what her three-inch, suede, *Calvin Klein* boots were going to look like after she left the club. She could barely take a sip of her drink without a random passerby nudging or brushing up against her. The weed and cigarette smoke was thick enough to cut with a knife. Asia was seconds away from leaning into Liaka's ear to plead with her to leave when Liaka smiled from ear to ear, throwing her hands up at a female approaching them.

"Hey, girl!" The female screamed at Liaka over the thumping music with a *Heineken* bottle in one hand and a fully rolled, freshly lit blunt in the other. She threw her blunt arm around Liaka for a quick hug.

It was baffling to Asia that anyone would have the audacity to leave the house dressed like that and, even more, that they would enter a nightclub that way. Cut-off blue jean pum-pum shorts, altered and cut so short that there was barely enough material to hold the crotch together. They were so tight that she couldn't, or didn't, bother to button them up, exposing a good portion of the front of her G-string. The top that she wore resembled a bikini top with just enough material to cover her nipples. The female took a long drag from her blunt and passed it to Liaka. It was the first time Asia had ever seen Liaka smoke weed. She knew from that point that there was definitely something different about this female and, in her presence, Liaka also became different.

"Lianna, this my girl, Kadiajah, but, everybody call her, Asia. Asia, this my home girl, Lianna," Liaka screamed. Lianna barely nodded in a 'whassup' fashion and her standoffish behavior caused Asia to curl up her lip.

"I got someone I want you to meet!" Lianna pulled Liaka close to her side and away from Asia. The dark room, combined with the large crowd of people, made it almost impossible for Asia to realize that Lianna actually approached them with four men behind her. A closer look at one of the brothers standing behind Lianna revealed his hand firmly attached to her ass. Liaka took a few steps away with Lianna, for Liaka to pair up with a light-skinned brother who lowered in closer to whisper something in her ear.

From amongst the group of four men, a brother who had to be at least six and a half feet tall and weighing probably three-hundred pounds parted the crowd to approach Asia. Asia widened her eyes and immediately turned her back to him, saying to herself, "*I just know this gorilla looking nuggah ain't 'bout to come over here to...*"

"Damn, princess! You shining like a motherfuckin' diamond, ya dig?"

Asia pretended to be surprised as she turned back around to face him. He was wearing a dark blue do-rag tied on his fat head, and when he smiled, every single tooth in his mouth was covered in platinum and diamonds. He was making a hell of a first impression because Asia hated both, the thug look and designer teeth.

"I'm here with somebody," Asia said sharply, raising her drink to her mouth and wrapping her lips around the straw. Asia squinted and began to look aimlessly around the club.

"Well, that nigga gotta be a fool to leave such a beautiful thing like you all by herself in here," his deep voice stressed, totally invading her personal space. His breath reeked of cigarette smoke. Asia crinkled her nose and turned her head, now seriously searching for Liaka. Once she spotted Liaka a few feet away giggling with her new male friend, Asia threw a menacing stare that said it all, *get me the hell outta here!*

Instead of Liaka running to her girl's aid, she threw back a pathetic look of her own, *come on girl, bear with me. 'Cause this nuggah is FINE!* Liaka laughed merrily at whatever the brother was saying to her, then gently rested her hand on his forearm. At that point, Asia couldn't wait for the night to be over, just to tell Liaka how much she owed her for subjecting her to that.

A song from *Busta Rhyme* came on and the whole crowd went berserk. Everyone within eye-distance began to *throw their hands up where their eyes can see* and jump or wild out with their best dance moves. Well, everyone except Asia. The brother in front of Asia began to dance his body close to hers. If she didn't know any better, she would have thought that it was his stiff erection being pressed against her waist. But, it was too hard to be an erection. A few more thrusts made her realize that it was actually a gun shoved in his waistband and being smacked against her pelvis. Grinding his body against hers, he rested his hand on the side of Asia's hip which she instantly removed.

A wandering hand from amongst the crowd held a blunt in the air for the brother in front of Asia to reach up and seize it. His free hand, for the second time, returned to Asia's hip, this time circling around to cup the line of her ass. His massive hand was strong, but Asia removed it again. A cloud of weed smoke was blown from his lips and inadvertently in Asia's face causing her to squint, throwing her head back and away from the cloud for any sign of fresh air.

For the third time, his hand found its way back down her waist, down her side, and around to cup her ass. He was obviously drunk and high. Asia sighed heavily, but she was fed up, so she left it there.

"Miss Beautiful, I ain't even catch your name. I should at least know your name if I'm gonna take you out to dinner tonight. So…"

"Oh, my God! I'm sooo sorry!" A drunken female apologized to Asia after she bumped heavily into her, spilling ninety percent of her drink all over Asia's face and hair. The ice cold drink shocked Asia to the point that it sucked the wind from her lungs. The whole left side of her body was soaked; her hair was ruined and her tan shirt was stained pink from the drink and stuck to her chest. Asia had enough. She smacked the brother's hand off her ass, plucked a squared ice cube from her cleavage and stormed off to the bathroom. Liaka turned when she saw the commotion of Asia walking off and quickly followed behind her.

"Asia, what the hell happened?"

She burst through the bathroom door to see Asia checking herself in the mirror. Asia rolled her eyes at Liaka, giving her a look of death. The drink caused half of her hairstyle to lay lifelessly flat on one side of her head, while the other side remained vibrant and still full of body. Her make-up wasn't any better. Asia cleaned the running mascara from under her eye with her thumb.

"I was gonna ask are you having fun yet. But…," Liaka said with an innocent smile. The bathroom door opened again, spilling the music inside, for Lianna to stumble in. She wobbly approached them, then slammed her cup on the sink's counter.

"Liaka, that nigga is sweatin' tha shit outta you!" Lianna slurred drunkenly, playfully slapping Liaka on the arm and then checked her hair in the mirror. "Yeah girl, you better get on that! He got a brand-new, money-green Range Rover, and I heard he got a big ass dick!" Lianna winked at Liaka in the reflection of the mirror. "You fucked around and got the good one! 'Cause this sorry ass nigga that I'm dealing wit', if he wasn't eating this pussy right, I woulda been done kicked his ass to tha curb!" Lianna drunkenly threw her arm around Liaka and laughed. The weed and alcohol on Lianna's breath hit Liaka like a punch in the face. Liaka cringed as if the stench was burning her nose hairs.

"Oh! And you, girl," Lianna blurted, "Link was asking about you. What's your name again? Egypt? Ethiopia? South Africa? Well, anyways, that nigga acted like every female in here had the plague 'til he seen you."

Asia ignored her.

"Lianna, my girl ain't feeling good. So, I think we…"

"Hey! You got a light?" Lianna blurted, cutting Liaka off. Two females were smoking weed themselves in a toilet stall behind them.

"I'll tell her we're leaving, okay?" Liaka sighed to Asia.

"Where do y'all wanna eat at? Red Lobster? The Olive Garden?" Lianna asked, the second she came back, sucking fiercely on the blunt.

"We 'bout to call it a night, Lianna. My girl don't feel good."

"What? But, it ain't nothing but...," Lianna looked down to her wrist. "Oh, shit! I ain't even got a watch!" Lianna said, and then burst out laughing. "But, I know it's still early, girl. Come on, hang out with a sistah."

"I would, I would. But, I came with my girl, and I'm her ride, so I can't leave her hanging."

"Hmph! You don't know what you 'bout to miss! We could go get a room, get smoked out, drink, and get our fuck on! These niggas is 'bout it, trust! You better get on it!"

"Another night. I can't dis' my girl. I..."

"What's wrong with her anyways?"

"What's wrong with me? What's wrong with me? What the fuck do you think is wrong with me? Look at me! Do I look like I feel up to going to some hotel to fuck some strangers? Do I look like I want to socialize with any of those thugs you with? Huh?"

Every female in the bathroom, including the three females who just walked in, focused on the irate female barking at her girls. Lianna stared Asia down for a few seconds before bursting out in laughter. In her intoxicated state, it took Asia to point out her hideous look for Lianna to even notice.

"What the fuck happened to your girl? She looked fucked up!" Lianna snickered, and then took a drag off her blunt.

"Liaka! I'm leaving! Are you gonna give me a ride home, or are you gonna stay with this nasty ass bitch?"

"Nasty ass bitch? Who the fuck you think you talking to, you monkey looking like bitch?" Lianna snarled, her smile instantly faded into a scowl. Asia and Lianna approached each other in a face-off, Liaka jumped in the middle to separate them. In spite of Asia being over three inches taller than Lianna, and outweighing her by at least thirty pounds, Lianna stood her ground.

Thinking back on it, Asia wasn't sure if it was the "liquid courage" of alcohol coursing through Lianna's system, or her project upbringing that gave Lianna that confidence stance. One thing was for sure, neither one of them had it in them to back down. The females in the bathroom looked on in silence, anxiously staring wide-eyed in anticipation of a fight. The intense stare off between Asia and Lianna lasted for all of a minute before Lianna snarled, "that's what I thought," then returned to her reflection in the mirror.

But, the moment Lianna turned her back on Asia—what she felt was a clear sign of disrespect—Asia lunged to grab a hold of the back of Lianna's hair, only for Liaka to intercept Asia's hand inches from Lianna's head. Lianna never knew the wrath she was so close to receiving as she casually raised the blunt back to her lips to recharge her high.

"This bitch ain't even worth me breaking a nail for! You can stay with this trashy ass tramp! I'm leaving!" Asia growled, bumping passed Lianna to storm out of the bathroom. Plowing her way through the crowded dance floor, Asia made her way out of the club, knowing there was nothing in the world that would make her want to associate with the likes of Lianna ever again.

Turning off the Interstate, Asia rolled to a stop at a red light. *Funny how time changes things*, Asia thought to herself. Over time, Asia began to slowly warm up to Lianna, with the last few weeks bringing them even closer. Deep in thought, Asia barely realized that she was rounding the corner to her street. She spotted Donovan immediately. There he was, all physically fit, two-hundred pounds of him, wildly chasing their daughter and son around in a patch of grass on the side of her building. Just the sight of him triggered something within Asia. She gently applied pressure to her brakes and the car slowed. She watched him, almost in a trance.

His powerful arms easily threw their son up in the air, only to catch him securely on his fall. Their interaction was picturesque. Yet, there was something missing, something lacking from the picture—Asia. Her presence would make that picture-perfect scene complete.

Adjusting her center rear-view mirror, Asia quickly examined her reflection. Between glances at herself and the road, she smiled, checked her teeth, her nose, her eyes, and finally her hair. No one could tell her that she wasn't cute that day. It couldn't have been a better time for her to have it going on. Asia leaned over to rummage through her glove box. *Orange Tic-Tacs.* She popped at least four of the tiny mints in her mouth and sucked on them like it was a race to strip the mints of their flavor. Passing a cupped hand over her mouth and nose, Asia exhaled hard to check her breath.

"Minty fresh," Asia whispered to herself with a smile. Her white Volvo station wagon rolled to a stop across the street from her house. Neither Donovan nor her kids had noticed her yet. Asia took that opportunity to

unbutton three of the top buttons on her blouse, revealing just the right amount of cleavage. A little more than she would normally show in public, but this was for Donovan. She intended to entice him and, if she had her way, Donovan would remove the other six buttons within the hour.

It had been a couple of weeks since Asia had sex with Donovan and, if Donovan wasn't ready, Asia sure was. Slamming her car door behind her, Asia emerged from the driver's seat to finally attract the attention of Donovan and her children. The sight of their mother walking in their direction prompted her kids to immediately stop playing with their father, bolting off towards her. Asia dropped to one knee with open arms and was actually knocked on her back from her kids running headlong into her.

"Mommy! Mommy! Mommy! Daddy took us to *Chuck E. Cheese's* and I ate five slices of pizza!" Her son cheered proudly about his accomplishment.

"Really? You ate that much? You must have really been hungry."

"Mommy, I didn't eat *that* much. He's so greedy," Asia's daughter said.

"Greedy? What about you, Miss Eat-half-of-your-birthday-cake?" Asia delivered, tickling her daughter's side. She laughed heartily, wiggling in her mother's arms. Asia raised her eyes to see Donovan approaching.

"How's everything? Is Maliaka holding up all right?"

"She's doing a lot better. I left her with Lianna, so she should be fine," Asia replied, slowly rising to her feet.

"That's good to hear. Tell her I'm sorry for her loss. As for the kids, you don't have to worry about feeding them. We just came back from…"

"Chuck E. Cheese's. I was told how a little someone ate all of five slices of pizza," she said, glancing down to her son who clung to her leg. Their daughter reached up and Donovan instinctively leaned down to pick her up, holding her on his side.

"Yeah, little D sure did have an appetite with him today," Donovan said with a half-smile. "Hey, Kadiajah, I can see today's not a good day so…I'll give you a call, okay? If you need anything, just give me a call," Donovan ended, giving his daughter a kiss before lowering her to the ground.

"Donovan!" Asia called out, "There…there is actually something you can do for me," Asia continued sexily, through lustful eyes. "You said you wanted to talk to me about something. Maybe we can go inside and…"

"Mommy, Daddy's friend is really nice. She bought me a race car," Asia's son blurted, then pointed to Donovan's truck across the street. The passenger side of Donovan's truck slowly opened. Asia's mouth dropped. She watched, speechless, as a female emerged from Donovan's truck, a blonde haired, blue-eyed female, standing about six feet tall. She wore a dark brown mini-skirt so tight that it left absolutely nothing to the imagination and a tight half shirt barely holding her double D breasts inside. It was obvious to anyone with eyes that she wasn't wearing a bra as she walked over to them, her large chest jiggling with each step. Donovan could only close his eyes, shaking his head as his female friend approached.

"That...that's what I wanted to talk to you about. But, I thought about it and figured the funeral, and...now just wasn't the best time," Donovan explained pitifully.

"Are you...Donovan! Are you fuckin' kidding me?"

"Kadiajah! The kids!"

"You took Donovan Junior and Sky, our kids, on family time with...with her?" Asia spewed, pointing at the female, with her eyes still on Donovan.

"Kadiajah, please! Not out here, not like this, not in front of the kids. We can talk about this…"

"I'm sorry. I don't mean to disturb y'all. But, I just wanted to come over and officially introduce myself. Donny has told me so much about you," the blonde said with a smile. "Your children are absolutely adorable, especially Donovan Junior. He's…"

"Maryann, now...now isn't a good time," Donovan spit, cutting her off. She appeared confused at his interruption, but said, "oh, okay. Well, hopefully, at a later date, maybe we can become more sociable. Get better acquainted."

"Get better acquainted? I don't fuckin' believe this! Listen here, Maryann! I swear, if my kids weren't here, I would beat your motherfu…"

"Maryann, please wait for me in the truck!" Donovan stepped in between them as Asia raised a closed fist, advancing towards her. Maryann's eyes widened as she flinched from Asia.

"Mommy, what's wrong?" Asia's daughter asked, behind curious eyes.

"Donny, Sky, let's go inside," Donovan gently nudged his kids towards Asia's front door. Donovan looked up to see Asia on the verge of exploding. "Kadiajah, please, let's go inside," he pleaded, noticing how both Donovan Junior and Sky watched their every move. Asia stared at Maryann walking back across the street to Donovan's truck with a look of death. If looks could kill, Asia viciously tortured, maimed, and then murdered Maryann, only to

 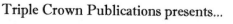

revive her to repeat the process. Donovan reached for Asia's arm to lead her up to her apartment.

"Don't fuckin' touch me!" Asia barked, wildly yanking her arm from him. Asia threw her jacket down to the floor the moment she burst through her front door.

"Sky, take your little brother to his room. Me and mommy have some grownup stuff to talk about, okay?" Donovan said sadly to his daughter.

"But, Daddy…"

"Sky! I don't want to hear another word out of your mouth! Take your brother and…," Asia screamed, as Sky grabbed her brother and ran off to her room.

"Kadiajah, let me explain."

"Explain what? What the hell could you possibly explain to me, Donovan? That you wanna be Mister Fuckin' Family-man with blonde Barbie out there? That you couldn't spend some quality time with your kids without dragging along… her! Is that what you want to explain?"

"Don't do this, Kadiajah. Please!" Donovan stressed, trying to rest his arms on Asia's shoulders. But, before he could get close enough to touch her, Asia violently pushed his hands away.

"Do what? From the looks of it, you're the only one doing anything around here! And with the kids? I'm telling you right now, Donovan, I don't want you bringing my kids around that bitch!"

"Your kids? Your kids? The last time I checked, Kadiajah, you didn't make them on your own! Unless you're the Virgin Mary, I think I had a little something to do with that!"

"Don't be a fuckin' asshole! So that's it? That's what you had to talk to me about? To tell me that you're dating a fuckin' white girl? What is it, sistahs just don't do it for you anymore? A flat ass and big tits floats your boat now?"

"Kadiajah! Lower your voice! The kids can hear you!"

"So, what? What's wrong, Donovan? Don't you want our kids to hear how you're leaving mommy for a white girl? What is it, Donovan? Was I too *black* for you?? No, let me guess. Miss Fuckin' Barbie Doll let you do whatever you want without a care in the world, huh? Is that about right, Donovan? Well, I'm nobody's fuckin' doormat!"

"Listen to yourself!"

"I can hear myself loud and clear! Oh, I get it, Miss Fuckin…"

Triple Crown Publications presents… Queen of Thieves *PART 1*

"Kadiajah, enough! Just stop!" Donovan yelled, the pierce of his voice echoed throughout the apartment. "All right, you wanna do this here? Now? Let's do this then! I tried to exercise a little restraint, but, fuck it! Let's put everything out there! Yes! Yes, I am with Maryann! And do you know why, Kadiajah? It's because she listens to me! Something you could never find the time to do! Well, unless it had something to do with you! But, that's only the beginning. She stands by me and any decision that I make. She respects them! She doesn't condemn me for having ideas, no matter how radical you think they are!"

"I didn't stand by you? By your ideas? That's bullshit! I stood by every sane decision you ever made! I…"

"No! It's my turn to talk!" Donovan hissed, "she respects me. She goes out of her way to make *me* happy. But, I wouldn't expect you to understand that. That's so typical of you. I knew you would act this way."

"How the hell do you expect me to act? You stroll up to my house, after you take our kids to a family outing with some bimbo! Then you tell me that you're leaving me for her? Hell! If you're gonna leave me, at least leave me for someone black!"

"Grow up, Kadiajah! Just grow up. Listen, I love her and I'm gonna be with her. We…"

"Love her?" Asia croaked. The rage that coursed through her body transformed into fear. *Love her.* The words repeated like an echo in her head.

"Yes, Kadiajah. I think I do love her. And we have plans to go away at the end of the month. And…and I'm gonna propose to her."

Wha…what are you talking about, propose to her?"

"I'm gonna propose to her. I'm gonna ask her to marry me," Donovan stated in a flat tone. His words cut through Asia like a knife. She knew that, for the rest of her life, she would never forget the words that just escaped his lips.

"Don't! Wait…listen…what are you talking about? That's crazy! You…"

"I'm sorry. I really didn't want to tell you like this," Donovan expressed, sadly.

"Please, Donovan! Okay, I'm sorry. I said it, I'm sorry. Let's slow down. We can talk about this."

"Talk about what? There's nothing to talk about. This is not something that's open for debate. This is how I feel."

"Donovan, please! I don't want to debate or argue with you. I just want to talk to you. Please, just tell me where all of this is coming from? We were just...together...a few weeks ago. It was...I thought we were gonna work things through. That you just wanted to take a break, but work things through. I came here today thinking…," Asia stopped, tears began to swell up in her eyes.

"Kadiajah," Donovan reached out to her, "I thought it would work, Kadiajah, I really did. I tried to make it work. Believe me, I tried. I thought about the few times I spent the night here. I thought maybe if we could connect again that it would work. I thought if we gave each other a little space, some time apart, that it would draw us back together, bring us closer. But, as the time passed, it only made me realize that we're not working. Kadiajah, it's not gonna work."

"Give it some time. Please! Just give it a little more time. For the sake of our kids, our family," Asia cried, tears now rolling down her face.

"I am thinking about the kids. How would our kids benefit growing up in a house with their parents always at odds? How would it benefit them to see us trying to hold on to a relationship that shouldn't be held on to? This is the best thing."

"The best thing? The best thing is you getting married to her?"

"I love her. I don't know how it happened. We actually became close when I confided in her about you. Then, I just fell in love with her."

"Don't say that! Stop saying that!" Asia cried. "Donovan, just listen to me now!" Asia clutched a handful of Donovan's shirt. "You *can't* love her! You just can't! Just give us a little more time. I promise you, I can make it work; I'll make us work. You can't marry her! You...you were supposed to marry...me," Asia sighed, pulling Donovan close to her chest. Donovan reached up to grab the back of Asia's hands to peel himself from her hold. She held on to him as tightly as she could, but, he broke her hold, removing her hands.

"I'm sorry, Kadiajah," he said, and then took a step back. "I'll be back next weekend to pick up the kids. I'm sorry," he turned to walk out.

"Please, Donovan, don't leave! Please don't do this!" Asia yelled out to Donovan's back. Her body shrank to the floor. She sat, crouched on her knees, resting in the middle of the kitchen. "Don't leave me," she whispered. But, he continued to walk out. Donovan was gone. Her head was heavy as it hung low.

Mustering up the little strength she could, she lifted her head to glance over her shoulder. Sky and Donovan Junior stood teary-eyed in the doorway leading into the living room; Donovan Junior cuddled up under his big sister, an overstuffed teddy bear as big as him, dangling from his arm. They stood frozen. Asia lowered her head again. Her eyes closed as the gravity of what Donovan had just told her weighed on her thoughts.

"Mommy," Asia heard from an innocent voice behind her back, a gentle hand resting on her shoulder. "Don't cry. Daddy will come back home. I promise," Sky said naively, through doleful eyes. Asia turned to hold her kids tightly. She cried hard, clutching onto their little bodies, clutching onto the only things she felt she had left.

# $C$hapter 14 | $T$oy

$A$re you serious? No, he didn't!" Liaka said, astounded. Asia sat across from Liaka in Liaka's apartment.

A couple of hours had passed since Donovan broke the news to her. It pained Asia to no end just thinking about it. Pulling herself together, Asia knew she couldn't stay home. Grabbing her belongings, Asia packed her kids in the car to be verbally assaulted with, "Mommy, what happened?" and "why were you and Daddy fighting," and a volley of other questions Asia didn't particularly care to answer; each question a teaspoon of salt being poured into the wound Donovan left in her heart.

Asia's only response was a 'not now!', until she dropped her kids off at her mother's house. The story she told her mother was along the same lines that she spit at her kids, purposely vague. She didn't have it in her to explain to her mother the falling-out that she and Donovan just got into. Not now. Not after so many visits of Asia convincing her mother that they were getting back together any day now. How could she break the news to her mother that, not only were they not getting back together to be a family again, but that Donovan had intentions of proposing marriage to another woman? Asia took losing her man to another woman as a personal blow to her ego. In her mind, she lost.

"I couldn't believe it. I still don't believe it," Asia related, her tone a

Triple Crown Publications presents... $Q$ueen of $T$hieves *PART 1*

testament of her pain.

"But, I don't understand. What happened?"

"I don't know, Liaka. I just don't know. I thought I had a pretty good read on how things were going. That just proves that my intuition is all fucked up."

"Come on, Asia. It's not all like that," Liaka sighed.

"He looked so good, Liaka. I've been with this man for so many years, the good, the bad, and the ugly. I've seen him from being naked, to being in a three-piece suit, to everything in-between. But, I swear to you, there was nothing sexier than seeing him playing with our kids like that. My heart melted. I don't know what it is. 'Cause it's not like I haven't seen him playing with the kids before. But, today...today there was just something different about him," Asia recounted, with a sadness in her eyes.

"Well, you know what, it's his loss!"

Asia exhaled heavily. "She was pretty," Asia mumbled, her voice trailed off. "She looked like a dingy cheerleader. Like some brainless, big-boobed, dingy cheerleader. Like he pulled her right out of a porno movie or something. But, she was pretty."

"And you're upset with that? That just lets you know where he's at with his!"

"I'm not prejudiced," Asia said sharply, her comment more of a self-conviction than a statement.

"Why would you say that? I know you're not prejudiced."

"Because, I kept saying that he was leaving me for a white girl. I didn't mean it all like that. Well, yes, I did! I mean, it's hard enough for a sistah to find a good black man who's got a good head on his shoulders, career-orientated, drug-free, and ain't on the 'down low'. Just because I think a brother should stick with his own sistahs, does that make me prejudiced?" Asia posed. Liaka let out a slight chuckle, shaking her head 'no'. "I mean, it ain't like it ain't enough white men that they couldn't pick from! I swear, if these brothers ain't running after some white girl, they now running after some Puerto Rican girl! And you already know them females is only looking for one thing, some black dick! That's all they want—a big, black Mandingo dick!"

"You're crazy!" Liaka laughed.

"No, I'm serious!"

"No, you're not! What you are is mad. You can't possibly think the only reason those females get with a black man is for his...manhood. And I'm sure at least some of those men are looking for something more than just a play toy. Not *all* black men are like that."

"No, just all the black men who can't handle a strong sistah!" Asia emphasized. "What is it with these brothers now-a-days? Let a sistah hold down a career, be strong-willed, a little assertive, and these brothers get intimidated."

"Don't be like that. There's still some good men out there."

"Well, I can't find any! But, you know what? I know what to do now, get on it just like these brothers do! I don't believe I was sitting back waiting for this... this asshole! Like some dumb, pathetic bitch! Keeping my shit *tight* for him and he's running around, sticking it in every blonde with two legs!" Asia spit. "You were lucky. I think Olu was the last good man left," Asia said without thinking. "I'm...I'm sorry. I didn't mean it..."

"No, it's okay. He was a good man. He took such good care of me. He robbed banks, but he still took good care of me," Liaka said, her eyes lowered to the floor; her voice leveled off as the thought of him entered her mind. "I knew," Liaka continued flatly. She raised her eyes back up to Asia. "I knew. I knew what he was doing."

"What? What are you saying?"

"He told me. On the day he proposed to me, I asked him and he told me. I asked him if there was anything he wanted to tell me, anything I should know about before we got married. I told him I didn't want any secrets between us if we were gonna get married. And, well, he told me."

"Told you what?"

"Pretty much everything."

Asia stared at Liaka in disbelief, mouth agape, slowly shaking her head. "And you mean to tell me that you knew all these weeks and couldn't even tell your best friend?"

"Well, it's a little difficult to tell someone that the man you love, the man you are about to marry, is a bank robber. He made me promise not to tell anyone anyways. But, even if he didn't, how do you tell someone something like that?" Liaka related, her face twisting up.

"So, you can tell me now. What did he tell you? Did he tell you about the bag? The bloody clothes? The gun?"

"No."

"Why not? Didn't you ask?"

"No! If I asked him, then he would have known I was looking through his stuff."

"So, what exactly did he tell you?"

"He told me a few stories. How he got started, a few jobs he'd done. Things like that. And if you thought I was turned on before when everything was mysterious with him, girl…," Liaka said, melting from the mere thought of it.

"That's crazy."

"Asia, you weren't there. Just to hear how he described some of his heists. How he strong-armed any scene that he went into. I could imagine such power. Everyone in the room being at your mercy. You can get them to do just about anything you tell them to do. The complete power to control them. Ummm…just that raw power," Liaka sighed, dazing off, contemplating the thought.

"Raw power? How about insane?"

"That's not insane. That's domineering!" Liaka said warmly. "You should have been there when he talked about it. I'm not sure if it was *what* he did or the *manner* in which he did it that turned me on the most. It was like, when he told me, the way he described it, it was like that's what he was destined to do. And I was a part of it."

"What you are is lucky. Lucky that he never tried to hurt you."

"Hurt me? Olu would NEVER hurt me!" Liaka snapped angrily.

"You know I didn't mean it like that, Liaka. I'm sorry."

"Olu would have never laid a finger on me. He protected me. He was… teaching me. He was teaching me how to protect myself."

"And exactly how was he doing that?"

"Well, for one, he taught me how to use a gun."

"He…you…what?"

"It was no big deal. He just wanted to make sure that if I was ever in a vulnerable position that I could fend for myself. Personally, I think he was training me to be his partner," Liaka uttered, followed by a snicker. "I wonder what it would be like," Liaka expressed, thinking aloud.

"You don't have to think about it, let's do it," Asia stated. Liaka turned to read Asia. A blank look was on her face. "I said 'let's do it' because you were staring off into space like you were actually considering it. But, obviously you lost your sense of humor, because it was a joke! Ha! Ha! Very funny, you know, a joke," Asia related, wondering why Liaka wasn't following her particular sense of humor.

"Don't you even wonder what something like that would be like? To do something daring like that?" Liaka posed.

"Uh, no! No, I don't. I don't think about crazy things like that."

"That's not really that crazy."

"Liaka, yes, it is! In fact, that sounds like something your crazy ass girl, Lianna, would say. You can't really be serious."

"Not anything like a bank or something. Nothing like that. But, to just be in total control of someone. To have the entire room at your mercy."

"Liaka, you're talking crazy!" Asia exclaimed, with nervous laughter. "I know what you need. I know what we both need, to go out! To have a fun night out on the town. To just put aside your experience, my experience, and just go out to have a good time. And to hear something like that coming from me, you know we really need it!" Asia chuckled. "Listen, call your girl, Lianna. I'm sure she knows at least ten different spots we can go to. Let's do it. How about it?" Asia asked. Liaka was slow to nod, still more concerned with entertaining her thoughts.

"You're right, we should go out tonight. Get our minds off what's going on," Liaka agreed.

"Then, it's settled. Set it up and let me know what we gonna do. I have to go and get these kids. I know my mother's going insane wondering why I just left the kids with her like that. I might as well get through the interrogation she's gonna put me through. But, Liaka," Asia paused, then stood to her feet, "...we're gonna be all right. We both been through it, but, we'll make it. Let's have some fun tonight and, next week, we start fresh. The beginning of the week will be the start of the rest of our lives. Maliaka, we'll make it," Asia ended, giving Liaka a long hug.

Liaka followed Asia with her eyes as she grabbed her *Fendi* handbag from the corner of the couch and headed out the front door. Liaka could hear Asia's car start and pull off. The hum of her engine faded off into the distance. Liaka turned to the phone. *That sounds like something your crazy ass girl Lianna would say.* Asia's words sang like a nefarious hum in her head, a hum that prompted her to call Lianna.

"Look! Right there! It's right there! He...hello?" Lianna stuttered.

"Looking for a lighter. Are you ever straight?" Liaka said.

Triple Crown Publications presents... Queen of Thieves *PART 1*

"Straight for what? If I could, I would stay smoked out, weeded up, twenty-four hours a day!" Lianna expressed with sincerity.

"I would ask if you were busy. But, being..."

"Damn, nigga! Is you blind? Ho...hold on, Liaka! 'cause this blind ass nigga act like he need glasses or something!" Lianna blurted, then dropped the receiver with a thud. If that was anybody else, their rude behavior would have angered Liaka. But, not Lianna. For some strange reason, Lianna's sharp attitude amused her. As she sat as a silent spectator, listening to the faint sounds through the receiver of the verbal lashing Lianna spit at her male companion, Liaka could only smile at her friend's behavior.

"Okay, I'm back. I swear, if I didn't tell this nigga to...Liaka?"

"Yeah, I'm here."

"Oh, 'cause I was about to say. I just know this girl ain't hang up on me!"

"No, I didn't hang up on you. I was just sitting here thinking about you, so I decided to give you a call. Are you busy?"

"Naw, I'm just laid up, chillin'. 'Bout to smoke this blunt," Lianna answered.

"Sounds like you're doing a whole lot better."

"Yeah, I took a long, hot bath to relax. And by the time I got out, Asia came over. Who you got over there with you?"

"It's just Kenny. He's...shut up, boy! You so stupid!" Lianna said laughing. "He talkin' 'bout just Kenny? Just give him back his blunt! This nigga fuckin' retarded!"

"Listen, do you hear me?" Liaka questioned, hearing rattling through the receiver. From the moment Liaka heard it was Kenny over there visiting, she knew she should have just hung up. Maintaining Lianna's focus on anything when Kenny was there was like trying to distract a hungry pit-bull from a half-pound of sirloin steak!

Not that Lianna was so into Kenny that she couldn't be pulled away from him. In fact, it was just the other way around. As far as the saying goes about having a man wrapped around your little finger, Lianna took that adage to a whole new level. Lianna had Kenny wrapped around her pinky finger, her ring finger, her middle and index finger, and possibly a couple of toes to go along with it. At first, Liaka thought Kenny was just another one of the many brothers that had fallen victim to Lianna's sexual prowess, basically—pussy whipped! But, Liaka saw that it was much more than that. She had some type of hold on Kenny that she couldn't understand. Probably never will.

"I'm sorry; I hear you. This nigga just keep playing. Kenny! Don't you see me on the phone?" Lianna exploded, but, couldn't help but to giggle from his constant playing.

"We gotta take Asia out tonight. 'Cause you ain't gonna believe me when I tell you what happened between her and Donovan."

"What did he do now? Tell her to stay in the house all twenty-four hours a day instead of twenty-two?"

"Girl, he ain't tell her to be in the house, to stay in the house, or even be around the house! Because he told her, get this, that he's leaving her for another woman!"

"Get outta here!"

"And that ain't even the worst of it! He's gonna have the nerve to tell her that he wants to marry the other female, too!"

"No! No, he didn't! You lying!"

"Girl, I'm more serious than a week in a rain shower without a weave!" Liaka spit. They both burst out in laughter.

"What...what Asia say? How she doing?" Lianna questioned, between puffs on the blunt.

"She's hurt. She's hurt that she knows it's finally over. But, she seems to be more upset at who he left her for. Donovan's gonna have the nerve to tell her that he's leaving her to marry a white girl."

"Um...that's...," Lianna mumbled.

"That's why I wanna take her out. She was actually the one who suggested it. But, I think we both need to go out. Hopefully, it will take our minds off the things that's been going on. Even if it's just for one night," Liaka said. "We should go to the mall first, though. They had a cute lil' jean skirt at... what was it, Banana Republic? I think I might get that."

"Um, uh huh."

"I was talking to Asia about something and she said something to me that made me think about you. She told me I was crazy. But, she don't know the whole story. She don't know everything me and Olu talked about, what we been through. She didn't know that I knew. He told me all about what he was doing. All I had to do was ask him and I knew he would tell me. He would never lie to me," Liaka declared, her tone more like she was trying to convince herself than anyone else. "Do you know what I was thinking about?"

"Um, what?"

Triple Crown Publications presents... Queen of Thieves *PART 1*

"Olu taught me how to use a gun. I know I could tell you that, 'cause I know you won't get carried away. I knew I shouldn'ta told Asia. I knew she would freak! Anyways, he used to tell me how easy it is, you know, to rob someone. How people act when they getting robbed."

"You right...um...I hear you, girl," Lianna sighed.

"You're not even listening to me! What are you doing?" Liaka questioned, hearing Lianna answer with a moan, followed by a rustling in the background.

"This...ummmm...this nigga got his head between my thighs, girl. He got his lips and, oh, his tongue right where it's supposed to be," Lianna whispered between moans.

"Oh, no you not! I just know you ain't...I thought you were smoking?"

"I am smoking. But, this nigga smoking on me!" Lianna moaned. Liaka had to fight the urge to burst out laughing. She couldn't believe Lianna would do something like that while she casually talked on the phone. Liaka found herself feeling slightly guilty for listening in, trying to hear the details of what was happening on the other end.

"Lianna, I just know you playing, right? He can hear you?"

"Yeah, he can hear me, and? Liaka, if you never tried it, have a nigga twist his tongue up in you, oh so gently, while you smoking on a blunt. There's no other feeling like it. Best massage you could ever have," Lianna pronounced, her breathing increasing.

"Here I am, trying to talk to you, seeing if we could do something tonight, and you...ewww! You so nasty!" Liaka said, with a chuckle.

"That's all you need, girl. To lay back, smoke a blunt, and have the right set of lips massaging your shit up for you."

"How could you even...and Asia say I'm crazy!"

"I'm for real. You...oh, toy, be gentle. Slow down. It ain't going nowhere," Lianna sighed, drunk with lust. "You know my toy will bless you too, right?"

"What?" Liaka blurted, with a hearty laugh. "What did you call him?"

"Toy. When I get into my zone with him, he has to respond to 'toy'. Toy is cool like that. I think Asia needs it more than you. No, Asia definitely needs it more than you! So, how about this, after we go out tonight, after the club, he can come over and bless all three of us."

"I see you've been clearly smoking too much weed! How do you look even saying something like that? Like I'm gonna sleep with your man."

"No, I didn't say fucking. I don't give him permission to give his dick out. He can only get my goodies when he's been good. I said you and Asia can *borrow* his tongue—that's it. Don't worry, he love that shit. He get off just from doing that. This nigga do what I tell him to do. Watch this," Lianna stated, her tone becoming slightly aggressive. "Toy! Tonight I need you to hit two of my girls off, just like you handling that right there. Got it? Yeah, just like that. Stay on that spot right there," Lianna uttered, her hand lowering to rest on the back of his head. "Nigga! Ain't nobody tell you to lift your head up to answer! Don't stop what you doing. Just moan—yes!" Lianna commanded. Liaka heard the groan of two um hmm's being hummed loudly on the other end.

"Girl, that's it! I heard enough, I gotta go!" Liaka stated, shaking her head with an indelible grin on her face.

"What? It ain't nothing wrong with that. These niggas do it! It's time to switch the game up. So, at the end of the night, I'll have my nigga bless you up properly. That's a nice way to end the night—no strings attached. He... umm, girl, he just lowered his tongue to where he know I like it. It's getting real now, ma. I gotta go!" Lianna cried out, for Liaka to hear some more rustling, and then the phone went dead.

# Chapter 15 | Who's Your Type?

The sun was going down. Liaka pressed the display on the face of her car stereo as she rounded the corner to Lianna's block.

6:54 P.M.

The fall season was stealing more and more of the daylight hours as the close of the summer rolled to an end. Liaka welcomed the fall season. She enjoyed the weather the most. But, that fall season would be different. It would be the first fall in years without Olu. Liaka fought to clear her mind. No more negative images. She had to think positively; she had to move on.

Ironically, turning into Lianna's neighborhood didn't help matters any. Lianna was her girl, but, going to pick Lianna up, or chill at her house, wasn't one of the top things on Liaka's lists. Aside from the inevitable ogling and verbal harassment she was prepared to receive if Angel or any of his boys were there, Liaka also had to be concerned with the safety of her vehicle. Leaving her pearl-white *Acura TL* parked blocks away from the projects, fully loaded with all the accessories—the TV's, the stereo, the twenty-two inch spinners—caused her more concern than all the 'baby, let me suck on that's,' and other illicit come-on's combined. The sardonic trade-off was, if Angel or any of his boys were "hugging the block," at least Liaka knew her car would have a set of eyes on it.

Unfortunately, those "eyes" would also be on her every move, literally undressing her with every step. That day, Liaka just wasn't in the mood for either of those hassles. Liaka glanced back and forth from the road to her *Ralph Lauren* bag on the passenger seat. She reached over, fumbling inside for her cell phone.

"I'm pulling up in front of your building right now. Hurry up so we ain't gotta be in the mall all night."

"I'll be right down. Give me five minutes," Lianna responded, then hung up as fast as she answered. Within seconds, Liaka rolled to a stop in front of Lianna's building. Angel, nor any of his boys, were anywhere in sight. At least that was a good sign; one less form of aggravation for Liaka. But, a minute didn't pass before Liaka spotted a brother wearing a black hoody—a hoody barely revealing his fitted hat pulled down low—approaching her. The swagger in his steps and his inspective glances into the car assured Liaka that he wasn't there to harm her.

Liaka knew the flashiness of her car, along with her looks, was like a magnet to brothers in the 'hood. He unveiled his head from under his hoody. Standing feet away from her driver's side door, he made a gesture for Liaka to roll down her window. Liaka regretted not picking up her phone again. At least with her phone in her ear she could have faked like she didn't see him, being engulfed in her call. But, there he was, cheesin' down at Liaka with a smile from ear to ear.

"How you doing today?" He chimed, then leaned over the hood of the car. Liaka barely cracked the window for him. But, the three inches on the driver's side was enough for him to try to gain access to Liaka inside.

"I'm a'ight. But, if my man come out and see you next to me, he's gonna have a problem," Liaka answered, hoping to discourage him. From the look on his face, it didn't.

"Your man ain't got nothing to do with me. I'm sayin' though, shorty. Why don't you slide me them digits on the low real quick, and I can ease up outta here before he even come out. Keep that shit on tha low, ya know? So we can work something out on a later date," he said slyly, with a devilish glint in his eye. He bit on the bottom of his lip—his attempt at trying to look sexy—searching over every inch of Liaka. He was actually kinda cute-perfectly straight teeth, nice, caramel skin tone, and the braids underneath his hat appeared tight. But, Liaka just wasn't in the mood.

"I don't cheat on my man. I..."

"Um, you wanna back the fuck away from my girl window?" the shrill voice of Lianna caused him to lean upright and peer over his shoulder.

"I thought you said your man?" The brother said. Liaka smiled with a shrug.

"Well, she meant her girl! That's my bitch! She ain't thinking about dick, nigga! She thinking about this pussy! So, get to stepping!" Lianna spit at him, walking around to open Liaka's passenger door. She just stood there, staring over the hood of the car at him with a twisted look on her face. The brother glanced down at Liaka, back up at Lianna, down to Liaka again and sucked his teeth.

"Dyke ass bitches!" The brother snarled under his breath, then turned to walk off.

"Yeah, yeah, dyke ass bitches! That's right. 'Cause of broke, walking motherfuckas like you! So, get to stepping, nigga! Kick rocks!" Lianna snapped, as he pimped away.

"Now you know you ain't right," Liaka chuckled.

"That nigga's a fuckin' scrub! I've seen him around. If he was 'bout it,' believe me, I woulda let you know," Lianna assured her, lowering the passenger side sun visor to check herself in the mirror. Liaka snickered as she watched Lianna out of the corner of her eye. Lianna rubbed her thumb across the lower line of her lip to clean the excess lipstick that smeared over the bottom. She was clearly wearing too much makeup for Liaka's taste, and too much lipstick for *anybody's* taste. On top of that, she had the nerve to be wearing bright, candy-apple red.

"So, we 'bout to go and get Asia?" Lianna questioned, like nothing happened moments earlier.

"Yeah, she should be home by now. She had to go to her mother's to drop off the kids." She pulled off slowly, cruising past the brother from a few moments ago. Liaka couldn't help but to glance up at her rear-view mirror. She felt sorry for him. The look on his face faded into a blur. There was no mistaking it, he was hurt.

From the corner of her eye, she could tell Lianna already forgot about it. Cold. Lianna was heartless when it came to things like that. Liaka remembered the talk she tried to have with Lianna over the phone. How she tried to relate her thoughts which were met with Lianna 'getting it just like she likes it'. But, now, as they cruised in silence, Liaka had Lianna's full, undivided attention.

"What's up with Kenny?" Liaka asked casually.

"Kenny? I don't know, it's just Kenny. Every girl gotta have her lil' flunky nigga on the side, right?" Lianna stated. She leaned forward to fumble with Liaka's car stereo.

"He be selling, right? Drugs? He be hustling?"

"He do his lil' thang. Nothing big. He's what I call a *Honda hustla*. He hustles just enough to buy a *Honda* or something. Like I said, nothing big."

"Anybody ever try to rob him before?"

"Rob him? How the hell would I know? I don't care about what the hell he does! I keep him around for two reasons and two reasons only: that nigga make sure I stay with weed, and that nigga eat pussy like he went to college for that shit!" Lianna said with a chuckle. "But, I bet if someone did try to rob him, his bitch ass would probably just give it up! He try to act all hard, like he's a real thug. But, I know he be stuntin'. Why you asking? What you all concerned about Kenny for? I told you, if you want him to bless you, all you gotta do is ask. Stop acting all prissy an' shit! You think when a nigga got a chick and they be like, 'yo, hit my boy off', he be acting all like that?"

"That's *not* why I'm asking," Liaka said, amused, "I was asking you something earlier. Do you remember what I was talking about?"

"Yeah, going out. I heard you. You was telling me what happened to Asia. That Donovan thing. Then you said you wanted to hit the club. I heard all that. So, I thought of two ill ass spots for tonight. *Gotham's* is hot! And it's guaranteed to be live! But, they also got that new club that just opened up on the South end. They was talking about that all week on the radio, so that shit should be jumping, too."

"Not that either."

"Then what, bitch? Stop speaking in codes! I ain't a mind reader. Just speak your mind!" Lianna snapped.

Liaka quickly glanced over to her, then back to the road. "I was talking about Olu. How me and Olu talked, how he taught me things."

"Taught you things? Things like what?"

"Just some things. We also talked about a lot of things."

"Hold up, slow down. Go back to those 'some things' that he taught you."

"For one, he taught me how to use a gun."

"That's it? You going on all like that 'cause you *held* a gun? Who don't know how to use a gun? I'm thinking you gonna tell me that he taught you how to crack a safe or something. Angel's been bringing guns around me for years. Nines, .38s, .45s, shotguns. But, since you so excited about it, what type of gun did Olu have?" Lianna said in a condescending tone.

"I think it was a nine. It was black," Liaka related, slightly embarrassed. She merged into highway traffic, heading to Asia's place. Liaka knew it would take about ten minutes to get there, fifteen if she slowed it down. She was pushing more for fifteen, hoping to have a little more time with Lianna alone to relay her thoughts. Liaka could see that Lianna was quickly losing interest; she had to get her back. "He was also telling me how he used to rob people," Liaka said in a flat tone. From the corner of her eye, Liaka noticed how Lianna stopped fiddling with the radio.

"How he used to rob people? So, wait a minute, you knew? You knew the whole time that he was gonna rob that bank?" Lianna asked, amazed. "Ooohh, y'all some sneaky ass bitches!" Lianna continued, with a hearty laugh.

"I ain't sneaky. I just know how to be discreet," Liaka returned with a smile.

"So, that ain't the first time he did it?"

"No."

"Hmph! You good, girl. I know my secret safe with you, 'cause I woulda never guessed that shit! So, what else did he do?" Lianna probed, her body shifting completely to face Liaka, her curiosity piqued.

"He told me about when he first got started. How he used to rob drug dealers. He told it all. And Lianna, that shit used to get me going," Liaka sighed. Lianna burst out in laughter, more like a celebrated cheer. She could hardly contain herself as she rocked in delight.

"Oh, believe me, I already know! Now I think you might finally understand why I loves me a thug nigga! It's just something about a brother who dominates shit everywhere he goes that's such a turn on. And don't even get me started about them in the bedroom. I be trying to tell these females, if they wanna make sure they shit is done up right, fucks with a *real* thug nigga! One of those mean, gangsta ass niggas! You know I had my share of niggas. But, I had this one dude, I ain't even gonna lie, he used to make *me* nervous! And I was his girl! He never smiled, laughed, nothing. He was always so serious. I used to see how some niggas would get when he came around. They was terrified of him. And I used to love that shit! They said he killed like four or five people and got away with it because people were too scared to turn him in. And, by the way he used to act, I believe it."

"What happened to him?"

"He eventually got locked up. He got like ten or fifteen years, something like that, for stabbing this brother up in broad daylight. So they say. I know he used to rob people, too. And, one time, he actually had the nerve to ask me to *help* him."

Liaka instantly turned to Lianna. "He asked you to help him?"

"Yeah, he came in one day and was just pulling out knots of money wrapped in rubber bands from his pockets. When I asked him where he got all that from, he told me how he knew some dude that was selling 'cracks'. He said the kid was a sucker to him, so he just robbed him. He said he didn't even have to shoot him to get it, either. Then he told me if I wanted to make some money that he would put me down. I told him 'whassup?' He told me my part would be simple: just set dudes up for him. Flirt with them, get them to go somewhere discreet, then he would come and rob them," Lianna described her tone nonchalant, as if she was describing what she ate for breakfast.

"What did you do?"

"I thought about it. I was just waiting on him. He just never brought it up again. But, it ain't like I ain't robbing these niggas anyways! You think when these niggas like Kenny, and these other brothers be coming to my house, or when we go to the room, that I don't be catching them? I be getting them for like two, three hundred a pop, and they don't even miss it. Once a nigga start thinking about pussy, they start thinking real 'one-sided'."

"Keep them in that frame of mind and you can do whatever you want! Some niggas don't even think a female would rob them like that. And the few times a dude did question me about touching his money, all I had to do was act all surprised and innocent, then go down and suck his dick. That *always* shuts them up," Lianna related with a shrug. "Why, you thinking about robbing someone now?" Lianna asked enthusiastically, her eyes grew wide with excitement. Liaka remained silent as she pulled off the highway. "You ain't gonna say nothing? It don't matter. The fact that you *ain't* saying something says it all."

"That's crazy, huh?"

"Hell naw! Do you know how easy that shit would be to rob one of these niggas? They would never see that shit coming! They don't expect females to do shit like that. Some of the smarter ones know that a female would set

Triple Crown Publications presents... Queen of Thieves
*PART 1*

them up. But, most of them would never suspect a female doing it *herself!*" Lianna explained convincingly. Liaka caught a glance at Lianna out the corner of her eye; Lianna stared back at her, unflinching. Liaka got nervous. The mere thought of carrying out that idea, turning that fantasy into a reality, echoed those same eerie feelings she had in the presence of Olu.

"How would you do it?"

"Me? It all depends on what type of nigga it is. The average nigga would be easy. *All* niggas want pussy, so getting him alone would be nothing. Then, all you gotta do is make him think that you into that S&M shit, being tied up, spanked, then just tie his ass up, simple as that. Because, once he's tied up, he's pretty much at my mercy. If he was a herb nigga, I would probably tie him up butt-naked, slap him up a few times, then just take his shit. But, if he was one of those hard ass niggas, I would probably pop a cap in his thug ass!"

"Stop playing! You ain't shooting nobody!" Liaka said, with a laugh.

"Shit! If I had to, I would. When you get down like that, you have to be ruthless! You gots to let a nigga know that you for real!" Lianna said sternly. "You still ain't tell me, you wanna do it, huh?" Lianna continued, anxiously. Liaka remained silent as she turned into Asia's neighborhood. "Tell me! Don't just leave me hanging like that!"

"Call Asia and tell her that we 'bout to pull up in front of her house and not to take all day."

"Uh, uh. Tell me!" Lianna insisted. Liaka simply smiled. Reaching for her cell phone, Liaka proceeded to dial Asia's number before Lianna stopped her. "I ain't gonna let you call until you tell me," Lianna threatened. Liaka threw her a mischievous grin then leaned on her car horn. "You dirty. But, it don't matter. I'm gonna find out," Lianna conceded. Asia's kids were the first to emerge from the front porch, running off towards the car. Asia wasn't far behind.

"Listen; don't mention what we were talking about to Asia. Okay? You know how she is."

"Only if you tell me. Are you gonna do it?"

"We'll talk about it later. Just promise me you won't tell her. I don't want her to…"

"Hi, Auntie Likey!" Asia's daughter cheered at Liaka's driver's side window. Liaka quickly turned back to give Lianna a distinct look. Lianna nodded reluctantly. Only then did Liaka open her door to let them in.

"What's going on, girl," Asia stated, as Lianna opened the passenger door for her.

"Mommy! Donny won't let me see his gun!" Asia's daughter whined, before Asia could even take a seat in the back.

"Look! Both of you. If either of you start, I swear! We won't even leave this street! I'll march both of your little butts right back up to the house and you'll both spend the rest of the night in your rooms! Do you hear me?" Asia threatened, pointing a menacing finger at them. The threat worked. They both sat quietly in the back seat as Asia began to strap them in their seatbelts.

"Come up here and sit with me," Lianna called out to Donovan Junior before Asia could fully strap him in. Lifting Donovan Junior between the spaces of the front seats, Lianna situated him on her lap. She immediately began to smother him with kisses.

"If you're gonna keep him up there, put your seatbelt on," Asia mentioned. Lianna secured her seatbelt over them as Liaka slowly pulled off. Little Donovan felt the warmth Lianna showered him with. He was happily receptive. As Lianna held him lovingly, she carefully inspected his little hands, fingers, and the soft curls on his head. *To have a little boy,* Lianna thought to herself.

"Where we going? The Buckland Hills Mall?" Asia inquired, leaning over to embrace Sky. It didn't take her mother's intuition to see that Sky was jealous from the attention Lianna showered her little brother with. Asia tickled Sky's chin with her index finger then reached in her purse for her compact make-up kit, something she knew would placate Sky from past experiences of Sky sneaking through her purse to play with it.

"Yeah, I wanted to stop by *Filene's,*" Liaka announced. Lianna squeezed herself forward, sliding little Donovan to the side to reach for her handbag on the floor. Once she got it, Lianna removed a half-smoked blunt from a cigarette pack. Donovan Junior studied Lianna over his shoulder curiously. It took for Lianna to place the blunt between her lips for Asia to observe her.

"I just know you ain't 'bout to smoke that in here."

"What? I'm a open the window," Lianna explained incredulously. A twisted look from Asia made Lianna return the blunt to the pack after sucking her teeth. Liaka shook her head at Lianna with a smirk. Lianna clicked on the radio and turned up the volume slightly as they drove. She danced in her seat with little Donovan in her lap, lifting his little arms with each snare of the beat. They arrived at the mall about twenty minutes later.

"Look, they got a sale at *Lord & Taylor*," Asia announced.

"Typical Asia," Liaka sighed.

"Why you say that? They got some cute stuff in there," Asia returned.

"Let's go to *Filene's* first before we start wandering," Liaka suggested. As the three of them entered through the mall's front doors, it wasn't long before brothers were on them. Liaka was the first to realize all the attention they were getting. Lianna was next, provoking a little extra swagger in her step, welcoming their lustful stares. Asia was oblivious to their glances, more concerned with keeping an eye on her children and window shopping, trying to find the best deal on display.

"Damn, girl! Did you see how them brothers were looking at me?" Lianna said, blushing after passing a group of teens.

"At you? You must need glasses!" Liaka chuckled. "All those eyes were on me!"

"Please! Them niggas was looking at me like I was on the menu!" Lianna affirmed. "One of them looked familiar, too."

"I can believe it. Knowing you, you probably knew him *real* good. Maybe even a few of his boys, too," Liaka teased.

"Don't hate! I ain't got no shame in my game!" Lianna returned.

"I know. Maybe that's the problem," Liaka snickered. Asia listened from the sidelines. She didn't have the energy to get involved; her mind was still preoccupied with the news Donovan shared with her.

"Ohhh, we gots to go up in here!" Lianna blurted, drawn to a display in a department store window. She didn't wait for them to respond before she dragged little Donovan by his arm into the store. Asia waited to see how Liaka would respond to Lianna. But, she didn't. Liaka only gave Asia that look that said it would be useless to argue.

"Now this shit is hot right here!" Lianna expressed, removing a shirt from a clothing rack. Lianna held it up, and then laid the shirt against her chest.

"That is cute," Liaka agreed. "That would look nice with a pair of tight blue jeans. Asia, what you gonna get?" Asia shrugged as she began to sift through a rack of skirts, every now and then glancing down to her kids.

"I gotta go and try this on," Lianna uttered, heading off to the dressing room. Asia waited for Lianna to walk off before she turned to Liaka.

"Why do you always do that? If I say we should do something, you never

agree. But, the moment *she* says let's do something, you jump at it!"

"It's not all like that," Liaka sighed. "What are you talking about anyways?"

"Like this, here! When I wanted to go to Lord & Taylor, you were quick to shut that down. But, right when she wanted to come in here, you didn't even make as much as a peep!"

"That's not fair, Asia. You know how she is."

"No! It's not about her. It's about you! It's about how you always choose her over me. How you always make excuses for her, just like you're doing now."

"Because I thought you would understand."

"Oh, I understand all right. I understand that..." Asia saw Lianna exit the dressing room out of the corner of her eye.

"Now tell me this shit ain't hot!" Lianna chimed as she approached, modeling the outfit she just picked. Their subtle nods were less than enthusiastic. "What? You don't like it?"

"Naw, it's real cute," Liaka assured.

"Then, what? Why y'all acting like y'all was talking about me when I left?" Lianna accused, her eyes darting back and forth between them.

"Now you know you ain't that important," Liaka said slickly. Asia smiled.

"Then y'all must be looking at me like that 'cause y'all hating how I'm wearing the hell outta this top! Asia, what you gonna get?"

Asia was somewhat thrown off by Lianna's inquiry. "I don't know. This store really isn't my style. I really don't see anything that I like," Asia answered, sorting through her third rack of clothes.

What Asia didn't relay was her particular distaste in the majority of the options she had to choose from. The department store Lianna decided to go to, catered to women who were more apt to revealing more flesh than Asia felt comfortable with. By the fourth rack of clothes Asia sorted through, she would have been lucky if she didn't run across a half-shirt that read *Princess, Spoiled Bitch*, or *Daddy's little girl* written across the front. Most of the other items weren't too far off; nine-inch mini-skirts or low-cut, tight jeans dominated most of the clothing racks. Asia collected what she considered to be the closest items to her style of clothes, removing two articles from the rack.

"That's not gonna cut it tonight. Here, try this," Lianna suggested, after her quick rejection of Asia's choice. Lianna removed a sky-blue tank by *Dolce and Gabbana* and a tight mini-skirt to match. Lianna walked over to hold

Triple Crown Publications presents... Queen of Thieves
*PART 1*

the outfit to Asia's chest and waist. "Wait! Let's put the finishing touches on this!" Lianna blurted, scurrying off. She came back seconds later with a pair of matching sky-blue leather and suede knee-high boots. "Now, that would be cute on you."

"Ah, I don't think so," Asia said.

"At least try them on. If you don't like them after you try them on, fine! Go back to your old ways of dressing like a mother."

"Hello, I *am* a mother," Asia said sarcastically, gesturing to her kids.

"And that's your problem. You act like just because you're a mother that you can't be sexy or dress sexy. You being a mother doesn't mean that you have to stop droppin' it'. Well, that is, unless you *can't* drop it anymore," Lianna said, slyly. Liaka stood there smiling. She waited anxiously to see if Asia would fall for the bait. Asia rolled her eyes at Lianna, followed by snatching the outfit from her hands.

"Don't think just because I don't drop it like it's hot that I can't!" Asia slurred, with a twist of her hips and a snap of her fingers.

"Oh, shit! Now that's the Asia I wanna see! I knew you had it in you, girl!" Lianna cheered, as Asia walked off to disappear into the dressing room. "These would be cute on you, Liaka," Lianna suggested, holding out a pair of *Apple Bottom* jeans.

"They are cute. And these are one of the few pairs of jeans that actually fit me right," Liaka said. "It's hard to find a good pair of jeans that fit me right."

"I just know you ain't complaining. Because if you are, I'd be more than glad to take some of that ass from you," Lianna said enviously.

"Oh, believe me, I'm not complaining. Because this ass right here stopped more traffic than a red light!" Liaka replied, as they both broke out in laughter.

"That looks really pretty, Mommy," Asia's daughter called out.

Liaka and Lianna turned to notice Asia standing shyly in front of the dressing room. In the history of their friendship, Liaka had never witnessed Asia wearing something so provocative, so racy, which revealed such ample amounts of flesh and accentuated every curve of her body. Asia gazed at Liaka innocently, waiting for a response.

"Kadiajah, girl, that shit look slammin' on you!" Liaka said thickly. Asia turned around to examine herself. She stood in the center of three six-foot mirrors. Her eyes traveled from the top of her head, carefully examining every inch of herself as they slowly descended to her feet. Her top was short, and it revealed more cleavage than she felt comfortable sharing with the world. But, the skirt was the worst. Asia knew from the moment she squeezed it on that there wasn't a chance in hell she would be able to sit and cross her legs without showcasing to the world her particular brand of panties. She grabbed both sides of the skirt and tried to wiggle it down to conceal more of her thick thighs. It was useless. The tight denim and style of cut on the waist made her struggling effort futile.

"What are you doing?" Lianna questioned.

"This skirt is showing way too much of...well, just too much."

"Just stop it. Since I've met you, I've never seen you wear the hell out of an outfit like that! And if I didn't see it with my own eyes, I would have never known that you had a body like that!" Lianna said, eying Asia. Asia gazed at Lianna who was lost in her new look. Lianna snapped back from her trance to notice the look Asia shot at her. "Don't flatter yourself, girl. I'm impressed, but, not *that* impressed! You don't have all the *attachments* that I need," Lianna slurred.

"Oh, 'cause I was about to say, you better get your girl, Liaka," Asia said, for them to break out in laughter. After Liaka gained her composure, she glanced up to notice a handsome brother stopping outside the department store window to watch them. Liaka wasn't quite sure where his focus was directed, but, she was sure that he was definitely looking at them.

Liaka glanced back over her shoulder to her girls. They were oblivious to their admirer. Asia was more concerned with covering herself, while Lianna was in the process of lifting the hem of Asia's shirt to disappear under the line of her breasts. Asia smirked at Lianna's attempt, and then lowered it back down to cover half of her stomach.

Liaka turned to their admirer for the second time to see that he was entering the store. He approached them keenly. Lianna was the second one to notice the brother, catching a glance of him in the reflection of a mirror. His approach prompted Lianna to rub her lips together, desperately striving to revive the luster of her lipstick.

"Excuse me," the brother announced, once he entered their space. Liaka and Lianna's eyes were already on him. Asia was the last to notice him. She immediately cowered, realizing that no man in years, aside from Donovan, feasted his eyes on so much of her flesh, and to have it be a complete stranger at that. "I was just passing by when I happened to notice you. I thought you were beautiful and I wouldn't have been able to live with myself if I didn't stop in and introduce myself," the brother said smoothly, introducing himself to Asia, and reaching forth, extending his hand to her.

Lianna's warm smile faded into an envious smirk. She rolled her eyes at him, and then returned to a rack of clothes. Liaka was happy for Asia, even going so far as to coax her kids away from them to give them some time alone. Asia was slow to extend her arm to accept his hand, her other arm unconsciously crossed over her chest.

"My name is Zachariah," he chanted in a deep tone, his firm hand closing around hers. He stood about six foot four, towering over Asia; almond complexion, shiny, bald head, and appearing to be in his late thirties. He was eloquently dressed in a dark blue pin-striped suit, a loosened tie, and the top three buttons on his pink dress shirt were undone to reveal the hint of a muscular chest underneath.

"I'm...I'm sorry. This is so embarrassing. You have to excuse me. I have to change," Asia sighed, attempting to release her hand from his.

"I'm sure no matter what you change into that you're still going to be beautiful."

"Thank you. But, I still have to change. I feel...uncomfortable standing here like this," Asia said, releasing an embarrassed chuckle.

"Do you mind if I wait for you to change? Because I still didn't get your name."

"I have to be honest with you. You are a very, very attractive man. But, I just got out of a long-term relationship with my children's father. So, right now, I'm not at a very good time in my life to meet someone. I'm really, really sorry," Asia related, pulling her hand from his.

"I don't want to step out of bounds or be out of line here. And I can fully appreciate your position. But, I would think that now would be the best time to probably move on. Maybe go out with someone who may possibly take your mind off of him." Asia let out an ambiguous sigh. From his position, he wasn't sure if Asia was giving in, or growing frustrated. "How about this," he dug into the inner pocket of his blazer, "take my card. If there's a chance that you might change your mind, give me a call." He flipped his card out to her. Asia reached out to accept it. "Before I leave, can I at least know your name?"

Asia couldn't help but to blush. "Kadiajah. My name is, Kadiajah," Asia returned shyly.

"Kadiajah. That's powerful. The name of the Prophet Mohammed's wife. It fits you. Kadiajah, the pleasure was all mine. Hope to hear from you soon." He ended with a subtle nod and a quick glance over her body before walking off. She finally raised the card up that he gave her. It was a business card; he was a real estate agent.

"Damn, girl, I'm scared of you!" Liaka said dramatically, approaching Asia from behind. "'Cause that brother was fiiinnneeee!"

"Do you see that? You had it in you the whole time! And just to think, all you had to do was show a little skin to get that type of attention," Lianna remarked.

"Exactly!" Asia said snidely. "THAT'S why he approached me! I'm standing here more than half-naked! I expect that from *most* men. Just another reason why I would never find myself like this in public. Why else do you think he approached me?"

"Uh, maybe because he like what he seen? Have you ever thought about that?" Lianna said, in a chastising tone. "So, let me get this straight. You gonna hold it against him because he happened to walk by you, seen something that he liked, and decided to come and talk to you? Yeah, you all fucked up! Now I see why your man left you! You don't even know how to take a compliment when you get one!" Lianna spit coldly. Asia's smile quickly faded, her cheerful demeanor diminished. Liaka saw the look on Asia's face and tried to step in.

"Forget about her. So, what did he have to say?" Liaka blurted.

"No! I want to answer that little comment she just made!" Asia spewed, stepping around Liaka to face Lianna. Lianna paid little attention to Asia as she returned to sift through another rack of clothes. "For your information, I CAN take a compliment! But, I would prefer to be complimented on my *intelligence*, on my *mind*, instead of how much tits and ass I can show!"

"Why you say it like that? Did I say something wrong?" Lianna said. "All I was saying is that he like what he seen. You can't tell me you wasn't checking him out. I'm sure when he walked up you wasn't looking at his *intelligence*. You was looking at him just like the rest of us."

"We were ALL looking at him," Liaka spoke up. "'Cause that brother looked better than a tall drink of water on a hot summer day!" Liaka continued with a smirk. Lianna returned to the rack, lifting a top out to examine it, oblivious to Asia's evil eyes on her. Liaka prod her with the tips of her fingers, trying to divert Asia's attention. It took a few seconds before Asia rolled her eyes at Lianna then turned to face Liaka.

"So, what did he say?" Liaka probed again.

"Nothing really. He just wanted to know if he could get to know me. He gave me his card," Asia returned unenthusiastically, handing the card to Liaka.

"A businessman. You can't go wrong with that," Liaka said energetically. Asia shrugged and stepped off to disappear behind the door of the dressing room. "You gonna call him?" Liaka questioned, talking to Asia through the door.

"Call him? Who said I was gonna call him?"

"Why not? You have to call him."

"Why?"

"Again, why not? Asia, weren't you the one saying that we have to move on? Well, who better to move on with than a brother like that?" Liaka announced convincingly. Asia heard Liaka's words as she stood in the tight dressing room with only her bra and panties on. She thought about Donovan. Lianna's words pierced through her. *Now I see why your man left you!*

*Did Donovan leave her because of her attitude? Was it something she did? Was there something she could have done in the past that could have possibly saved their relationship? Was she being too uptight?* Asia picked up the clothes from a small wooden bench behind her, the clothes that Lianna picked out for her. She held them to her chest and waist again.

She never wore clothes like that for Donovan. Didn't even own something like that in her entire wardrobe. Was it possible that Donovan viewed Asia more as a motherly figure than a sexual object? Asia began to question if it was even possible to be both—a wholesome mother and the facade of a sexual being. Previous thoughts about how Donovan openly lusted over the scantily clad women in the music videos, the magazines, sometimes even in her presence when they were out, stealing glances at them, came to Asia like haunting images.

Then, an image of Maryann came to her mind. Maryann reeked of sexuality. From her helpless, innocent attitude, to her scantily clad wardrobe, to her voluptuous shape. Could it be possible for Donovan to see Asia as this epitome of a sexual siren, not just as a mother, outside of the bedroom? What if she could show the world, in the presence of Donovan of course, that she could drip sexuality and remain classy at the same time? Could this be done, all while maintaining that wholesome, motherly image? A mischievous smirk spread across Asia's face as she remained with the clothes still pressed to her body. At that moment, she had an epiphany.

"I know you hear me! Hello?" Liaka repeated, tearing into Asia's thoughts.

"I heard you. I was just thinking when I was getting dressed," Asia said, walking through the dressing room doors, Lianna's chosen outfit flung over her shoulder.

"Well, if you heard me, then you heard that Lianna said if you don't want him, then give him to her," Liaka said, waving the brother's business card in her hand.

"Yeah, give him to me. I'll definitely know what to do with all that fineness! One night with me after what I would do to him, and I guarantee he'll forget that you even exist! And if he's a real estate agent, I might even get a house up out of the deal," Lianna said with confidence, reaching for his card. Ironically, Asia smiled in return.

"I don't think so. I don't think you're quite his *type*," Asia remarked, snapping the card from Liaka's hand. Liaka smiled to herself thinking, *that's my girl!*

"Not his type?" Lianna croaked with a chuckle. "Let me give you a little newsflash, Kadiajah. I'm EVERY man's type! Unlike you, I'm not that naïve to not know what a man wants. You continue playing 'Miss Suzie-homemaker,' being that's working out so well for you and all. And I'll continue being every man's deepest, darkest fantasy! You see, when I gets a brother, I know how to gets down and dirty for mines and gives him just what he likes. That's the big difference between you and me."

"You see, you're the type of bitch who *spits*, I *swallow* and lick my lips when I'm done! You're the type of bitch who's worried about her hairstyle if he wants to pull your hair. *I'm* the bitch who would offer him a handful of hair for him to pull, beg him to spank me, then bend over and give him *options*! You starting to see the difference, Kadiajah? Every *nigga* may *say* that he wants a good, wholesome, wifey-type girl. And he does, for outside appearance, for the public to see. But, once you both get behind closed doors, that nigga want a bitch that would make a porn star blush! But, that's the problem with bitches like you. After you let a nigga fuck *you*, you're the type of bitch who starts to question if you've done everything correctly. After I fuck that nigga, I KNOW that there ain't another bitch breathing that made that nigga toes curl, or cry out, like I just made him."

"To put it bluntly, I'm the type of bitch that women like you worry about. The type of bitch that you fear. But, strangely enough, it's of your own doing. Bitches like you keep me in business. Just ask yourself: why do you think those rap videos are so popular? What do you think he's thinking about when he's watching them females do the 'booty clap'? The lyrics of the song? Her intelligence?"

"If females like you knew how to handle your business, then most of your niggas wouldn't come to females like me saying, 'you just ain't doing it right'. In the end, you're the type of bitch that's afraid to lose her man, while I'm the type of bitch a nigga is afraid to lose!" Lianna narrated harshly, and then returned to casually sift back through the rack of clothes.

Liaka and Asia were speechless.

Lianna's words hit them like a slap in the face. It was disturbing for Asia to think that she fought so hard to create and maintain a certain image for Donovan, to keep Donovan; an image that possibly contributed to the demise of their relationship. Asia flipped the clothes over her shoulder and looked at them again.

"How much are those?" Lianna asked Asia indifferently.

"The top is ninety-five dollars and the skirt is one-hundred and thirty dollars. Way too rich for my blood."

"Is that what you wanted to wear tonight?"

"I was thinking about it. Especially if it will help to put bitches like you out of business," Asia said adamantly. Lianna smirked at Asia, but, said flatly, "get 'em."

"I wish I could, but, I can't. Two-hundred and twenty-five dollars is a little too steep for me."

"Just get 'em! Wear them out tonight, make sure you don't get anything on them, and then return them tomorrow for a refund. Then I'll come back and get them for you. Because, trust, I seen three pairs of jeans and a few tops I'm gonna get this 'booster-girl' I know to get for me. She'll come in here, boost them, and then sell them to us at half price. Just tell her your size and what you want, trust, she'll get them for you," Lianna assured, with a wink.

"Now do you see why I like her," Liaka said to Asia with a smile.

The three of them continued their shopping, each purchasing their selected items they planned on wearing out that night. With bags in tow, they all headed over to the food court section of the mall. Throughout the course of their meals, different brothers approached them, each in turn.

Lianna tended to attract the younger, more thugged-out brothers; like bees to honey. While Liaka and Asia were clearly more popular with the older, more mature crowd. More numbers were taken than given out. Asia didn't give her number out to anyone, but did manage to get five different numbers, including Zachariah's.

Liaka gave her number out to two brothers, two of the brothers who she felt had the most potential. She also received about five numbers from brothers as well. Lianna was the worst, giving her cell number and home number out to almost every brother who approached her. Out of the three of them, Lianna was clearly the most popular with the brothers.

Liaka and Asia wasn't sure if it was Lianna's particular style of dress—she wore a pair of skin tight, painted on *Allure* jeans, with a tight, half-shirt that read *Superhead* in red letters across the front—or the fact that she perfected the art of flirting down to a science; batting her eyelashes, seductively licking her lips at just the right time, that mesmerizing, hypnotic stare that now became her trademark, or her arsenal of other tricks. Whatever it was, although Liaka and Asia couldn't quite put their finger on it, there was no denying it—men wanted her.

"So, y'all never said if y'all decided where we going for the night," Lianna mentioned, greedily licking her fingers clean after devouring a plate of barbecue chicken.

"I really don't care. I'll leave that up to y'all. But, one thing's for sure—I definitely want to get my drink on!" Liaka stressed. "What do you think, Asia?"

"You asking me? I have no idea. Miss Thang here is the expert on things like that," Asia said, pointing to Lianna. "Did you come up with anything yet?"

"Well, before we came and got you, I was telling Liaka about that club *Gotham's*. That should be live tonight. But, they also got that other new club that just opened up. So, you never know," Lianna conveyed.

"If you had to pick, which one would you go with?"

"Why do we have to pick? We can go to both! Check out the new club, see what type of crowd they got, what type of niggas they working with, and if it ain't live, we slide out to *Gotham's*. I like *Gotham's*. The brothers who usually go there got more money, bigger cars, bigger rims, bigger...ummm," Lianna hummed with a smile.

"Mommy, I have to go to the bathroom," Asia's son complained.

"Can't you hold it? We're about to leave and go straight home from here," Asia sighed, popping the last of her hot fries in her mouth.

"Noooo! Mommy, I have to go!" he moaned in an annoying whine. Asia sucked her teeth. She licked her fingers and grabbed two napkins from the dispenser on the table.

"Come on, Sky. 'Cause I know right when I get back, you're gonna have to go, too," Asia said, standing from the table to lead her kids away. As Asia passed a trail of pay phones lining the hallway to disappear around the corner, Lianna noticed a brother hang up one of the same phones, staring off in their direction.

One thing was for sure, within a few seconds of staring at him, Lianna knew his face was familiar. She had definitely seen him around before. He was a baller. Lianna immediately got into flirt mode. The transition was easy for her; she lived it. The only difference was in the degrees in which she displayed it.

"Remember what you was talking about earlier?" Lianna posed to Liaka. Liaka was busy slurping on the last of her soda, the straw sifted through the ice on the bottom, searching to get the last of it.

"I remember, but, I'm still not telling you."

"You don't have to. Because what's walking over here right now, I just might do it myself," Lianna stated. Liaka peeked over her shoulder.

"How you, ma?" he chimed, staring down at Liaka.

"Don't I know you from somewhere?" Lianna asked.

"I don't know. But, I'm definitely trying to get to know her," he returned, brushing Lianna off. Lianna rolled her eyes. "What's really good, ma?" he continued, chanting down at Liaka.

"I'm good. But, I didn't know I was your ma," Liaka said teasingly.

"Figure of speech, beautiful. My name is Niheem. What's yours?"

"Maliaka. But, my close friends call me, Liaka."

"Well, Maliaka, soon enough you can trust I'll be calling you Liaka, too," he stated confidently. Lianna sat across from them, a hostage to their conversation because she would be damned if she was going to get up and leave. She didn't care that her presence could be taken as an envious attempt to cock-block Liaka, hating on the fact that he picked her.

As she listened in on their conversation, the moment she heard him say his name, it hit her. His face was just familiar at first, but, coupled with his name, Lianna was now positive that she knew him. Niheem dated an old girlfriend of hers, an old girlfriend who severed ties with Lianna after her friend found out that Lianna gave a man she was dating head late one night in the back of a bathroom stall at a nightclub. That was one of the few times Lianna truly regretted her licentious ways.

At first, she tried to defend her actions, claiming they weren't together at the time, so she did nothing wrong. Then, she even tried to cop a plea to her friend, hoping to salvage their relationship, blaming her actions on too much weed and alcohol. But, her friend wasn't having it. Sleeping with your friend's ex was just off limits and Lianna crossed that line.

"Do you really know him?" Liaka posed, after he walked off.

"I said I knew him, didn't I?" Lianna spit with attitude. "So, what you gonna do? You gonna do it?"

"Do what?"

"Take that nigga shit! If you scared to do it, let me know. Fuck it! I'll do it myself!"

"Are you serious?"

"Why not? My girl told me about him. The nigga's weak! Don't let that hard shit fool you. Behind closed doors, the nigga turns into a bitch! Fuck with me, I'd have that nigga grabbing his ankles! I'm glad he pushed up on you. I didn't want his bitch-ass anyways," Lianna claimed. "Now the only question is, are you still down? Or, was all that shit about Olu teaching you how to use a gun and all that other shit just talk?"

Those words triggered something in Liaka. "I don't just talk! I act. I just wanted to see where *your* head is at!"

"You ain't gots to test me. I'll show you where my head is at. Trust, I'm the motherfuckin' one! And when the time is right, I'll definitely see where yours is!"

# Chapter 16 | The Baddest Chick

Lianna dropped her big, brown shopping bag indifferently on her sofa as she and Liaka entered her apartment. She headed straight to the kitchen; Liaka took a load off on the couch. They dropped Asia and her kids off at home before heading to Lianna's place. Liaka grabbed the TV remote. The blackened screen slowly lit up to reveal the image of a news broadcast. BANK ROBBERY—UNDISCLOSED AMOUNT UNRECOVERED— SUSPECTS STILL AT LARGE! Lianna walked back in the living room with two drinks in her hand.

"What did you end up getting?" Lianna took a sip from her glass, she handed the other glass to Liaka.

"I ended up getting those low cut *Apple Bottom* jeans and the *Apple Bottom* half-shirt to match. The red letters in the logo will match perfectly with my red G-string that will be peeking out the side, and the red and white cross trainers I got. Braid my hair into two pigtails, put on the red barrettes at the tips, and I'll be comfortable enough to get my groove on and be the cutest girl up in there."

"I don't know about all that, being the cutest girl and all. But, that does sound cute. But, this right here," Lianna reached for her outfit in her bag, "this sure enough gonna have all eyes on me!" she stressed, laying out a pair of faded, ripped jeans across the couch; she pulled out a matching ripped shirt that went with the outfit.

"You know, I wanted to thank you for what you did earlier in that store," Liaka mentioned.

"What did I do?"

"With Asia. Picking out that outfit for her. I know if it was just me and her, she would have never tried something like that on, let alone buy it. Do you know how long I tried to get her to wear something like that? But, she would never listen to me. But, the first time you get on her, she put it on."

"That just goes to show you that she always wanted to put something like that on in the first place. Her problem is she's more concerned about what other people are gonna say about her than what she thinks of herself."

"Speaking of Asia, why you so rough on her?"

"You think *that's* being rough on her?"

"You know what I mean."

"'Cause, she don't appreciate nothing! Look at Donovan. She had a good man, but, ran him off, and now expects everybody to feel sorry for her. She had a good thing and blew it! I bet he got tired of feeling deprived and went to the next chick who he felt could do the job. I wish I could get a man like that," Lianna expressed harshly.

"Hold on, wait a minute, Miss God's-gift-to-men! What happened to being every man's deepest, darkest desire?"

"Oh, don't get it twisted! I AM every nigga's dream come true! But, having the gift of making a man melt at my mere touch can also be a curse. You see, unlike Asia, my problem isn't keeping a man. It's getting a man to take me serious. Men tend to look at me as only a play toy."

"No! Say it isn't so! I would have never guessed that!"

"I'm being serious. That's one of the few things she has over me. Because at least when she deals with a man, he looks at her as a person. Unfortunately, because she gives off that 'friend-vibe,' he may begin to *only* look at her like that. But, at least she can get that. And even if she didn't get that, at the end of the night, at least she got her kids to go home to," Lianna sighed. It was rare for Lianna to take on such a dismal tone. Lianna avoided eye contact with Liaka, purposely keeping her eyes on the images flashing on the screen.

"Lianna, what did you say?" Liaka clicked the power button. Lianna rolled her eyes up at Liaka.

"I just said 'at least she got her kids'. And she don't even appreciate that! Look at how she treat that little boy she got! He is so adorable. I could only imagine having my own little son. I would teach him EVERYTHING! I would braid his hair up, put him in the flyest gear, and when he got older, teach him all about females. That lil' nigga would be the man! He would have bitches fucked up!" Lianna said happily.

"Oh, my God! I never knew you wanted kids. Why didn't you ever tell me?" Liaka stated. The smile on Lianna's face quickly disappeared. She rose from the couch with her cup.

"Are you done with that? 'Cause we gotta get ready for the club and I gotta take a shower," Lianna stated coldly.

"Lianna," Liaka called out, "you want kids?"

"It doesn't matter if I want kids or not!" Lianna snapped angrily, turning her back to Liaka. She spun around so quickly that she spilled a drop of her drink on the carpet. Lianna raised the half-filled glass to her lips, but, she didn't drink. She simply lowered the glass back down and turned to face Liaka. Lianna stood for a moment, facing Liaka before resting her glass on the coffee table and lifting up the bottom of her shirt. About an inch above her belly button, Lianna revealed a four-inch scar. She gently ran her fingers over it.

"Have you ever seen this?"

"Yeah, I've seen that before. That was for your spleen, right? It looks like a scar when someone had their spleen taken out. But, that shouldn't stop you from having kids, could it?"

Lianna lifted her shirt a little more. She exposed the bottom of her bra, then lifted it slightly, exposing another two scars; one about two inches running parallel to the line underneath her breast, the other one about the same size in length, about a half-inch under it.

"When I was seventeen, me and three of my girls crashed this house party on the South end. Because we wasn't from around that way, and because we was different, you already know the dudes were on us. Well, my girl started dancing with this one Spanish kid. I guess his girl, or some girl that was sweating him, was there and seen it. Anyways, she ended up approaching my girl with her girls, and the next thing you know, they started fighting. Her girls tried to jump my girl, so we all started fighting. It was four of us against about seven of them."

"Then, when the dudes started to break it up, I heard screaming. But, it was so many fists being thrown, and so many bodies around, that I couldn't see who was screaming, or what they were screaming about. The next thing you know, I felt like I was getting punched in my chest. It wasn't until I took a step back and took a look down and felt my shirt getting wet that I see the blood," Lianna narrated, lowering her shirt to take a seat back on the couch next to Liaka.

"The last thing I remember was getting lightheaded and some dude dragging me out of the party and throwing me into his car and driving me to the hospital. They ended up just dropping me off in the emergency room parking lot and just left me there. I guess they was scared to bring me in because of the police. When I woke up, I was in a hospital bed with all types of bandages and tubes coming out of me. I remember the doctor saying something about a collapsed lung, a punctured something, and something else. I was still weeded up, high from the party, so when the hospital started filling me up with all types of drugs, I was just outta it. I don't even know who stabbed me."

"After a couple of months, I went to the doctor for a check-up and that's when he told me. The stab wound damaged something inside of me. The doctor was breaking it down for me, but, once he said ninety-two percent probability that I may never have kids, I just blocked the rest of it out," Lianna explained, her voice lowering to a depressed hum. "But, then I thought it was a good thing," Lianna continued, with a muffled chuckle."

"You know how dudes are. Most of them don't want to be bothered with a kid anyway. So when I started telling dudes that I couldn't get pregnant, they loved me! Shit! I even loved the thought of it for a while. Never worrying about birth control, the pill, or some lazy ass nigga forgetting about condoms. But, then I met this one guy, Sean. Oh, Sean," Lianna sighed, her eyes closing to reminisce. "Sean was different. He treated me like a queen. I've never had someone treat me like that before. He had the money, the style, he was fine as I don't know what, and, Liaka, his sex game was so good it wouldn't even make sense to cheat!"

"So, what happened?"

"We were together for about six months when I finally told him that I couldn't get pregnant. At first, he didn't believe me. He said *most* females say that. So, I just left it alone. Then I began to notice how he...kept it in, even after he was done. ALL THE TIME! I just thought he was buggin'. Then, one day he told me how he was trying to get me pregnant. That he wanted me to have his baby.

"I didn't know what to say to him. So, we tried. Believe me, we tried! Five, six times a day, every day, for weeks, we tried. Then he asked me if I was serious about not being able to get pregnant. I couldn't answer him because I knew he was serious; he really wanted a baby. All the other guys I used to be with just wanted to hit and run. Or were dogs with five other girls on the side. But, Sean, he took me serious. He really loved me," Lianna said painfully.

"After we tried for so long and I didn't get pregnant, I started to see the changes in him. He started acting different towards me. I would see how he looked at the girls with kids. Especially the girls with like two or three kids. Then, he told me straight up that he wanted kids and I couldn't give them to him. I should have known from that point it was over. But, I loved him so much, so I tried my best to keep him. I tried everything. But, then it happened.

"One day, he came and told me how he got this other chick pregnant and how she was having his baby. Again, I should have left him alone then and there. But, stupid me, I loved him, so I stayed. Because, after all, it was *my* fault, wasn't it? He wanted something that I couldn't give him. So, how could I get mad that he went out and got it from someone else, right?" Liaka began to see the tears swell up in Lianna's eyes.

"I wasn't *woman* enough to give him that baby! So, he got it from another woman. We were still together 'cause I sure enough wasn't gonna leave him. So, he eventually brought the baby around. He had a little girl. And, Liaka, I swear, she was so cute. She looked just like him. I looked at that little girl and I knew that was supposed to be *our* little girl, not some other bitches! Then, he told me that she was pregnant again! This time with twins! So, here I am, thinking, I can't have ONE baby, but this bitch is popping out two at a time! How could I compete with that?"

"Then, he had the nerve to tell me that he didn't want to cheat on her anymore, and how he wanted to be serious with her and start a family. Cheating on her with me! How the fuck did that happen? How did I become the jump-off bitch? If anything, he was cheating on me with her! I was his girl! That bitch was the jump-off! How the fuck did that shit get reversed like that?" Lianna exclaimed, still having a hard time accepting that part of her history.

"But, you know what? I said from that day forward, I would NEVER let that happen to me again! Fuck being a pathetic bitch! I had to learn to live with the fact that I can't give a man kids. That my womb is barren; that I'm a mule! But, I told myself to make up for it that I was gonna be the baddest, most freaky bitch a nigga could dream of! Since I can't give him that baby, then I could make up for that...flaw, in other ways. I knew that I had to be that much more of a woman so a man would still love me," Lianna explained, single teardrops rolling down the sides of her cheeks.

Liaka found herself crying as well. She reached for Lianna's hand and pulled her close to her side on the couch. She used her thumb to clean the trail of tears from Lianna's eyes.

"A man is gonna love you one day once he gets to know you. So, I really don't know why you crying, girl. You know you gonna have kids one day," Liaka stated, followed by wiping the tears from her own eyes. Lianna lifted her eyes to Liaka. "And I can tell you why you haven't been having babies," Liaka continued, "It's because it's impossible to have kids if you keep swallowing them all!" Liaka joked, playfully nudging Lianna's arm. Lianna's mouth dropped in shock. "See? That's exactly what I'm talking about!" Liaka said, pointing at her open mouth.

"Oh, no, you didn't!" Lianna chuckled, snatching a throw pillow from behind her back and began to pummel Liaka with it.

# *C*hapter 17 | *R*iddles

Liaka sat at her desk on that early Thursday morning. She had just finished typing the final certification on a motion. The printer to the right of her on the floor began to slowly churn out page after page with a mind numbing buzz. Hours of staring at her computer screen left Liaka with irritated eyes. She closed them tightly, rubbing her outer eyelids in massaging circles. There was a bottle of spring water in the bottom drawer of her desk. She reached for it, took a large gulp, and then returned it.

9:57 A.M.

*This is going to be a long day,* Liaka thought. She began to manipulate her computer mouse over its pad, searching to pull up her next scheduled assignment. It just happened to be an appellate brief, a lengthy appellate brief with a separate appendix for one of the firm's larger clients. Liaka was confident in her research that it took to prepare the brief. She just didn't have it in her to begin the monumental task of preparing it. She began to look around the office from her desk. She noticed a co-worker by the coffee pot tapping a spoonful of creamer into a spoon to mix it in with her cup of coffee.

"How is it today?" Liaka posed.

"Do you mean me? Or this joke that they serve called coffee?" she answered, taking a sip of her coffee, then turned to face Liaka.

"I guess you answered it for the coffee. So, how are you doing?" Liaka reached for a styrofoam cup and a single packet of tea at the office's break station.

"Aside from Peter running around here trying to make my life miserable, everything is fine. And you?"

"As well as things could be, I guess," Liaka answered. Liaka didn't have it in her, or felt it relevant to discuss Olu's death with co-workers at the office. Through Liaka's behavior, it was hinted that she experienced the death of someone close to her. Who it was that died was never discussed.

On several occasions, co-workers stopped by Liaka's office inquiring about the comely looking gentleman in the picture with Liaka. Liaka hated to lie about the prior relationship she had with the man in the picture on her desk. So, all the curious inquires of when Liaka would finally introduce them to the handsome man were always met with subtle evasions to change the subject. Well over a month had passed since Olu's death, but, Liaka still didn't have it in her to remove their picture from her desk. So, it remained. A daily reminder of one of her more memorable moments with him.

"What's Peter bitching about?" Liaka inquired, pouring some hot water over the tea bag in her cup.

"You know him. If it's not one thing, it's another. Today's 'moan-of-the-week' revolved around the results of last week's *Pell* settlement. He believes if we had, and I quote, 'meticulous preparation', then settlement negotiations would have reached into the low six figures. Forget about the fact that *Pell* was a no-win case! We pretty much made something from nothing out of that one. Ungrateful little prick!"

Liaka let out a little chuckle as she ripped the top off three individual sugar packets and dumped them into her cup. The woman swallowed the last mouthful of her coffee before finally getting fed up with it. She tossed the two-thirds filled cup in the trash in frustration.

"If anyone should file a lawsuit, it should be us! It should be against the law to serve us crap like this!" she snapped, gesturing to the simmering pot of coffee. She followed Liaka's lead and began to make a cup of tea for herself. "So, how is James' caseload working out? Especially that Johnson file. Did you guys survive the opposing party's summary judgment?"

"Yeah, but, I think we got lucky on that one. It went before Judge Rittenband."

"Lucky is an understatement if you went before him. And, as much as I would love for you to explain how you guys pulled that feat off, your phone is ringing," she said, pointing to Liaka's phone on her desk. Liaka looked over her shoulder to see the light on her phone fluttering with each ring.

"Duty calls," Liaka announced, raising her cup in obeisance and headed off to her desk. "Good morning. You have reached the law offices of Hertzberg, Hertzberg, Fox, and Green. How may I be of assistance this morning?"

"Ah, good morning. This is Detective Todd Willhelm of the Hartford Police Department, Special Investigation Unit. I'm looking for a, Miss Sikes," the man announced on the other end. Liaka could still feel the eyes of the woman on her. Liaka glanced up to give her a slight nod, followed by a smile, before turning back to fully face her desk. Once she had her back to her, Liaka's smile instantly faded.

"This...this is Miss Sikes. May I ask what this call is in reference to?"

"Ah, the purpose of this call is that your name came up in a subsequent investigation that our office was conducting. I would much rather prefer to discuss this matter with you in person."

"An investigation? What sort of an investigation?" Liaka questioned, a slight twinge of butterflies twisted in her stomach.

"Again, I would rather discuss this with you in person than over the phone," the detective returned in a solemn tone. Liaka sat in silence. Her heart began to pound in her chest. *What in the hell could a detective want to talk to me about?*

"In person? Ah, sure."

"Good. How's this evening sound? My office. Say, five o'clock?"

"Five o'clock? Could we make it five thirty?"

"Five thirty it is. See you then," the detective ended.

Liaka removed the phone from her ear and stared at it for a moment before she placed it back down on the receiver. If her day wasn't going fast enough before, the detective's phone call definitely didn't help matters any. To say that she was distracted from her work for the rest of the day was an understatement. Yet, slowly and surely, the workday rolled to an end, and not a minute too soon. Liaka thought she would have lost her mind if she didn't get out of that office.

Within a few blocks of the precinct, Liaka began to get an eerie feeling and, when she pulled her car into the police station's parking lot, she was suddenly overcome with anger. A huge truck could be seen parked at the end of the parking lot, the acronym S.W.A.T. written across the side panels in big, bold, white letters. The truck was a distant reminder of that fateful day, a tragic reminder and a vivid scene of a day she knew she would never forget. Tossing the strap of her purse over her shoulder, Liaka slammed her car door behind her and headed off towards the station's front entrance. There was a lone female receptionist at the front window in the lobby.

"Good evening. I have a five thirty scheduled appointment with a Detective Willhelm," Liaka announced politely, forcing a pleasant smile to her face.

"And your name?"

"Maliaka Sikes."

The receptionist returned the same warm smile. She spoke briefly on the phone. Liaka tried to eavesdrop, but could find out nothing as the receptionist whispered a few more hushed words and then hung up.

"Yes, Miss Sikes. He's been expecting your visit. He'll be out in a moment. Please, make yourself comfortable," the receptionist said, gesturing to a row of seats in the lobby. Seconds away from taking her seat, Liaka was diverted to a glass encased cabinet which held trophies, awards, and a few other accolades given to that department. Liaka slowly approached it out of curiosity until she stood inches away, peering in through the glass.

Liaka was instantly rocked to her core.

She felt her knees grow weak beneath her as she unconsciously took a step back. A brief image that remained a blur in her memory, an image that haunted her on so many sleepless nights, had now made itself concrete. Not only was this image now tangible, this image also had a name—Detective José Dominguez. There he was, shrouded in his prestigious honorary metals, even deemed 'Cop of the year' the last two years running. Liaka swallowed the urge to vomit all over the glass.

"Now there's an example of a superior detective." Liaka spun around to face the presence behind her. "Oh, I'm sorry. I didn't mean to sneak up on you," Detective Willhelm apologized, noticing Liaka jump at his sudden appearance. He held a single brown folder in one hand, extending the other to Liaka.

"I'm Detective Willhelm, and I thank you for coming in." Liaka slowly extended her hand to meet his. His hand was cold, clammy, just as Liaka expected. She barely let one shake go its full revolution before pulling away. "Please, follow me," the detective added, not particularly reading Liaka's distant behavior.

"Right in here, Miss Sikes," the Detective said, opening a side office and stepping back for Liaka to enter. Liaka took her seat in a single chair across from his desk as the detective, in chivalrous fashion, waited for Liaka to take her seat before he took his. "Well, where do we start?" The detective began, shuffling a couple of papers around on his desk to make room for the folder in his hand. Flipping the folder open, the detective stared down at its contents for a few seconds before returning his gaze back up to Liaka. "I'm going to cut straight to the chase. Your name happened to come up in one of our investigations. Does the name Oluwan Zayes sound familiar to you?"

From the moment she heard Olu's name, she was hoping her shirt wouldn't reveal the rapid flutter of her heartbeat pounding in her chest. "Why?"

"I'm just asking the question. Does the name sound familiar to you?" the detective pressed.

"Again, I have to ask, why?" Liaka returned. She wasn't budging and he knew it.

"Because, you were listed as his primary contact in one of his documents. In fact, you were the only contact we could find."

"He was a very close friend," Liaka returned, in the same flat tone.

This time it was the detective who paused before saying, "A close friend? Interesting. Well, would you mind telling me about this close friend?"

"What's there to tell? He's dead, isn't he?" Liaka delivered coldly.

"Unfortunately, he is. And with his death, came many unanswered questions. I was hoping, with your help, that just maybe we could answer some of them."

"Is this an interrogation?"

"Interrogation? No! I..."

"Am I under arrest?"

"Of course not! This is simply..."

"Then if I am free to leave on my own accord, I would rather not sit here and subject myself to reliving the painful memory of a dear friend and his untimely death!" Liaka stressed, standing to her feet.

"Ma'am! Miss Sikes...I apologize! Let's start over," the detective stuttered anxiously, bouncing to his feet from behind the desk. Liaka stopped and turned to face him feet from the door. "Please, just five minutes," he pleaded, gesturing her back to her seat.

"If your sole purpose of this meeting was to ask me questions which I obviously don't have the answers to, then it doesn't make sense for me to sit here and waste both of our time," Liaka delivered, standing in her place by the door. She could read the emotion on the detective's face—defeat. He shook his head then leaned behind his desk to lift up a white, rectangular cardboard property box.

"Being that our investigation is complete, and you were labeled as his primary contact, by law, I am obligated to turn this material over to you," the detective said, as if it pained him to release it. He pushed the box on his desk a few inches in Liaka's direction.

"Just sign these release forms," he instructed, as he busied himself marking a few X's where she was to sign. FIRST NATIONAL BANK OF CONNECTICUT - INVESTIGATION, was written across the top in black marker, with the date of the incident in red marker on the side. "Sign here, here, and here. And I guess we're through," the detective ended, pointing to the spaces on the multicolored page. Liaka slowly approached him as he held the pen out to her. She made brief eye contact with him before removing the pen from his hand, and then placed two large X's in the spot where her signature was supposed to be.

"Please! Wait a minute!" the detective called out, stepping from behind his desk to approach her. He reached into his back pocket for his wallet, pulled out his business card and placed it on top of the box. "Here's my card. It has my office and cell phone number on it. If there's anything, and I mean anything, that you may think of when you go through the contents of this box, please don't hesitate to call," the detective stressed in a pleading tone.

Liaka looked down to the card, and then slowly back up to make eye contact with the detective. There was desperation in his eyes. Liaka rolled her eyes at him and purposely spun around with the box so fast that the card slid off the edge and flipped into sort of a dance as it fell to the floor. The detective peered on with sad eyes as Liaka stepped over the card and walked out of his office.

Placing the box on her passenger seat, Liaka fought the urge to tear the lid off the box and search through the contents right there in the parking lot. The only thing that stopped her was a marked patrol car entering the parking lot; the cop driving, staring at her every move. Liaka reached her apartment in record time.

Tossing all of her belongings with each step on her living room floor, she

Triple Crown Publications presents... Queen of Thieves
*PART 1*

headed straight to the coffee table with the box. It was taped shut. It took Liaka all of four steps to make it to the kitchen and back with the first knife she could find. Kneeling on the floor in front of the coffee table, Liaka sliced wildly at the tape that secured the box closed.

At first sight, Liaka noticed folders, a few files, and an assortment of different papers. Liaka bunched them all together and lifted them from the box. Lining the floor of the box was a cell phone, a BlackBerry PDA, a set of keys, some receipts, and a wallet. The next item she saw caused Liaka to pause frozen, staring.

It was the velour box which held the ring Olu proposed to her with. It must have been in his pocket the whole time. She gazed at her hand, her ring finger, which still wore the ring that Olu placed on her hand from that night. Liaka's lip twitched to form a half smile. From the night of Olu's funeral, Liaka made a promise to herself—a promise that, for the rest of her life, she would never remove that ring from her hand. She removed the cell phone and the BlackBerry, and placed them neatly on the coffee table. The wallet was next.

Opening the dual sided wallet, Liaka removed a wallet-sized photo of Olu and herself stuffed into a slot where a credit card would fit. The photo was taken in a photo booth at the mall over a year ago. Liaka recalled the day she dragged Olu into the photo booth, mainly to smother him with kisses as the machine flashed its five photos, capturing their every move. She had long forgot about that day until that lone photo instantly jogged her memory. She could only imagine what happened to the remaining four photos.

There were a few credit cards, business cards of various sorts, and five hundred and eighty-two dollars in cash. Liaka was a second away from placing the wallet down when she noticed an unusual piece of paper stuffed flat behind a credit card. It was littered with numbers, a configuration of numbers with no distinct pattern.

To anyone else, Liaka could only imagine to the detectives as well, the numbers didn't make any sense. A product of random scribbling. But, to Liaka, the numbers were familiar, very familiar. She pushed the box aside to clear some space on the table for the lone sheet of paper. She rested the paper flat on the table to stare at it, mesmerized by the numbers, where she remembered seeing them.

Then it hit her.

Liaka snatched the piece of paper up from the table and bolted off towards her bedroom. The top of her dresser drawer was the first place she looked. Tearing through the dresser, Liaka flung her panties and bras aside wildly as they rained on the floor behind her. At the bottom of the drawer, there it was, five of the numbers. She remembered the lower opening of her nightstand. She dropped to her knees to the left of her nightstand by her bed. Four more numbers.

"The closet!"

She ran to the closet and threw the door open. There were four more numbers on the inside crack of the door; they were somewhat faded, the two most visible being on the top. Liaka's eyes made a slow descent to the floor. The numbers stopped. There was something else Liaka noticed at the bottom.

The corner of the carpet was no longer nailed to the floor. It appeared as if someone had ripped the carpet up and just laid it back down without bothering to bind it. The corner lifted with relative ease as she walked it along the edge, lifting feet of carpet with each step. One of the floorboards was visibly loosened. Liaka reached down to wiggle it a little, removing a single wooden strip. The small crevice in the floor revealed a safe.

The safe was small, white, and covered in a light film of dust. The box was a lot heavier than it appeared, and tilting it from side to side made Liaka concluded there was a heavy, blunt object inside. But, she couldn't open it. The only way to gain entry into the sturdy box was with a key, a key which Liaka didn't have. She quickly rose to her feet and sped off to the living room to snatch up the keys that were in the bottom of the property box. Aside from about three sets of car keys, there were four other miscellaneous keys attached to the key chain. The key most resembling a safe key was inserted into the face of the safe.

It fit.

With a final turn of the key, the lid of the safe popped open. Liaka slowly lowered herself to sit Indian style with her legs crossed on the floor at the side of her bed. A black glock 9mm, the gun Olu taught Liaka how to assemble and take apart. There were four stacks of hundred dollar bills wrapped in bank denominations of five thousand dollars.

Liaka lifted out the twenty thousand dollars in cash to see a diamond encrusted *Cartier* watch. She kept rummaging through to see a purple velour bag with a gold braided string securing the bag closed. Unraveling the bind, Liaka dumped the contents in the palm of her hand. There had to be at least one hundred thousand dollars' worth of diamonds, rubies, and other precious stones; the biggest being a twelve karat, princess cut, canary diamond.

There were a few scattered pictures in the box, the four remaining pictures she and Olu took together in the photo booth at the mall, along with a few other photos they took together in Cancun. As Liaka began to examine each picture, reminiscing on past times, she came to realize that the contents in that box, a safe, hidden away from even herself, held what Olu considered his most valued possessions.

How *could a man's most valued possessions be a picture of his girl?* Placing the few photos back inside the safe, Liaka removed the last of the miscellaneous papers at the bottom. The papers were documents, records of the car dealerships that Olu owned. But, there was one document that had an address of a residence in Brooklyn, New York. It was a bill pertaining to rent of an apartment.

*Why would Olu be paying rent for a place in Brooklyn? Olu didn't have a place in Brooklyn anymore. He got rid of that apartment years ago, along with his place in Queens, didn't he?*

Thousands of dollars in cash and valuable jewels in her possession were inconsequential compared to the revelation of this new address. Liaka sighed heavily, leaning back against the bed, wondering what other secrets Olu kept from her.

# $C$hapter 18 | $B$rooklyn

$A$ beep from a car horn shattered Liaka's trance as she sat staring off into space in her living room. Talking to Asia a couple of hours earlier, Liaka made plans to drive with Asia and Lianna to Brooklyn to hopefully figure out the truth of the mysterious address on Olu's bill.

The couple of days Liaka sat on the information in the property box from the police station, and the documents in Olu's hidden safe stashed away in her house, gave her time to think. Liaka thought she was positive from the conversations she and Olu had, that he related everything to her concerning his double life. But, she was wrong, painfully wrong. Liaka now came to question everything about him.

*Was this the address of another woman? Did Olu's separate double life include another relationship, maybe even a child? Did Olu even love her?*

She could see why the police chose to contact her. All of Olu's information in the property box led back to one destination—Liaka's apartment. But, the documents in the miniature safe, hidden in the floorboards in her room had the address of the apartment in Brooklyn. Yet the address in Brooklyn didn't have Olu's name on it. Liaka was more confused than ever. She had it in her to just jump in her car and go to Brooklyn by herself, to just take off and shoot up to New York to put an end to the mystery that clouded her for the past couple days. But, Liaka didn't have it in her to face the unknown. Her first

Triple Crown Publications presents... $Q$ueen of $T$hieves *PART 1*

idea was to just take Lianna. She knew Lianna wouldn't give her the third degree on wanting to travel to Brooklyn on such short notice.

The promise of a few blunts and maybe something to eat would keep Lianna content. But, Lianna was too reckless. So Liaka needed the lucidity of Asia's character. Clicking the power button on her TV, Liaka grabbed her fall jacket and headed for the door. But, before she could reach it, the car horn beeped again, this time with more urgency.

"All right! I'm coming!" Liaka screamed to no one but herself. Liaka walked out her front door to see Asia's car with Lianna already in the passenger seat. Liaka was shocked. She spoke to Asia about picking Lianna up prior to arriving at her place to avoid the trip of back-tracking to Lianna's, but, Liaka didn't expect Asia to do it. Liaka could only imagine what the fifteen-minute drive must have been like with only the both of them alone in the car. As Liaka approached, Lianna opened the passenger door to step out.

"Damn! Took you long enough!" Lianna barked, making her way to the back seat. Liaka knew she didn't take long at all, two minutes tops, from the time she heard the first beep of the horn until she made it outside; the awkwardness of them being alone in the car probably made fifteen minutes feel like an hour.

"Calm down. I'm here now, ain't I?" Liaka answered, taking her seat on the passenger side.

"So, are you finally gonna tell me what we're going up here for? Or are you gonna keep everything a secret from us on the whole trip?" Asia posed sarcastically. "I know that it has to be something big. Just look at the look on your face." Liaka could feel Asia's eyes burning a hole in the side of her face. Without saying a word, Liaka let out a conceded exhale and dug into her pocket for the bill.

"What's this?" Asia questioned.

"That's the address where we're going," Liaka stated. The car bounced as Lianna jumped to nosily stick her head through the space of the front seats. Asia studied the bill carefully, every inch of it, even flipped it over to look at the back.

"The other day a police detective called my job. He told me to come down to the station because he wanted to talk to me. I didn't know what it was about, and he clearly didn't want to tell me over the phone. When I got there, the first thing he started asking me about was Olu. At first, that freaked me out! Because I'm thinking, what the hell do you wanna talk to me about Olu for? Then I started thinking my name may have been caught up in something he did. Luckily, it wasn't. Olu had my address listed as his place of address. So, being that my address was the only address they had, they had to turn his stuff over to me."

"What stuff?" Lianna asked from the back seat.

"Just a box full of stuff that I guess was no longer useful to them. So I took the box home, began to go through it, and started finding some things. You know, you can drive while I talk," Liaka said sarcastically to Asia, signaling to the road. Asia rolled her eyes at Liaka and pulled off.

"While I was looking through it, I found a couple of things. Nothing major to them. But, stuff that was priceless to me. Mainly, a few photos of us together. Then, I found his wallet. There was this small piece of paper in it with some strange numbers on it. Either it didn't make sense to them, so they left it alone, or they never found it. But, once I started looking at it, the numbers, they were definitely familiar to me. I remember the numbers because some of them were written in my room, my bedroom. So, of course, I went in there to look around. The whole time I'm thinking, what could I possibly find in my own bedroom that I don't know about? I've been in there ump-teenth times and knew every inch of it. So I thought," Liaka said.

"So? What did you find?" Asia asked anxiously.

"I started matching the numbers on the paper to the numbers in my room. To make a long story short, he hid something in there, a safe. He was actually hiding a safe underneath the floorboards in my bedroom. After I found it, I started going through it. That's when I found these..." Liaka pulled out a few other bills from her pocket. She divided them between Asia and Lianna.

"See? That's why I say men ain't shit! I don't know why they always have to be like that—all sneaky and shit!" Asia exclaimed. "You would start to think that you can't trust ANY of them! Because right when you think you know something about them, there's ALWAYS something you don't know!"

"Hmph! Men ain't the only ones like that," Lianna announced.

"What did you say?"

"Men. They ain't the only ones who do shit on the sly. Us females can get on that same bullshit too. The only difference is, we can keep our shit discreet better than they can. How many times have you been dealing with a dude and found some girl number on him, in his cell phone, on a piece of paper in his pocket, and he come up with some lame ass excuse about whose it is. Ah, my boy left it in my pocket. Ah, she just gave it to me. Please!" Lianna said.

"Their fault is they don't know how to handle their business and keep it on the low. Females do. Shit, when I start getting caught up in my own shit, all I gots to do is put them on the defensive, start accusing them of all types of shit, and they'll be so busy trying to explain their life away that they won't have time to be concerned about mines!" Lianna described convincingly. Asia focused on Lianna through her center rear-view mirror.

"Not *all* females are like that."

"There you go again, Miss Naïve," Lianna sighed. "So let me get this straight. You trying to tell me that if you was still with Donovan and some NBA player or some football star approached you, you wouldn't creep with him on the low?"

"Um, no! When I was with Donovan, I was loyal. I was faithful to him. I could'a crept around on him many times, but, I didn't. I got approached, but, I turned every one of them down. I had respect for him, my kids, and most important, I had respect for myself!"

"Respect? What the fuck respect gots to do with getting money? I'm gonna get mines! You think if I had some nigga who was driving a bucket, that I wouldn't be quick to upgrade his ass and trade him in for a nigga with a Beamer? Or upgrade that nigga in a Beamer for the next man in a Bentley? How would I look staying with some broke ass nigga who wasn't trying to do better for himself? Shit! If I DIDN'T leave him, I would look just as stupid as him! It ain't nothing wrong with a girl trying to better herself."

"What the hell does that have to do with what we were talking about? Or, are you two gonna start up and keep going back and forth with that bullshit women's liberation shit again? Can I finish telling my story?" Liaka blurted, scanning back and forth between Asia and Lianna. They both remained silent. "Anyways, that wasn't the only thing I found in there. There was also jewels in there, diamonds, a diamond watch, money."

"Money? Now that's what I'm talking about!" Lianna spit enthusiastically. "How much money?"

"About...about twenty-thousand dollars."

"Oh, hell, motherfuckin' yeah! Now I see why you wanted to go to the city! We going shopping! I know I'm good for at least five outfits!" Lianna cheered joyously.

"We're not going shopping. I just wanna go to the address in Brooklyn and see what it's all about," Liaka said flatly.

"Why can't we do both? Go to Manhattan first, being that it's on the way. We can grab them cute..."

"She said we ain't going shopping! Is it even possible for you to just once stop thinking about yourself?" Asia snapped curtly. Lianna sucked her teeth, cursing Asia under her breath before she sat back pouting in her seat.

"Maybe we can grab something on the way back. One outfit apiece. But, let's just see what this is about first, okay?" Liaka said, referring to the bill. Asia mumbled under her breath, disgusted at Liaka's attempt to appease Lianna, but remained silent. Lianna remained silent herself; silently smiling. One outfit was better than nothing, she thought.

Lianna opened her pack of cigarettes and removed a half-smoked blunt and lit it. She inhaled deeply, and then blew the exhaled cloud of smoke between the front of the seats for it to crash and dance across the back of the front windshield. Asia immediately stared at Lianna through the rear-view mirror again with angry eyes. Lianna threw a stare back at her; the remaining cloud of smoke being blown from her lungs as if to taunt Asia. Asia merely rolled her eyes and cracked her driver's side window, circulating some fresh air on her side. They made it to New York in good time. The streets of New York were congested with traffic.

Yet, with Asia driving to some music, almost in a trance, she handled the heavy traffic gracefully, maneuvering her car in and between traffic. They drove through New York for about an hour before finally making it to Brooklyn; something it would have taken a normal New Yorker fifteen minutes to do.

"You're going down! The numbers on the streets are going down. You gotta turn around," Liaka announced, scanning the numbers on the street signs. Asia glanced down at the bill in Liaka's hand and up to Liaka before spinning the car around to drive in the opposite direction. Her eyes suddenly lit up. "Stop! This is it!" Liaka cried, pointing wildly to a house on the right of her. Asia screeched the brakes on the car, throwing all three of them forward as they came to an abrupt stop.

"Damn, bitch!" Lianna cursed, almost on the floor in the back seat. The quick stop caught both Liaka and Lianna off guard, but, Lianna was the one most affected by it. Asia cracked a mischievous smile as she peeked through her rear-view mirror to see Lianna getting situated back in her seat. The car rolled in reverse a few houses, backing up to the house Liaka pointed at. Liaka matched the numbers on the house with the number on the bill one last time, and then just stared at it.

"I know we ain't drive all the way up here for you to just look!" Asia said waspishly. Liaka turned to Asia with somewhat of a fearful look in her eyes, then back at the house. Liaka took each stair of the building slowly, her heart pounding faster with each step. The three of them finally made it to the top of the steps with Liaka centered in between them. Liaka stood frozen for about a minute just staring at the door before Asia sucked her teeth, then stepped forward to knock.

Asia rapped on the thick, wooden door, but there was no answer. Liaka reached out for the buzzer. After two minutes, still nothing. Liaka removed Olu's keys from her pocket, searching through them for some type of key, any type of key that was similar to a house key. There were three sets of keys. Liaka tried the first one. It didn't fit. Then the next one. Nothing. She inserted the third.

"Hey! What are you doing?" a deep male voice called out, after swinging his door open in the adjacent building. The three of them jumped from his halting, sharp tone of voice. The three women eyed him, all of them at a momentary loss of words. He was an older black man, probably in his mid-forties. His hair was slightly graying, balding. He had on a pair of wire-rimmed glasses, holding on tightly to his red and black plaid robe as he stared at them menacingly in his doorway.

"My man...my fiancé. I was trying to surprise him," Liaka stuttered, saying the first thing that popped into her mind. "He didn't answer when I rang the bell. So I was just using the key he gave me," Liaka continued, jingling the key in her hand, explaining herself through innocent eyes. He eyed the three of them one at a time, suspiciously. He looked past them to the car they were driving. The Connecticut license plate on Asia's car stood out to him. He stepped out of his residence, closing his door behind him.

"Let me see some identification."

"Um, yeah, sure," Liaka replied, digging through her handbag. She pulled out her driver's license and handed it to him.

"Connecticut? Far from home, are we?"

"Yeah, but, not too far to keep me from my man," Liaka returned warmly, forcing a smile to her face. The man just stared back at Liaka for a couple of seconds with an investigative look in his eyes, then slowly cracked a smile.

"Lucky man. To not have one, but three beautiful women to come and visit him. He must really be a special guy," the man said, his voice becoming warmer. "I definitely have to say that this is a little unusual. In fact, you're the first visitors that I ever seen him have at his home. Yeah, I've never seen anyone come and visit him. I was beginning to think he was some type of loner or something. But, that don't too much bother me, though. Because he is probably one of the best tenants that I've ever had."

"What do you mean?" Liaka probed.

"Well, for one, he's one of my only tenants who paid their rent for the entire year! I mean, to pay a year's rent in advance? Go figure. He's also clean, respectable, and quiet as a mouse. I guess on account that he's hardly ever home. But, even when he is, it's sorta like he isn't. I guess you coming here sorta explains why he's never home. He must be spending all of his time in Connecticut visiting you," the man explained, smiling to reveal the top of his teeth.

"I keep telling him to pack up and move to Connecticut with me. But, he likes it here. He has family here. And he's been here for what, one, two years?"

"Actually, three years."

"That long, huh? Time really flies," Liaka returned.

"I guess I'll let you girls attend to your business. You don't look like you're going to rob the place or anything. Not after I got your license plate number and all," he said facetiously, but, serious about his comment. Turning to step back inside his apartment, he swung the door back open chanting, "Oh, hold on a minute! Wait right there!" then disappeared back into his place. Seconds later he came back out with a stack of envelopes handing them to Liaka. "These began to stack up in the mailbox. So, to avoid it flooding out all over the place, I figured I'd collect it for him," he delivered. "By the way, I normally wouldn't allow tenants to give out an extra key to their girlfriends, or anyone for that matter. But, for you, I'll make an exception." He ended flirtatiously, a grin plastered on his face as he stepped off to disappear into his place.

Liaka focused back on the door. She returned the last key into the lock. It fit. The room was dark. Sunlight forced thin slices of light on spotted areas of the room. The living room was moderately furnished: an eight-foot cream colored sofa, a matching loveseat and recliner, and a metallic silver and glass coffee table was in the center of the living room atop a black Persian rug.

Triple Crown Publications presents... Queen of Thieves *PART 1*

A few plants hung from the ceiling by the closed window blinds; they were withered and decadent. The wooden floorboards creaked under the pressure with each step as Liaka walked into the living room. Asia and Lianna walked off in different directions of the apartment.

The only other furniture in the living room was a large entertainment center. To the side of it hung a fifty-inch Magnavox flat screen TV secured against the wall, and a small bronze and glass bar set in the corner. The bar was empty of liquor; its glass tumblers and crystal bottle the only items decorating its shelves.

"I'ma see if he got something to eat, 'cause I'm starving!" Lianna stated, heading off to the kitchen. Liaka sat on the couch with the stack of mail the landlord gave her. A few credit card bills and a bill for a membership at a *Bally's* fitness center in Brooklyn were in the pile. "What type of nigga don't have shit to drink in his crib?" Lianna screamed out from the kitchen. Liaka ignored her. Liaka glanced up from the couch to see Asia rummaging through a drawer in the entertainment center. Liaka tore the *Bally's* envelope open.

*Membership expired! Last chance to renew savings!* The information on the page revealed the membership expired three months ago. Small print revealed that the membership was officially opened four and a half years ago.

"Would you believe he had...," Liaka began, and then stopped when she looked up over her shoulder to see that Asia was gone. She searched around, but, Asia was nowhere in sight. She crumpled the membership paper into a ball, slightly flustered and flung it to the floor.

"Liaka! Come here, you gotta see this!" Asia yelled out from the back bedroom. Lianna emerged from the kitchen stuffing the last bite of a cinnamon raisin bagel in her mouth. Liaka turned the corner towards the bedroom to see Asia standing in front of the bedroom closet.

The bedroom was just about as lightly furnished as the living room, only the basic essentials; a king-sized canopy style bed and two reddish oak dresser drawers. Liaka began to approach the closet. Half the row of hangers which held Olu's clothes was swept to the side. Behind the closet full of clothes held a safe, a large, black, cast-iron safe, standing almost six feet tall.

"I wonder what's in there," Lianna uttered listlessly. Lianna was the first to step forward to take a hold of the safe handle. She tried to twist it to the left, then right, but, it didn't budge. Liaka remembered the small sheet of paper with the random numbers on it which led her to the safe in her floorboards.

Something told her to bring that small piece of paper with her, and she was glad she did.

Lianna stepped back with Asia to watch anxiously as Liaka spun the knob on the combination, matching the numbers on the dial to each number on the page. Clicking the dial on the last digit, Liaka took one last look over her shoulder at Asia and Lianna before grabbing at the handle. It didn't budge. A deflated sigh escaped Liaka's lips. Lianna sucked her teeth.

"Backwards! Try the numbers backwards!" Asia blurted. Liaka eyed her strangely. "Just try it backwards. Olu wasn't like other brothers. He was different. So why would he set the combination normally?" Asia insisted. Liaka shrugged lightly, and then turned back to the safe. She spun the combination dial wildly to clear the previous numbers, stopping the dial on the last number on the page. She went through each number again, this time in reverse. The last number entered, which was actually the first number on the page, produced a faint click. It couldn't have been louder than a pin drop, but, they all heard it.

The lever was tight, but, it slowly began to move as Liaka applied pressure. She turned the lever a full one-hundred and eighty degrees for the heavy door to pop open an inch. It took the strength of both hands for Liaka to pull the heavy door open. Their eyes widened to the size of tea saucers once Liaka opened the door fully and took a step back.

There were three shelves inside. The top shelf was completely filled with stacks of money, hundred dollar bills wrapped in bank denominations of ten thousand dollars. The second shelf was littered with jewels; diamond encrusted watches, diamond encrusted bracelets, gold and platinum rings, and other small, expensive trinkets. The most visible thing on the bottom shelf, along with the most unusual in the safe, was a nine by twelve inch photo album. Liaka had her eyes stuck on the photo album as Lianna reached in to pull out one of the watches.

"This...this is an eighty-thousand dollar watch!" Lianna announced in awe, staring mesmerized at the expensive jewel.

"How would *you* know?" Asia said in a condescending tone.

"I saw it in a magazine. And this is definitely it!" Lianna declared, her eyes glued to the opulent piece of jewelry in her hand. Lianna was so enthralled by the watch that she didn't even catch the snide remark Asia threw at her.

"There has to be at least a quarter million dollars in here," Asia announced, reaching in for a stack of hundreds.

"Put it back! Don't touch it! Don't touch anything!" Liaka cried.

"What? But, we..."

"But, nothing! Just put it back!" Liaka snapped angrily, cutting Lianna off. Both Asia and Lianna looked on with sad eyes, reluctantly placing the items back in the safe. "Just give me a second by myself. Please," Liaka expressed. It didn't take a genius to see that Asia, especially Lianna, didn't want to leave the room and walk away from the amassed wealth empty-handed. Yet, out of respect for Liaka, they both turned away, sorrowfully trudging out the room.

Liaka walked over to close the door behind them. She walked back over to the safe and removed the photo album. Opening the front cover revealed a six by nine photo of her and Olu. Her lip twitched, tears swelled up in her eyes. She flipped through each cellophane covered cardboard page.

The first few pages revealed photos of individuals Liaka wasn't familiar with; a painful reminder of how much of Olu's life that will always remain a mystery to her. Close to the center of the album, Liaka did happen to run across a photo of a face that was familiar to her. He was one of the men at the bank with Olu.

The brother had a large, radiant smile on his face with his arm thrown over Olu's shoulder in an embrace. Olu, as usual, remained with the same expressionless scowl on his. Liaka lifted the cellophane sheet from the white cardboard page. The four by six picture was peeled carefully from it. Liaka raised the photo close to her face, examining theirs.

"Asia! Lianna!" Liaka yelled out. The door flung open for them to rush in. It was obvious that they never made it a few feet from the door. "Lianna, find some type of bags. Duffel bags, garbage bags, I don't care! Just any type of bags so we can gather some of this stuff. But, not all of it," Liaka instructed. A Kool-Aid smile spread across Lianna's face as she bolted out of the room without further instructions.

"No more being in the dark about what's going on. Now, I find out the truth," Liaka vowed, concentrating back on the picture in her hand.

# $C$hapter 19 | $S$hakin

Three sets of lights embedded, almost hidden in the plush grass, shone on both sides of a large wooden pillar at the foot of the road. FEDERAL PENITENTIARY. Liaka cut her steering wheel right off the main road onto the side street leading to the penitentiary. Asia was in the passenger seat with her. The prison was about two blocks up the road, hidden by the cloak of foliage, neatly tucked away from immediate society.

The crimson sky painted the roof of the building; rows of razor wire lined the top, a chain-link fence surrounded its entire outer perimeter. Liaka rolled into a parking space in the visitor's parking lot. After packing up half of the belongings at Olu's place in Brooklyn—at least half of the most valuable items—the three of them headed back to Connecticut with the wealth Olu had accumulated in his safe.

A tally of the cash stashed in the safe totaled a little over two hundred and thirty thousand dollars; all of the jewelry equaled just under a quarter million dollars as well. It took nothing short of a miracle for Liaka to calm Asia and Lianna down after they counted out the small fortune of cash in the safe.

Liaka figured she heard about every excuse in the book from Asia and Lianna as to why they should split the money and jewels three ways between the each of them. But, Liaka refused. It wasn't that she didn't want to share the wealth with her girls, but, Liaka had to make sure there were no ties attached to the safe; ties that would eventually lead back to her.

To keep them at bay, Liaka gave each of them twenty-thousand dollars in cash and a diamond encrusted watch to calm them down, more or less to shut them up. Asia accepted the cash and jewels with gratitude. But, Lianna was dissatisfied, she wanted more. Liaka was uncomfortable storing the possessions that she removed from Olu's safe at her house, which prompted her to secure all the merchandise in a small handbag and open an account for a safe deposit box at a bank.

The drive back from Brooklyn, although rampant with harassment from Asia and Lianna, also finalized one thing in Liaka's mind: she was going to do it; she was going to rob someone. The feel of almost a half million dollars in cash and jewelry running through her fingers, coupled with the thrill of how it was obtained, was almost too much for her to handle. She wanted more, and that desire for more ironically led her to prison.

Back in Connecticut with Olu's photo album and several of his documents, it took a few days, but, Liaka found out the identity of the man in the picture with Olu, the man involved in Olu's last robbery heist: Shalimar Santiago. He was alive. He was the only one on that fateful day to survive the shower of bullets rained on them by the authorities at the bank.

It was nothing short of a miracle that he survived. Eleven gunshots hit him, two from high powered rifles. Even more miraculous for him was, after several months in the prison's intensive care, physical therapy unit, he managed to recover with ninety percent of his original mobility. Aside from thirty percent of his left calf muscle blown off, leaving him with a permanent limp, and several other bullet holes in his body—the massive scars on his chest a testament to the extensive surgery—Shakim was pretty much normal. With a little investigation and a few strings pulled, Liaka found out what prison they were housing him in and what they charged him with.

Four counts of first degree murder in the commission of a felony, six counts of attempted murder of a Federal Agent, seventeen counts of first degree kidnapping, one count of bank robbery, one count of felony resisting arrest, and one count of trying to flee from the scene of a crime. Shakim was facing the death penalty. Even if he did, by some miraculous feat, escape lethal injection, the totality of the charges he was arraigned on made him face 21,240 months or 1,770 years in federal prison! The DA was more than determined to nail the coffin shut on his fate; nail the coffin shut, wrap it in chains, and seal it in cement!

Liaka found out where he was and decided to reach out to him. From the beginning, she was met with resistance. Receiving a call from an anonymous paralegal employed at some private law firm, as Liaka described herself, triggered Shakim's senses. His radar immediately went up. Yet, conversing with the soft-toned female over the phone, who assured that she may be of some help to him, even possibly possess some legal information to assist in his case, managed to calm him down. The mere mention of Liaka finally relating to Shakim that she was retained by a man who only went by the name "Olu" was the final determining factor in him deciding to meet her.

The visiting hours at the prison that night were between the hours of six and ten P.M. The digital clock on her dashboard read six twenty-seven. Liaka's goal was to get in under the semblance of a professional legal visit, increasing the chances of them securing more privacy. Liaka killed the engine and was about to step out.

"Liaka!" Asia announced, placing her hand on Liaka's shoulder before she could exit the car, "I hope you know what you're doing," Asia related with sincerity. Liaka exposed a confident smile followed by a slight nod. Retrieving her black leather briefcase from the back seat, Liaka closed her driver's door and headed towards the penitentiary's front entrance. The lobby was filled with people. Liaka headed straight to the front counter to check in.

"Good evening. My name is Maliaka Sikes. I work for the law offices of Hertzberg, Hertzberg, Fox, and Green. And I have a scheduled legal visit with a...," Liaka paused, and then reached into her briefcase to pull out a file. "...a Shalimar Santiago," Liaka continued, making eye contact with the female correctional officer at the desk. Liaka rested the file on the counter with Shakim's name in full view, and then reached into a compartment in her briefcase to hand the woman her paralegal business card and driver's license. A peculiar gaze was thrown at Liaka from the correction officer as she typed Shakim's name on the computer, she then flashed a suspicious glance at Asia behind her.

"Who is she?" the correction officer asked bluntly. Liaka peeked over her shoulder.

"I apologize. She is also a paralegal hired by the firm that represents Mister Santiago. Her name is Kadiajah Wilkins. She should be listed as well," Liaka conveyed, in a respectable tone. Asia immediately stepped forward to hand the correction officer her identification.

"Please, have a seat. Let me check the schedule and run this by my lieutenant," the CO related. Liaka picked up the file from the counter and gave the female a friendly smile before she stepped away. There were no double seats in the lobby where they could both sit together, so they stood, in silence.

A long fifteen minutes passed before the correction officer at the desk called out, "Sikes! Wilkins! You can go in now," pointing to a sliding metal door. They walked into a second waiting room and took their seats at a two-seated partition divided by glass.

The glass had faint smudges of palm prints on it, vestiges of someone's past attempt to reach out to their loved ones incarcerated; or the incarcerated reaching out to embrace a touch of freedom. The single seat opposite them was empty. So they waited, again. Ten minutes passed before a correction officer led a brown-skinned brother draped in a baggy one-piece orange fluorescence jumpsuit to their station.

Shakim stood about six foot two. He was sporting a nappy afro with a razor sharp edge-up lining his forehead and outer face. Shakim approached them stone-faced, his eyes focused intently on Liaka. He cut his eyes at Asia for the span of a blink before returning to Liaka. They picked up their phones when Shakim stood a few feet in front of them.

"You're very photogenic," Shakim uttered smoothly, taking his seat across from them.

"Excuse me?"

"You look just like your picture, Maliaka. Olu had a picture of you. You know Olu wasn't, how would you say, the sociable type. So, I doubt if he showed it to anyone else. But, he showed it to me. I know it was one of the few things he held close to his heart." Liaka bent down to reach into her briefcase on the floor, pulling out the photo of Olu and herself that she found in his safe. "That's it, that's the one. Where did you get that?"

"Olu shared a lot with me. A lot of things," Liaka stressed, with a furtive look in her eyes. Shakim caught it. They shared a knowing look between them. A few seconds passed before he broke eye contact with Liaka to glance over to stare at Asia.

"Who's this?"

"This is my girlfriend, Kadiajah," Liaka introduced, flashing a quick glance to Asia. Liaka had to do a double take. Because, from the corner of her eye she saw Asia smiling; not only smiling, but, actually blushing.

"Why did you come up here?" Shakim asked bluntly. The smile quickly faded from Asia's face.

"Be...because of Olu," Liaka stuttered, thrown off by his sudden harsh tone.

"What about Olu?"

"You know the type of relationship me and Olu had. So..."

"No, I didn't! I knew that he loved you and held you close to his heart. But, you were a part of his private life. None of my concern," Shakim delivered thickly.

"But, you do know that we were close. I loved him more than any other man in my life."

"That's good to hear. What's your point?"

"The point is I want you to tell me about him."

"Tell you about him? Tell you what?"

"Everything! I want to know about Olu, the Olu that I didn't know. The Olu that only you knew," Liaka pleaded.

"Who is she again?" Shakim questioned defensively, staring at Asia.

"I told you, this is my..."

"Open your shirt!" Shakim snapped at Asia. Asia's eyes widened. She unconsciously leaned back. She fixed her mouth to say something, anything, but, nothing would come out. Shakim's stare was intense as he locked into Asia's eyes. Liaka couldn't understand why fear encompassed her entire being. Shakim didn't yell his demand, he wasn't even threatening. Not to mention they were protected from him by at least two inches of bulletproof glass. Liaka stared at Asia with nervous eyes. She didn't know why she didn't respond to Shakim outright, refusing his request, or why she didn't say something to Asia herself.

But, if a response was elusive to Liaka when he first posed his request, Liaka soon found herself in complete awe as she watched in amazement as Asia hesitantly began to slowly unbutton the top buttons of her white dress shirt. Liaka was speechless. She couldn't believe her own eyes as she watched Asia slowly proceed down each button, innocently yet seductive, to finally open the front of her shirt with both hands, holding it open for him, exposing her bra covered chest.

Liaka realized that Asia never even bothered to inspect her surroundings to see if someone was watching her audacious display before she so easily complied with his request. It was subtle, but, Shakim's lip twitched into a perverted smirk as his eyes quickly ingested her rich, dark chocolate skin—her ample cleavage pressed together by a white lace bra—before he nodded a slight sign of approval, prompting Asia to close and button her shirt back up.

"You can never be too safe. Not even in this place, especially in this place," Shakim declared, his stance growing more lax. He leaned slightly to his side in Asia's direction, stealing one last glance as her fingers played with the buttons on her shirt. He couldn't help but notice how her manicured fingers stopped buttoning her shirt on the fourth button from the top, still revealing an ample amount of cleavage.

"What specifically do you want to know?"

"Just tell me about him. I knew him. But, there was so much that I didn't know about him," Liaka said painfully.

"I can tell you that, by far, he was one of the realest individuals I've ever met in my life! I've never met anyone like him, and I doubt I ever will. He was the last of a dying breed. The type of brother in a past lifetime who would have been an Egyptian king, a Black Panther, a Prophet. Someone who was destined to live great and die young. His fate was inevitable. Brothers like him, so powerful...It was only a matter of time. He was too great for this existence," Shakim delivered eloquently.

"Olu was the type of brother who could make things happen, move crowds with just his words. He was the type of person who could walk into an environment in a state of total chaos, and bring peace. Or vice versa. He was a man of honor. If he gave you his word on something, you could stake your life on it. So, when you profess to have loved no other man as deeply as you loved Olu, I believe you. I loved him myself, more than some of my own blood!"

"How long did you know him?"

"As long as I can remember."

"Did he...did he ever talk about me?"

"Olu was a man of very few words. I'm sure you know that. He rarely spoke unless there was some substance behind it. So, as for his personal life, for the most part, he kept that a closed book," Shakim related. Liaka let out a heavy sigh of disappointment. "But, he did mention you," Shakim uttered. The life instantly came back to Liaka's eyes.

"One day, he conversed with me about you. And, for Olu, that was pretty unusual. He told me for the first time in his life, he was in love. And as a result,

his every waking moment was spent thinking about you, thinking of ways to make you happy. How he couldn't see living life without you. I think he related this to me because you were becoming a distraction. You were the main reason why he officially wanted to get out," Shakim related. He could see that his words pained Liaka.

"But, he still had the apartment in New York. Why? Why, if he loved me, would he keep something like that from me?"

"I can't answer that. But, if I had to guess, I would have to say that it was probably to protect you. Olu lived a life that he didn't want to expose you to, that he didn't want you involved with. A life he wanted to keep separate from you."

"Did you ever go up there?"

"I knew about it. But, that was his place for privacy. A place to collect his thoughts."

"You know, I didn't know everything about Olu, but, I do know more than what most people think. More than you probably think," Liaka said mysteriously.

"I bet you do."

"He taught me things."

"I wouldn't doubt that either," Shakim said. He read into Liaka's colloquialism, but, he wasn't biting. "Let me ask you, how did you get them to schedule us under a legal visit?"

"Because I really am a licensed paralegal. I work in a law office, so I just scheduled us as a professional visit so we could talk more...privately."

"So, you know about the law?"

"I would say so. I graduated at the top of my class. And, within six months, secured a position with one of the senior partners at my law firm. So yes, I would say that I know a little something about the law."

"Then, you can help me?" Shakim spit with eager curiosity.

"I may be able to help you. But, you have to help me first."

"Help you? I'm looking at close to a thousand something years! How could I possibly help you?" Shakim spit, slightly amused.

"Tell me everything I want to know about Olu and the game!" Liaka spit greedily, the mere thought of the robberies Shakim and Olu committed together, what Olu shared with her in the past, causing chills to run up her spine.

"The game? What are you talking about, 'the game'?"

"For one, I wouldn't insult you. So please, don't insult me. You know what I'm talking about. And for two, this is a professional legal visit. So, any breech of this conversation would infringe on attorney-client privilege and would be inadmissible in court. So we are the only ones privy to this conversation," Liaka said, gesturing to Asia. "Now, if you want my help, which I will offer to give you, even extend the resources of the law firm that I work for, I need you to help me understand the game," Liaka repeated insistently.

Shakim switched the phone from his right ear to his left, studying both of them before him. He wasn't sure why the female before him was so interested in the stick-up game, or what possible benefit she could gain from him exposing that life to her. But, now he needed her and the carrot she dangled in front of him was too tempting to resist.

"Say I did tell you a little something about that life, about the life of a professional stick-up artist. I would only be speaking from a hypothetical point of view. You do understand that, right?" Shakim related, his eyes indicating to the phone on his ear, then a quick jerk of his neck motioning to the CO standing about twenty feet behind him. Both Liaka and Asia nodded in agreement.

Shakim leaned in towards the glass, the phone pressed tightly against his ear, and began to share with them, in excruciating detail, a few of the most infamous heists Olu and himself committed, all narrated under the guise of a third party. He spared no detail, painting the most vivid picture, giving them everything he thought they wanted to hear.

Shakim described how the strongest men crumbled in fear and trembled like children at the mere sight of them in some circles. How their lust for money and thirst for power became an unquenchable desire that could never manage to be filled, no matter how much wealth they obtained. How the mere thrill of robbing someone became an aphrodisiac like no other.

Liaka and Asia listened to his descriptive accounts, entranced by his every word. With each story, Shakim could see the physical changes Liaka was experiencing; her body language, her sudden movements, the way she squirmed and adjusted herself in her seat every so often, sometimes being so lost into him that she had to snap herself out of it. Asia was also drawn to Shakim's previous lifestyle, not as captivated to the degree which she noticed Liaka to be, but, drawn in no doubt.

She had to admit, prior to Shakim describing their notorious lifestyle to them—for her to hear with her own ears—Asia began to think that Liaka was losing her mind when she expressed the strange surge of excitement she felt every time she listened to Olu relate one of his stories to her. But, there she was, sitting in a federal penitentiary visiting room, clinging on to Shakim's every word, every juicy tidbit of his adventurous life, finding herself experiencing the same pleasure Liaka so passionately talked about. Shakim seen the pleasure both Liaka and Asia received from his tales, prompting him to get more graphic, more descriptive, more explicit with each story, until he was done. Giving them what he felt was just enough to satisfy their illicit craving, but sparing enough in his mental arsenal, leaving them thirsty for more.

"A little something like that?" Shakim said slyly, leaning back and to his side, slicing squinted eyes between them. Forty minutes had passed by like five. It took a moment for Liaka to gather herself and come back down to reality before she finally had the composure to respond.

"Exactly like that!" Liaka slurred thickly, a mischievous glint now in her eye. It didn't take for Shakim to finish elaborating on one of his first heists for Liaka to know that he was going to be an intricate part of her schemes. He was a gold mine of information to that life, and she planned to play him close, keep him at her disposal for any further insight she might need in the future.

"How are you doing in here? Do you need anything?" Liaka questioned, changing pace. Her comment generated the first form of expression from him, an evident curl of his lip into a smirk. Yet, as quickly as the smirk appeared, it faded back into the same insipid mien he held throughout the visit.

"What you could do for me is look into my case. See if all the I's were dotted and the T's crossed. Give me something to work with, anything! That's what I need," Shakim related aggrieved.

"I give you my word; I will look into it for you. I will personally call in a favor and ask my boss to help me. But, what about money? Do you have any?"

"Money. How ironic is that? I fought to make my millions, only for me to lose it all, unable to spend a penny," Shakim related with a satiric chuckle and a shake of his head. He focused on Liaka for a moment, lost in thought before saying, "Why are you doing this? To hear old war stories? Why are you really here?"

"Because you were close to Olu. I know you and Olu were very close. You probably knew him better than anyone, even myself. So, if I can help a close friend of Olu, then I feel it's my duty to do it. I would like to be here to help you," Liaka explained sympathetically.

"My case is what's important. If you want to do anything for me, do that."

"I can do that, too. But, I'm talking about in here."

"I can't deny that I could use a little help," Shakim said humbly.

"I'll put five thousand dollars on your commissary account by the end of the week. Anything else?" Liaka said energetically, happy that he was receptive to her help.

"I'm good."

"What about a female?"

"Huh?" Shakim gasped, slightly amused.

"I didn't mean any disrespect by that, and if it was taken as such, I apologize. I just thought...you being in prison, that..."

"No need to apologize," Shakim said with a smile, "I was just a little thrown off by your comment. A female. It would be nice to trade thoughts with someone. It can get a little lonely in here, despite the masses. To have a little escape from this existence, maybe look into the face of an angel every now and then would be nice," Shakim said smoothly, his eyes cutting over to Asia. She found herself blushing again. She could see Shakim literally undressing her with his eyes.

"I got someone perfect for you. I think you'll like her. It's my girl, Lianna," Liaka said enthusiastically. "I think she'll..."

"Santiago! You got five minutes!" The correction officer announced harshly, approaching Shakim from behind. Shakim got the CO to back off with a sharp look over his shoulder.

"I will be coming back up here again. I give you my word on that. I'll also send you the authorization forms you're gonna need to sign, to allow me to gain access to your entire criminal file. It was very nice to meet you. I will see you again, Shalimar."

"Shakim. I go by, Shakim," Shakim related, for Liaka to gather her belongings. "Maliaka," Shakim spit, seconds away from Liaka hanging up the phone, "I can see why Olu felt that way about you. You're...you're different. Take care of yourself," Shakim ended sincerely, slowly rising to his feet.

"You, too, Shakim. You're definitely different, too," Liaka said smiling, hanging up the phone.

"Bye, Shakim," Asia sighed sexily, speaking the first two words since she arrived.

"It doesn't have to be," Shakim uttered, followed by a subtle wink. Asia, who remained a silent spectator to their interaction, winked back then slowly hung up the phone. Shakim remained glued to his side of the table as he watched Liaka and Asia walk away. He processed that mental image of them in his mind, his mental rolodex, to take that back to the cell block with him.

Asia threw a few flirtatious glances over her shoulder back at Shakim who drank in her every move. She toyed with his illicit thoughts. Asia wanted to leave him with a vivid memory of her to take away with him, provoking her to strut away with a little extra swagger in her step. She turned the corner without needing the confirmation that he was still looking.

"What was that all about?" Asia asked, the moment they reached back at the car.

"Nothing. I just wanted to talk to him. Hopefully get some closure," Liaka explained unconvincingly, taking her seat behind the wheel. "And hold on a minute! You're asking me what that was all about? I need to be asking you! He tells you to just open your shirt, and you just do it? You, of all people?" Liaka snapped, still somewhat amazed at Asia's nonchalant attitude at his request.

"I only did it for you. I mean, if I didn't, he wouldn't have talked to you, right? Then our entire visit would have been for nothing," Asia conveyed altruistically.

"Uh huh, yeah. I'm buying that," Liaka said with a chuckle.

"And Lianna? Why would you tell him that you were gonna hook him up with Lianna?" Asia spit angrily.

"Think about it, it's Lianna! I figure, he's in prison, so he might want a female that's gonna take care of some of his...desires for him. And who better than Lianna. She loves doing shit like that. To know that one man will give her his sole, undivided attention, she lives for that shit. You know her; he could ask her for anything and she would do it! Phone sex, naked, freaky pictures, you name it!" Liaka described casually, thinking about her girl's wild antics.

Asia didn't respond. She just threw a twisted look at Liaka from the corner of her eye. What Liaka was painfully unaware of is, from that encounter in the mall when Asia and Lianna traded those words; Asia had been playing with some newfound thoughts on her introverted views on sexuality and how to go about expressing it. Now that Donovan was officially out of her life, Asia made up her mind that she was going to explore that unknown side of herself.

Shakim's charismatic stance, and the stories he related to them, were only a few factors convincing Asia that he would be the perfect person to test her newfound liberation on. Not only could Shakim conjure up that raw passion Asia knew she had within her, that she was dying to explore, but, she also concluded she could be as free as her heart desired, expressing her most illicit desires without the fear of her behavior getting out. Because, at the end of the day, who could he possibly tell—a bunch of other prisoners? She would be able to explore herself and keep her reputation intact.

"When are you coming back to visit him?" Asia asked, feigning any real interest.

"I don't know. A couple of weeks, maybe a month. I'm okay for now. I got what I came for," Liaka assured, driving down the main road leading away from the prison. *I got everything I came for*, Liaka repeated to herself in her mind, a mischievous grin forming on her face.

# $C$hapter 20 | $J$ack $M$ove

$B$eads of water rolled down Liaka's body to drip in the tub. Tightening both faucets in the shower, Liaka leaned out to reach for a large dark green towel hanging on the rack by the sink. She quickly grabbed for the heavy towel to pat her body dry. Wiping the steam from the mirror with the palm of her hand, Liaka cleared an opening big enough to get a clear reflection of herself. She lifted the transparent shower cap from her head; her hair was wrapped tightly in a circle on her head. A few condensed beads of water rolled down the face of the mirror.

She was in no mood to prepare for the date she had scheduled. She thought her face appeared to be a little chubby, mainly as a result of her 'monthly friend' popping up on her. But, having a chubby face was the last of her concerns. It was only on rare occasions where her period snuck up on her a week early, or a week late, and hit her that hard. Unfortunately, she was experiencing just one of those tormenting kind of days.

Strangely enough, unwrapping and running her fingers through her hair managed to make her feel a little better. She ran a hot comb through it, and as she suspected, it was easily styled to perfection. Looking fabulous on the outside, but, feeling like crap on the inside, caused Liaka to play with the idea of canceling her date. But, she couldn't. She had to go through with it because this was far from one of her ordinary dates.

Triple Crown Publications presents... $Q$ueen of $T$hieves
*PART 1*

Playing with the idea for the past couple of weeks on if she was going to actually go through with her plans and rob someone, she finalized that she was—and that night was the night. A few weeks prior, when they all visited the mall to do their shopping, Liaka purposely took the numbers of some potential 'victims', mainly the drug dealing type, for the climatic date when she finally decided to do it. The perfect victim came in the form of a brother named Donta.

Donta was the last type of brother Liaka could ever imagine finding herself with. His initial approach had to be one of the most memorable, and the corniest, she could remember. She could only imagine what type of females would fall for his best Mack lines like: "I know you're tired, because you've been running through my mind all day." And, "You gotta be related to a bee, because you look as sweet as honey." But, such a cheesy approach only contributed to her position that he would be the perfect victim to begin her excursion of heists on. Not only did he carry himself in a manner which would label him a wannabe thug, but, based on Lianna's certainty that she was familiar with him, in her opinion, he was the perfect mark to take. At a minimum, at least the perfect herb to juice money from.

Ironically, money wasn't the main factor driving Liaka to rob someone. It was the thrill. Olu and Shakim sparked something in her that she knew could never be quenched until she finally went through with it; commit that first robbery. She had to experience that thrill for herself. After talking to Donta only a few hours earlier, with his trite remarks, Liaka was convinced that he was definitely the one. Now the only problem was those damned sharp pains that kept twisting in her stomach.

Tossing the towel that was wrapped around her body on the bed, to find a pair of cheeky panties and matching bra, Liaka walked over to the closet and slid the door open. A pair of skin tight, faded blue jeans almost jumped out at her. They would be perfect. The weatherman predicted the slight possibility of snow on that chilly November night, prompting Liaka to slip on a heavy cream turtleneck sweater. Liaka glanced at herself in the mirror, giving her hair and body a quick once over before focusing back on her bedroom clock.

7:23

Donta told her he would be there at eight.

As the time slowly passed, Liaka grew nervous at the prospect of what she planned on doing. She sat on the edge of her bed, deep in thought, before reaching for the phone on her nightstand. She dialed Lianna's house. Ten unsuccessful rings concluded Lianna wasn't home. Making it down to her kitchen, Liaka yanked open the refrigerator door.

The pain in her stomach slightly subsided, but, underneath, she could feel a twinge of hunger. She thought to snack on something light. Past experiences led Liaka to understand the 'Rules of Engagement' when it came to first dates. A light snack was a safe precaution. Not that Liaka had any qualms about gorging out on a first date in fear of making a bad impression. But, more in line with the unpredictability that comes with a first date. If he was cheap, that would definitely put a damper on Liaka getting her eat on, because she would be damned if she was going to come out of her pockets! Or the other possibility—in the middle of the date, when it became plainly evident that he wasn't going to get any action, that he would instantaneously transform into—MR. EQUALITY! Make a woman pay for her own meal faster than a speeding bullet. Able to calculate fifty percent of his portion of the bill faster than a locomotive. Able to wrap up the date and drop her off in a single bound.

So much for chivalry.

Prior to Olu, Liaka experienced a few trifling brothers who possessed such un-super powers. Just the thought of that type of brother was a painful reminder that made Liaka know it would be almost impossible to replace Olu. A thin sliced turkey sandwich was quickly slapped together.

7:41

She knew time was slowly closing in. Sinking her teeth into the sandwich, Liaka ventured off to the living room for her handbag to retrieve her cell phone.

"Hey, Donta, what's up? It's me, Shanice." Fully prepared to go through with her plans from the very beginning, Liaka gave him, along with a few other brothers, a fake name. "I'm not sure if you remember my address, so here it is..."

The address Liaka gave him was from an apartment complex about three blocks away. Liaka peeked out through her window blinds. Luckily for her, the weatherman failed to be accurate in his prediction; not a snowflake in the sky. In fact, he couldn't have been more inaccurate, because in the clear night sky there wasn't a cloud in sight. The full moon and a million and one stars glowed like miniature lamps to light the night.

Liaka was pleased it didn't snow. Now she would finally be able to sport her suede knee-high boots she just purchased. Slipping them on, followed by her dark brown, waist level faux fur, Liaka headed for the front door. Liaka caught a last glance of herself in a large five-foot mirror by her front door.

"You can do this, girl," Liaka whispered to her reflection, boosting herself up, before giving a vision of herself an assuring nod. She shrugged her shoulders up in hopes of warmth as a sudden burst of frostbiting air bit into her. She still felt like total crap on the inside. But, one thing was for sure, she knew she looked slamming on the outside.

Liaka didn't even make it off her block before two cars pulled up on her, almost one after the other, trying to get some play. Liaka politely turned them down. She finally made it to the building where she planned to meet Donta. She warmed herself in the lobby a quick fifteen minutes before Donta arrived.

He pulled up in a black, two-door *Acura Legend* coupe at a high rate of speed. The front end of his car did a nose dive as his vehicle screeched to an abrupt stop in front of the building. The muffled bass of his car stereo thumped as she began to approach the front door. Her phone rang the second she reached for the handle.

"Yo, Shanice, I'm out..."

"Front. Yes, I know. I see you," Liaka said dryly.

Emerging from the front lobby, with each step down the stairs towards his car, Liaka could feel a twist of nervousness churning in her stomach. Yet, the moment Liaka reached for the handle of the passenger door, it instantly faded. When she opened the door, she was hit with a cloud of weed smoke in the face. The Dipset's *Back in the building* crashed through the speakers until he turned down the volume for Liaka to take her seat.

"Oh, my bad, shawty. Let a nigga move them shits," Donta slurred, handing her the remains of a half-smoked blunt. He leaned over to the passenger seat floor to lift out two shopping bags. He pushed them through the center of the seats to the back, to see Liaka still holding on to the blunt.

"You could hit that shit if you want, shawty."

"No, I'm straight," Liaka said, with a shake of her head, passing the blunt back to him. Donta shrugged and immediately lifted the blunt back to his lips. He inhaled deeply. The flame of the blunt lit up the dark interior of the car, bouncing and glistening off of the diamonds on his platinum chain.

"I ain't know you was a good girl like that," Donta said, with a devilish grin,

the street light glowing off his caramel face.

"Well, now you know," Liaka cooed sexily.

"It's like every lil' shawty smoke weed now-a-days. So to find a lil' shawty who don't, that's different," he said, inhaling deeply on the blunt again.

"You said it right. Because I am different," Liaka assured. Truth be told, Liaka was only a second away from raising the blunt to her lips to take a drag as she held it in her hand.

"So, what's on your mind?" He shifted the car into drive and slowly pulled off.

"I was thinking a movie. Maybe a little dinner after that," Liaka conveyed. Donta nodded.

"I see you don't smoke, But, if you wanna sip on something to drink, I got a lil' Hennessey in the glove box."

The heavy, half-pint bottle of Hennessey fell from the glove box the moment Liaka opened it. When she picked it up, she could see that it was a fresh, unopened bottle. Liaka glanced at him from the corner of her eye. Donta was focused on the road. Liaka cracked the seal on the bottle and took a small sip.

"I guess that good girl shit went right out the window, huh?" Donta said with a smirk, peeking at her from the corner of his eye. Liaka cracked a half smile, but, didn't respond. She took another sip and handed it over to him. Donta rested the blunt in the ashtray and took about four large gulps from the bottle, before greedily licking his lips and resting it on his thigh. Liaka noticed how he swallowed about a fourth of the bottle in one swig. It was nothing. He took another two gulps, without even so much as a flinch, before handing it back to Liaka.

They eventually made it to the movies. They caught a screening of a new *Tyler Perry* movie. Between laughs, Liaka began to study Donta, how he revealed subtle, yet distinct things about himself. Liaka noticed how he snuck the bottle of Hennessey in the movie theater with them. How they didn't make it fifteen minutes into the movie before Donta blatantly poured out about three-fourths of his extra-large soda on the floor, to refill the rest of his cup back up with his drink. His behavior wasn't much different after the movie when they went to dinner. Between appetizers, Donta ordered shots of Tanqueray and washed them down with a pitcher of beer. He barely picked at the large meal he ordered, being more concerned with nursing on his drinks.

It was obvious from the beginning of dinner to Liaka that he was determined to get drunk more than anything else. As the hours passed, and the strong liquor merged with his system, Liaka could also notice the evident changes in his behavior. He went from being a little corny, yet charming at the beginning of their date, to a complete and utter jackass within the span of four hours. It was a little amazing to Liaka to witness his complete transformation right before her eyes.

"Yo, you seen how that motherfuckin' waiter was actin' in that bitch?" Donta slurred, followed by a slight chuckle. They drove down a well-lit road at about one in the morning. Liaka cut a look at him out the corner of her eye in the darkness of the car. She could see his eyes jumping back and forth between her and the road. Liaka had it in her to relate to him that if he wasn't conducting himself like such an asshole that the waiter wouldn't have responded in turn. But, she decided to bite her tongue. The car rolled right through a stop sign as Donta boldly rested his hand on Liaka's knee.

"I don't even think I told you this shit. But, damn, shawty! You look good as fuck! I told you that shit though, right?" Donta drawled, weakly massaging her knee. Liaka could see that he was clearly paying more attention to her than the road as his eyes spent more time on her than the few cars of passing traffic. She gently removed his hand from her knee.

"No, you didn't. Thank you. But, I really think you should pay more attention to the road." She noticed his difficulty keeping the vehicle between lanes.

"Now, how the fuck is a nigga supposed to concentrate when he got some sweetness like this sitting next to him?" Donta slurred, slapping his hand right back on her knee. Liaka left it there. She quickly became more concerned with *not* distracting him, hoping he would pay more attention to the road. For the span of a second, a thought flashed into her mind that an unfortunate stroke of fate would cause him to drunkenly careen his car off the road and kill them both.

"Why don't you let me drive," Liaka posed nervously, as Donta continued rubbing her thigh.

"Come on, shawty. Let a nigga do this. I ain't new to this shit," Donta sighed, finally removing his hand to rummage through the inside pocket of his large leather jacket. He found the cigarettes that he was searching for and lit one. It took the flame of his lighter kissing the tip of his cigarette to spark the idea that Liaka had no idea where they were going.

"Where are you going?" Liaka questioned, as she noticed him traveling in the opposite direction of her house.

"I got this," Donta assured. Twenty minutes later, Donta pulled his vehicle into a hotel parking lot. His inebriated state caused him to scrape the front end of his vehicle on the entrance of the parking lot, and even clip the bumper of another vehicle at his drunken attempt to park. Liaka grabbed at the dashboard to brace herself in fear before the car finally came to a stop. She felt her heart skip a beat.

"Damn! You scary like that?" Donta laughed. "Don't worry, I ain't gonna hit nothing. I told you I ain't new to this shit." Donta roughly yanked the transmission into park. Liaka almost snapped her neck to look at him in amazement. She was wondering if he was joking or if he really didn't realize that he already hit something! Twice!

"Give a nigga a minute, ya heard. I'll be right back. You...you just sit there looking as delicious as you wanna be!" Donta slurred drunkenly, stumbling out the car. Liaka watched him with angry eyes as a turn of her neck followed him out the back window. He took one last drag from his cigarette and tossed it carelessly in the wind, then disappeared into the hotel lobby.

The lights from the hotel parking lot lit up the interior. The two shopping bags in the back seat were the first things to pop into Liaka's mind. With no movement coming from the lobby doors, Liaka spun in her seat so fast that she caused the car to bounce as she reached for the bags in the back. A pair of baggy navy blue *Sean John* jeans and a thick baby blue *Sean John* turtleneck with white lettering. The other bag held a brand new Blackjack and a portable PSP game, along with two disks. Lifting her eyes up out the back window to the lobby, Liaka could see him drunkenly stumble out of the front doors.

"A nigga was on some shit, thinking we could smash tha room, na' mean? Bless that shit love-love, ya dig, shawty?" Donta said, waving the key in his hand. Liaka forced a smile. "Grab them pack of Philly's in the armrest. It should be like two or three of them left in there," Donta slurred, slamming the door to walk off towards the room.

Liaka stood for a second, staring at the back of his head in disgust as he stumbled away. She rolled her eyes then yanked open his armrest for the blunts. Trailing about twenty feet behind him, Liaka noticed how Donta reached into his pocket for his cell phone to check the number calling. It didn't take a genius to know that he was talking to a female from the secretive demeanor he insisted on taking; speaking in a hushed tone, hanging up within a minute's time.

"I don't even know where my head is at. I knew a nigga forgot something. I shoulda stopped by the bootleg and grabbed my boo a little something to wet her throat with," Donta said, struggling with the key in the hotel door. That was a joke. Liaka knew if there was any alcohol in their presence, it would immediately be devoured by his alcoholic ass! He finally managed to get the front door open. Liaka followed him inside to watch him plop down on the first chair by the bed. Before taking the time to even inspect the room, he shoved a cigarette in his mouth and lit it. Liaka closed the door behind herself and made her way to the edge of the bed.

"Ho...hold on, beautiful. Slow that down. Let a nigga capture this moment for a second."

Liaka was mid-way from taking her seat. Before her ass could hit the edge, Liaka paused to think about it, and then rose back to her feet. It took every bit of self-control Liaka could muster to avoid spewing out the fiercest epithets she could throw at him. But, she had a bigger agenda. So instead of speaking her mind, she merely placed her hand on her hip and weakly modeled a few poses for him.

His glassy, blood-shot eyes lustfully traveled over Liaka's entire body. He boldly beckoned her over. A sinister smirk spread across Liaka's lips. Her stride was deliberate as she exaggerated the sway of her hips approaching him. With each step she studied him, watched his body language, his mannerisms, his squinted eyes, thinking how was she going to pull this off. His behavior revealed the obvious: he was drunk and high out of his mind. Liaka knew the combination of weed and alcohol coursing through his system would make him an easy candidate to be physically overtaken.

Two years of *Tae-Bo* and strength training would enable her to take out a drunken man any day. But, she couldn't allow his inebriated state for her to make her final decision, because Donta still had some size on him. Being close to six feet tall and weighing about two hundred pounds, Liaka knew despite her strength and him being drunk, that if he put up a fight, she would definitely have one.

Liaka came to a stop about three feet in front of him. She stood over him, staring down at his face, his eyes. From where she stood, they appeared to be closed. But, then she noticed his hands slowly rise from his sides to reach out for her hips. They massaged in firm grips down her thighs, then back up to her waist.

"Yeah, this that shit right here!" Donta growled. He rubbed his hands over her curves, working them around to fill both hands with her ass. With a firm grip he squeezed, pulling her closer.

"Okay, okay, calm down," Liaka sighed humorously, removing his hands from her to take a step back.

"Damn, shawty! Your shit is tight as fuck, for real! I can tell you be hitting the gym cause your shit is firm as fuck! You could bounce a quarter off that ass!" Donta shook his head as he watched her take a seat at the edge of the bed. Rising to his feet, Donta unzipped his heavy leather coat and tossed it into the chair where he just sat. The heavy leather hit the back, fell to the seat and rolled from it to fall to the floor. Donta ignored it, grabbing for the pack of blunts.

She sat in silence as he emptied the blunt tobacco with no regard on the carpet. The empty blunt wrapper was moistened with his saliva for him to reach into his jean pocket to pull out a healthy dime bag of weed, spilling the entire contents into the blunt. Liaka began to wonder if this clown ass joke of a brother really did think there was a remote chance that she was going to give him the goodies. How in the world did he plan on 'functioning' high and drunk out of his mind? He flicked a lighter to kiss the flame on the tip. He kicked off his cream construction Timberland boots, took a deep inhale and reclined with his head rested against the headboard.

"Damn, Shanice. Take your coat off. Get comfortable with a nigga," Donta suggested, through chinky eyes. His words made Liaka realize what she must have looked like; fully clothed, still wrapped up in her fur at the edge of the bed.

"Uh...give me a minute. I have to use the bathroom," Liaka stated, excusing herself from the room. The bathroom door was swung closed and locked before Liaka even had enough time to click on the light. She opened the sink's faucet, breaking the silence of the bathroom with running water, and then lowered the lid on the toilet to take a seat.

This shit isn't gonna work! Liaka cursed to herself under her breath, growing restless. *I wish I still had that Hennessey bottle. I'd smash him in his fuckin' face with it and just get it over with!* Just the thought of doing something like that caused a wicked smirk to spread across her face. She chuckled. She couldn't believe the predicament she found herself in, locked in a hotel room with a complete stranger, contemplating on how to rob him! Then, reality began to set in.

*Who am I kidding? I'll never be able to do this!* She reached up to shut off the running water in the sink for silence to fall back over the small bathroom. The next thought to engulf her was, how in the hell was she going to get out of there? Rehearsing an array of excuses to throw at him, Liaka concluded that it would be best to just tell him the truth; that she was on her period and nothing was going to happen. Hopefully, that vision of her 'monthly friend' would be enough to take some of the steam out of his tank and bring the night to an end.

Tapping her cell phone in her pocket, Liaka figured if he caught an attitude that she could just walk out and call Asia to come and pick her up. Taking a deep breath, Liaka checked herself in the mirror then opened the bathroom door; about ten minutes passed since she first entered.

"Uh…Donta, we got a little problem. My *girlfriend* just decided to visit me for the month, so…," Liaka began, as if she was disheartened, taking a seat on the bed. "I'm sorry. But, maybe we can do this another night." Liaka kept her back to him. She waited a few seconds trying to figure out what type of response he would come up with. But, there was none. He just laid there silent, unmoving.

"Donta, did you hear me? I wanna go home," Liaka said, raising her voice a little, looking over her shoulder at him. Still nothing. Liaka stood to her feet, turning full circle to face him. He lay, motionless. Peering down at his face, Liaka leaned in closer to see if his chinky eyes were still open. This time there was no mistaking it, they definitely weren't. Yet, strangely enough, the blunt remained burning between his fingers, a trail of weed smoke dancing from its tip to evaporate in the air.

"Donta! Come on, now! I'm serious! Stop playing!" Liaka cried, poking at his leg. Still nothing. Liaka studied him with curious eyes before saying, "You gonna mess around and burn this place down! Give me that!" reaching to remove the blunt from between his fingers. But, removing the blunt from his hand made no difference; his fingers remained in the same position in which he held it. Liaka put both hands on his leg and shook him aggressively. Nothing.

*No this nigga ain't pass out on me!* Liaka chuckled under her breath in disbelief. He was so out of it, it would appear that he wasn't even breathing. Liaka leaned over for the second time, shaking him frantically, chanting, "Donta! Donta!" shoving his body with such violent thrusts that the entire bed shook underneath him. But, he was out of it. The only response Liaka got in return was a deep grunt under his breath followed by a twitch of his nose. Rocked with the same nervous feeling Liaka felt when she first approached Donta's car at the beginning of their date, Liaka knew if there was ever an opportunity that was going to present itself—that this was it!

Throwing caution to the wind, Liaka leaned in closer with deliberate movements to hover over Donta's lifeless frame. She patted him down. Her hand stopped at the pocket of his jeans. His left pocket was flat. Her hand traveled over to the right side of his baggy jeans, all the while staring at his face with nervous eyes.

She felt something in his right pocket. There was a huge lump. She found herself swallowing so hard that she just felt like she digested a golf ball. Liaka was so nervous that her hands were visibly shaking. But, she boldly reached out to squeeze the exterior of his mysterious lump. It was definitely money. Liaka looked around the room, not necessarily knowing what she was looking for, until her eyes spotted it, a heavy crystal ashtray on the nightstand by the head of the bed.

Liaka told herself that if by some freak chance of fate he awakened while she was digging in his pocket, that she would reach for it and smash him in the face with it, then run out the room screaming bloody murder! Liaka took a breath and held it. With one hand she lifted up the edge of his pocket and tried to squeeze the other hand in. The way his body was laying, his jeans were pressed tightly against his leg, so she struggled. Her fingernails, the first knuckle, then the second, was forcefully pushed into his pocket until she felt the tip of her nail hit the lump. Pulling at his pocket even harder, with one final thrust, Liaka pushed her fingers in until most of her hand disappeared into his pocket. The tips of her fingers caressed a wad of bills.

"The drinks is on...," Donta mumbled incoherently in his sleep. Liaka jumped back about fifteen feet. If there was ever a point in her life of being close to a heart attack, Liaka was past it as she stared down over him, frozen, her heart beating uncontrollably in her chest. It took a few seconds for Liaka to realize he was only talking in his sleep and just happened to roll over and

 Triple Crown Publications presents... Queen of Thieves *PART I*

mumble something. Because, for that brief second, Liaka felt like her life flashed before her eyes. But, just as fast, Donta was lifeless again; the only movement or sound coming from him was the smacking of his lips and an incessant hum grumbling from his lungs.

Liaka waited for a moment and reached for his pocket again, this time with unwavering boldness. She easily dug her hand in to remove a knot of money. The outer bills on the knot were all hundreds, at least fifteen of them, followed by a few fifties, then some twenties. A quick run through made Liaka realize that she was holding three thousand two hundred and fifty-two dollars in her hands. Liaka continued rifling his items; his platinum chain with medallion, his *Movado* watch, a platinum bracelet, and two diamond encrusted rings set in white gold on his ring and pinky finger.

Stuffing the items of jewelry and money in the pockets of her fur, Liaka did a quick scan of the room to see his leather coat crumpled up into a ball on the floor. Going through the jacket, she found another small set of bills, but, most importantly, his car keys. With one last look at Donta over her shoulder, still passed out, Liaka tossed his keys in mid-air and caught them in her hand thinking, *it can't be this easy.* Then, she chuckled, walking out of the room.

# $C$hapter 21 | $I$nnovate

$I$nnovations was packed that Saturday afternoon as Liaka and Asia sat in the hair salon patiently waiting on a stylist. Liaka didn't get home until about two forty A.M. the following night after leaving Donta. It didn't feel like she got more than four hours sleep before she was awakened by Asia pounding on her front door a little before eleven A.M.

Liaka crossed her leg over the other, an *Essence* magazine taking up space on her lap as thoughts of what happened the night before with Donta played on a continuous loop in her head. Immediately after rushing out of the room and to his car, she began to ransack his vehicle before she even pulled off. She searched the glove box and the armrest, but, there was nothing out of the ordinary in them. What did manage to slow Liaka's pace and capture her attention was his stereo system.

The entire trunk was filled with stereo components; speakers, amplifiers, crossovers, equalizers, and other gadgets Liaka couldn't even recognize, custom designed in the walls and floorboard of the trunk. This left Liaka with the harsh reality that it would have been almost impossible for her to remove all the equipment without the assistance of some professional help and time wasn't her friend that late at night. So, as much as it pained her, she decided to leave it.

Snatching up the two shopping bags from the back seat, Liaka thought she

Triple Crown Publications presents...    $Q$ueen of $T$hieves
PART 1

spotted what appeared to be the edge of a cellophane bag stuck in the crack of the seat. When she reached to tug at it, out popped from the crevice two and a half ounces of ready rock cocaine in two large balls. She decided to pocket that as well. With the two shopping bags in tow, Liaka parked his car about six blocks away from her apartment and jogged the rest of the way home with all of his spoils in hand. Angel was the first person that came to Liaka's mind when she thought of the clothes and who could possibly take the drugs off her hands. But, the Blackjack and portable PSP were hers.

Liaka was dying with anticipation to see the reaction Lianna was going to give her when she finally told her about what she done. Glancing to her right at Asia, who was busy flipping through an *Essence* herself looking at hairstyles, Liaka knew she could never tell her. Asia wouldn't know how to respond to something like that. But, Lianna, that was right up her alley. She would get a wicked kick out of something like that.

Sitting there in that candy apple red leather chair, watching all the commotion going on in the tight salon, Liaka smiled to herself thinking of how easy it was to pull it off. From everything she heard Olu and Shakim describe, she didn't think it would happen like that. Where was the excitement, the thrill, the rush? Aside from being rocked with that sudden bolt of fear from Donta turning over in his sleep, Liaka felt none of that.

The feelings she experienced when Olu described one of his glamorous heists didn't even register compared to the dull feelings she felt driving away from the hotel. But, she knew at that moment, there was a distinct difference between what she did, pillaging a sleeping man's valuables, and what Olu had done, storm a bank with guns blazing. And the distinct difference was *force*.

They used force, power, as a means of obtaining their wealth. While what she did was the equivalent of taking candy from a baby. Liaka knew that force was the determining factor, the essential ingredient that turned her on, that set her heart afire, the missing element in the equation. Force had to be used if she wanted to come even close to mimicking the effects of the excitement she chased after.

With a wily eyebrow raised, Liaka could only imagine what Donta's reaction must have been when he woke up the next morning to find all his valuables gone. Shock, amazement, utter disbelief? To think, when he brought Liaka to that hotel room, he had every intention of getting some action. Liaka thought to herself, *he got some action all right! He didn't get any pussy, but, he sure got fucked,* as a slight chuckle escaped her lips.

"What the hell is so funny?" Asia asked, once she noticed Liaka staring off into space, silently entertaining herself.

"Nothing. I was just thinking about this brother I went out with last night."

"I didn't know you went out on a date last night. Why didn't you tell me?" She stopped flipping through the pages of her magazine.

"Because, trust me, there's nothing to tell. He was a joke! He spent most of the night in a race to see how drunk or high he could get. Which lead to the grand finale of him passing out. Like I said, a joke!" Liaka explained with a shrug, lifting the magazine up from her lap.

"Still, you could have at least told me about it," Asia returned, feeling left out. She shrugged it off. "What do you think about this?" Asia held a page up in her magazine for Liaka to see.

"I don't like it. It's too short," Liaka said, scrunching her face.

"It is kinda short, huh? Well, what about this?" Asia said, pointing out a different hairstyle.

"Now that's cute. I like that," Liaka assured. Asia nodded, inspecting the hairstyle for a second time once she received her friend's approval. "What are you gonna do?"

"Just touch up. Nothing major. I just got it done, so I should be good for at least another week. But, I am gonna get a pedicure."

"And not a second too soon, because you sure need it."

"Oh, no you didn't!" Liaka gasped in shock, playfully slapping Asia on the arm. "I don't know why you said that. I got cute feet," Liaka whined, slightly embarrassed.

"Girl, you know I was just playing. But, they sure ain't as cute as mines. I will say that they are better than some of these other females in here," Asia said, subtly gesturing to the other women around the shop. "Can I ask you something?" Asia posed, taking on a serious tone. "The money in Olu's safe in Brooklyn, what do you plan on doing with all that?"

"I don't know. I haven't given it too much thought yet. I don't want to do anything too drastic, nothing out of the ordinary. But, I was thinking about treating me and my girls to some shopping, maybe a trip to Jamaica," Liaka said with a smile. The serious look on Asia's face faded into a smile herself.

"Hey, I sure wouldn't be mad at you," Asia chuckled.

"Um, Ms. Honey, you're up next," A male stylist called out to Liaka, beckoning her over to his chair with a single curling finger. Alexis was one of the most flamboyant gay men Liaka ever met in her life. He was soon becoming Liaka's favorite stylist after her normal stylist, Sasha, went out on maternity leave.

"So, Miss Liaka. What can I do for you? 'Cause I just know you ain't here to get your hair done," Alexis stated, boldly running his manicured fingers through Liaka's hair as she took a seat in his chair. His fingers weaved through Liaka's hair, from the scalp to the tips, as if to massage and inspect it at the same time.

"Really, I just…"

"See? Some of you bitches need to take notes on this shit here!" Alexis blurted out to no one in particular, still playing in Liaka's hair. "This is how your shit would look if you kept your shit tight! Moisturize and texturize, ladies. Moisturize and texturize. I can't tell you that enough. I can do some of my best shit with hair like this! Now, what was you saying, honey?" Alexis stated, gently pulling Liaka's head back by her hair to look up at him.

"Just a shampoo and some moisturizer. I came mainly for a pedicure," Liaka answered, enjoying the massaging strokes he gave her head.

"Yeah, girl, because even though you stay on the money with your hair, those feet look so crusty and ashy that you look like you been kicking powdered doughnuts!" Alexis said playfully with a chuckle. Everyone within ear's distance broke out in laughter.

"Uh, uh! You better leave my feet alone!" Liaka said, blushing with a chuckle herself. "Y'all gonna make me feel bad about my feet and give me a complex or something. I got cute feet."

"Tsk, tsk, tsk. Denial is not a cute thing, girl. Throwing a coat of nail polish on them do not make them cute. The best thing you got going for you is at least they small. So you're not that bad, they can be saved. A couple of weeks of soaking should soften them up," Alexis explained candidly.

Tearing down the little confidence Liaka had in her feet, a female worker approached Liaka on a rolling cart reaching for her boots. Liaka was a little hesitant in allowing her to take them off after their playful ribbing. The female unlaced and removed Liaka's quarter length pink Timberland boots, then peeled her white bobby socks from off her feet. Alexis nosily leaned over to get a better look.

"They're not as bad as I thought. But, they could still use a good soaking,"

Alexis said dryly. Liaka reclined her head back over a black porcelain sink and closed her eyes. The warm water, along with Alexis' fingers, relaxed her as they both massaged her head. Every thought in her mind, even those of Donta and the night before, seemed to merge and evaporate with the cloud of smoke rising from the sink. The only thing to distract her was the stylist who was working on her feet; she lifted her foot from the basin to push the cuticles back on her toenails.

"Another cop shoots another black man and gets away with it!" Liaka heard being spit from a woman to the left of her. Liaka had the urge to sit up and see who the voice came from, but, felt Alexis in the middle of lathering her hair up. So, she sat still, her eyes closed, trying to make out the contents of their conversation over the running water by her ears.

"It doesn't surprise me. But, let that be a little white kid from the suburbs, and you better believe you would have the National Guard in here trying to figure out what happened!" the same voice slurred.

"Think about that black man in New York. Shot forty-one times? I mean, come on! How can anyone justify shooting someone forty-one times?" another voice interjected.

"You can't! But, because it's *just another black man*, they can get away with it!"

"Forget New York. Think about what they did to those brothers who robbed that bank a few months ago!" Alexis stated.

Liaka's eyes immediately popped open.

"They didn't have to do those brothers like that!"

"But, they were robbing a bank. That's a little different," the first woman returned. Liaka knew she would never forget that voice and couldn't wait to sit up just to see who it was coming from.

"Still, I think that was wrong. They damned near executed those brothers! They just didn't want them to get away. And they would have done anything in their power to stop them. Even if it meant killing every last one of them!" Alexis spit dramatically. Liaka smiled, knowing Alexis was going to have an extra tip coming to him that week.

The rest of their dialogue was muffled due to Alexis extending the sink's nozzle over Liaka's forehead to run the warm water through her hair to rinse the shampoo out. The water showered in and out of her ears, leaving their voices broken fragments of sound. But, it was enough to remind Liaka of Olu's dying declaration: AVENGE ME! KILL DETECTIVE JOSÉ DOMINGUEZ!

"It's okay, though. 'Cause one day, they gonna start getting theirs!" was the last thing Liaka heard Alexis spit with attitude. Cracking a smile, Liaka thought to herself, *and who better to start with than Detective Dominguez.*

# $C$hapter 22 | $S$chemin'

A song from *Jadakiss* caused the crowd to erupt into frenzy on the dance floor, leaving Liaka, Asia, and Lianna visible at the bar. Convincing Asia to go out on that Saturday night wasn't too difficult. Liaka thought maybe it had something to do with Asia's hairstyle. There was no question—Alexis did the damn thang on her head! Not to mention her outfit. Strangely enough, she actually managed to squeeze into the outfit Lianna picked out for her. Sure, it was something clearly right out of the repertoire of Lianna's style of dress, but, Asia slowly rolled her hips in that tight mini-dress as if they made it for her!

"Y'all ready for something else to drink?" Lianna screamed out over the music. Liaka and Asia both nodded in agreement. With a wave of her hand, a large dark-skinned brother with six cornrows noticed Lianna's signal and walked over to the bartender. The brother whispered something in his ear for him to take notice of Lianna and her girls at the other end of the bar.

"I'll have two shots of Tequila and a strawberry Remy Red," Lianna chanted.

"And for you two ladies?" the bartender said. Liaka thought about it for a second, shrugged and said, "You know what, just give me the same." Asia looked at her with raised eyes and smiled.

"What the hell, me, too!" Asia said energetically. Both Liaka and Lianna stared at Asia with a stunned look on their faces.

Triple Crown Publications presents... $Q$ueen of $T$hieves *PART 1*

"What got into you?" Liaka questioned, as the bartender nodded at them and walked off to fill their order.

"What got into her is she wanna have some fun tonight! Shit, she looking fly as hell, we at a live ass club, and we got my nigga who will buy the bar out for us! She doing her thang. Don't hate!" Lianna snapped at Liaka, nodding to the music.

"Mind as well. It ain't like I got a man to worry about or go home to."

"Trust! With you looking like that, wearing some shit like that, it won't be long before somebody in here try to lock that shit down!" Lianna assured with a smile. Liaka couldn't believe how they were interacting with each other. It had to be one of the first nights Liaka could remember them being together for so long without them trying to tear each other's heads off. For some reason, they just had that type of effect on each other. Yet there they were, laughing and joking as if they were the best of friends. Within moments the bartender came back with their drinks.

"This is to my home girls. My down ass bitches that I know got my back, no matter what! To y'all," Lianna announced, raising one of the Tequila shots in a celebrated fashion. Liaka and Asia followed in suit. The three of them met with a three-way clink of their shot-glasses. Lianna downed the shot like a pro, without even a twitch of her nose. But, Asia and Liaka's facial expression spoke of their inexperience of drinking such a strong drink. That didn't stop them from downing their other shot in unison with Lianna.

"Oh, shit! This my jam right here! Come on, y'all!" Lianna shouted energetically, dancing off to the crowded dance floor. "Go! Go! Go!" Lianna chanted with the chorus, pumping her fist in the air singling along with 50 Cent's 'In the club'. She danced herself towards the dance floor a couple of feet in front of Liaka and Asia with her drink in hand, but, stopped short before getting lost in the crowd to turn back to Liaka.

"Don't forget what to do. 'Cause it's enough of them type niggas in here tonight, Shanice," Lianna whispered to Liaka with a wink of her eye, before disappearing onto the crowded dance floor. Liaka watched Asia out the corner of her eye hoping she didn't hear what Lianna said. Chances are she couldn't. The music was deafening.

On the drive to the club, and even when they arrived, Asia noticed how Liaka and Lianna whispered amongst each other, a little more than usual. It was obvious to her that they were sharing something juicy between them. But, they were being extremely discreet about it, so Asia was left in the dark.

The secret that eluded her was Liaka and Lianna made a pact prior to going to the club to seek out the biggest drug dealers as potential victims to possibly set up. After Liaka shared her little secret with Lianna about her night with Donta, she got the exact reaction she was expecting from Lianna, she went crazy! She loved it!

When Liaka first related her little heist to Lianna, Lianna didn't believe her. But, once Liaka convinced her that she was actually telling the truth, showing her proof as evidence, Lianna's reaction was congratulatory. Liaka executed her first heist, all on her own. Although mediocre, it created sort of an insidious bond between them, where Lianna fashioned Liaka as coming to the *other side*. The assurance that Liaka would actually follow through with what Lianna only considered idle rambling was a revelation to Lianna. For her, it was only the beginning to follow through with something bigger.

On the dance floor, Liaka and Asia were doing their thing. Whenever a brother danced in front of Liaka who she found uninteresting, she had no problem dancing over to the next brother who did capture her interest. But, Asia remained stuck on one brother pretty much the whole time. Four songs played through before Lianna emerged from out of nowhere with a full blunt in her hand, her now empty drink in the other. She took a long drag off the blunt and passed it to Liaka, followed by shaking the ice in her empty cup. Liaka shook her head no; she was still working on the first drink in her hand. Lianna shot a quick glance to see the three-fourths filled drink in Asia's hand and didn't even attempt to ask her if she was ready for another.

But, being full of surprises that night, Asia raised the drink to her lips and slowly gulped down the rest of it in one shot. Squeezing her eyes tight, Asia opened them, shook her head and handed Lianna her empty cup indicating her desire for another.

Lianna figured Asia had it in her all along. You know what they say: 'The quiet ones are always the worst ones'. Lianna knew it would only take a little coaxing to bring it out of Asia, and Lianna knew she was the perfect person to do it. Liaka kept to the beat, dancing with the brother now grinding on her from behind, but, stared at Asia slightly amused. She wondered what got into Asia as of late. Taking two drags off the blunt Lianna handed to her, Liaka was about to hand it back over to Lianna only for Asia to reach out and intercept it. If Liaka wasn't stunned enough with Asia's behavior before, her

Triple Crown Publications presents... Queen of Thieves
PART I

reaching for the blunt completely blew her mind!

There was Asia, soccer mom of the year, dancing wildly seductive, half-naked, in the middle of the dance floor, drunk, and smoking on a blunt! Three pulls on the blunt and Asia handed it back to Lianna who disappeared back into the crowd. Still amazed at Asia, it now came as no surprise for Liaka to see Asia lose all inhibitions and begin to grind herself on the brother in front of her. The brother could only lock his hands around the flesh of Asia's hips and hold on to the ride she was giving him.

It wasn't long before Lianna returned with a shot and another drink for Asia. Asia downed the shot with fervor and handed the empty shot-glass back to Lianna. Asia was definitely not the same person. But, coincidentally, Lianna was. Because before the next song came to an end, Liaka noticed her locked in a passionate tongue kiss with the large brother with the cornrows treating them to drinks; both of his hands explored every inch of her ass over her tight mini-dress. And if Liaka's eyes weren't playing tricks on her, she would have sworn that one of his hands slipped in front of her to disappear in between her thighs. Liaka chuckled, and then continued to dance with the brother behind her.

Once the dance floor calmed after about another five songs, for heads to wander off to the bar, bathroom, or lounge area, Liaka and Asia followed in turn. As far as Asia was concerned, it couldn't have happened at a better time, because the blinking lights, the heat of the tight crowd, and drinks left her head spinning. Lianna was only a few steps behind, forcefully peeling herself from the brother who had a tight hold on her, reluctant to let her go. The second floor of the bar was equipped with pool tables, two large screen projection TV's and several couches lining the outer room. They all managed to find their way there, seeking out an empty couch in the corner.

"I know you're ready for another drink by now!" Lianna said to Liaka. Liaka and Asia plopped heavily in the couch.

"Are you crazy? My head is spinning as it is!" Liaka said, with a smile plastered across her face. Lianna brushed her off, and then turned to Asia.

"What about you, girl? I know you 'bout ready for another one, right? You hanging like a real trooper tonight!" Lianna asked energetically, egging her on.

"Girl! Messing with you, I drank so much tonight that I'll be lucky if I'm not throwing up in the next half hour!" Asia slurred in a queasy tone.

"Well, we better get what we can out this nigga now! "Cause he swear he's getting some pussy tonight. And when he find out that he's not, the bar will officially be closed!" Lianna announced humorously, taking a seat on the third cushion next to Liaka. "Speaking of drinks and getting wide open, what was really good with your girl tonight, Liaka?"

"Did you see her? I was just as surprised as you! I was like, Damn! Look at my girl get live!" Liaka cheered, as they both turned to Asia. She began to blush.

"Blame that on your girl. She's the one that got me out there drinking like I done lost my mind!" Asia said.

"Don't put that on me! 'Cause I sure didn't force those drinks down your throat, *or* inhale that weed in your lungs. But, I always knew you had that in you all along," Lianna said convinced.

"I couldn't believe my eyes! I'm thinking to myself, look at her, backing that thang up, damn near doing the booty-clap on that brother like that! Like you took a page right out of Lianna's freak-a-nigga handbook!" Liaka said dramatically.

They all laughed.

"Shit! You know my saying—ain't no shame in my game! I gets it in!" Lianna announced, slapping a high five with Liaka.

"And like I told you before, don't act like just because you don't see me doing something like that, that I can't do it! You'd be surprised at what I can do to my man behind closed doors," Asia said with a grin, snapping her fingers.

"Man! What man? You ain't got no man! That nigga left you for the next bitch!" Lianna said sharply, and then burst out laughing. Liaka chuckled, but, then turned to Asia. The smile quickly faded from her face. Lianna was oblivious; she took another deep breath and laughed even harder, slapping her knee for added effect. It took a poke to her side and a twisted look from Liaka for Lianna to calm down. "What? I know she ain't thinking about that nigga no more! 'Cause he sure ain't thinking about her!" Lianna huffed unmercifully, casually taking a sip of her drink.

"Still, that's not funny. You don't say shit like that! You..."

"No, she's right," Asia spoke up. "For once, this crazy ass heifer is actually right. Donovan ain't thinking about me. And the quicker I realize that and put him out of my mind, the better off I'll be," Asia said painfully.

"You damned right, I'm right! With all these fine ass brothers in here,

Triple Crown Publications presents... Queen of Thieves *PART 1*

sweating the shit outta you, as good as you look, and you sitting here worried about him? That nigga is pushing up in the next bitch! You think he's thinking about you when he's doing THAT? Shit! You better wake up! I know just what you need—you need a big ass dick! A thug nigga that will tear your shit down! Because the problem with you is, you been messing with Donovan for so long, that that's all you know. You spent all those years fucking *one* dick, that you think that's all you deserve! Like you not supposed to move on with your life, even though he clearly moved on with his. Trust me, find that diesel brother that you was grinding on, take that nigga home with you tonight, and fuck that nigga until every thought of Donovan is gone!" Lianna said sharply, followed by a wink, downing the rest of her drink. The smile returned to Asia's face.

"That brother was fine, and big. What was he wearing, like a size fourteen sneaker? And the way he was grinding on me, I wonder if he could put those hips to work like that in the..."

"Asia!" Liaka blurted, playfully slapping Asia's arm with a smile. Asia giggled.

"Girl, you know I'm only playing. You both managed to convince me to walk out of the house with these 'fuck me' clothes on. But, I don't think I'm quite ready to take it to the level where I can live up to my appearance."

"Well, if you don't wanna do that, you know I can still call Kenny," Lianna said casually.

"Yo, lil' cutie, how you..."

"We ain't interested!" Lianna spit harshly at a brother who leaned down to talk to her. The brother quickly leaned back up, his smile faded into a scowl. He eyed her evilly, sucked his teeth, and spewed, "stuck up bitch!" then rolled his eyes and walked off.

"I wasn't a bitch one second ago when you was trying to get at this bitch!" Lianna yelled out, causing everyone within ears distance to look over at them. The brother simply threw his middle finger up over his shoulder without looking back and disappeared into the crowd.

"Anyways, back to what I was saying. Yeah, I can call Kenny for us tonight," Lianna said, as if nothing happened.

"Kenny?" Asia said curiously.

"Girl, don't ask. Trust me, you don't wanna know," Liaka said with a chuckle.

"No, serious. What is she talking about? Who the hell is Kenny?"

"That's my lil' jump-off, my lil' side thang. Every bitch gots to have one. And Asia, girl, that nigga got a degree at the university of *eating pussyology!* He mastered that shit! I trained that nigga to perfection. After we leave here, I can call him and have him hit you off. Trust, he will bless you lovely. Best head you ever had," Lianna stressed with a stern nod. Asia spun to Liaka with an amused look on her face.

"Is she serious?"

"You thought I was playing? I told you not to ask," Liaka answered, with a shake of her head.

"You say it like that's a bad thing. Asia, when I told you to put that outfit on, was I wrong? No. 'Cause that shit look slamming on you, and you know it! When I told you to come out tonight and promised that we would have a good time, was I wrong? No! 'Cause you was just out there ten minutes ago, damn near doing the *Beyoncé* on that nigga, laughing, having a good ole time! So, just trust me on this one. All you gots to do is lay back and let my toy do the rest. Just look at it like this: consider him a massage therapist who is just gonna give you a massage. A really, *really* good massage. But, instead of using his hands, he uses his tongue and...ump! No, that's it! It's final. I'm calling him," Lianna said, closing her eyes as a chill came over her just thinking about him.

She unclipped the cell phone on the waist of her mini-skirt. Liaka smirked at Lianna, and then turned to Asia to see her sitting silently with a devilish look in her eyes. Asia watched eagerly as Lianna flipped the phone open and dialed.

"Um, aren't you gonna say something? Tell her to stop, something?" Liaka said humorously, as if she let the joke go on long enough. She noticed Asia staring at Lianna greedily, biting her bottom lip.

Asia broke from her daze, shot a glance at Liaka, then turned to Lianna saying, "Um...yeah, don't...don't call him. I can't do that."

Lianna turned to Asia in mid-dial to see if she could read her. Their eyes locked, a wicked smirk spread across Asia's face. Their brief moment spoke volumes and told Lianna all she needed to know. Lianna worked too hard to pull Asia out of her shell for Liaka to rain on their parade. Lianna opened her mouth to speak, but, stopped as all of them looked up to see the large brother Lianna was dancing with part through the crowd to approach them.

"Y'all sure y'all don't want something else to drink? 'Cause I'm 'bout ready for a refill," Lianna said, with a deliberate look at them, slicing unknowing eyes to the brother over her shoulder. Asia caught on.

"You know what? I think I am ready for another one. Nothing too strong though. Just a beer," Asia said, as a smile spread across Lianna's face.

"I'm good. I'm still working on this one," Liaka stated, lifting up her drink. A subtle sigh escaped Lianna's lips.

"Papi, get my girl that beer. And come on, 'cause I need you to beat this nigga ass! He gonna come over here disrespecting me and my girls cause we didn't wanna give him no play! I told him we was with you, but, he still started calling us bitches and all that! And I just know you ain't gonna let him get away with talking to your girl like that," Lianna purred innocently, rubbing up against him. His lip curled and his eyes squinted into an evil glare as Lianna snuggled under his arm, leading him off into the crowd.

"I know she's not serious?" Asia said.

"I thought you would have learned by now. Lianna is crazy! Knowing her, she's probably pointing out that kid that came over here and gassing that big brother up so much that he'll just beat the kid up without even saying a word! Don't be surprised if any minute they shut the club down because a fight breaks out. She love putting shit in the game like that: get two brothers fighting and swear they fighting over her!"

Lianna came back minutes later to drop Asia's beer off, But, didn't stay long enough to say a word, vanishing back into the crowd with her male friend. For the rest of the night, Liaka and Asia remained in the upper lounge with Liaka occasionally stepping off with a few random brothers who approached her. The new alias, Chanel, was given out to each of them as Liaka insisted on taking their numbers, refusing to give out hers.

The club began to let up at about two thirty in the morning. Liaka was so tired and drunk, trying her best to keep focused on the road, that she paid little attention to Lianna in the back seat being secretive as she whispered into her cell phone. Asia was in the passenger seat pretty much out of it herself; eyes closed, head leaned back against the headrest.

"Asia, you coming over to my house, right?" Lianna questioned eagerly from the back seat, piercing the silence of the car. As tired and drunk as Liaka was, she shot a glance at Asia to the side of her, then back to the road, unsure of what was going on.

"Wha...what?"

"You still coming over, right?" Lianna repeated. The glance was quick, a split second at most, but, Liaka caught Asia peeking at her out the corner of her eye.

"Yeah, I don't care," Asia mumbled weakly, and then closed her eyes to rest her head again. Nothing more needed to be said. Because in the history of their associations, Asia spoke most passionately about her reluctance of even hanging out with Lianna, let alone spending the night at her house. Liaka knew what time it was, but, decided to keep her two cents to herself. She didn't blame Asia.

She figured Asia needed a little comfort to help her alleviate some of the tension she still held in from Donovan. Hell! Liaka even entertained the thought that if her 'girlfriend' wasn't visiting she would have probably taken Lianna up on the same offer herself. Because from Lianna's description about the skills Kenny possessed and the notorious tongue he had, that would be just the type of massage she could use. Olu was the last man Liaka had sex with, and the pressure was building. Being deprived of Olu's touch left that void in Liaka and her body began to feel it.

Although it was close to three A.M. when Liaka pulled up in front of Lianna's building, there were brothers hugging the block at the end of Lianna's corner. Asia opened the passenger door and stepped out without saying a word or looking back. There wasn't much to say. Liaka knew that any attempt to explain her reasoning behind staying the night at Lianna's would only reveal the obvious. Silence was better.

"All right, girl. I'll get up tomorrow," Lianna said, lifting the passenger seat to step out. Asia flashed one last innocent glance at Liaka before walking off with Lianna. As tempting as it was for Liaka to speak out and tease Asia, being the words were on the tip of her tongue, Liaka let her go, knowing it had to be hard enough for Asia to do something like that without the extra harassment coming from Liaka. Liaka was actually proud of her girl for attempting to break out of her shell. She snickered and pulled off.

The drive to Liaka's house, although only a few minutes away, presented extreme difficulties for her. She was drunk, high, and physically drained from such a long day. The silence of her car only contributed to the sleepy feeling overcoming her. Struggling to keep her eyes opened and focused on the road, Liaka swerved in and out of traffic; the white lines dividing the lanes formed a solid blur. Liaka tore through a few stop signs, and even a red light, inevitably gaining the attention of a patrolling police car. Just a few blocks away from her apartment, Liaka was snapped awake by the sound of two chirps of a police siren behind her. She forced her eyes up to the rearview to see the red and blue flashing light behind her.

"How you doing tonight? Is everything okay?" The cop directed the bright beam of his flashlight in Liaka's face; she squinted from the glare.

"Ah, yeah. Just heading home. The club...I just came from...is there a problem?" Liaka stuttered, trying to avoid eye contact with him.

"Well, you just ran a red light, blew through the last two stop signs, and seem to be having difficulties staying in between the lines, not to mention you were speeding," the officer narrated in a calm, yet stern tone.

"Are you serious? I'm so, so sorry. I'm just really, really tired. I just had a long day, so..."

"Can I please see your license and registration?"

"My license? Um...yeah, sure," Liaka fumbled through her handbag. The cop flashed his light in Liaka's handbag, watching her every move. "Here you go. I was just trying to get home. I'm sorry. If..."

"Could you please step out of the car, ma'am."

The cop opened the driver's side door for Liaka then took a step back. She rose from the car, wiggled her skirt down in two steps and closed the door behind her. The short mini-skirt, her calf high, three-inch black leather boots, and her tight-half top, exposed most of the flesh on her body causing the nippy night air to give her the chills. Her teeth chattered in her mouth, and the frigid wind contributed by the occasional passing car, prompted Liaka to fold her arms over her chest.

"Have you had anything to drink tonight, ma'am?" the officer posed bluntly, after inspecting Liaka's driver's license. Liaka knew her last attempt now was to try to seduce him or, within the hour, she would probably be headed for a jail cell. She put on the most innocent mien she could muster; doe eyes, a sad pathetic look, her lip poked out.

"Mister Officer, I...I only had a couple of drinks. Two drinks, that's it. But, I'm not drunk or anything, I promise. I'm just tired," Liaka sighed, in a remorseful tone.

"Do you know that you almost hit a parked car from you being so *tired*?"

"No, and I'm so sorry. I was just really trying to get home," Liaka pleaded, her body visibly trembling from the cold. The cop looked at Liaka, her body trembling considerably, and said sympathetically, "you can get your coat from the back seat, Miss Sikes," waving her off to her car.

Leaning in the car, Liaka peeked out her back window to see the cop staring at her. But, instead of being concerned with her fumbling in the back seat, his eyes were glued to her ass and thighs sticking halfway out the car. Liaka purposely arched her back a little more, teasingly, the back hem of her skirt rising a little higher to expose more of the back of her thighs. After giving him more than an eyeful, she rose from the back seat with her coat.

"I'm going to have to give you a sobriety test to determine your blood alcohol count," the officer announced flatly and he turned to walk off to his car.

"No! Wait! A what? But...but, I'm NOT drunk! Please, Mister...what's your name?" Liaka called out to him. He stopped to turn around to face her. Walking back to approach her, Liaka had the first opportunity to get a good look in his face. He was a brown-skinned brother, probably in his mid to late twenties, a clean-shaven face. His uniform hat prevented Liaka from seeing his hairstyle, but, it was short on the sides; probably waves and a fade. He stood over six feet. The comment Liaka made didn't quite produce a smile, but, it did help reveal his row of top teeth.

"My name is Officer Cooney. And, I'm sorry, but, I have to..."

"No, your *name* name. Your first name," Liaka pressed avidly. The cop looked at Liaka with curiosity; curiosity fading into interest.

"David. David Cooney. But..."

"David. Can I call you David? Look, David, I'm a paralegal at a prestigious law firm, the Hertzberg firm. I'm on my third year of study to take the bar exam, because it is my goal to become a lawyer one day. Here, look...," Liaka said impulsively, quickly sprinting off to her car to return with her handbag. She handed the officer her paralegal business card.

He raised his eyes from the card and attempted to speak before Liaka spit, "...I was out celebrating tonight with a few of my girls, and we had a couple of drinks. Not too much, just a couple. Just a couple of drinks to celebrate a special occasion. But, I'm not drunk at all. So, please, I can't get a ticket or something popping up on my record and possibly hurting my chances or affecting my future. Please!"

The cop sighed heavily, saying, "Miss Sikes, I can't..."

"Maliaka," Liaka said, through innocent eyes.

"Maliaka, I..."

"I live less than five blocks from here. Not even two minutes down the street. Please, I'm going straight home. *Please!*" Liaka stressed. The officer stared blankly at Liaka for a few seconds before finally cracking a slight smile. He returned his attention back to her license and her business card in his hand, examined it, and looked around to where they were, then back to Liaka.

"Just a few blocks. Right around the corner. You could practically throw me from here," Liaka said playfully. He let out a slight chuckle. He took a deep breath and exhaled heavily, handing her back her driver's license and card.

"Maliaka, you're gonna make a great litigator one day. Look, tonight's your lucky night. Straight home! I don't want you out here hurting anybody, especially yourself," the office said, with a warm smile.

"Thank you, David. I really mean it. Thank you," Liaka purred, receiving the items back from him, purposely caressing his hand. Liaka turned to walk off to her car breathing a sigh of relief.

"Miss Sikes...Maliaka, if I can call you, Maliaka. It is extremely unusual for me to do something like this. But...but, I was wondering, would it be...would you like to have dinner some time?" the officer asked, somewhat embarrassed. Liaka looked up at him as he approached; how his stern, firm demeanor evaporated, exposing his vulnerable side.

"Um, sure," Liaka answered, thrown off herself by his invitation.

"Great. Here's my card. Maybe when you're not so tired you can give me a call," he returned energetically, pulling a card from his pocket. Liaka took a seat behind the wheel and watched as he rounded the back of her vehicle to pull off with a honk. As his taillights faded into the darkness of night, Liaka lifted his card to her face. David P. Cooney, Hartford Police Department. The corner of her lip curled. The conversation from the hair salon began to ring an eerie tune in her head. Cops killing black men—cops killed Olu!

"AVENGE ME, MY WIFE! AVENGE ME!" Olu's dying declaration struck her. Liaka squeezed the card in her hand, partially crumpling it, until she tossed it in her passenger seat and pulled off.

# Chapter 23 | His Name Is Tylon

Liaka closed Lianna's refrigerator door after pouring herself something to drink. A few days had passed since their night out at the club. From the start of the week, Liaka had been so swamped with work that she barely had enough time to get a good night's sleep, let alone hang out with her girls. But, the following Thursday, after three successfully prepared depositions, Liaka finally managed to squeeze some time in to go see Lianna.

"Damn! So much for thinking about me!" Lianna snapped, as she watched Liaka rest wearily into the loveseat next to her, raising the ice cold drink to her lips.

"Stop complaining. I work all day. And this is your house, so you supposed to be serving me," Liaka returned, swallowing another mouthful.

"Serving you? Please! What I look like, Florence from the Jefferson's?" Lianna spit humorously, clicking through the channels on her TV remote. "And you working ain't got nothing to do with you getting your girl something to drink. Shit, you was right there."

"I know, I know. My mind was just someplace else. I was thinking if I remembered to reference this case in this motion that I filed today."

"Well, what you should be thinking about is if you handled your business on Saturday night. Or were you so drunk that you forgot what we went there for?"

"I should be asking you that! The way you was all over that brother, I just know you ain't get no numbers."

"Shit! You must not know who you talking to! I always gots to have my lil' nigga on the side that will get us the drinks, maybe treat us to dinner after, shit like that. But, I always handle mines!" Lianna related with a smile, kissing a flame to the tip of a cigarette.

"Oh really? And how you handling your business with the next man all over you?"

"Hun? I got six numbers right up under his nose, and I could have got more! Being hugged up with the next nigga at the club ain't gonna stop the next nigga from approaching you. All you gots to do is flash a nigga a smile, maybe wink at him, and the minute you step off from the nigga you with, TRUST, the next nigga will follow you. Shit! I was hugged up with that big nigga and this brother literally handed me his number right over his shoulder! I just cuffed it in my hand and kept it moving like nothing happened."

"Girl, you a mess," Liaka chuckled.

"If I'm a mess, then them niggas is a mess too! Don't think them niggas don't be with they girls, they wives, and right when I step off from the nigga I'm with to go to the bathroom or something, they on me! Trying to get some ass on the sly, or get up in my mouth. And shit! If the next bitch can't handle her *business*, and if the nigga look good and he 'bout it', I might hit that nigga off with a lil' somethin'-somethin'. And what do you think gonna happen after that? They gonna go right back to their girl like nothing happened. And me? I'll go back to the nigga I'm with, sipping my drink, and no one's the wiser. From that point on, me and the next nigga know—we got a secret. And I know I just got another nigga up under my wing. I didn't invent *The Game*, or make the rules. But, I'll be damned if I'm not one of its best players!"

"Every time I think there's absolutely nothing else you could say to surprise me—you say some shit that surprises me!" Liaka said amused.

"Liaka, that nigga was fine! He put the "F" in fine. I had to get a piece of that! And the way he pushed me in the bathroom stall, all them people around, and took control of me like that...um! He had me like putty in his hands," Lianna confessed, with a wicked smirk.

"And you truly went right back out there to that big brother you was with!"

"So. And? At least I didn't kiss him after that."

"What are you talking about? Yes, you did! I saw you kissing all over him when we left the club!"

"Correction—I never kissed him, he kissed me. There's a big difference," Lianna said calmly, blowing a cloud of cigarette smoke.

"Girl, you ain't shit!" Liaka said laughing.

"Where do you think I got shit like that from? Niggas! And speaking of niggas, back to what I was saying. Did you get some numbers or not? Or was my little confession of hitting a nigga off your way of distracting me from the question?"

"No. I'm not trying to distract you from the question. And yes, I did get some numbers. But, not only did I get a few numbers, I got the number from the perfect one we can get," Liaka explained confidently.

"No, you didn't."

"And why didn't I?"

"Because *I* got the number from the perfect one we can get first!" Lianna stressed. "I damn near patted that nigga down right there in the club. And his pockets were on swoll—with money! And I can tell by the way he move and his game, that he's sweet. Easy money. But, listen to you, talking 'bout how you got the perfect one. Like you really know what you doing. Like you a gangstress or something."

"If you don't remember, I already got one. So as the saying goes—I'm one up on you," Liaka said, with one eyebrow raised.

"What? Pickpocket a nigga that was sleeping? Wow! Whoopee. Who can't do that? I'M talking about taking a nigga shit while he's *awake*! Some gangster shit! This time we gonna do it right. Don't get me wrong. I give you your props for even doing that. You surprised me on that one. To keep it real, I thought you were just talking out the side of your neck. But, you really came through. By the way, what about your girl, Asia? Did you tell her about your little stick yet?" Lianna asked, extinguishing her cigarette in the ashtray, reaching for a blunt.

"Asia? Are you crazy? Miss goodie-goodie would lose her mind if I told her something like that! She would have a fit."

"Hmph! I don't think she can act all like a goodie-goodie anymore," Lianna said in an ambiguous tone, tearing the wrapper off the blunt.

"Why you say it like...oooohhh! What happened that night? Tell me she didn't do it?" Liaka asked eagerly, leaning in her seat towards Lianna.

"Do it. Do what?" Lianna said, feigning ignorance. Liaka instantly hit her with a twisted look, watching Lianna as she took the nail of her thumb to slice the blunt down the middle. She dumped the blunt tobacco in the ashtray with a blank look on her face.

"Don't play stupid with me! You know what the hell I'm talking about. Kenny! Your little 'toy' thing! All of a sudden she just wants to mysteriously hang out with you and spend the night at your house? Yeah, like I wasn't gonna see clear through that! So tell me. Did you call Kenny? Did she do it?" Liaka pressed, the anxious look on her face revealing how badly she wanted to know the answer. Lianna reached into the crack of her couch and pulled out a small Ziploc bag of weed. She began to fill the empty blunt wrapper in silence. Securing the blunt closed and raising a lighter to the tip, Lianna took a few pulls and turned to Liaka with a huge smile plastered across her face.

"Liaka, let me tell you. Kenny had that girl wide open!" Lianna exclaimed dramatically. Liaka exploded in laughter, throwing herself back into the loveseat, stomping her feet.

"No! No! You lying! You can't be serious! You playing! I just know you playing!" Liaka cried, hardly able to contain herself. "Tell me. Please! I gotta hear *exactly* how it happened!"

"Well, when we got back here, Kenny was already here waiting. He was chillin' in his car smoking a blunt. But, I knew he was gonna be here anyways. I don't care what time it is. All I gotta do is call him and tell him to come over, and he'll be over here in record speed! And when I told him that I needed him to do me a favor and hit off my girl, I could damn near see that nigga smiling through the phone. And then when he finally seen Asia, that nigga had a look on his face like he was a kid in a candy store. I gave Asia my house keys and told her to go up to my place and I'd be there in a minute. Then I met up with Kenny and schooled him to what time it was. You know, being Asia was new to that type of shit and all. And girl, you should have seen how 'green' she was right when me and Kenny went up into the living room."

"She was sitting on the couch all nervous an' shit. So, to put her at ease, I told her we wasn't gonna do it anymore. I said I changed my mind and that he was just gonna give her a regular massage. I told her to go to my bedroom and I was gonna get us something to drink. Do you know, as long as I've known her, I never seen her acting all like that—all shy and nervous. So I brought her a drink and told her to just relax. She damned near drank the whole glass in one gulp! I purposely kept the lights off so it was pitch black in there. Kenny came in there a few minutes later. Right when that nigga walked in, you already know, I had him in 'toy-mode', so I put him right on the floor, hands and knees, and told him to crawl the rest of the way to the bed.

"I couldn't really see Asia's reaction, but, I know she was buggin'. I then ordered Kenny to take off Asia's boots and to give her a foot massage. He did it. But, that nigga started to piss me off, because, without me even telling him, he began to lick and suck on her toes! That wasn't part of the fuckin' deal! But, instead of buggin', once I seen Asia starting to relax, I left. I figured I'd discipline that nigga later," Lianna narrated, sucking in a mouthful of smoke from the blunt. She extended it to Liaka who shook her head no. She was more concerned with the story Lianna was telling her. Lianna shrugged.

"Okay, keep going. 'Cause I know that ain't it. Tell me," Liaka said impulsively. Lianna exhaled a large cloud of smoke trying to suppress a smile.

"I waited like fifteen minutes and peeked my head back in to see what was going on. And girl, Kenny was going to work on her! I taught my toy well, so I saw he was taking his time. But, soon enough, he had her crying out like he was killing her! And I know she heard me walk in. But, he had her so fucked up and she was holding his head so tight between her thighs, I was surprised she ain't suffocate him!" They both burst out in laughter. "And now that I think about it, that bitch owe me some money! 'Cause she sure enough fucked my sheets up! I thought I was bad. But, you would of thought she ain't get none in a year! And you know what...," Lianna paused, as she stared off with a pensive look on her face.

"What?"

"I saw how Kenny was acting when we dropped Asia off, how he was looking at her. 'Cause I sure wasn't letting them both leave my house together, alone! But, now that he knows where she lives, let me catch that bitch creeping with my *toy* on the low after I tried to do her a favor!" Lianna huffed, in a cynical tone.

"Yeah, Asia's really gonna do something like that!" Liaka said sarcastically, with a roll of her eyes.

"Shit! Don't put it past her. If I left it up to you, from what you thought, she would have never let Kenny get at her like that in the first place! Understand human nature—everyone got the potential to travel to dark places in their heart. And everybody sure enough got it in them to get they sneak on," Lianna returned sternly.

Liaka had no comeback. She knew Lianna made a good point. Because never in a million years would she have thought Asia to indulge in such behavior. Lianna accepted Liaka's silence as a sign that she was right. Lianna tapped the ashes from the blunt in the ashtray and disappeared off to her bedroom; a cloud of smoke trailed her head in a whirlwind from behind. Thinking about Asia's little tryst with Kenny, Liaka glanced up a few minutes later to see Lianna entering the room.

"Are you crazy? Where did you get that? Put that away!" Liaka gasped wide-eyed, as Lianna whipped out a gun that she was concealing behind her back.

"Stop acting so scary. It's my brother's gun. And *this* is how we gonna do our stick-up!" Lianna stated, waving the gun in her hand.

"Give it to me! You don't know what you're doing. You're gonna mess around and have that thing go off!" Liaka stressed, ducking and dodging from the line of fire as Lianna swung the gun around, her finger dangerously circled around the trigger. The blunt was held between Lianna's lips causing the smoke to hug a cloud up her face. The cloud of smoke partially shielded the mischievous smirk on Lianna's face as she stood with the gun like a *Bonnie* without a *Clyde*. Liaka had to admit, Lianna looked a little menacing in that position. But, with the smoke fogging her vision, and Lianna being a little high, Liaka knew she had to remove such a deadly weapon from her hands.

"Give it to you? What you know about a ratchet?" Lianna stated in a mocking tone, still waving the gun in her hand. Liaka carefully reached out with both hands to point the gun away from her and remove it from Lianna's. It was a .380 semi-automatic.

Engaging the safety, Liaka clicked a lever for the magazine to pop out. The eight shot clip held five bullets in it. Liaka inserted it back in. She snapped back the head of the gun and looked into check the chamber. A single bullet popped out and fell to the floor. She released the head for the gun to click back in place, a bullet chambered and ready to fire. Liaka pointed the gun at the floor and slowly lowered the hammer into the weapon, all the while with Lianna staring at her dumbfounded.

"How did you know how to do all that?"

"I told you, Olu taught me how to use a gun. He taught me on a nine, but, this doesn't look too much different," Liaka answered casually, picking up the bullet from the floor. Lianna instantly went to grab for her sneakers and coat without saying another word. "What are you doing?"

"We 'bout to do this—right now! The nigga name is Tylon. He lives in New Haven. Trust, this nigga's easy money."

Triple Crown Publications presents... Queen of Thieves
PART 1

# $C$hapter 24 | $L$et's $D$o $T$his!

$H$ey, Papi, you busy? No, it's me, Stephanie. Yeah, I told you I was gonna call you by next week. Well, here I am, Papi. I'm calling," Lianna said, with Liaka by her side. Liaka occasionally glanced around at the late evening downtown traffic. "Yeah, tonight. I don't know, you tell me. Where am I? Right now I'm in downtown Hartford. I just picked a couple of things up. But, I'm 'bout to go back home. I live in Meriden," Lianna said, winking her eye at Liaka.

"Yeah, I'm going home now. I want you to pick me up at my house. Matter of fact, do you know where the *McDonalds* is on Main Street in Meriden? You ain't got to say it all like that! You silly. Well, this is how you get there. Where you coming from, New Haven? Okay, just get off the first exit in Meriden, take that left, and you'll see the arrow's directing you to a *McDonalds*. No...no...it's easy. Yeah...Okay...yeah. I'm going there now. You already know, baby. That sound good. It better be one with a Jacuzzi and room service. Holla! All right, forty-five minutes. I'll see you then, Papi," Lianna ended with a purr, hanging up the phone. Lianna and Liaka shared a brief glance before jumping back in Liaka's car and taking off.

Liaka pulled into a parking lot across the street from the *McDonalds* in Meriden. She found the most secluded spot out of view from the road and parked. Lianna walked right up to the counter and ordered; a Big Mac, extra-large French fry, and a large coke. Liaka couldn't understand how Lianna could eat at a time like that, especially when her stomach was twisting in knots with nervous anticipation. Taking money off a sleeping Donta was one thing. But, with Lianna now involved, armed with a weapon, Liaka knew she had to expect the unexpected.

They both sat at an empty table with Liaka taking occasional sips of Lianna's soda. Lianna munched down on her burger and fries as if she didn't have a care in the world. Seated at a table facing the parking lot, Lianna flirted with just about every cute brother who entered the place. Liaka sat in silence, running through countless scenarios in her mind of how they were going to pull it off. Close to twenty minutes passed before Lianna began to tap excitedly on the window, signaling to a jet black four-door *Jaguar* creeping into the parking lot.

"You ready?" Lianna asked, slurping on the last of her soda. Liaka returned a weak nod. Throwing her trash in the garbage, Lianna boldly emerged through the restaurant doors headed straight for his vehicle. "I need you to do me a favor, baby..." Lianna opened his passenger door to stick her head in, "...can you just drop my girl off? She only live right down the street from me. It's not that far." The driver looked over his shoulder back at Liaka. He nodded a quick yes for Lianna to jump in the passenger seat, Liaka in the back.

"Just tell me how to get there, 'cause I ain't never been out this motherfucka! This shit look crazy as fuck out here," the driver said. He reversed, and then pulled out of the parking lot onto the street.

"Yeah, take this right and go straight ahead. I'll tell you where to go next," Lianna instructed, having no idea where she was going herself. She didn't know a soul who lived in Meriden and was only familiar with the *McDonalds* based on a previous date. The driver did as she instructed, then slightly turned up a track from *Lil' Wayne* on his car system.

The butter-soft, green leather interior hugged Liaka's curves, yet Liaka was anything but comfortable as she sat, staring nervously at the back of Lianna's head. The spontaneity of what they were doing left Liaka with no idea as to how Lianna planned on going about it. Little did Liaka know; Lianna didn't have any set plans herself. She was just playing it by ear as they went along. Lianna took mental notes of the streets they traveled, the distance they were driving, from the two rights they just took, and exactly how to get back.

"Take this right," Lianna instructed, as they approached a stop sign. The street was pitch black and fairly secluded. "Do you mind if I smoke?" Lianna posed. The driver shrugged. Lianna passed a glance over her shoulder at Liaka who stared back at her with paranoid eyes. Lianna smiled as she turned back in her seat. Reaching into the inside pocket of her leather coat, Liaka's eyes widened the second she witnessed Lianna pull the gun out.

"Pull over, motherfucka!" Lianna ordered thickly, pointing the gun in his direction. Liaka shot her attention at him to see that he casually glanced at Lianna, down to the gun, and then smirked before focusing back on the road.

"Go 'head, ma. Stop playing. Put that shit away before you hurt someone, or get hurt, all right?" he responded nonchalantly. "You know, if I was the wrong type of nigga, I mighta taken that shit serious. That's really cute, though. Which way do I go now to take your lil' friend home?" he said, as they rolled through a stop sign. The look on Lianna's face transformed from a nervous fear into pure rage. She began to lower the gun and Liaka thought that was pretty much it, until...

BLAP!

Lianna's hand jerked from pulling the trigger. A thunderous clap rang from the barrel, producing a flash of light in the tight interior. The bullet tore into his right thigh causing him to scream out in agony and almost lose control of the vehicle.

"You think I'm playing now, motherfucka? I said pull this shit tha fuck over, bitch!" Lianna screamed, aiming the gun directly to the side of his face. Every muscle in Liaka's body tightened, even her legs. But, not fast enough to prevent the squirt of urine that shot from her in fear. With only one leg, the expensive automobile careened sideways—his chrome rims shredded up as they scraped the curb on the side of the road—before smashing head on into another parked car at about thirty miles per hour.

The abrupt stop caused the three of them to be thrown forward in their seats. Before Lianna could even gather herself, she was met by the driver throwing himself at her, reaching for the gun in her hand. Liaka finally picked herself up from the floor of the back seat to see the four hands of Lianna and the driver both struggling for control of the weapon.

BLAP! BLAP!

Another two shots rang out, one blasting through the sunroof to rain down fragments of glass on them, the other through the roof of the car.

Liaka jumped in fear, crouching for cover behind the seats from the aimless shots.

"Come on! Hit this motherfucka!" Lianna cried out, struggling with every ounce of her being to retrieve the gun. Liaka was paralyzed, her mind raced, she didn't know what to do. Before her mind could register the gravity of their altercation, she witnessed the driver release one hand from the gun and throw a wild haymaker punch at Lianna's face.

The punch barely missed her, and from what Liaka could see, he was cocking back for another. Something came over Liaka. A pure rush of adrenaline prompted her to jump from the back seat, run around to swing the driver's door open, and begin to yank wildly on the back of his coat. As Liaka yanked with jerking thrusts on the back of his coat, and Lianna still tussling for the gun, another shot went off, that one fatally close to Lianna's head, shattering the passenger window behind her. It took close to a minute of them struggling with him before the loss of blood and energy began to take its toll. With the last of his energy drained, Lianna finally managed to snatch the pistol from his hand.

"You wanna shoot at me, motherfucka? Huh?" Lianna screamed dementedly, recklessly swinging the handle of the gun at his face, violently pistol whipping him. The butt of the gun instantly broke his nose and split him open above his eye. Blood spilled from his face, even splattered a bloody spray across her own.

"I told you to pull this motherfucka over! If your stupid ass woulda just listened, none of this shit would have happened!" Lianna screamed, hitting him with almost every word she spoke. Her hands and the butt of the gun were covered in blood from the blows she inflicted on him. Lianna then aimed the blood-stained gun at his head, and was a second away from pulling the trigger, before a final yank from Liaka made his head and upper body fall lifelessly halfway out the car. Lianna leaned forward to dig her hand into his pockets, the other holding the gun pressed to his temple. Liaka immediately followed in turn as they both ravished his flaccid frame like a pack of wild dogs ripping into all of his pockets.

A few weak moans escaped his lips, followed by slight movement. With each of his pockets forcibly turned inside out, Liaka held a knot of money in one hand as Lianna swung the gun handle down on his groin with one final blow. He wailed out in excruciating pain. Lianna began kicking his

Triple Crown Publications presents... Queen of Thieves PART 1

lower body, trying to force him completely from the vehicle. With one final yank from Liaka, he fell to the pavement with a thud. Liaka stood over him, staring down at his mutilated body at her feet.

"What are you waiting for? Let's get the fuck outta here!" Lianna cried hysterically, spinning her head wildly to survey the scene. Headlights could be seen creeping in from the corner end of the street. Lianna shot a second look at Liaka with panic stricken eyes. Liaka looked down at the driver again on the ground, and then squeamishly stepped over him to take the wheel.

The driver's seat was covered in blood, but, Liaka took the seat, slamming the door behind her. She grabbed the steering wheel. It slid between her fingers from the blood coating it, but, she still managed to shift the transmission into first gear, backed up over his legs, and turned to screech off.

# $C$hapter 25 | $O$fficer $C$ooney

$L$iaka immersed herself in work trying to distract her mind from the stick-up she and Lianna engaged in a few days prior. The altercation generated conflicting feels within her. On the one hand, all the blood their violent beating produced rocked her to her core. Rushing straight to her bathroom when she finally arrived home, Liaka clicked on the light to see the amount of blood staining most of her clothes. The darkness of night distorted the actual bloodshed of the scene. Liaka knew it was severe from the way his drying blood stuck her hands to the steering wheel. Liaka drove at dangerously fatal speeds to get back to her car. His bullet-ridden vehicle was the scene of a crime, and Liaka wanted to get out of it and distance herself from it as soon as possible.

A reflection of herself in the mirror when she got home revealed splatters of blood all over her clothes, even a spray of spots across her face. Liaka remembered her hands. A thin layer of blood coated them, made her fingers stick together. She knew she would never forget the amount of blood. This ironically produced the second conflicting feeling within her.

From gazing down to the dried, sticky blood on her hands, Liaka raised her eyes to stare deeply at herself in the bathroom mirror. An evil smirk spread across her face. The stain of blood had now become a reminder, a visual memory of the heist they pulled off. The crimson stain on her hand, physical evidence that she actually did it.

For the first time since Olu shared his wickedly intriguing tales, Liaka felt remnants of those feelings, the feelings that set her soul afire. But, this time, instead of living vicariously through Olu or Shakim, the mere glance at her own reflection in the mirror, staring into the windows of her own soul, produced those feelings.

Throughout her workday, Liaka was constantly revisited by those images. Another reoccurring image was Lianna's reaction to it all; the extreme sense of pleasure she seemed to derive from it, the fiendishly diabolical laugh she heckled as they drove off back to her place. Lianna stressed to Liaka how despite only making off with a little less than fifteen hundred dollars, how the extreme rush of excitement she received from robbing someone, how she felt so alive, that she couldn't wait to do it again. Taking a break to stretch her legs from her workstation, Liaka returned only a few moments later sipping a bottle of spring water to see the light on her phone blinking.

"Hello, you have reached the law offices of Hertzberg, Hertzberg, Fox and Green. This is Maliaka Sikes speaking. Are you presently represented by us?" Liaka posed politely, taking a seat behind her desk.

"No, I'm not. But, I was still wondering if you could help me?"

"I'll see if I can."

"I was looking to retain the services of an attorney for a slight problem I've been having."

"I'm not an attorney. But, what sort of problem?" Liaka asked sincerely, scurrying to grab a pen and yellow notepad on the side of her desk.

"It's been my mind. Ever since I've met this beautiful young lady, I can't seem to get her off my mind," the voice elaborated. Liaka lifted the pen from the pad, a smile spread across her face.

"Who is this?" Liaka asked brightly.

"Just a man who had his heart touched by your mere presence. So, do you think a lawyer will help me with my case?" the voice asked. Liaka sat back in her chair, still beaming.

"Sure. I'm sure someone in this office has the legal expertise to help litigate matters as serious as yours. May I have your name please?" Liaka said playfully.

"Yes. My name is Officer David Cooney."

"David?" Liaka said with a chuckle. "Why you playing?"

"Who's playing? I was dead serious about the comment I made. I really haven't been able to get you off my mind since the night I first met you. Are you busy?"

"No, not really. I have the rest of the day to do my research for the few motions I have left."

"Good. Then have dinner with me tonight," David returned quickly.

"Kinda bold, are we?" Liaka said, slightly amused.

"Usually I'm not. But, I have to see you again. Soon. So what do you say? Dinner at about, say seven o'clock? Maybe we can go to that new Norwegian restaurant. How does that sound to you?" David pressed anxiously. Liaka waited a few moments, savoring the silence.

"Tonight? Well, tonight I was going to..."

"They have delicious food there. It's discreet. Tucked away on the outskirts of the city. And just think about it, going to dinner with me tonight will save me thousands in legal fees," he added charmingly. He could hear Liaka chuckle in the background. "Was that a yes?"

"Well, I wouldn't want to be the cause of you blowing a small fortune on legal fees. Because lawyers can get expensive. So, okay, it's a date. I guess we can have dinner tonight."

"Great! Pick you up at your place around seven?"

"Sounds good. I'll see you then."

The black, full-length wool evening dress Liaka picked out for her date with David was chosen for two specific reasons. The first was it would be freezing out that night; the weatherman predicted the temperature to drop in the mid-thirties and the thick material would provide that extra warmth needed. The second and most important to Liaka was that the long material, although form-fitting to hug each and every one of her curves, covered more than three-fourths of her flesh. The night David pulled her over, she remembered being half naked in her club attire. So to shatter any ill-conceived impression David may have formulated in his head, Liaka wanted to wear an outfit that spoke of the message she wanted to send—she was not an easy lay and there would be no indulging in her goodies that night.

As Liaka continued to apply some eyeliner in her bedroom mirror, she began to ponder on what it might be like to seriously date a cop. Could it be possible that close associations with David would allow a virtual field day of what she could actually get away with; no speeding tickets, smoke weed like it's legal? Could David be a proverbial 'get out of jail free' card? Liaka heard her doorbell ring at about six thirty to shatter her comical thoughts. *Punctuality.* One of the many traits Liaka found so appealing in a man. At least he headed out to a good start.

"License and registration," David announced playfully, the moment Liaka opened her front door for him.

"And what did I do this time?" Liaka said with a smile, placing her hand on her hip.

"I'm sure there's some law on the books that says it has to be illegal to look that good," David returned thickly, eyeing Liaka up and down.

"You're so silly. But, thank you," Liaka said blushing.

Arriving at her front door without his uniform was a real good look for him. The porch light reflected off his face to reveal his dimples. As Liaka suspected, he did have waves and a faded haircut, tapered razor sharp. He was dressed casual, wearing an olive colored heavy sweater under his quarter-length leather, a pair of black slacks and black shoes to match.

Closing the door behind her, Liaka noticed how he hurried a few steps ahead to open his passenger door for her. The restaurant David spoke of was just as he described; discreet, cozy, and the atmosphere produced a comfortable setting giving Liaka a relaxing feel that she was definitely appreciative of. After a captivating meal, they began to enjoy each other's company over a bottle of wine.

"So, how do you like being a paralegal?" David posed, sipping at his glass of Chardonnay.

"I enjoy it. It gets a little hectic sometimes. Preparing for trial can be stressful. But, it's preparing me for my future as a lawyer. How about you? What's it like being a crime fighter? Almighty defender of justice!" Liaka said dramatically. He laughed.

"Crime fighter. You make it sound as if I'm some type of superhero. It has its days. Some can be very rewarding. Helping people, trying to solve problems. It leaves you with a pretty good feeling at the end of the day. Other days, it's not so great. The things you see. I've been doing this for a few years, but, sometimes it still gets to me. Believe me, being a cop doesn't get any easier."

"How long have you been a cop?"

"Well, let's see. I graduated from the academy with top honors and was pretty much on the beat within weeks. So I would say, close to seven years now," David stated, taking another small sip on his wine.

"Seven years?" Liaka said, an eyebrow raised.

"Why, does that surprise you?"

"Yes! It looks like you could have been in junior high seven years ago!"

"I guess I'll have to take that as a compliment. I get that a lot. It does have its advantages. It's easier to relate to a younger crowd. But, it's a little more difficult to get the same respect from some of the senior officers. I guess I don't look tough enough for them," David stated with a shrug.

"I think you look pretty tough to me," Liaka cooed sexily, finally taking her first sip of wine.

"Really? Well, I know I'm tough enough to protect you," David returned smoothly, leaning forward to gaze into Liaka's eyes.

They spent the next hour and a half on a bottle of wine, engaged in small talk. Liaka surprisingly found herself enjoying his company. He was sweet, charismatic, and a total gentleman throughout the entire evening. At the end of their date, David walked Liaka to her front door. Liaka climbed her first step and turned back to face him.

"I would like to thank you for such a wonderful evening. It's been a really long time since I went out on a date and really enjoyed myself," Liaka began, peering up at him. David took a step in closer.

"The pleasure was all mines," David returned slyly, leaning in to give Liaka a kiss. Liaka allowed him to give her a peck on the lips, but, took a step back when his hands reached out to wrap around her.

"I think it's a little past my bedtime," Liaka sighed, with a sneaky look in her eye. David licked his lips as if he was trying to taste Liaka on them.

"I hope I'm not being too forward, but, I would love to see you again. Hopefully soon. I had a very good time myself tonight. How about this weekend?" David invited, leaning in for another kiss. Liaka leaned in like she was about to allow another kiss, only to let him get inches away from her to twist her head and walk off.

"Call me," Liaka said with a smile, peeking back at him over her shoulder. She winked at David on the bottom of the steps then stepped inside her apartment.

# $C$hapter 26 | $I$ $W$ish $I$ $H$ad $A$ $B$lunt

$L$iaka unzipped and stepped out of her boots, kicking them next to her sofa. It was a relief to get them off. The style of boot was annoyingly uncomfortable on her feet, but, they were cute and they went perfect with the outfit Liaka wore out on her date. Unbuttoning each button down the front of her dress, she rolled it from over her shoulders, down her waist and stepped out of it. She let it fall to the floor then reached around to unclasp her bra. Liaka let out a sigh of relief as the tight brassiere let up from her chest.

Liaka walked naked from the waist up, in only her panties and booty socks, through her apartment to the bathroom. With a quick brush of her teeth and a wet nap removing the light application of make-up from her face, Liaka made her way to her bedroom and plopped on the corner of her bed.

11:23 P.M.

Lifting the comforter from the edge, Liaka noticed the time and thought it was too late to call Asia. She dialed her number anyways. Liaka clicked the power on the remote for her TV to slowly shine a dim glow from the flashing images on the screen.

"Hello?"

"Wassup? What you doing?" Liaka asked, snuggling under her thick blanket.

"Nothing. Just laying here watching TV. What time is it?"

"About eleven thirty."

"Eleven thirty? Why you calling me so late? And where were you? I called your house and you weren't home."

"I just came back from going out with that cop, David. The one I was telling you about. How he pulled me over, and then eventually asked me out."

"So *that's* how you got out of that ticket! What did he do, bribe you to go out to dinner with him, or he would arrest you?" Asia said with a chuckle.

"No! You stupid!" Liaka answered, with a chuckle herself. "He was actually on the verge of letting me go. But, right when I was about to leave, he asked me out. And I mean, could you blame him? As good as I was looking that night, there was no way he was gonna pass up an opportunity to at least ask me out!" Liaka continued sarcastically.

"Um hum."

"He actually surprised me. Going out to dinner with him really wasn't that bad. I enjoyed myse...Asia, hold on. My other end is ringing," Liaka paused, clicking over to her other end. "Hello?"

"Yo, Liaka! Waddup!" Lianna chanted on the other end.

"Wassup?"

"What you doing?"

"Just talking to Asia on the other end. Why, what up?"

"Nothing. Just sitting here chillin'. Thinking about the other day. That shit was crazy, right?"

"Hell yeah!"

"And you gots to admit, that shit was funny as fuck too!" Lianna said fervently, breaking out in laughter.

"At the end it was. But, at first you scared the shit outta me! I would of never expected you to do that!"

"It's his fault! All he had to do was pull over and I woulda never...well, I ain't gonna front. I probably woulda popped a shot in his corny ass anyways!" Lianna said with a chuckle. "That nigga was..."

"You know I told you I got Asia on the other end, right?"

"So? I know you ain't 'bout to hang up with ME?"

"I'ma call you back. I was in the middle of telling Asia about this brother I went out with."

"And, so? You can't tell me?"

"Yeah! I'll tell you when I call you back!"

"Just hang up and call me back with her on the phone, three-way," Lianna suggested. Liaka remained silent. "What?"

"Naw, it's just that...you know I ain't tell Asia what happened, and..."

"I ain't gonna say nothing! But, I swear! The both of y'all kill me. What she gonna do? It ain't like she ain't gonna find out one day anyways!" Lianna said dryly.

"I know, but..."

"Go head, call her. I said I wasn't gonna say nothing. But, for a chick who just did some gangsta shit like that, I don't know why you still acting all scary."

Liaka paused for a second before saying, "All right. I'ma call you back."

"You better not have me here waiting! Call me RIGHT back!"

"All right, damn!" Liaka huffed, clicking back over to Asia.

"I was about to say! Another minute and I was about to hang up on your ass! Leaving me waiting all long like that!" Asia snapped with attitude.

"You wasn't about to hang up on nothing. Shaddup," Liaka said.

"Who was that?"

"Hold on. It was Lianna. She want me to call her back three-way," Liaka explained, clicking over before Asia had a chance to get another word out.

"It's about time! You took long enough," Lianna said sarcastically, the moment the call connected. "Is Asia on the phone?"

"Yeah. Wassup, girl?"

"Asia! Whaddup, my nigga! How my girl doing?" Lianna said in a mocking tone. Asia knew why Lianna addressed her like that—it was because of Kenny. Regardless of the secret pleasure Kenny gave her on that night at her moment of weakness, Asia knew at that exact second she would live to regret that night.

"Chillin'. Just trying to hear the rest of what happened on Liaka's night out with 'Mr. protect and serve.'"

"Protect and serve? Liaka, what the hell is she talking about?"

"Oh, she ain't tell you? Miss Liaka is dating a..."

"Damn! Can I tell it?" Liaka snapped over Asia. She took a deep breath and said, "It ain't no big deal. I just went out with this guy tonight."

"Who just happens to be a cop!" Asia blurted.

"A cop? You fuckin' with tha police?"

"She had to! It was either that, or don't pass go and go straight to jail!"

Asia said jokingly.

"He didn't threaten to take me to jail!" Liaka said harshly.

"Hold up! Liaka, you fuckin' with a cop?" Lianna repeated, unable to get past that.

"Yeah, Lianna. Damn! Keep up with us. She's...messing. . . with...a...cop," Asia said, dragging out every word to tease Lianna.

"What the fuck would possess you to fuck with a cop?

"'Cause, she had to work that shit to make sure she didn't go to jail."

"Asia, would you please shut up! Lianna, that night when all of us went to the club, after I dropped y'all off, I got pulled over. And the cop that just happened to pull me over happened to ask me out and I said yes. So I went out with him. It's no big deal."

"No big deal? That's the fuckin' Jake! They the motherfuckin' enemy! Of course that shit is a big deal! You know how I hate them motherfuckas! You know what they did to me and my brother! You know how they are. And you fuckin' with them? I don't know how you could do some stupid shit like that. Especially after what they did to Olu!" Lianna spit with attitude. There was a moment of uncomfortable silence.

"First of all, don't get it fucked up, Lianna! I would NEVER forget what they did to Olu! And second, I know you have a hard time controlling what you say out your mouth. But, don't you ever, EVER say some fucked up shit like that to me again! Do you hear me?" Liaka growled.

"I was just saying...you know what I meant, Liaka. Them motherfuckas is dirty," Lianna said thinly.

"A y'all, I'll be right back. I think I hear my whining ass son crying," Asia spoke up, dropping the phone.

"Liaka, you do know what I mean, right? I ain't mean it all like that. But, I woulda never thought, out of all people, that you would be fucking with one of them! I woulda thought that you would have wanted to kill one of them."

"Who said I don't," Liaka said flatly. A moment of silence passed over the phone again, the only sounds that could be heard was the faint hum of Asia talking to her son.

"I shoulda known! How could I have not seen it? You scheming on that motherfucka, ain't you?" Lianna chanted into the receiver. Liaka remained silent. "You ain't gotta say nothing. I already know."

"Do you really think I would ever forget what they did to Olu? I loved Olu

Triple Crown Publications presents...

Queen of Thieves
*PART 1*

more than life itself! And I made a promise to him. So when that cop pulled me over and asked me out, I seen that as an opportunity—and took it! I know exactly what I'm doing. The next time he calls me and..."

"I swear, that lil' boy get on my nerves! He need his father to toughen him up so he stop crying up under me!" Asia said, returning to the phone. "So, did y'all kiss and make up yet? 'Cause I gotta get off this phone and go put that boy back to sleep."

"Yeah, we straight. I'll talk to you tomorrow," Liaka ended.

"Lianna, you relax yourself, okay?" Asia said to her.

"Oh, I'm relaxed. Why, do *you* need to be relaxed?" Lianna returned in a peculiar tone.

"Bye!" Asia blurted, hanging up.

"Now, back to you. What you gonna do?"

"I don't know. I'm still trying to figure it out. It's not like I'm used to doing shit like that—like I'm in the habit of avenging dead boyfriends. I...who's that?" Liaka heard a voice in Lianna's background.

"Angel. He just...come on, Angel! I'm hungry. Please!" Lianna cried to her brother. "Well then I know you at least got a blunt. Then here. Here go the money. Go get some," Lianna said in a whiny tone.

"Are you gonna listen to me, or keep crying about some weed?"

"I hear you. But, this nigga ain't shit! This motherfucka...don't worry about who tha fuck I'm talking to! You see me sitting here hungry and you can't even get your sister something to eat! You always do this shit to me. You can't even go get me a bag of weed, and I'm telling you I got the money. Come on, I'll smoke with you," Lianna continued, pleading. "It's Maliaka. And I'll tell her if you do that for me."

"Tell me what?"

"That stupid ass nigga he brought to the house the other day. The nigga that was on you like he ain't never smelled no pussy before. Angel want me to tell you that he said he wanna get with you. OK, there! I told her. Now will you do that for me?' Lianna stressed.

"I'll talk to you tomorrow, Lianna," Liaka said curtly.

"No, cause we gotta talk. I'm listening to you. But, this bitch ass nigga act like he can't never do nothing for me. Even though he lay up in my house every fucking night! You fucking asshole!" Lianna cursed out, her voice gradually increasing with each word.

"I told you. I don't know what's gonna happen with this cop. But, Olu told me to promise that I wouldn't let him die in vain and to avenge him. So I vowed to keep that promise."

"I ain't talking about that. I wanted to talk about the other night."

"What about the other night?"

"That shit you was doing! What the fuck was that? You was just sitting in the back seat! You was supposed to set that shit off! For a minute, I didn't even know you was still back there. You was the one talking about how you wanna get one of them niggas. So I ended up getting the perfect nigga, and you just froze up!"

"I ain't freeze up! I just ain't know what you was doing. And the way you just pulled that gun out...damn! Give your girl a warning or some type of signal next time. Something!" Liaka said humorously.

"How in the hell I'm gonna give you a warning doing some shit like that?" Lianna said in a twisted tone. "Ah, Liaka, I'm 'bout to pull the heat out and rob this nigga. Are you ready?"

"Stop being stupid. You know what I mean."

"Well, we gonna have to set up some type of signal or code for when we do the next one."

"What next one?"

"I got another nigga we can get. But, I guarantee you, this nigga is much sweeter. I mean, butterball sweet. Are you down?" Lianna questioned.

Butterflies began to churn in Liaka; she was experiencing that feeling again; that tingly feeling in the pit of her stomach. Liaka unconsciously squirmed her naked body under the covers from the mere thought of it; her breasts rubbing up against the fabric, her nipples growing firm as a result. Liaka turned to the right of her Queen sized bed. It was empty—void of Olu. He related one of his torrid tales to Liaka in that very same spot, only for them to engage in the most primitive sex when he was done. A smile spread across Liaka's face from the memory. She quietly slid her panties down around her thighs and rubbed two fingers across her lips, slowly.

"Yeah, I'm down," Liaka said thinly.

"Good. And this time don't leave me for dead."

"I ain't leave you for dead! If you don't remember, I was the one who got that nigga off you," Liaka reminded her. Just the visual of Lianna taking her back to that night—their ruthless stick-up—aroused Liaka to part herself with two fingers and gently slide them in.

"The nigga shoulda never been able to get on me in the first place! That's why on this next one, YOU gonna be the one to set that shit off!"

"Oooohhh, yeah," Liaka breathed heavily, "you ain't said nothing but a word. I'll set it off. I'ma set that shit off lovely!" she moaned, taking herself on an erotic ride that Lianna had no idea she was steering. But, even her diddling fingers and the pleasure she gave herself couldn't take back the words that came out of her mouth; she knew she was now committed.

"All right. We'll see. Look, I'll see you tomorrow. 'Cause I'm damn sure about to get this nigga to get me some weed and something to eat!" Lianna ended, hanging up the phone; she had no idea Liaka dropped the phone once she pushed enough buttons to set off her first orgasm; she was working quietly, mouth agape, on the second and third.

Lianna placed the cordless phone on the table and lifted her eyes to see Angel walking back from the bathroom zipping up his zipper, headed into the living room. The mere fact that he didn't come out screaming was a good indicator that he didn't check the gun that she and Liaka used for the robbery. Lianna figured Angel must have been content that the gun was still there, than to bother to check the clip for bullets.

Because unbeknownst to Angel, from the five bullets that were originally in the weapon, only one remained. As Angel took his seat on the recliner, paying her absolutely no mind, Lianna attempted to put on a pouty face hoping to gain some sympathy from him, possibly make him feel guilty enough to go and get her something to eat.

"Mira, you ain't hungry?" Lianna asked softly, through sad eyes. Angel ignored her. "Angel, papi, por favor," Lianna continued, growing whinier.

"Yo, what the fuck? Leave me alone! Damn!" Angel barked, trying to block her out.

"But, pa. I'm hungry."

"Then get your stupid, fat ass up and go make yourself something to eat! You the only fuckin' Spanish bitch I know that don't know how to cook! You get that shit from your black *Moreno* side!" Angel slurred, rolling his eyes.

"But, it ain't nothing to cook. I already checked."

"Then call one of the many niggas that you fuckin' and have them bring you something to eat! What? The only way they fuck with you is if you sucking they dick, or if they getting some pussy? That ain't my fault you a

lil' hood-rat, jump-off bitch! Do what you do best! Tell one of them niggas you'll suck them off for a happy-meal. I ain't your man. So leave me the fuck alone!"

Normally, Lianna would have lost her mind from such a comment. But, she was starving and didn't have a joint of weed to her name. Angel was her last hope. And lashing out on him at that time would most definitely destroy any possibility of him doing her a favor. Lianna mustered up the strength to bite her tongue.

"Come on, Angel. Please! I'll buy you whatever you want to eat. At least take me to get some weed. I'll smoke with you *and* give you some to keep."

"Yo, just sit the fuck down and relax for five minutes. Damn! I just left this stupid ass bitch 'cause she was nagging me to death! Now I gotta come home and deal with this shit? Is you gonna shut the fuck up and let me watch some TV in peace?" Angel barked, giving Lianna a twisted look.

"Only if you gonna go get me some weed and something to eat," Lianna returned, throwing the same look back at Angel. Angel exploded.

"I fucking can't stand y'all dumb ass bitches!" Angel yelled at the top of his lungs, jumping to his feet to stomp out.

"Good! I'll be a dumb ass bitch, you fuckin' cabrón! That's why your girl fuckin' two of your own boys behind your back, puta! They runnin' *trains* on her, you little dick faggot! She's taking it—front and back—both of them at the same time! And don't come back home either, 'cause I'm double locking the doors, bitch!" Lianna yelled out.

Lianna quickly jumped to her feet and ran to the front door. She swung her front door open to see Angel starting his car and peeling off. Lianna had a look of death in her eyes as she followed his taillights speeding off to disappear up the street. Within seconds, he was gone. Lianna stepped out onto her front porch and looked both ways up and down the street.

Surprisingly, there wasn't a soul in sight. She turned back and slammed the front door behind her. She immediately double locked it out of anger. Huffing back towards the sofa, Lianna plopped down in the cushion, reaching for the phone again. She called Kenny for the fifth time in two hours. Still no answer. Lianna sighed heavily. The food was an issue, But, Lianna knew she would never be able to get a wink of sleep without taking a few tokes on a blunt; especially in the heated state she was in. Lianna began to run through the options in her mind. Taking that twenty-minute walk down to the Village housing projects was tempting. But, it was freezing out, and Lianna thought, *what if nobody was out selling weed?* She would have taken that long walk for nothing.

Leaning forward to search in the ashtray, Lianna removed the extinguished butt of a cigarette and used it to sift through the ashes, hoping to find any remnants of a sizable blunt roach to smoke. There was only one, and it was hardly worth the effort to take it out. But, she did. Raising it close to her lips, Lianna blew on it heavily; it was covered in ashes. Cleaning it as best as she could, Lianna lit it and inhaled fiercely. Within the span of three quick intakes, the blunt roach disintegrated into ashes, she burned the bottom of her lip trying to get it all. Her fingers would have been burned in the process as well, But, the amount of weed she consumed on a daily basis, left the tips of her index finger and thumb permanently stained brown and tolerant to the fire.

Reaching for a cigarette on her coffee table, totally frustrated, she lit it, But, before she could sit back and exhale the cloud of smoke, she was stuffing her hand in the crack of the couch. It was useless. She knew deep down there wasn't any weed in there, But, she still checked hoping to miraculously find even a dime bag. Lianna began to look around her apartment. Not for anything in particular, just out of aggravation.

She had it in her to storm into Angel's room and cut up some of his best clothes out of sheer spite. Anything to somehow pay him back. Entertaining the thought, Lianna's eyes stopped on the recliner where Angel was sitting. She leaned forward and squinted her eyes to get a better look. She seen something, But, couldn't make out what it was. Taking another long drag off her smoke, Lianna dropped the full cigarette in the ashtray and stood to approach the recliner. She reached and pulled from its crack, ten pieces of small yellow paper, folded in rectangles, wrapped in a rubber band.

She looked down at it in her hand. She immediately knew what it was— dope, heroine. Her mind flashed to the *good* and *bad* things she heard about the drug. The good: it made some men sexually insatiable, and would give him what is notoriously labeled—*the dope dick*. Meaning, he could last for hours without ever achieving an orgasm. Rumor had it that it made a woman just as insatiable. But, then there was the bad—the drug was physically more addictive than cocaine!

As a result of Angel storming out of the house, he must have mistakenly dropped a 'bundle' of his dope. Lianna held it in her hand as she walked back to take a seat on the couch. She never took her eyes off of it as she reached for her cigarette again. She inhaled on it deeply, followed by licking her lips. Exhaling a cloud of smoke, Lianna looked around her empty apartment again, then back to the folded up pieces of paper in her hand.

Almost a minute had passed of dead silence with Lianna occasionally looking towards the front door, then back to the product in her hand. She dropped her cigarette in the ashtray again and pulled one of the individual pieces of paper out. Inside there was a fine, crystal-like, light brown powder. It was smashed flat against the paper. Lianna manipulated the paper into sort of a paper cup to break it up. She licked her lips again. Staring down at the paper, Lianna kept thinking to herself, *damn I wish I had a blunt to smoke.*

Triple Crown Publications presents... Queen of Thieves PART 1

# $C$hapter 27 | $T$he $S$plit

$T$he gym wasn't too crowded on that Tuesday evening. There was a lot less people in there than Liaka expected. During the week, Tuesdays and Thursdays were normally the worst. Finding an empty exercise bike or Stairmaster to work out on was hell. Another thing Liaka took pleasure in was the fact that she and Asia managed to persuade Lianna into going to the gym with them on that evening.

Asia was prepared to get into the full rhythm of her workout; her strict regimen designed by a professional fitness trainer to target all the main points of her body; not that she was always strict enough to follow it. Lianna, on the other hand, was just the opposite. The only workout program Lianna would probably adhere to would involve being naked with some brother in her bed.

Slamming her gym door closed, Liaka led the way as the three of them made their way out to the main fitness area. Liaka noticed how they only traveled from the locker room to the fitness area, yet Lianna's focus was clearly more directed at the few passing brothers than any workout they planned on doing. It was as if Lianna couldn't help but to stare, wink, or flirt in some fashion with every cute brother with a nice body that passed her by. After pulling Lianna away by her arm from the last brother headed into the men's lock room, they finally managed to get her focused on the exercise equipment instead of a nice pair of buns. Both Liaka and Asia took their seats on a stationary bike. Lianna, on the other hand, walked a half circle around it, staring at it as if it was a creature from another planet.

"It's not gonna hurt you," Asia said teasingly. Lianna rolled her eyes at her then turned to Liaka.

"This is what you want me to do? Ride a bike?" Lianna huffed, with a twisted look, staring down at the bike.

"For starters. It's a good warm-up. The bike ride will get your blood pumping and your heart going. Burn off some of those cheeseburgers that you love eating so much," Liaka said cheerfully with a smile, as she began to pedal herself. Lianna sighed, shook her head with an angry look, and then finally managed to climb on the bike.

The way she struggled to get comfortable on the seat, her curious look as she examined the display on the handlebars, and her whole posture screamed of how out of place she was in that environment. They also noticed how Lianna made it a point to keep looking around at the passing men, or a quick glance at Liaka or Asia out of embarrassment due to her unfamiliarity.

"What you need to do is be more concerned with the bike in front of you instead of all the men you can't seem to stop staring at. Can't you pay attention to something else for just one hour? At least to get your body right. Don't worry; they'll be there when the hour is up. I promise you," Asia said.

Yet, to make such a comment to Lianna was somewhat misplaced. Because despite the continuous abuse she inflicted on her body from the amount of weed, cigarettes and alcohol she consumed, not to mention every sort of junk food imaginable, Lianna still managed to have an exceptionally nice shape.

Her stomach was relatively flat, she had a slim waist, a round firm ass, and her chest was still perky enough that she didn't even need the support of a bra. All of that despite Lianna never stepping a foot into the gym, or even doing as much as a squat or single crunch. Asia even knew that her comment was more directed at her lifestyle than her shape, because as much as it pained Asia to admit, Lianna did have a naturally nice body. Asia wasn't sure if she could attribute Lianna's nice shape to good genetics, or if it was all the "sexin'" she engaged in that kept her body looking fit. But, whatever it was, it was working for her. Asia watched her as she began to pedal on her bike and knew it would only be a matter of time before Lianna would...

"Get my body right? For one, you better take a real good look at me! 'Cause trust, THIS is what niggas want!" Lianna stressed, waving a single hand over

Triple Crown Publications presents... Queen of Thieves
PART I

her body. "Secondly, niggas ain't thinking about shit like that! They don't give a fuck about a health conscious bitch! Niggas want a female with a cute face, a slim waist, thick thighs, and a fat ass! The only thing them niggas want a bitch *working out* is her pussy! And I got my *Kegel* exercises dead right! So when a nigga want me to *'flex my muscles'*, I'll squeeze my pussy around his shit so tight, he'll think my pussy is bench pressing five hundred pounds!" Lianna said chuckling.

"Y'all chicks ain't learning shit that I'm teaching y'all, huh? You keep on thinking that niggas be thinking about shit like that. You think when a nigga run up on you and try to talk to you, that he really concerned with how many sit-ups you can do? Or how many miles you can pedal on some stupid ass bike? The first thing that nigga thinking about is how good you look, how good that pussy might be, and what your *'head game'* is like."

"Well, how about this. I got an idea. How about working out and taking care of your body for...hmmm...let's see—YOURSELF! You always go straight to the issue of pleasing some man, or how good you can make some man feel. What about yourself? Do you even consider looking good or keeping yourself healthy for yourself? Why do you always seek to validate yourself by how many men you sleep with, or how well you can please a man? It's like you measure your self-worth as a woman by how well you can please a man or take dick. Sadly for you, you have no idea that that doesn't work. You can't seek to gain validation from *outside* of yourself. The only way to gain true validation is from *within*," Asia related sincerely. Lianna gazed at Asia with a blank look on her face before turning to Liaka.

"Spoken just like a chick with no man!" Lianna spit with a chuckle. Asia just shook her head, and then focused back on the blinking display across the handlebars to monitor her progress. An uncomfortable silence passed as the three of them concentrated on their workout.

Their exercise on the stationary bike consisted of them trekking two and a half miles over the course of fifteen minutes, with the last five minutes involving spurts at partial to full speed. But, within five minutes of Lianna even touching the bike's pedals, she began to show signs of fatigue. She got winded quickly. Lianna cut glances out the corner of her eye to Asia on her right, then over to Liaka on her left. They were both pacing themselves and getting a decent sweat from their workout. It was soon becoming humanly impossible for Lianna to pedal another minute, so she found herself slowing her pace to a stop. She sucked her teeth.

"Wha...what are you doing? Just a couple more minutes," Liaka huffed at Lianna, lightly panting. Liaka grabbed her towel from the handlebars to pat the few beads of sweat that dampened her forehead, But, continued her pace.

"Th...thi...this is stupid!" Lianna wheezed heavily between breaths.

"It's only stupid 'cause you can't do it," Asia teased. Lianna rolled her eyes at Asia.

"Y'all can stay here doing this stupid shit if y'all want. I see all the working out I'll ever need right over there," Lianna said, making eyes at a brown-skinned muscular brother knocking out pull-ups on a Universal gym at the other end of the room. Lianna slowly stepped off her bike. Asia cracked a smile as she watched her. It was evident that she was in pain; she took careful steps as if bracing herself for a possible collapse.

Asia remembered her first time on a bike, and figured if Lianna thought she was feeling it then, she would curse the gym and its very existence from what she was going to go through in the next few days. Steadying herself, Lianna took a few wobbly steps for Liaka to call out, "Hold up," to Lianna, slowing her pedaling to a stop.

"Okay, we'll do something else," Liaka sighed, patting her forehead again, stepping off her bike.

"Liaka, but, we haven't..."

"Asia, let's go stretch. We did enough on the bikes. We got a good sweat. Come on," Liaka said to Asia. The expression on her face spoke of her intention. It was a reminder to Asia. Prior to going to the gym, they both agreed if they could somehow, miraculously, get Lianna to actually go with them that their workout would be more geared to cater to her.

They both knew it would be a big enough deal just to get her there. And now that they had her there, they had to do something to keep her intrigued. Frustrating her would only work in contradiction of ever possibly convincing her to go back. Liaka had something else in mind. And fortunate for Liaka, the look she threw at Asia worked; Asia nodded in return. Lianna remained oblivious to their little scheme.

"Do what?" Lianna snapped aggravated.

"Stretch. And don't worry, you're not gonna have to get all sweaty doing it either. And it will make your legs feel better too. You always talking about how nice you are in the bedroom. So let's see how flexible you really are,"

Liaka said energetically, flinging her towel over her shoulder, headed towards the aerobics room.

Liaka made her way to an open spot near the corner of the room with Asia and Lianna close behind. She lowered herself to the floor in an Indian-style position. Asia was familiar, causing her to follow suit. Lianna remained standing, staring down at them with a look on her face as if she smelled something funny.

"What do I have to do?"

"For one, you have to come down here and sit with us. You could start with that," Liaka said sarcastically, remaining in high spirits. Lianna cast her eyes around the room then let out a heavy sigh before lowering herself to the floor in front of them. From the stationary bike, Asia had been timing herself in her mind how it would be only a matter of time before Lianna got fed up and stormed out.

"Okay, the first thing you need to do is relax. Kick your legs out in front of you," Liaka instructed, unfolding her legs from an Indian-style position, "and begin by massaging them." She continued, applying light, firm massages from the top of her thighs, gradually proceeding down her legs.

"This is stupid!" Lianna cursed, as she watched them.

"Then just do something stupid for once. Just try it," Liaka suggested, continuing down to her calf muscles. Another sigh escaped Lianna's lips before she slapped her hands on her thighs in frustration and began to rub massaging strokes on them. Liaka massaged each leg with a smile, Asia, with an expressionless look on her face, and Lianna, with a look of anger, teetering on the edge. Asia estimated five minutes and counting before Lianna would finally lose it and explode.

Yet, to both of their surprise, with each circular massage of her hands, Lianna began to concentrate more, seemed to be more relaxed, applying firm squeezes, alternating between each leg. Her newfound focus not necessarily to placate Liaka, but, more as a relief to relieve the pain in her legs as a result of the stationary bike.

"Okay, now that we got our muscles relaxed, feet together," Liaka began, closing her legs together out in front of her, "now slowly lean forward and touch your toes. Count to twenty." Liaka leaned forward with both hands to curl her fingers over her toes. Asia was able to follow Liaka's directions with relative ease, the second knuckle of her fingers reaching over her toes.

Lianna struggled, but, with considerable effort was able to touch her ankles. Liaka was the most flexible of the three, and after a few seconds of warming up, folded over completely to rest her face against her thighs, the palms of her hands wrapping to touch the bottom of her feet. Lianna was content and kept at it. Her hamstrings felt like they were on fire from the new experience of stretching them to their limit. She watched Liaka in disbelief.

"... and twenty," Liaka sighed, returning to an upright position. "Legs apart. Same count. Start with our left leg, and go...," Liaka instructed, her legs now apart about ninety degrees in the shape of an L. This position proved to be even more difficult for Lianna as she fought to even remain folded over. Alternating between each leg, Liaka positioned her legs to her sides to do a complete split on the floor.

"Daaaammmnnn!" Lianna said dramatically. Liaka followed her split by leaning forward to press her chest flat against the floor. "Now THAT'S what I want to learn how to do! Doing some shit like that, I know you's a nigga's dream come true!" Lianna continued emphatically.

"If I was able to do some shit like that, splits and shit, or put my legs behind my neck, I'd have a nigga in tears!" Lianna pressed, staring at Liaka mesmerized. Lianna turned to Asia who was a close second; she was able to force herself into a full split, but, that was clearly her limit.

A shadow appeared in the corner of Lianna's eye for her to look up and see a tall, slender brother who was ripped with muscles walking by. His eyes were glued to the three of them on the floor, yet his only reaction was a slight smile as he continued past them. A grunt escaped Lianna's lips as she forced herself to her feet.

"Where are you going?" Asia called out to her.

"Y'all go head and keep stretching. I see all the stretching and working out I'll need!" Lianna said impulsively, and then took off after him.

# Chapter 28 | Video Vixens

The snow rained down unmercifully on that wintry night. Close to eight inches blanketed everything on that side of the world, and it appeared that Mother Nature had no intention of letting up any time soon. Traveling down the Highway at less than fifty miles per hour, Liaka found herself on the passenger side of a Hummer H3. The driver, a dark-skinned brother in his mid-thirties, was squinting with much effort out the front windshield.

Lianna was in the back seat sucking down on a cigarette, her eyes glued to 'The Matrix' playing on an eight-inch screen in the passenger seat headrest. There was another ten-inch screen mounted underneath the face of the car stereo playing the movie as well, but, Liaka was having a hard time paying attention to the action on the screen. Tonight was the night for her to initiate the stick-up; the brother driving, one of her choices.

Liaka was thrown off by the driver's willingness to travel out and get them on that hellish snowstorm of a night, especially after repeated warnings broadcasted over the television and radio that driving should be limited to extreme circumstances only. Yet, it took less than a half hour of Liaka enticing him over the phone to convince him that picking them up would be well worth any inconvenience it would take in driving to get them.

They chose the Village housing projects for him to pick them up. Close to forty-five minutes had passed with Liaka and Lianna standing in a freezing project hallway waiting for him to arrive. Liaka seriously entertained calling the whole thing off figuring he wasn't going to show up anyways due to the snowstorm. But, within the next ten minutes, he finally arrived.

Liaka opened the graffiti-laced doors hearing the honk of a horn. A gust of wind blew a cloud of snow flurries in the hallway, showering the entrance with a drift of snowflakes. Liaka shivered as a few snowy crystals trickled in the hood of her coat and down her neck. The truck was barely recognizable due to the amount of snow covering it. It was buried under a blanket of snow, but, it was the same truck he was driving the night Liaka met him at the club.

Prior to entering the club that night, Liaka and Lianna made a secret pact to hunt for potential targets to "jack," and the parking lot was established to be their first place of business. The most expensive vehicles had to be matched with their owners. A sky-blue Hummer H3 with thirty-inch chrome rims was the focus of Liaka's attention that night as she watched the driver emerge from the truck, draped in a full length, sky-blue and white mink and chinchilla fur coat. Liaka made it a point to walk by him to get a good look at his face, partially concealed under the large fur hood of his coat.

Throughout the night, Liaka studied him; who he mingled with, the drinks he ordered, and made sure to keep one eye glued on him. And when the perfect opportunity presented itself, she took it. Under the guise of getting herself a refill, Liaka stepped off from Asia the moment she noticed him standing at the bar alone.

Within feet of him, Liaka thought all chances of making his acquaintance were blown when he began to focus on a petite, light-skinned female at the other end of the bar. But, Liaka wasn't so easily deterred. Raising her hand in an exaggerated fashion, Liaka ordered her drink with a raise of her voice, purposely bending over the counter in an inviting manner. It did the trick. Because before Liaka had time to receive her drink from the bartender, the brother was positioning himself on the barstool besides her.

After a few soft whispers in her ear, trading names, and a few brief formalities, his words merged into a constant blur as Liaka began to dissect him; platinum and diamond teeth covered every tooth in his mouth, they appeared to be two solid bars of crushed diamonds embedded in platinum. A sly ploy for the request for time made Liaka take notice of his watch. The face of his *Aquanautic King Cuda* was surrounded by diamonds, with quarter karat stones embedded in each hour.

Triple Crown Publications presents... Queen of Thieves *PART 1*

Before Liaka left, she made sure to take a page right out of Lianna's handbook and purposely felt him up for any potential knots in his pockets. Liaka knew that little trick was probably an unnecessary gesture, as everything about his whole demeanor screamed of money. Unleashing every seductive trick in her arsenal, Liaka made sure to leave him drooling for more before she accepted his number and stepped off. Only a few short weeks had passed before Liaka found herself sitting comfortably in the heated seats of his large truck.

"Yo! This shit is crazy!" Lianna blurted from the back seat; the movie had her entranced. Neo was throwing a fury of punches and kicks with precise accuracy, fending off countless 'Agents' that approached him. Liaka faced the small TV screen in front of her, but, she was actually watching the driver out the corner of her eye. Pulling off from the atrocious driving conditions of the highway, the driver managed to take a heavy sigh of relief as they rolled to a stop at a red light. Familiar with the exit, Liaka knew that they entered the town of Farmington.

"Chanel, what up with the smoke?" Lianna called out.

"In the bag it should be two boxes of blunts, and huh…" The driver returned, digging into his inner coat pocket to pull out about a half ounce of Purple Haze weed, pushing it to Liaka.

"I got that, Chanel. You can watch the movie. I'll roll it," Lianna announced anxiously, reaching through the front seats to intercept the clear cellophane bag. Liaka rummaged through the paper bag on the floor by her feet. The flashes of light from the TV screen revealed a half-gallon of *Belvedere* Vodka, two packs of *Dutch Master* blunts, and a twelve pack of *Magnum* condoms.

There was something else at the bottom of the bag as Liaka felt around; an extra-large pack of *Dentyne* gum. Liaka removed the pack of blunts and the gum, and handed the blunts back to Lianna. She knew why Lianna was so eager to roll the blunt. Liaka ripped the top off the pack of gum and popped one in her mouth, thinking, *this brother would be lucky if he was left with one blunt in that bag after Lianna got through with it!*

"Let me get one of those," the driver requested with his hand out. Liaka's first instinct was to pull out a stick and give it to him. But, she went against that. Instead, she pulled out a stick, removed the individual wrapper and placed the tip of the gum between her lips. Using the center console for support, Liaka sexily leaned over with the gum between her lips, inches from his face.

The driver turned to see the stick of gum trapped between the pearly white smile of Liaka, a hypnotizing seductive look in her eye. Although the truck was slowly rolling, he leaned in her direction to nibble down on the gum, and then planted his lips firmly on hers; he simultaneously slipped her his tongue. Liaka allowed him to taste her before she leaned back.

"I just thought it would be a little sweeter from my lips. But, you just had to try to get some from the source, huh?" Liaka said in a seductive tone. A small chuckle escaped his lips. Stripping the toothsome sweet of its flavor, he chewed the gum with no regard; Liaka's gesture forgotten about as fast as the act was committed. Yet to Liaka, the act was huge. It was a subtle reminder to herself that she had to step it up.

"Papi, you got a light?" Lianna questioned, leaning through the seats with the blunt in her hand. Liaka noticed how Lianna made no attempt to hand him back his weed, and was even more shocked that he didn't care to ask.

"Check the glove box. It should be a lighter in there."

A small light shone on the registration and insurance papers as Liaka clicked the glove box open. A few other knick-knacks cluttered the insides along with a small gold-plated lighter. But, Liaka noticed something else—the handle of a gun. Liaka removed the lighter, unflinchingly, and handed it back to Lianna. A succession of smoke poured from the back seat to slowly fill the car. Liaka looked down at the TV screen to see the movie coming to an end. But, no sooner than the credits began to roll, did they pull off the main road and into a well-lit, semi-circle driveway.

"We're here," the driver announced. The driveway to the door was only about thirty feet, yet they all bundled up in their coats to sprint up the walkway. The ten-foot, heavy oak and glass door was opened to reveal his living room.

"Oh, shit!" Lianna screamed, jumping behind the man as a huge Rottweiler dog charged them at full speed.

"Killer, easy, easy!" he announced thickly, kissing his teeth, bending down to one knee. The vicious beast jumped energetically around its owner, panting and wagging its tail uncontrollably.

"Yo! Get this motherfucka away from me!" Lianna cried out nervously, her body still pressed to him with a vice-grip like clutch on his arm.

"Don't worry. He's harmless. Unless I command him *not* to be. Killer, sit!"

the man barked, the energetic dog sat on cue.

"Could you please put him away," Liaka pleaded through frightened eyes.

"I paid a lot of money to get this nigga trained dead right. He can be as harmless as a kitten. Or..." The owner kissed his teeth in an arranged code for the beast to growl, show his teeth and prepare to strike, "....the most vicious killer."

"Okay, daddy. I see. But, please! He's scaring me and my girl," Liaka pleaded again as they cowered behind him, trying to distance themselves as far from the dog as possible.

"Make yourself comfortable. I'll go and lock him up in the back." He roughly snatched the thick leather collar around the dog's neck to lead him through the living room and out the back.

"That stupid ass dog blew my motherfuckin' high!" Lianna cursed. She took a sigh of relief watching the dog being dragged away. She raised the blunt to her lips and sucked on it fiercely trying to rekindle the flame. Liaka began to look around and examine the living room. The room and its contents had to be one of the most lavish she ever been in.

"It would sure be a shame to lose a connection like this," Liaka sighed, sliding comfortably into the corner of an eight-foot black leather sofa.

"What? Don't tell me you bitching up on me!" Lianna spit with venom, spinning around to Liaka from examining a seventy-inch flat screen TV built into the wall.

"No. I was just saying. To live like this. If we..."

"Look! You think this nigga is trying to *wife* either of us up? This nigga don't give a fuck about us! This nigga thinking about a threesome, he's thinking about some pussy! Trust, before this week is out, he'll have another two bitches in here trying to do the same thing to them! Come on, Liaka. Stay focused. This nigga ain't looking for a wife, and we ain't looking for no husband! We looking to rape this nigga pockets, take his cream! Bottom line, we here for the money!" Lianna hushed in an aggressive tone. Liaka didn't have a response. The revelation rang harshly true to Liaka.

"That's my bad. You right."

"I know I'm right! I..." They turned to see the brother emerge from the back room.

"You could have made yourselves comfortable. Let me get them coats from y'all," he requested, walking around to the back of Liaka. Liaka was wearing a one-piece, skin tight blue jean bodysuit. Lianna untied the strap on her full length, cream Shearling and removed the heavy coat from her body. The brother smiled when he received the coat from her. Lianna was scantily clad in a tight, cream leather mini-skirt, which barely covered her thighs, a pair of black leather thigh-high boots, and a black suede top, exposing half of her stomach.

"Now I see why you was bundled up so tight," the brother said with a slight chuckle, admiring Lianna.

"I'm from Miami, so I'm a southern gal. I feel more comfortable like this," Lianna cooed, "I'm not used to all this cold weather and three layers of clothes. And being that I'm still a little chilly, maybe..."

"...something to drink will help to warm you up," the brother said smoothly, tossing Lianna's coat on his arm over Liaka's. Stepping off to a custom bar at the edge of the room, he returned moments later with three tumblers filled with ice and a half-gallon of liquor.

"You have a really nice place here," Liaka mentioned, as he took a seat next to her on the sofa. "What do you do?"

"I'm a record executive for a prominent rap label. But, I also got a couple of other hustles on the side," he said, twisting the cap off the bottle, topping off one of the glasses. Lianna walked over to take a seat on the opposite side of him. She flicked his gold plated lighter that she pocketed from his car and lit the blunt again.

"Is this your place?" Lianna asked, ingesting a mouthful of smoke.

"The company owns it. We conduct business here, use it for rap videos every now and then. When I first seen you in the club, I thought about staring you in one of our up and coming videos," he mentioned, with a quick glance at Liaka, then returned to fill the second glass. Lianna shot Liaka a subtle look over her shoulder behind his back like, *I told you so!* with a smirk.

"With a body like that, have you ever considered modeling, or being the star girl in a video?" he posed to Liaka, lifting one glass to hand it to her. He reclined back into the plush sofa after handing the last glass to Lianna. The comment he made helped to put things back in its proper perspective for Liaka. He was looking for potential video girls! Liaka took a sip of her drink, and then turned to give him eye contact, silently imagining how many other females he ran the same lines on.

"Thank you. But, no. I wouldn't even know how to get involved with something like that," Liaka said dryly.

"I got connections. That's my thing. Actually, you would both look real good on TV. How long have you two been friends?"

"Friends? Who said anything about us being friends? That's my girl!" Lianna spoke out, standing from the couch. She swallowed a mouthful of her drink, then rested it on a coffee table in front of them as the brother watched her every move. Lianna made it a point to graze her body against his before crossing over him to sit on Liaka's lap. Liaka didn't know what to think, let alone what to do, as she had no idea where Lianna was taking things. But, with Lianna assuring Liaka with a subtle wink, Liaka decided to improvise and play along.

"Sometimes she can be a little shy, maybe that's why she didn't tell you. But, I *had* to come. She can't go out on a date with a man without me, and vice versa," Lianna related. She began to run her fingers through the back of Liaka's hair. Liaka was extremely uncomfortable with Lianna lovingly caressing her hair down her back, but, with the watchful eye of their admirer lusting over them, Liaka swallowed her aversion and lovingly wrapped her hands around Lianna's waist.

Inhaling the blunt again, Lianna held it between her fingers as she lowered it to Liaka's mouth. Liaka abandoned any last bit of restraint and wrapped her lips around the tip of the blunt to smoke from it. She fed from the blunt in Lianna's hand, even rested her hand on top of Lianna's fleshy thigh.

"That's what I'm talking 'bout right there. That's what's up! How long have y'all been together?" he asked, receiving the blunt from Lianna.

"Almost three years," Liaka answered, applying a light squeeze to Lianna's thigh.

"It's actually a pretty funny story. This guy I was dating, well, he wasn't just a guy. He was my live-in boyfriend of two years. I started to have this strange feeling that he was cheating on me. So, I went through his cell phone one day and happened to find her number programmed into it," Lianna began to narrate. "It took a few days, but, I finally conjured up the courage to call her. We talked over the phone and she told me how my man was trying to get at her, even promising to wife her up! And I believed her, because I remember him running the same lines on me. But, at that point, I just had to see who she was. Was she pretty? Did she have a better body than mines? I had to know. 'Cause I know my shit ain't nothing to sleep on.

"So we finally met. And when I first laid eyes on her, I was like—Damn! She is blazing! I always knew I had this secret attraction to women, as I find them so sexy, especially women as beautiful as my girl. So as we continued to talk, one thing led to another, then we eventually just kicked that nigga to the curb and got with each other! And hey, if the nigga woulda came at me real, and wasn't trying to be so sneaky with his shit, he probably coulda had both of us. But, now, he has neither," Lianna related, lifting Liaka's hair from the side of her neck to kiss a few small pecks on the side.

Gradually working her way down to Liaka's earlobe, Lianna feigned nibbling on it as she whispered, "The chair to your right, the one with the arms," then finished by sucking on it. Liaka rocked her head with drunken lust, her eyes squinting to focus on a high back, Victorian style chair, decorated with engraved wooden arms.

Lianna was starting to get heavy on Liaka's lap, and their plan was beginning to take form, prompting Liaka to gently pat Lianna on her ass. Unfortunately, Lianna read that playful gesture a little differently; she leaned over and planted her lips flatly across Liaka's. Liaka proved that she was more than willing to play along with Lianna's little facade of them being bi-sexual, but Liaka soon had a hard time believing if this was all some elaborate act to throw him off guard, or if Lianna was actually deriving some secret pleasure from the act.

"Let me get that blunt, momma. You know I'm trying to get my smoke on," Liaka said, nudging Lianna for her to get up. Lianna finally took the hint. She got up and walked over to a small end table against the wall with her drink. Lianna placed her drink down and reached for a huge universal remote. She began to press buttons at random. A brick encased fireplace covered in a brass shell burst into flames. The three of them turned to it upon ignition. Another button dimmed the lights; a third caused a flat screen TV on the wall to come to life.

"All right, all right. Let me see that 'cause you going crazy," the brother said, walking over to Lianna to remove the remote from her hand. The images of Nelly's 'Grillz' music video flashed on the screen, enticing Lianna to slowly bop her head to the music. Her hips came to life as she began to slowly grind to the beat.

She brought her drink to her lips again and downed it to about half, before lowering her eyes, beginning a hypnotically alluring dance. The brother watched her in a trance, his eyes lowered to her ass rolling underneath her skirt. Liaka smirked as she watched him. Lianna had him stuck.

"Yeah, I could definitely see the BOTH of you in videos. I can see that you got a blazing ass shape up under that!" The brother slurred lustfully, stuck on the back of Lianna's skirt. "You got the shape, the face, the entire look that we seek to put in the spotlight." He turned to see Liaka stand from the sofa to approach him. A trail of smoke danced from the tip of the blunt in Liaka's mouth curling around her head, as she rhythmically moved in their direction.

She inhaled deeply, and then removed the blunt from her mouth, placing it between his. He could feel the presence of Lianna dancing up behind him. They sandwiched him in the middle of the living room, all three of them swaying to the beat. Liaka turned from facing him, offering her backside to him. A light grind on his crotch enticed him to lower his hand to fill it with Liaka's fleshy ass cheek.

"So, y'all share everything, huh? So, if I can get at this shit right here," he began slyly out the corner of his mouth, gripping Liaka's ass, "then I can get at this shit, too," he continued, turning halfway to fill his other hand with Lianna's ass. Lianna finished off the rest of her drink, and then bent over in front of him to place the empty glass on the white tile floor.

Rising back up, Lianna removed the blunt from his lips and pulled the back of his head down to plant her lips over his. Liaka circled her hands around his chest and began to unzip his heavy sweater, exposing his naked chest underneath. Liaka ran her fingernails through the curly hairs on his chest, but, he was more entranced, engaged in a passionate tongue kiss with Lianna to pay her much mind.

His hands reached down to yank up the back of Lianna's skirt, exposing her fleshy g-stringed ass. Lianna began to slowly walk him back, never removing her mouth from his. Liaka lowered her hands to unfasten his belt buckle, followed by unbuttoning and zipping down his pants, for them to fall to the floor around his ankles. His semi-hard erection bounced through the slit of his silk boxers, but, Liaka still grabbed the elastic and pulled them to his feet. They guided him to the chair for Lianna to finally remove her lips from his and nudge him back. He fell into the chair with a bounce for Liaka and Lianna to stand in front of him on both sides.

"So, you can make us video girls? And just what do we have to do to get that spot?" Liaka questioned, and then leaned down to begin kissing up the side of his neck.

"Shit! You already know! Keep doing what you doing. Y'all bitches know what time it is! Handle your business like you supposed to, and I'll have y'all be the main feature!" he slurred. Liaka began to run her tongue down his chest, transforming a soft lick, to a nibble, to a light bite. With each bite, Liaka sunk her teeth into his flesh a little harder.

"Ah, shit! Yo, ease that shit up, ma," he sighed, once he felt the clutch of her jaws.

"You gotta watch her. She likes to get a little rough. Trust me, I know," Lianna moaned, and then lowered herself to her knees to begin kissing on his inner thigh.

"Oh, so y'all bitches like that shit rough, huh? Then y'all in luck. 'Cause I'm just the right nigga to know how to beat that pussy up!" he growled, yet leaned back to allow them to take complete control. Passing a quick glance at Lianna, Liaka recognized the brief gaze she gave her, and then sliced down to his boots. It hit Liaka immediately. The brother had on a pair of dark brown leather 40-below Timberland boots that came up to his calves. The laces weren't tied, or even threaded three-fourths of the way up.

Liaka began to pull at them, unlacing them until one of his laces was pulled free from his right boot. His face took on a look of partial confusion mixed with desire as he watched Liaka, but, Lianna's snake-like tongue traveled up his right thigh to bring his full attention back to her.

The last thing Liaka noticed from the corner of her eye was Lianna wrapping her fingers around the shaft of him, gently pulling, as she nibbled on his inner thigh. A powerful sigh escaped his lips, he leaned his head back, lost in the moment. Unlacing the other shoelace from his boot, Liaka slowly rose to her feet and reached for his arm. Gently guiding his arm to the handle of the chair, his eyes slowly opened to look down to see Liaka wrapping the lace around his wrist, securing it to the chair's arm.

"Naw, naw! I ain't with all that tie up shit. I...I...naw...," he sighed ecstatically, in a partial stutter, as Lianna silenced him by wrapping her lips around his stiff erection. "Wait...no...oh, yeah...but, hold up...," he babbled incoherently, barely resisting as Liaka secured his wrist tightly to the arm of the chair. Lianna lowered her head over him, taking him deeper in her mouth; his breathing increased, his resistance slowing to a slight tug.

"Just relax, baby. Let us take care of you. I promise you, this will be a night you won't forget," Liaka purred, walking around the back of him to begin wrapping the other shoelace around his other arm. Lianna worked magic on his manhood with her mouth; her tongue, suction, and lips working exquisitely in union. His head fell back lazily against the chair, his eyes drunkenly rolled in his head.

Liaka wrapped the shoelace repeatedly around his wrist, yanking it tight before tying it into a knot. He let out a whimpering moan, but, Liaka wasn't sure if it was the result of the shoelace cutting into his skin around his wrist, or Lianna working her mouth on him, taking him deeper in her throat. His moans became more animated; he squirmed joyously in his seat as Liaka tiptoed whisper-quietly back to the sofa, her hand slipping under the cushion.

"Yo,...ma, you got that shit on the money! I'm putting you, I'm putting the BOTH of y'all in the next five videos that I shoot!" he cried out emphatically, his head flailing back and forth.

"And all my girl had to do was suck your dick to get it!" Liaka spit thickly. His eyes popped open. They came back into focus for him to stare wide-eyed down the barrel of his own gun which Liaka held inches from his face. Then he felt it—Lianna's teeth lightly sunk into his flesh around his rock hard erection. Lianna had him fully immersed down her throat; her lips nestled against his pubic hairs, and if she bit down, would have severed his entire penis clean off at the base.

"A place as nice as this, and all the money you *claim* you make, I just know you got enough dough lying around her somewhere. So, this is what we're gonna do. You're gonna tell me where the money is, all of it, and my girl won't bite your dick off and give you an instant sex change!" Liaka stated sharply, snapping the hammer on the gun.

"Is y'all bitches stupid? Do you know who the fuck I am? I'm fuckin'... aaggghhhh!" he screamed out in agony, as Lianna silenced him by sinking her teeth down on him. The pressure of her jaw broke through his skin as a trickle of blood slowly rolled down his inner thigh.

"Bitches? Now that's no way to talk to a woman. Especially a woman who got a gun pointed at your head and my girl like a pit bull on your dick," Liaka said calmly, then leaned forward to smash the butt of the gun in his face. The blow split his eye open. "Let's try this again. Lil' Sexy, do you think you could teach this disrespectful brother some manners?"

Her jaw tightened around him again.

"All right! All right! My jacket! Check my pants and my jacket! It's all in there! Now please...aaagghhh...just get this bitch the fuck off me!"

"That's a start," Liaka said dryly. "Lil' Sexy, ease up, baby girl. Give him a breather," Liaka tapped Lianna on her shoulder. She released her grip slightly. Liaka did a quick scan around the room, keeping the barrel of the large weapon aimed at him the whole time. The leather coat he was wearing rested in a chair by the foyer. Liaka cut her eyes back at him, a look of pain still evident on his face, then back to his jacket at the other end of the room.

Holding his manhood in her throat for that period of time began to present difficulties for Lianna; his erection obstructed any clear passage for her to take a deep breath. Lifting her head from him, a sordid trail of saliva clung from her lips to the head of his quickly fading erection. Lianna inhaled deeply, filling her lungs with much needed oxygen. But, the moment Lianna took her second deep breath, the brother lifted his legs and kicked Lianna in her chest with full force. Lianna went flying across the room, landing on her back to slide ten feet on the tile floor. Liaka shot back around to see Lianna lying on the floor out of breath, the wind knocked out of her from his mule kick to her chest, and him wildly yanking at the binds on his wrists.

"Don't! Stop...don't fuckin' move! Stop! Don't..."

BLAP!

A shot cut through Liaka's voice, she mistakenly squeezed the trigger. The bullet barely missed his head, shattering a bronze encased mirror behind him. He instinctively ducked from the sound of the shot, but, with one final, frantic yank, broke the wooden arm of the chair. With one arm still secured to the chair, he dragged it with him as he lunged for a lamp on a table.

"Shoot him! Fuckin'...(cough)...shoot him!" Lianna screamed at the top of her lungs, cowered on the floor, still trying to catch her breath. But, as Liaka tried to steady the shaking gun in her hand, he reached for the lamp and hurled it at Liaka, unmercifully. Liaka threw her arm up to protect herself just in time for the porcelain lamp to shatter over her elbow. The impact caused Liaka to drop the gun. With one violent blow from his free arm, he swung down on the wooden arm of the chair, snapping it in two.

"I'ma kill you, you stupid ass bitch!" he growled dementedly, yanking his pants up to charge at Liaka. He jumped at Liaka with full speed, but, Lianna intercepted him by throwing herself at his legs. Her arms wrapped around his ankles for him to fall face first to the floor with a thud.

Shaking it off, he reached down to Lianna, holding on to his legs for dear life and filled his hand with a fistful of her hair. Yanking her head back, he delivered a vicious punch to the side of her face. But, Lianna throwing herself in the throes of danger gave Liaka just enough time to scoop the pistol up from the floor. She swarmed down on him with a vengeance, swinging the gun with pistol-whipping blows. Each blow beat a little bit of life from his body. With the last bit of energy he had, he swung a desperate punch at Liaka, connecting square on her mouth to split it open. The blow was enough to lift Liaka from her feet, throwing her back on her ass.

"Unh!" Lianna grunted loudly, swinging the half gallon of liquor at his head. He turned just in time for the three-fourths filled bottle to smash directly across his face, shattering into a million pieces, showering him with alcohol. He stumbled back and tried to recover, but, Liaka jumped to her feet and kicked him with all of her might on the side of his knee.

Posted in a boxer's stance, Liaka delivered a quick one-two punch with precision, dropping him hard on his back. Liaka ran to the gun that slid on the floor halfway under the couch. She held it down on his weakly, moaning body. Their violent altercation left him semi-conscious. Blood covered his face and the top of his naked chest. The front of his open sweater was drenched in alcohol and covered in blood. A gash from the gun handle to the back of his head caused drops of blood to puddle on the floor.

"You...you okay, mommy?" Liaka called out weakly, she watched Lianna slowly pull herself to her feet.

"I...I'm all right," Lianna answered faintly, lowering her skirt that was hoisted up around her waist. She winced and squinted her eyes and reached up to feel the swelling on the side of her face. "It ain't nothing. This nigga hit like a bitch!" Lianna cursed thickly, and then kicked him in the nuts with the toe of her boot. He let out a sharp grunt and curled up into a fetal position.

Lying motionless on the ground, Liaka held the gun on him, staring down at him. She could taste the blood in her mouth from a split lip. A drop slowly rolled down the center of her chin. Liaka raised the palm of her hand to her mouth to wipe it. A bloody smear stained the center of her palm. A wily smile spread across her face. She was beginning to feel the nefarious sting of excitement course through her veins; she could feel the power. Standing over his stilly moving frame, she squeezed the handle of the gun. She visualized the bullets in the clip, each one representing an individual claim to power. At last

she finally captured the feeling she was searching for.

"Sexy," Liaka said thinly, never taking her eyes or the gun off him, "what do you wanna do with him?"

"Fuck him! Let's get what we came for!" Lianna spit with attitude. Lianna did a quick survey of the room. Everything within distance of their altercation was completely destroyed. The expensive chair they tied him to was in shambles, a few blood puddles stained the seat. Shards from a broken mirror littered a side table and floor at the other end of the room as a result of the stray bullet. Splatters of bloodstains spotted random area on the white tile floor.

The porcelain lamp he threw at Liaka was smashed, disintegrated into pieces. The only thing remaining was its warped electrical cord. It was just what Lianna was looking for. Snatching up the cord from the pile of broken fragments, Lianna forcefully pushed the semi-conscious brother on his stomach and tied his hands with the cord behind his back.

She was merciless, wrapping the cord with violent force around his wrists, cutting off the circulation of blood to his hands, and then went down to his feet. Bound into some perverted human version of a calf roping, Lianna savagely yanked him to his back and began to aggressively dig through his pockets. Lianna wasn't done. She snatched the platinum chain by its medallion from around his neck, followed by stripping him of his diamond encrusted watch, then lastly, his bracelet and two pinky rings.

"Open your fuckin' mouth!" Lianna commanded, punching him in the stomach. He coughed from the blow, giving Lianna just the access she needed. She snapped out the blood-stained diamond and platinum fronts that covered his upper and lower teeth. "I'ma get these shits to fit MY mouth, bitch! Have my shit looking like *Paul Wall!*" Lianna chuckled, admiring the saliva drenched, platinum teeth in her hand.

"The safe! I know you have to have one around here. Where is it?" Liaka barked down at him, pressing the barrel of the gun deep in his cheek.

"I...I...I don't know what you're talking about," he moaned out, a glob of bloody saliva dripped from his mouth. Roughly flipping him over, Lianna noticed the tip of his dick still hanging out the front slit of his boxers.

"What...what are you doing?" Liaka cried, as she watched Lianna dive her head down to his waist.

"Yo...I...aaagghhh!" the brother cried out in a blood curdling wail as Lianna, without a moment's hesitation, sunk her teeth in to bite off a chunk of skin on the head of his dick.

"Did that jog your memory, motherfucka? You think you know where the safe is now, nigga?" Lianna huffed, spitting the chunk of flesh in his direction, wiping the blood from her mouth with the back of her hand.

"I'm...I'm not gonna ask you again. The safe!" Liaka stuttered, surprised she managed to get the words out. Crying out in pain, he attempted in vain to curl his body up. It was useless. The bind held his hands firmly behind his back. A few seconds of moaning passed, only for Lianna to dive down at his crotch again.

"All right! All right!" he cried out in fear, cringing at Lianna's lunge, deathly terrified of Lianna taking another bite. "The master suite! The last room to the left! Behind the portrait on the wall, there's a safe behind it. Please! It's behind the picture!" he cried.

"The combination, what is it?" Liaka commanded.

"Seventy-five, eighty, thirty-seven, fifty," he whimpered, weakly dropping his head to the floor.

"Sexy, go handle that! I'll watch him," Liaka instructed, with the gun still on him. Lianna nodded. She bolted through the house with lightning speed into the room he described. A portrait of *Nefertiti's* head hung in the distance at the far end of the room. Lianna made a beeline towards it. She examined the sides of its outer bronze frame to see a set of hinges fastening the large painting to the wall. She tugged at it gently for the portrait to swing open revealing a large wall safe behind it.

"Seventy-five, thirty-seven, eighty, fifty," Lianna said to herself, locking in each number on the combination dial. She reached for the handle and attempted to turn it. "Eighty, seventy-five, thirty-seven, fifty," she sighed and tried again. "Fuck!" Lianna cursed aloud, slapping the back of the picture in frustration. She let out a heavy sigh and tried again. "Seventy-five, eighty, thirty-seven, fifty?" Lianna said to herself, now unsure if she even remembered the proper combination. She held her breath as she spun the dial to the last number. This time she heard a faint click. Lianna's smile revealed her whole top row of teeth. She reached for the handle again. This time it put up no resistance as she turned it.

The inside was divided into two levels. The first thing visible on the top shelf was about ten stacks of bills wrapped in $5,000 tape denominations.

Immediately pushing her hand into the safe, Lianna peeked over her shoulder as she took one stack of bills and sneakily stuffed it down the front of her skirt. She looked down to examine herself to see the rectangular shaped stack forming a slight bulge on her crotch. She pushed it down further, securing it snugly, almost between her thighs in the crotch of her panties.

*"She already got money,"* Lianna said under her breath, trying to convince herself and find any form of justification for pocketing a portion of their take; a take her and Liaka were supposed to divide fifty/fifty.

There were a few other expensive trinkets—which Lianna quickly pocketed in a pillowcase that she snatched from the bed—but, what stood out to her, and the most unusual thing to catch her eye, was a small digital camcorder on the bottom shelf. It oddly stood out of place compared to the other valuables.

She folded open the side window screen and pressed the power button for the small screen to light up. Lianna wasn't sure if she pressed play, or if there was even any recordings on it. A second away from folding up the screen and tossing it into the pillowcase as well, a blurry picture faded in and out before coming into full focus on the screen.

The home-made video jumped shakily before the cameraman steadied his hand for a clearer picture. The picture on the screen quickly became familiar to Lianna—it was the living room of the house she was standing in. A date on the top right screen revealed that the activity shot was filmed less than two weeks ago.

A lone female sitting on the edge of the sofa came into view; a fearful look clearly evident on her face. As the lens zoomed in to get a close-up of her face, Lianna estimated that the female couldn't have been more than fourteen or fifteen years old. Her innocent face screamed of her being an adolescent, but, the scanty attire she wore on her over-developed young body, gave her a much older look. Lianna listened in closely to the small speaker on the camera to hear the young girl speak. Her words were muffled, her demeanor timid, but, there was no mistaking it—she was just a young child.

Another voice could be heard, the voice of the cameraman, but, Lianna still couldn't make out what was being said. From the way the single hand of the cameraman popped in and out from the corner of the screen, Lianna could only assume that he was trying to put the young girl at ease. From what she could see, he was being effective, based on the few slight blushes forming on her shy face.

 Triple Crown Publications presents... Queen of Thieves *PART 1*

The voice soon became clearer, more recognizable. It was the voice of the brother they had tied up in the living room. Lianna's lip curled in disgust as she listened closely to the brother relate how beautiful the young girl was, how she should be proud of her body and how she had such a promising career in modeling.

The young, light-skinned girl responded with childish enthusiasm; she was sucking it all up. His hand then reached forth from the bottom of the screen to rest gently on her knee. She flinched. A few convincing words from the charming, older brother calmed her as he began to softly caress her. The camera zoomed in on his hand, which was slowly moving up her thigh to the hem of her skirt. The camera was then lifted back to her face.

She blushed, passed a few glances, but, held her head down in embarrassment. Her innocent eyes pained Lianna as she listened to the brother feed the naive girl an elaborate dream of riches and stardom. With each elaborate praise the brother showered her with, Lianna could see his hand fondle and manipulate itself higher, until it disappeared between the naked flesh of her thighs.

Lianna squinted her eyes angrily, as the pain registered on the young girl's face from his fingers penetrating her. Lianna found herself repulsed to the point where she could watch no more when the brother rested the camera on the coffee table pointed on her, only to mount the young female, replacing his fingers with his erect manhood. The images of that subtle rape triggered painful memories from Lianna's past.

*Sly Biggie.*

The name of one of her mother's secret lovers when she was younger was tattooed in her memory. He was considerably younger than her mother, a mere nineteen to her mother's twenty-nine; Lianna was only thirteen at the time. She could remember the countless nights when she heard *Sly Biggie* and her mother making no attempt to conceal their passionate sex; her mother's animated moans of ecstasy singling like a melodious tune throughout the small apartment. Lianna remembered how she tried in vain to block out the sounds, finally solving the problem by blasting her boom box on the nights he came to visit.

*Sly Biggie* lived up to his name when it came down to concealing their secret affair from her father, even jumping out of her mother's second story bedroom window when her father came home unexpectedly one night. He was even craftier in his ability to keep his growing lust for a young developed Lianna under wraps from her mother.

Day after day, he grew bolder in his behavior as he exposed his growing attraction to Lianna, sneakily feeling her up, all at Lianna's vehement disapproval. Lianna's threats to expose his unconscionable conduct to her mother was met with fearless arrogance, his only comeback being, "it's your word against mine." In the end, Lianna thought her mother would never believe her over him, possibly not even care, prompting her to keep his conduct to herself. Then on one fateful day, it happened.

As a 'favor' for her mother, *Sly Biggie* went to pick Lianna up from school. At the first sight of *Sly Biggie* in his car, alone, Lianna had it in herself to never step foot into his vehicle. But, he assured her that he was just there to pick her up and bring her straight home. But, when he drove to an abandoned train yard, Lianna knew what was to inevitably come next. She fought, kicked, scratched, bit, but, it was no use. He outweighed her by well over one hundred pounds, and spewing one final threat of killing her father and little brother if she didn't submit, slowly took the fight out of her.

Lianna loved her little brother and would never be able to live with herself if her actions brought any harm to him. So for close to four months, she came to cringe at the mere sight of *Sly Biggie* when he came to her house late at night, knowing when he was done with her mother, leaving her passed out from the sex, the liquor, the drugs, or all three combined, that his next stop was to sneak into Lianna's bed to have his way with her. Lianna angrily slammed the side window on the camcorder and stormed out of the room.

"Did you get it? What took you so long?" Liaka asked anxiously, the second Lianna emerged from the back room. Lianna remained silent as she rounded the sofa to stare down demonically at the brother on the floor. "Did you..."

"Yeah, I got it," Lianna huffed, and then dropped the pillowcase full of valuables on the floor. "I also found his little home-made video, you child molesting motherfucka!" Lianna spewed with hatred, waving the camcorder in her hand. "Fucking women is a little too much of a challenge for you, huh? So, I guess the only way you could satisfy a female is if you mess with little girls!" Lianna continued painfully, tears swelled up in her eyes. Then she snapped. Lianna began to kick him all over his body, anywhere her foot could land. The brother on the ground inadvertently took on the form of *Sly Biggie* and any other pedophile Lianna could think of.

 Triple Crown Publications presents... Queen of Thieves
*PART 1*

"Okay, Sexy! Stop!" Liaka cried, pulling Lianna off of him. Lianna easily broke from Liaka's hold and dove for a vase filled with flowers, smashing it over his head. "That's it! Enough!" Liaka screamed, pushing Lianna back with a violent thrust. "We got what we came for! Now we have to figure out what we're gonna do with him."

"Nothing! Just leave his pedophile ass right there!"

"But..."

"But, nothing! Fuck him! He's not gonna tell anybody about tonight! He's not gonna tell anybody anything ! There's over six hours of video on this camera. Why do you think he kept it in a safe? So you could only imagine what else is on there! How many other girls he did that to, that he...raped! We're gonna take the tape with us, and if he even *thinks* about calling the police or telling anybody, copies of this tape will be sent to every television station, every newspaper, downloaded on every website I can think of, and then  sent to the police! Show the world what type of pedophile motherfucka he really is! Have him go to jail labeled as a child molester! Would you like that, motherfucka? How long do you think you would last in there, huh? Maybe you'll get a little taste of your own medicine and have them rape you, you bastard!" Lianna spewed down at him.

"Yeah, but..."

"Fuck him! Leave him right there! Let's go!" Lianna ended, snatching the sack of valuables from the floor. Liaka took one last look at the brother on the floor, shook her head and took off after Lianna. They bolted for their coats and ran to the front door, flinging it open. A gust of wind from the snowstorm blew in a cloud of snow, coating the entrance of the door and half the foyer with snowflakes. With his H3 keys in Liaka's hands, they ran headlong into the blanket of snow, disappearing into a blur of white.

# $C$hapter | $O$ne$-O$n$-O$ne
## 29

$L$ianna sat on her toilet early that morning. The porcelain seat was cold on the back of her naked thighs; she sat there in only her panties and an extra-large T-shirt. She barely noticed it. Her focus was heavily directed on a small space at the edge of the sink.

"Sniiiifff...sniff." Lianna inhaled deeply, ingesting half of a ten-dollar bag of heroin. It was her first bag of the day. The fine, brown powder tickled her nose, causing a few involuntary twitches. But, after another hearty snort, with her head leaned back, the slight tingle subsided. She leaned forward again to sniff the rest of the bag in her other nostril, infamously known as a '*one-on-one*'.

Unbeknownst to anyone, Lianna had been sniffing dope for close to a month, and sniffing a good amount of it. With her addictive personality, coupled with the disposable income she managed to acquire as a result of their few heists, heroin had now been added to her repertoire of insatiable addictions; each bag only feeding the monstrous beast within her, leaving the quench of her original high never fulfilled.

The first night, when she found the bundle of dope that Angel mistakenly dropped, had been long forgotten. From the absence of a bag of weed on that lonely night, Lianna decided to substitute her regular bag of weed, her narcotic of choice, for a bag of dope.

The first bag she sniffed actually made her sneeze a few times, followed by a feeling of sickness to the point of violently retching. Strangely enough, the body's signal of trying to expel the powerful narcotic from her system wasn't enough to deter her from trying it again. The second bag stuck. The direct blast of heroin up her nose shocked her system, and the foreign drug coursing through her body gave Lianna a euphoric feeling like no other; a high unlike any blunt of weed she ever smoked.

Even for Lianna, incorporating the drug into her repertoire of other stimulants, without detection from others, was no easy feat. Constantly disappearing off to the bathroom, a car, or any other private area to quickly sniff a bag of dope had now become synonymous with her character. It began with one bag a day split in half, a one-on-one. She quickly graduated to two bags. And within the span of a few short weeks, escalated to the point where Lianna was easily devouring close to seven or eight bags a day.

Given Lianna's history of only smoking weed and drinking, maybe indulging in an occasional ecstasy pill, Angel was left with no direct indication to link Lianna's erratic behavior to anything other than her possibly having a bad day. Or, could it have been the constant money she fattened his pockets with, buying his dope, blinded him as to what was going on right under his nose? Better yet, under *her* nose! Lianna wasn't sure if Angel cared that his own sister was getting high on heroin, or if he even bothered to give the idea serious thought, as long as he continued to benefit from it.

Another factor helping Lianna mask her newfound addiction was she managed to keep herself up. She understood the stereotypical views surrounding the typical addict; always broke, a drab appearance, and an array of other fallacious traits that went along with it. Lianna was just the opposite. She was still considerably 'thick', she maintained her voluptuous shape, kept a tight wardrobe, wore enough jewels, and aside from the dark circles forming under her eyes, which she easily masked under the concealment of heavy make-up, she didn't exhibit any traits that would fit the drug addict type.

Despite the miraculous feat of being able to hide her new lifestyle to everyone around her, the sole person who she remained so convincingly elusive to in revealing her drug problem to was, herself. If you were to ask her, she would state most adamantly that the dope was just another form of 'get-high', something she could easily refrain from on any given day, if she wanted to. Yet, the all-elusive 'any given day' that she wanted to never come.

In the short month that she'd been heavily consuming the highly addictive

drug, her body began to feel the symptoms of withdrawal if she didn't consume that first bag in the morning. She found out this painful revelation one morning after a reckless over-indulgence the night before, with Angel nowhere to be found the following day to purchase her morning bag. So she was forced to go without.

Because searching out on the street to purchase that morning bag of dope from any random drug dealer on the corner was unheard of. That would be the equivalent of a mental concession that she really needed it, and in her mind, she didn't. So the absence of the drug in her system on that dreadful morning was attributed to *anything* But, the deprivation of heroin. She could remember, vividly, how her whole body ached, how she experienced cold sweats, watery eyes, and even lost her ever-present appetite. Lianna knew from that morning that she had to remain 'prepared' as to never experience such a dreadful morning like that again.

Removing a second bag from a bundle of nine others wrapped in a rubber band, Lianna opened the small piece of paper, and with now familiar behavior, devoured the second bag up her nose. She held her head back with her eyes closed and sniffed again heartily for a second time, making sure any possible residue trapped in her nose was fully in her system. Lianna took a quick mental count of the eight other bags on the sink's counter behind water eyes.

*Bang! Bang! Bang!*

The sound tore through the pin-drop silent bathroom; Angel rapped on the other side of the door. Lianna jumped from the toilet at the unexpected outburst.

"What the fuck is you doing in there?" Angel cursed, banging on the door again, jiggling the door's handle.

"I'm coming! I'm coming! Damn! Can I take a fucking shit in peace?" Lianna blasted back at him through the locked door. She quickly snatched up the other eight bags from the sink's counter, flushing the other two empty bags down the toilet. She did a fast once over the sink's counter, wiping down any possible evidence with the palm of her hand. Sniffing for a final time, Lianna leaned her head back slightly and checked her nose in the mirror for any signs of the drug. A last glance at the empty toilet, Lianna wiped her watery eyes and opened the bathroom door.

"What the fuck, man? Put some clothes on! Don't nobody wanna see your stank ass!" Angel snapped.

Passing by him with her head down, she sucked her teeth and said, "then don't fuckin' look!"

It was a little before eleven A.M. The bright morning sunshine lit up her entire bedroom on that frigid winter day. There had to be at least two feet of snow outside, accumulated from the last few weeks of snowstorms that rocked the state in that first week of December.

Lianna slipped into a pair of skin tight blue jeans and an extra-large heavy wool sweater, followed by some extra thick, wool socks. Wrapping her thick curly hair in a bun with a dark blue bandana, she grabbed her pack of cigarettes and headed out to the living room. Angel was out of the bathroom and sitting on the couch, leaned over the coffee table gorging on spoonfuls of *arroz con salchichas* right out of the pot. A few chunks of potatoes and scattered kernels of rice littered around the pot on the coffee table, some even spilled on the floor around his feet.

"For a *Moreno* that can't cook, you sure are fucking my food up!" Lianna snickered as she observed him. "And you better clean all that shit up when you're done! Damn! You act like you in the chow hall in prison or something, or like you ain't never ate before!" Lianna tossed her smokes on the coffee table next to him.

Angel kept his head down over the pot, guarding it like an over-protective pit bull, But, sliced his eyes at her for a second. He went back to shoving spoonfuls in his mouth. The *Jerry Springer Show* flashed on the TV. Two females wearing only their skirts and bras with their shirts were ripped to shreds from them fighting, were being pulled apart by Steve and some other security, only to break free and charge at each other again. Chants of 'JERRY!' vibrated from the crowd in unison. The only thing competing with the sound of the TV was Angel chomping down on the food in his open mouth.

"Don't eat it all! Save me some!" Lianna whined, leaning over to nudge Angel on his arm. Stuffing one last spoonful into his mouth, he dropped the huge spoon in the warm pot and sat back with a sigh. Fishing out the handle of the spoon, Lianna dug in and fed herself. Angel picked up her pack of smokes and lit one.

"What the fuck is wrong with your face?"

"What the fuck is you talking about?" Lianna spit between bites.

"Your shit look fucked up! Y'all bitches be looking crazy when y'all ain't got no make-up on!" Angel said, with a hearty laugh.

"At least I can get made up to look good! What can you do? Nigga, you look fucked up and can't nothing help you!" Lianna said, going back at him.

"Yo, I'm for real. Your shits is all black underneath your eyes. You look like a cross between a dusty bird and a wounded raccoon!" Angel stated, and then burst out in laughter again.

"Suck my dick, bitch!" Lianna cursed, flinging the spoon with frustration in the empty pot.

"I bet you wish you did have a dick. But, knowing your nasty ass, you'd probably try to fuck yourself, trick!" Angel said slickly, relentlessly ragging on her. Lianna rolled her eyes at him and lit up a smoke.

"Yo, you got some weed? Smoke with a nigga, ma."

"Nigga, you gotta be playing! You was just talking all that shit about me, how I was just a 'trick' two seconds ago, then you got the nerve to ask me to smoke with you?" Lianna chuckled.

"For real, ma. I ain't trying to drive out in all that shit to get some weed. You got some trees?"

"Yep! I got some good ass weed too! Some head-banger shit! Like a half-ounce of it. But, remember when I asked you to get me some weed that night and you left me for dead, huh? Remember that?"

"Come on, man! Don't do that stupid ass tit-for-tat shit! Man, I told you I just left that stupid ass chick house 'cause she was chirping in my ear on some pigeon-head shit! Then I come home for some peace, and you start barking on me. But, come on, sis. You know I wouldn't do you like that."

"Nigga, fuck you! I ain't trying to hear all that shit! That shit ain't have nothing to do with me! But, you gonna take it out on me cause you ain't got no control over your bitches? Take that shit out on me 'cause your *dick game* is all fucked up? Step your game up, nigga! Stop crying like a little hoe and handle yours. Then maybe next time you'll be able to control them lil' pigeons you be dealing with. And then maybe, just maybe, you'll be able to smoke some of this blunt," Lianna teased, pulling out a crisp five pack of blunts from the crack of the couch.

She did a little mocking dance squirming in her seat, humming in a taunting manner as she split the blunt down the middle. Angel watched her for a second before diving to reach his hand in the crack of the couch on his side of the sofa. He turned back to look at Lianna. She didn't even flinch as she emptied the blunt tobacco in the ashtray.

"You feel stupid, huh?" Lianna said, with a chuckle. "You're a little late. I don't stash my weed there no more. This cross between a dusty bird and wounded raccoon 'trick' found a new hiding spot," Lianna said mockingly. She stood to her feet, licking the empty blunt wrapper to moisten it for easier manipulation. She disappeared to her bedroom and returned seconds later carrying a half-ounce of weed in a clear cellophane bag.

"Come on, ma! Don't do that! Smoke with a nigga!" Angel pleaded in a whiny tone, the second his eyes feasted on the healthy bag.

"You just sit there and wait on that," Lianna taunted, plopping back down on the couch. She hummed a little melody as she held the empty blunt wrapper in one hand, and dug her other hand into the bag on her lap, extracting a large bud of weed to break it up over the moist leaf.

"All right! You wanna be like that? Man, fuck you! Watch! See what happen the next time that nigga you fuck with come through looking for a bundle of dope. Your dumb, stingy, stank ass ain't getting shit! I ain't new to the fuckin' dope game. So I know you ain't getting that nigga dope for nothing! I know you getting your little cut of the money off the top. I ain't stupid! I was gonna give you a play, too. But, the next time that nigga come around, I ain't giving you shit!" Angel threatened, staring angrily at her as she twisted the blunt closed with the tips of her fingers.

"And? Who do you think you hurting? That's just less money for you! I'm still gonna get mines," Lianna bluffed, sparking a lighter to the tip of the blunt. Angel remained silent, stewing in his anger. His silence began to make Lianna uneasy.

*What if he wasn't bluffing? Would he really turn her down the next time she went to purchase off him, all out of spite? Would he turn down her money just to get back at her? Would he call her on her bluff?* Lianna knew within herself that the only one who would really be affected by the sever in their transactions would be her.

Angel was her only dope connection and having a secret dope connection so close, literally living under the same roof, was too invaluable to lose. She had to play herself cool in that situation. Giving him the blunt too quickly would most likely expose her sole reliance on him; but, refusing to give him the blunt altogether could very likely sever that valuable connection.

She took a few pulls off the blunt, playing it cool; her demeanor like she didn't have a care in the world. Out the corner of her eye, she could see Angel

now angrily absorbed in the TV. The closing credits of the show rolled up off the screen. A few moments had passed, enough time as to not look too desperate, before Lianna exhaled a cloud of smoke, saying, "look at you. Whining like a little bitch! I'ma smoke with you," then leaned forward to tap the ashes in the ashtray.

"Man, fuck you! Keep that shit! You wanna act all stingy with your shit? All right, watch. The next time..."

"*Ay, dios mio*! Shut tha fuck up, nigga! Tomar, here!" Lianna spit, pushing the blunt at him. He looked at her with angry eyes for a second before reaching for it. Raising it to his lips, Lianna watched as he greedily sucked on it, filling his lungs, the look of anger quickly fading as the powerful narcotic entered his system. A strange dichotomy existed within Lianna—one of an outwardly annoyed person conceding to the pressure, the other, inward relief at salvaging her connect. Passing the blunt between them until over half of it was consumed; they both looked up upon hearing a knock at the door.

"Go get that shit," Angel said dryly, behind bloodshot eyes, receiving the blunt from Lianna.

"I ain't getting it. You know it's just one of your stupid ass boys," Lianna returned, kicking her feet up on the coffee table. Angel huffed at the incessant rapping on the door, forcing him to get up. "Yo! Don't take the blunt with you!" Lianna called out as he stood to his feet, walking off towards the front door with the blunt still between his fingers.

"Man, I ain't going nowhere. Calm down," Angel assured, disappearing around the corner to answer the door. From the couch, Lianna could hear Angel talking with what sounded like two of his boys at the front door. Their voices went in and out for over five minutes, with Lianna sitting on the couch debating on if she should get up from her comfortable position to get the blunt from him. She got lost in the previews of the *Maury Show*.

"....and the lie detector test determined that was a lie!" Maury pronounced, as Lianna turned up the volume over Angel and his boy's voices, focused on a young couple on the stage. Watching the young brother angrily jump to his feet and fling his chair with rage from underneath him after Maury read his third alleged lie; he cursed a few choice words, adamantly professing his innocence, as his teary eyed girlfriend screamed in his face and ran off the stage.

Lianna chuckled under her breath, and then said to no one, "Aha! You got caught out!" taking pleasure in his misfortune. During the commercial break, Lianna lowered the volume on the remote to listen for Angel. She heard nothing.

"Angel!" Lianna screamed out, pressing mute. There was no answer. She immediately popped to her feet and stormed around the corner to the front door. She couldn't believe it, he was gone! Leaving with her blunt and all. Lianna swung her front door open to see that his car was gone from its parking space. Lianna was fuming. More than fuming. She knew Angel was grimy, but, leaving with her blunt like that was unforgivable.

The cold weather from outside wasn't cold enough to cool Lianna down from her heated state. It didn't even have enough time to give her a chill before she slammed her front door in anger behind her. Cursing every obscenity under her breath that her mind could conjure up, Lianna turned back to walk in her living room more upset at Angel than ever. Because not only did he leave with half of her blunt, he left her living room a complete mess without cleaning up before he left.

Lianna knew if she left it like that, waiting for Angel to come home only God knows when to clean up after himself, that within a half hour, there would be a million cockroaches having a feeding frenzy on her living room coffee table. She knew she had no choice but, to clean it up. Cleaning up as minimally as possible, but, just enough to prevent a cockroach carnival, Lianna soaked the pot in the sink followed by a quick vacuum before walking off to the bathroom.

A glimpse in the bathroom mirror triggered the memory of the insults Angel spewed at her earlier that morning. She examined her face, particularly under her eyes. The spots under her eyes were considerably darker, to the point of being noticeable. She tried to put the image out of her mind. A heavy application of cover-up was applied to her face, enough to satisfy and mask any flaw that was evident in her appearance. The brief moment she spent at her front door searching for Angel gave her an idea as to what the weather was like outside.

Brushing the kinks out of her hair, Lianna sliced it down the middle, braiding each side into two Pocahontas-style braids. She braided them forward so they rested on her chest outside of the black hoody sweatshirt that she put on. Wrapping another navy blue bandana around her ears and slipping on a pair of black quarter length Timberland boots, Lianna threw on her black

leather coat and headed out the door.

The walk to the store was brief, but, Lianna still received enough honks from the few random cars passing by her. That particular attention put a smile on her face, cheering her up from the irate mood Angel put her in. Purchasing a half bag full of junk food, some soft drinks, and a few other items, Lianna exited the small corner bodega to see an *Infiniti* truck pulling up into the parking lot a few spaces down.

He was a brown-skinned brother, and from what she could see, he was cute. She purposely slowed her pace, until he jumped out of the driver's seat headed her way. Within steps of each other, their eyes locked; Lianna was the first to crack a slight smile.

"Word to the Gods, Chili. You got T.L.C. up in there with you?" He chimed, stepping in front of Lianna. The line was corny, and she was tired of being told that she had an uncanny resemblance to *Chili* from the R&B group, T.L.C. But, he was cute, and he did have a nice truck.

"What you worried about them for? I'm right here," Lianna answered, playing along. They traded introductions in front of the store. Lianna learned that his name was Shalon, and he was from the other side of town. Exchanging cell phone numbers, Lianna turned and was seconds from walking away. But, once Shalon seen that she was walking, he offered her a ride that she quickly accepted.

Making plans to get together later that night, Shalon drove Lianna the few blocks to drop her off back at her apartment. Lianna stood on the edge of the road watching his truck speed off up the street, his muffler spewing out a thick white cloud of smoke behind it. She was momentarily lost in her new acquaintance until the sight of Angel's car brought her back to reality. Doing a track star jump over the large snow bank, Lianna ran off up the stairs to her apartment intent on giving Angel a piece of her mind.

# Chapter 30 | Stunt 101

I t was only a little after six P.M., but, it was dark out as a result of the winter solstice robbing that side of the world for at least two hours of daylight. Liaka, Asia, and Lianna walked through Liaka's front door. Asia headed straight to the kitchen. Liaka was more concerned with stripping her coat from her body, followed by her cream pin-striped blazer. Unclasping her bra through her white silk dress shirt, Liaka unbuttoned the back of her tight business skirt and plopped down on the sofa. She breathed a heavy sigh of relief from the long day she had. All morning she had her ASA training, studying with her boss for the Bar exam. She was beat.

Lianna was the first to call Liaka before she left work, asking Liaka to pick her up before she went home. Trapped in the house all day, Lianna just wanted to get out. Asia, on the other hand, was having trouble with her car for the last week, thereby obligating Liaka to pick her up every day from work. Hoping to steal a few hours of quiet time before she went to pick up her kids at her mother's house, Asia had no problem spending those few hours at Liaka's with her girls.

"Bring me something to drink, Asia," Liaka called out, leaning over to zip down her calf high leather boot.

"Yeah, grab me something, too," Lianna added, walking off to the bathroom.

"Damn! Again? You gonna have your insides fall out!" Liaka teased, before

Lianna could leave the room.

"Shaddup! I think it was something I ate," Lianna explained with a scrunched face, disappearing around the corner. Moments later, Asia returned carrying a two-liter bottle of soda with three empty glasses.

"Where this chick go?" Asia asked, removing her blazer and took a seat on the sofa next to Liaka. "Not to the bathroom again?" Liaka chuckled with a nod. "Let me ask you. You don't think she's been acting a little strange lately? Always disappearing off to the bathroom, acting all weird and stuff?"

"That's just Lianna. You know she just gets a little weird sometimes. I'm surprised you're just noticing that now," Liaka answered dryly, reaching for an empty cup.

"No. I mean *different*. For the last few weeks, she's just been...different," Asia repeated in a hushed tone, taking a few glances over her shoulder.

"I haven't noticed her doing anything she wouldn't normally do. Her going to the bathroom, I think..."

"Your boss said what?" Asia blurted the second she witnessed Lianna heading back into the living room. Liaka eyed Asia curiously, but, cast a glance over her shoulder to see Lianna approaching them from behind. Lianna didn't catch it. "So, how's the Bar exams coming along?" Asia asked, filling her glass with soda.

"It's a royal pain in my ass! Mainly because I'm so far behind. The other two girls that I started studying with are way ahead of me. I mean, so many hours and I don't even know how many exams ahead of me. I'm just catching up. I don't care if it will take a month of sleepless nights, I'll do it. And if...or should I say *when* I pass the Bar exam to become an attorney, it will all be worth it," Liaka said dreamily.

"That's the problem with my job. There's not too much room for me to advance, and I sure do need the money," Asia said disheartened.

"Why? Can't you push for a raise, a promotion, something?" Liaka asked.

"Promotion to what? No. My best bet is to just look for another career. Because with the money I'm making, and the little bit of money Donovan gives me every now and then in child support, it's just not cutting it."

"What's going on with Donovan?"

"Fuck him! That bastard can kiss my black ass!" Asia spewed, with a roll of her eyes.

"Damn. Why you say it like that?" Liaka said.

"Because, he did it! He really went through with it and married that bitch! That six o'clock, no curve, straight up and down, pencil bitch! I really didn't think he would actually do it. But, he did. But, the bitch wasn't even worth a *real* wedding. They just went to the Justice of the Peace at the Town Hall. And would you believe the day he tied the knot, that his sorry ass has been coming up short on his child support payments?

"Personally, I just thought he wanted a break. Maybe play in a few female's *'yards'* before he realized what he had and come *home*. I thought the chick was just a fling. I would have never thought in a million years that he would have allowed another female to come between him and his kids," Asia said, "and that's sorta a problem I was hoping you could help me with, Liaka," Asia continued sympathetically. "You know I would never ask you if I really didn't need it. But, the money in the safe in New York. Olu's safe. Do you...do you think maybe...Liaka, I need some of that money." Liaka looked over to her; Asia was unable to mask the sadness in her eyes. Liaka sighed.

"The rest of it is gone," Liaka said softly.

"Gone? What do you mean, gone?" Lianna spoke up, jumping into their conversation.

"Liaka, if you don't wanna lend me the money, fine! But, you don't have to insult me by saying all of that is gone," Asia spit, slightly offended.

"Come on, Asia. You know I would never deny you something like that. I could lend you some money. No! I can *give* you some money. Because you know I took half the money out of the safe the first time we went up there. But, the rest of the money is gone."

"I don't understand. What do you mean when you say it's gone?" Asia questioned incredulously.

"I went up there by myself a few weeks ago. I went there to check on some things, and to get the rest of the money. But, the locks were changed. And when I looked in through the window, the entire apartment was empty. I even kicked in a window and broke into the place. But, when I went into his room, the safe was gone," Liaka related in a dejected tone.

Asia sunk in her seat. That was not the news she wanted to hear. The twenty-G's Liaka gave her a couple of months ago came through when she needed it. But, it was more just to catch her up. Asia secretly counted on Liaka to come through for her, and the sad reality is she wasn't going to get what she thought.

"You ain't got to worry about the money. 'Cause I got the perfect dude we can get," Lianna said casually. Liaka shot her head to Lianna, wide-eyed, as if she just seen a ghost, unable to believe what Lianna just said.

"A dude we can get? What...what are you talking abou..."

"You know Lianna. Always saying something out of her mouth without thinking! Things that don't make no sense!" Liaka said sharply, cutting Asia off. She sliced squinted eyes at Lianna that screamed, *what the hell are you doing? Shut the fuck up!*

"You know what? Both of y'all bitches kill me! Y'all both *claim* to be the best of friends, but, y'all both act like y'all scared to let each other know how you *really* get down! So, since y'all both too scared to tell it, I will!" Lianna spewed.

"Yeah, Asia. If you need to get your paper right, I got this kid we could set up to rob. Me and Liaka done robbed two niggas already, and that's why she can fix her mouth to just give you some money. So I don't know why she's still frontin'. Shit! She's the one that put me on to robbing niggas! Hell, she even robbed one of them niggas by herself, and that's how the whole thing got started!" Lianna confessed, spilling the secret Liaka worked so hard to conceal; the secret she thought they both tried to conceal. Asia was floored, speechless. She could only slowly turn to Liaka and stare at her in disbelief.

"And now to you, Asia," Lianna continued, "I don't know why you sitting there acting all surprised, cause you be frontin', too! And if you wanna act like you got a case of amnesia, I'm talking about Kenny! You remember him, right? My little toy. The nigga that I called to my crib that night and had him give you some head to the point where you fucked my sheets up? Yeah, bitch! You owe me some new sheets! Is it all coming back to you now?" Lianna spit. Asia couldn't help but, to transform her look of astonishment, from the revelation of Liaka's secret, to sheer embarrassment from Lianna exposing hers.

"And the funny thing is, you would think as close as the both of you *claim* to be, that you would at least be yourselves around each other. But, both of y'all be stuntin', STUNT 101. Putting on y'all little masks of that perfect image, trying to convince *each other* that y'all something that y'all really not! And hey, I'm all for throwing on the mask and being that chameleon, changing faces, moods, styles, and clothes for the occasion. But, not around my best friends!

"Liaka, just admit it—you loved that shit! Robbing them niggas gave you that rush, that adrenaline rush. You don't think I was watching you? I saw how you was looking, how you was acting. You was thinking of Olu! How he got down, how he was building you. That shit is in you now, mama. Get your thug on."

"And Asia, bottom line, you's a fuckin' freak! And the worst part about it is, you really got YOURSELF convinced that you're not! I'm all up for you to live and portray that little church-girl, goodie-goodie image to niggas. I understand. You wanna be seen in their eyes as some wifey-type shit. If that works for you, fine. I wouldn't even care if you lied to Liaka and me. But, don't lie to *yourself.* Keep it real, you like your pussy ate out! You like dick. You like getting fucked. Ain't nothing wrong with that. You're human. That's just part of human nature," Lianna explained in a more casual tone, taking a sip of her soda.

She shrugged, and then placed a flame to the tip of a smoke. Complete silence fell over the entire room. Lianna was the only one who remained visibly animated; scanning back and forth between Liaka and Asia. She found it humorously amusing to watch them.

Yet, the irony in Lianna's little speech of redemption was that she clearly forgot to include *herself* into the equation. It was quite simple for her to 'free' Liaka and Asia from the secrets they held close to themselves, but, Lianna would never come clean with the little 'bone in her closet' of the new daily activity she'd been participating in—sniffing dope almost as frequently as she lit up a smoke. They both made every effort not to make eye contact with each other; their body language expressing how uncomfortable they were.

Lianna finally sucked her teeth, and spit, "look! I only did that so we could get that shit out in the open, so we could be real around each other! And now that we got all that shit out, we can handle this shit like a team! All the masks are off. I'll tell it like it is. Liaka, that shit got me open! So you already know I got the next nigga we can get. I studied him, and he got a tight little crew, but, all of them is sweet. That's another reason why I put that shit out there, 'cause we got to put Asia down. We need her on this one. You said you needed the money, right?" Lianna stated, focusing on Asia. Asia kept her head down, she remained silent, but reluctantly nodded.

"And, Asia, on the right day and time, Liaka would have traded places with you in a second! If her 'monthly friend' wasn't visiting, she would have been right alongside you, legs in the air getting tossed up, too! Tell me I'm lying, Liaka?" Lianna spit, throwing a twisted look at Liaka. Liaka blushed, but remained silent herself as well. Lianna scanned back and forth between them again.

After a few moments of tense silence, Lianna huffed, and spit, "I'm done! I'm done! Both of y'all can remain comfortable in your little secluded shells. But, just know, the only people you're fooling is yourselves!" then got up to storm off to the kitchen.

They watched Lianna walk out, for Asia to say in a soft tone, "That day when we went to the Federal Prison to visit Olu's friend, Shakim, when he told me what he used to do, the robberies, I left there and couldn't get him off my mind. It was just something about the way he described it that...that gave me the chills," Asia confessed, taking occasional glances at Liaka, but, never for more than a second. Liaka looked over and stared at her.

"That's exactly how I felt when Olu first confessed to me what he used to do," Liaka revealed. "It was just something so seductive in the way he described it. So powerful. And I kinda figured from your reaction, that you were having the same feelings that I was having when I first heard them."

Asia finally lifted her head to Liaka. "So you really did it? You actually robbed someone, Liaka?" Asia questioned, still amazed.

"Well, the first time, it wasn't really like that. I was curious. It was actually the guy I was in the hotel with, the one I was telling you about that passed out on me. When he passed out, I just kinda took all of his stuff," Liaka explained innocently. For the first time since Lianna put them both out on Front Street, did they lock into each other's eyes. Then it happened, they both broke out in hysterical laughter.

"What do you mean; you just kinda took all his stuff? When you told me about your date that night, you sure enough left that part out!" Asia said, still giggling. "Liaka, are you crazy?"

"I don't know. I just wanted to see what it would feel like. And I knew I couldn't tell you something like that. But, I had to tell somebody. So I told Lianna. And I know you're not gonna be fooled by Lianna's little theory of us robbing those guys being all my idea. I admit, I told her about how I felt when Olu told me all those stories, and even when I got that brother that night. But, it's not like I had to twist her arm to do it with me! And Asia, if you thought Lianna was crazy before, you wouldn't believe how she got down when she did that!"

"I could imagine. But, I kinda expect something like that from her. I'm still kinda buggin' that you actually did it."

"Well, what about you? Miss dedicated-and-loyal-to-Donovan! You don't think I knew something was funny that night when you went home with her? Picture you and Lianna hanging out together. Yeah right!"

"Shit! That night at the club when she started telling us about him, you know it had been awhile since I been with Donovan, and girl...I had to get mines!" Asia said thickly. They broke out in laughter again. "And I don't know what she's talking about; I owe her some new sheets? Shit, that's her fault! She ain't warn me that it was gonna be all like that! Liaka, girl. What that brother can do with his tongue...ump!" Asia said smiling, her eyes closed, a shiver shaking her whole body.

"So, did y'all finally stop with that ole bullshit?" Lianna questioned, walking back into the living room, taking a bite out of a sandwich she just made. "Because if y'all finally managed to get past the bullshit, then we can finally link up and become a team."

"A team? What do you mean, a team?" Asia posed.

"What the fuck does the word team mean? All three of us would be working together. Partners, associates, hermanas! Working together as a group."

"Um, I think you better lay off the weed, or whatever else you're on. 'Cause it's no way I'm doing some crazy shit like that! Hearing someone talk to me about it is one thing. Even being aroused by it is another. But, actually doing it, um, that's out of the question.

"Do you know if someone told me a year ago that I would do something like that, I woulda thought they were crazy too," Liaka said, "But, when I did it, I mean *really* did it, it was like...words can't describe it. When Lianna shot this one dude..."

"What? You actually shot someone?" Asia blurted, whipping her head around to Lianna.

"Yeah, but, that was the first time, after she made him crash his car. But, the second time..."

"The second time? You say that like...just how many times have you both done that? I mean, wow! What are you? Bonnie and Clyde? Well, Bonnie and Bonnie!" Asia sighed incredulously.

"You still ain't get off that bullshit yet? Look, me and Liaka got this shit on and poppin'! We done mapped it out on how to get these niggas, how to spot 'em, get them alone, get them off point, and finally rob them! All that! Now you said you needed some money, right?" Lianna snapped at Asia.

"Yeah, I said that I needed some money, But..."

"But, nothing! Asia, it's easy money! These niggas are drug dealers. It's not like we're robbing niggas that actually *need* the money! They woulda gave it to us slowly But, surely anyways trying to get some pussy. So, all we're doing is speeding up the process."

"But, what about getting caught?"

"Caught? Caught how? Who the fuck is a drug dealer gonna call when you rob him, the police? Them niggas just gots to take that shit as an L, a straight loss!" Lianna stressed. Just then, the phone rang. Lianna continued talking to Asia, more or less trying to convince her, as Liaka got up to answer it.

"Hello?"

"Hello, Maliaka." The voice was familiar, but Liaka just couldn't seem to put her finger on who it was. "Almighty defender and justice," David said, after a couple seconds.

"David. I knew who you were. What's up?" Liaka said enthusiastically.

"Just sitting here thinking about you. Since the last time we went out, I haven't heard from you. I've called, left messages, But, you never got back to me."

"I'm sorry. I've just been really swamped at work lately."

"Oh, because I thought we had a really good time on our first date."

"I did. I had a really good time," Liaka assured.

"I'm glad to hear. I had a really good time myself. A great time. And I was wondering if maybe...do you have company over? I'm sorry, are you busy?" David asked, hearing faint voices in Liaka's background.

"No, I'm not busy. I just got a couple of my girlfriends over. But, I can talk." She turned to see Lianna standing at the foot of the couch pretending as if she was holding a gun; obviously relating one of their heists to Asia. Asia was entranced as she gazed up at Lianna, hanging on to her every word, until they broke out in laughter.

"Sounds like you guys are having a really good time."

"They're just being silly," Liaka chuckled, watching Lianna be so animated.

"Now that I finally managed to catch up with you, and you told me it's not a product of you dodging me..."

"I wouldn't dodge you, David. I really did have a good time out with you."

"Good. Then I was wondering if I could ask you something. I've been invited to this annual *charity event* this weekend. And I was wondering if you would do me the honor and attend it with me—as my date. I've attended them for the last three years now, and it's for a really good cause. But, it's also, how should I say this..."

"Boring!" Liaka blurted.

"Bingo!" David said with a chuckle. "To sum it up, it is boring. But, I know if I went with you by my side, that our evening out would be the last thing but boring," David said in a suave tone.

"Is that so?"

"I know so. And this would be a great way for you to make up for leaving me in suspense so long," David stated. Liaka remained silent for a moment, thinking about the invitation. A charity event, Liaka thought. That was definitely something different, something new. It sounded interesting. Liaka was hit with an idea.

"Well, since you put it like that, how could I say no," Liaka answered. The few moments Liaka was on the phone began to attract Asia and Lianna's attention. Liaka could see Asia silently mouthing, 'who's that?' for Liaka to raise her index finger. Asia pressed the issue, for Liaka to wave her off like she was swatting flies away, and then turned her back to listen to David.

"Sure, I'd love to attend and be your date, David."

"Great! As I said, it's a formal event, a Black Tie affair. It's Saturday night. The invitation says eight P.M., so I'll pick you up, say, seven-ish?"

"Seven-ish sounds good. I'll see you then," Liaka sighed in a sexy tone.

"Until then," David ended.

"Who was that?" Asia asked, before Liaka even had enough time to place the phone back down.

"That was David."

"That cop? You still fucking with the po-po, huh?" Lianna spit in a disgusted tone. "What the fuck did he want?"

"He was just calling me to invite me to a charity event," Liaka said to Lianna, who rolled her eyes in the air at the thought.

"Are you going?" Asia inquired.

"I have to go. There's a few things I have to do there."

# Chapter 31 | Past Acquaintances

David's gold Jeep Cherokee pulled to a stop in front of the large cathedral-type building where the charity drive was taking place. CHARITY DRIVE: *Hartford Police Fights Multiple Sclerosis.* The frigid ten degree gusts of wind abused the thin nylon banner, whipping it savagely into a squiggly, snake-like dance against the building's bricks. David opened his driver's door, but, before he could take one step out, Liaka was pleasantly greeted by a valet opening her passenger door for her.

A four-inch *Jerry Wong* pump crushed the scattered remains of rock salt sprinkled over the street curb leading up to the entrance. Liaka was led by her hand as the valet assisted her from the car. She caught the eyes of the white teenage valet stealing a quick glance at her muscled calf, leading up to her milk chocolate thigh, as she slowly rose from the vehicle. Pulling her coat tightly against her body, Liaka snuggled up in her full length, dark brown fox fur, to protect herself from the frigid wind nipping at her skin.

"Shall we?" David said with a smile, his elbow extended to Liaka. She immediately pushed her arm through his, for them to walk side by side up the steps of the main entrance. The below freezing temperatures was enough incentive for them to double their pace to the front doors. Feet from the door, a doorman bundled up for the chilly night, flashed a smile and slight nod at them before courtly opening the door.

Triple Crown Publications presents... Queen of Thieves *PART 1*

Once inside the main foyer, they were greeted by two young blonde females who appeared to be in their late teens, handing them each a pamphlet chronologically detailing the nights' events.

"Madam," came the voice of a coat man approaching Liaka from the side to take her coat. David was already in the process of removing his coat from his shoulders, as the gentleman helped Liaka with hers. The warmth from the heated room began to caress over Liaka's body, loosening her shoulders in the process.

Liaka couldn't deny that she was smiling on the inside. Being invited to such an event, being treated like semi-royalty made her feel good. Attending the law office parties over the years couldn't compare to the feelings Liaka was having at that social event. Removing his overcoat to hand it over to the coat man, who placed it over his forearm, followed by Liaka's fur, David gazed at Liaka finally able to take in the stunning dress she wore.

Her black cashmere dress, although loosely fitted, still managed to accentuate every voluptuous curve on her body. Her hair was styled into a tight bun on the back of her head, a platinum chain with a two karat diamond hung from her neck, thick diamond tennis bracelets weighed down her wrist and ankle.

"You look beautiful," David sighed with earnest sincerity.

"Thank you," Liaka cooed, blushing.

"You are by far the most beautiful woman in here."

"And how would you know? You haven't even seen all the women in here."

"I don't have to, to know that they couldn't hold a candle to you," David said smoothly, extending his elbow to Liaka again. He was mesmerized by Liaka, eyeing her up and down.

"You clean up pretty nicely yourself," Liaka returned warmly, taking his arm.

David did look nice in his three-piece tux; the waves on his head were crisp, three-hundred and sixty degrees spinning, and razor sharp edge-up lining his forehead, all the way down to his pin-stripe goatee. Proceeding arm and arm into the main area, Liaka was somewhat awed by the prospects of the room; a massive crystal light chandelier in the center of the hall, hanging low from the fifty foot ceiling, with four smaller identical chandeliers squaring off the center; Roman style pillars juxtapose each other about twenty feet apart, lining down the center entrance of the room. A jazz melody that Liaka was familiar with echoed liked an enchanted serenade throughout the spacious room, as

Liaka laid her eyes on the finely polished wooden dance floor in the far right corner; couples were ballroom dancing on it.

Liaka then feasted her eyes on a huge ice sculpture of a swan, back dropped in a purple light, surrounded by a banquet of various hors d'oeuvres. The hall was packed to near capacity with everyone dressed in their finest apparel. Liaka and David walked arm and arm. A few random eyes turned to gaze upon them as they made their entrance down the steps to enter the crowd.

"Madam," came from another servant at Liaka, offering her a crystal flute filled with champagne from a silver tray. They both took two glasses with smiles and nods at the servant who nodded in return, disappearing into the crowd with the remaining drinks as quickly as he arrived. David was the first to raise the glass to his lips to take a small sip. Liaka followed in turn.

"This is really nice, David," Liaka confessed, after swallowing a mouthful of the sparkling bubbly liquid.

"I'm just really happy that you decided to join me here tonight," David returned, gently pulling her closer to his side. "Please, come with me. I want to introduce you to some people," David insisted, placing his free hand on the small of her back to guide her through the room.

The first person David guided Liaka to, as they weaved through the tight crowd, was a face that needed no introduction. Liaka soon found herself shaking hands and chatting with the Mayor of Hartford. She came to find out that David was no stranger to some of the major key figures in the Hartford area, as one after the other; David formally acquainted Liaka with each of them.

Liaka was introduced to heads such as the Attorney General, the Chief of Police, the first African-American Secretary of the State in Connecticut, to judges, and more city representatives than Liaka could keep track of. She tried her best to remember the names, faces, and position of each person she considered important, hoping to make a lasting impression on each of them as she was introduced. David was meticulous in his desire to introduce Liaka to everyone he recognized, leaving Liaka unsure if David was trying to impress her with his circle of associates, or show her off as some type of trophy girl.

"Would you care to dance?" David finished off his champagne, to place the empty glass on the edge of a podium, and then extended his hand to Liaka. Liaka lit up into a bright smile.

"I'd love to," Liaka beamed, placing her hand in his.

Liaka was pleasantly surprised by the way David moved on the dance floor; he was light on his feet, his movements were graceful, he led, but not aggressively, rhythmically swaying Liaka in a one-two step. Liaka noticed how David remained a complete gentleman the entire time. They danced a few songs as David constantly entertained her by whispering whimsical comments in her ear.

"You're so crazy!" Liaka giggled, with a playful slap on his arm. They made their way off the dance floor to the buffet table.

"No, I'm serious. Did you see him? He was dancing like he had a stick up his butt," David joked, causing Liaka to snicker again. David was the first to focus on the delicatessen of thinly sliced meat and cheeses displayed across the table. Reaching for a napkin, he picked at each tray, raising hors d'oeuvres to his nose to smell it before placing it on his napkin. Popping one into his mouth, then another, Liaka watched him as he snacked on his treats, scanning around the room.

"Maliaka, please excuse me for one minute. I see someone I have to talk to," David informed her, crumpling up the napkin, then stepped off from her side. Liaka followed David with her eyes as he snuck up behind a light-skinned brother with a tight tapered afro, who appeared to be in his late twenties. The brother threw his hands around David and hugged him tightly with laughter.

Turning back to the buffet table, Liaka looked over the different selections and picked the most visibly appealing treat before she heard over her shoulder, "Excuse me, may I have this dance?" Liaka turned back to look up at a white, salt and pepper haired gentleman, who was clearly in his mid-fifties.

"I'm sorry. But, I just got off the dance floor, and..."

"Please. Do me the honor of one dance. One dance with such a stunningly beautiful woman would really make this a memorable night for me. Just one dance," he implored, slowly reaching for Liaka's hand. Liaka blushed.

"How can I say no to that?" Liaka sighed with a smile, placing her hors d'oeuvres filled napkin back on the table. The man led Liaka back out to the dance floor. His movements weren't nearly as graceful as David's, but, he was still a very good dancer, nonetheless. The dance began normal; the older gentleman led, one hand extended to their sides, the other on the small of Liaka's back. But, if Liaka wasn't mistaken, by the turn of the second song, his hand was subtly lowering until it rested on the top of her ass.

"I saw you out here earlier, and I wouldn't have been able to live with myself if I didn't at least ask for one dance," he stated, looking deeply into Liaka's eyes.

"I don't know what to say. Thank you," Liaka blushed, as they gracefully two-stepped in small circles.

"What do you do for a living?"

"I'm a paralegal for one of the senior partners at Hertzberg, Hertzberg..."

"Fox and Green. I'm familiar. They're a really good firm. I've presided over a few cases from that firm. Most of them favorable."

"Oh, so you're a judge?" Liaka said brightly.

"GA 19, out of Rockville. I've been there for eight years. How do you like it over at Hertzberg?"

"Working for James has been great. He's actually mentoring me right now as I study for the Bar."

"Really? Beauty and brains. I had no idea that I was in the arms of Connecticut's most prominent up and coming future attorney. You know, I've guided many young women such as yourself through the pitfalls that come with taking the Bar," the Judge said, taking on somewhat of a seductive tone.

"Pitfalls, huh? And how might you be able to...ah!" Liaka gasped, as the Judge quickly spun Liaka around, dipped her into a bow and brought her back up in one smooth motion.

"Because there's many surprises that come with the practice of law. But, with the right gentleman in your corner, such as myself, I might be able to walk you through any roadblocks, even pull a few strings for you," the Judge stated, wrapping Liaka in one arm, spinning her out, then pulled her back close to his chest.

"You're quite the dancer," Liaka said, keeping up with every twirl and bend he put her through. "And if I didn't know any better, I'd think you were flirting with me," Liaka cooed, with a bright smile.

"Now that would be completely unethical on my part," the Judge said lightly, followed by a wink. "What I am doing is offering you an internship, if you'd like one. It would require a lot of late night hours with us working side by side. But, I could almost assure you..."

"May I cut in?" David asked, tapping the Judge on the shoulder. The Judge peeked back to see David standing behind him. Liaka could see that he was reluctant to let her go. But, he eventually did.

"The pleasure was all mine. Here's my card. Give me a call if you decide

Triple Crown Publications presents... Queen of Thieves
PART 1

to take me up on my offer," the Judge stated, pulling a card from the inside pocket of his black blazer. He placed it in Liaka's palm, but, instead of letting go, he raised her hand to his lips to plant a peck on the back of it.

"Sir," the judge ended, with a nod at David. He took one final glance at Liaka, then handed her over to David and walked off through the crowd.

"Should I be jealous?" David said, taking the judge's place.

"Maybe. He was pretty smooth," Liaka teased.

"But, not nearly as smooth as me," David returned keenly, pulling Liaka tightly in his arms.

"Not even close," Liaka assured with a sexy smile.

"What was that about? I introduce you to a few people, turn my back, and by the time I return you're networking like you've been doing it for years. Quick learner."

"I had a good teacher, Mr. protect and serve. Actually, he was a judge who is familiar with my firm. We were talking about me studying for the Bar and he offered me an internship with him."

"I see you just have that type of effect on people, huh? Come on. I want you to meet someone else."

"Is there anyone left? I woulda thought you already introduced me to everyone in here by now," Liaka said sarcastically.

"Ha, ha. Very funny," David sighed. "This guy here is a really good friend of mines. He is one of the guys who I really look up to on the force. He helped me out a lot," David said, leading Liaka off the dance floor. He led her to a group of about ten men mingling. They were rowdy. From first appearance as they approached, Liaka could see that they were pretty rambunctious; pulling and tugging at each other, drinking heavily at the bar. They seemed oddly out of place at such a function, their behavior more fitting to a corner bar than an elegant charity event.

They were crowded in a circle; about six of them faced Liaka. They all appeared to be fellow cops; all of them were either black or Spanish, clean cut, military issued haircuts. The ones that faced them focused on Liaka and David as they approached. The remaining four were oblivious.

"Fellas. Zay. This is the very special lady I was telling you about," David began, acknowledging all of the brothers there with a quick nod, But, focused on one of the four men with his back turned to them.

"Maliaka, I'd like you to meet a good friend of mines. Maliaka, José.

José, Maliaka," David said proudly, introducing them to each other. He turned around for Liaka to stare wide-eyed into the face of the man David introduced her to. It was José, José Dominguez. The detective who killed the love of her life.

Liaka couldn't believe it. But, there she was, standing face to face with the man who murdered Olu. The last time she seen him in person was at the bank; him being whisked off in the back of an unmarked patrol car, Liaka on her knees with Olu bleeding out on her lap. Liaka had nightmares of this man's face, the face that stood only feet from her.

José stuffed the last of an hors d'oeuvre in his mouth, cleaned the crumbs from his fingers in a napkin, and then extended his hand to Liaka. She stood frozen. Liaka didn't notice it, but she couldn't move, all she could do was stare up at José with a paralyzed look. José's hand hung in the balance.

A few seconds of tense silence passed, with all of them staring at an appalled Liaka, before José said, "You see the type of effect I have on women," looking around to the group. They all broke out in laughter.

"Maliaka, are you okay?" David asked gently, snapping Liaka out of her trance. It took the sound of David's voice to bring her back to reality.

"I'm...I'm sorry. I'm fine," Liaka stuttered, extending her hand to José. "It's very nice to meet you," Liaka said, taking his hand, speaking in a more casual tone. It took every ounce of willpower Liaka could muster to force a fake smile on her face.

"The pleasure is mines," José returned, gently squeezing Liaka's hand. José studied Liaka's face up close, getting lost within her eyes, subtly venturing down to her thick lips, then back up to her eyes. "Hey Dave, would you mind if I took this beautiful lady for a few spins on the dance floor?" José announced, never taking his eyes off Liaka.

"Well, I don't think she's..."

"It's okay, David. I think my calves can hold me up for one more round," Liaka spoke up, nodding at David. José guided her off to the dance floor before David could speak another word. Liaka peeked over her shoulder to see the sad look on David's face. But, she quickly erased his feelings from her thoughts. They had to be irrelevant at the time. She soon became more focused on her feelings. The extreme hatred she had for José, strangely enough, caused her to put things in perspective on why she went there in the first place.

 Triple Crown Publications presents... Queen of Thieves PART I

"So, what's a beautiful woman like you doing with *David?*"

Liaka was a little taken aback by his question, but answered, "he invited me here. So, I didn't see any harm in coming," finding it impossible to maintain eye contact with him.

"Oh, so you two are not an item?" José probed enthusiastically.

"We went out a couple of times. We're friends."

"Friends? I see. Well, is there any possibility that we can be *friends*, too?" José said slickly, pulling Liaka closer to his body. Liaka flashed a look up at him.

"I don't know. How do you think David would feel about that?"

"David? David who? What does David have to do with you and me?"

"Nothing, I guess. I just thought he was your friend."

"Don't get me wrong. David's a good guy. But, I think, no, I know, we'd be much better suited as friends. A woman like you, I'm more your type of guy."

"Really? And just what type of guy do I need?"

"A guy like me!" José said thickly.

"I guess we'll have to see about that," Liaka answered.

José was smooth on his feet. Liaka could tell he was quite a dancer in Salsa or Merengue, but, he was even smoother with his tongue. The way he moved, spoke, if Liaka didn't know for a fact that he was a cop, she would have never believed it. He reminded her more of a gangsta; one of the many thugs she remembered growing up with. Taking his eyes off her, Liaka noticed how something began to distract him. He glanced quickly over Liaka's shoulder, then back to her.

"Here!" José hushed, removing a card from his pocket, "take this. Put it away," he continued, pushing the card in Liaka's hand. Liaka looked back over her shoulder to see David weaving his way through the crowded dance floor, then back to José in front of her. Liaka took the card from his hand in a nonchalant manner and sneakily stuffed it down the front of her bra. A devilish smirk spread across José's face when he realized that Liaka would engage in his little scheme. Securing it on her chest, Liaka looked up at him to return the same mischievous mien as their eyes locked.

"All right, bro. You hogged up my date long enough," David said, trying to gently break them apart. José kept his eyes locked into hers. He licked his lips then finally broke his hold.

"That's my bad. But, the time just seemed to fly in her presence," José slurred. "Maliaka, it was a pleasure to make your acquaintance. Take care," José said, and then turned to David. "Hey Dave, you take it easy, all right buddy," José ended, patting David on the shoulder, then flashed Liaka one last look before taking off through the crowd back to his boys.

"Were you okay back there? When I first introduced you to José, you had a look on your face like you seen a ghost. Then a few minutes later, you're out here dancing with him," David said curiously.

"Naw, I was just a little thrown off. He reminded me of someone from my past," Liaka answered, "someone I vowed to keep a promise to."

To be continued...

CPSIA information can be obtained at www.ICGtesting.com
Printed in the USA
LVOW12s1521190913

353227LV00002B/264/P